cry
of the
daughter

cry
of the
daughter

A NOVEL BY

KIT REED

E. P. DUTTON & CO., INC. NEW YORK 1971

Published simultaneously in Canada by Clarke, Irwin & Company Limited,
Toronto and Vancouver

Library of Congress Catalog Card Number: 70-133580

ACKNOWLEDGMENTS
With thanks to the Abraham Woursell Foundation for its five-year grant.
Thanks to Richard Wilbur for permission to use the line from his poem,
"Complaint," which is quoted in the dedication.

SBN: 0-525-08832-6

For Joe
In this and the other kingdom

Jeremiah 8

15 We looked for peace, but no good came; and for a time of health, and behold trouble . . .

18 When I would comfort myself against sorrow, my heart is faint in me.

19 Behold the voice of the cry of the daughter of my people because of them that dwell in a far country: Is not the Lord in Zion? is not her king in her? Why\have they provoked me to anger with their graven images, and with strange vanities?

20 The harvest is past, the summer is ended, and we are not saved.

21 For the hurt of the daughter of my people I am hurt. . . .

I

Lily

§§§§ §§§§

All his/life long Thad would remember his mother at the bedroom window, looking toward the street with such concentration that he knew she expected to see her brother Harry any minute; he would come along in his white suit, swinging through the gate with gaiety and assurance, just in time to change everything for the better. As a small child Thad had sat by his mother and listened until he could almost see Uncle Harry rising up in the room between them, freshly-minted in the mold of his last photograph, dapper and heroic in the white suit, with his dark hair parted low and lights glistening in his handlebar moustache. To his surprise Thad held on to the image longer than he wanted to, past the point when he understood that his uncle was no better than anybody else and might never even come. Uncle Harry was strong, he was taller than Papa, and if Thad's mother still looked for him it was because he alone was not altered or damaged by the years; for her he was still as gallant and hand-some as he had been at twenty; wherever he was, he was exactly as he had been the night he ran away from home. Even though Thad had grown past his mother's vision he could not help seeing what she saw and each time he found her at the window he would have to try to find a way to beg her not to hope for too much. Then she would lash out at him, and after that she would hold out her arms, begging him to let her forgive him. Half a century later he would look back through the funnel of the years to one particular day when he was twelve, seeing his mother and himself as from a great distance, a boy and a woman both nodding and gesturing in unheard conversation, both poised in her silky, beautiful room in that handsome white house some time in the middle of the great golden age. He would not choose to examine the moment any closer because he knew his

II

mother had talked without hearing and they had touched without feeling, agreeing without conviction because it was the only way to make it possible for both of them to go on.

At the time she had turned quickly to face him, perhaps trying to make a double image: Thad, Harry, so that some day Thad might equal Harry although he could never replace him. Before her first son was born Mama had set Harry as a model for all her children; Thad had never seen his uncle, Harry would not come into their lives until he was ready, but Thad had already heard too much about him, about his manners, his prowess at fencing and shooting, what a gentleman he was. Harry had always been a superb student, while Thad complained about school; Harry never lost his temper, while Thad was prone to argument and occasional fits of rage; Harry was always gracious and respectful to his elders, Harry would never speak to his mother that way; Harry was Mama's beloved older brother, the emblem of all her hopes.

Coming into Mama's room, Thad understood what his mother hoped to see, and that he had fallen short once more, because she turned back to the window again, her head bent slightly in an angle he remembered from her favorite picture of herself, her arm so gently rounded that it looked as if it had no bones. Her dressing gown was pale silk velvet, falling in folds over the rose velvet chaise as if she had planned the effect, but pretty as it was, the room was too close, and rising and falling about them was the miserable cry of a baby who is going to keep it up all day; at thirteen months, Thad's brother Edward was still frail.

Fixed on the window, Lily said, just as if he had asked her:

"You can tell Papa I'm feeling much better, I'm almost myself again."

"Yes, Mama."

"There were times when I thought I might as well die."

"Yes, Mama." Thad thought: Edward, it was all his fault. He had seen all the new babies, Cora, Lila, Flo, and the only one he couldn't like was Edward, perhaps because he had made their mother so sick, perhaps because he was the only other boy.

"I thought we ought to celebrate."

He knew instinctively that he ought to forestall her but she was his mother and so he only said, "Yes, Mama."

"I thought we would give a party for Edward's christening."

He waited, knowing there would be more to it than that.

"I'm almost well now, and it's time for Papa and me to re-enter society. I'm going to have Papa send a telegram to your Uncle Harry, he's going to be Edward's godfather . . . Are you listening?"

"Oh, Mama."

"We'll all go to the church in the carriage and then we can come back here and our friends will all come for a champagne luncheon. Don't frown like that, it won't be too big, we're only asking the best people . . . What's the matter?"

There was no way to tell her so he said, "Oh Mama, you'd think Edward was the Prince of Wales."

She turned from the window to look at him. "Why Thad, Edward is your baby brother and you love him, everybody loves Edward because he's so helpless and so sweet."

He sighed, because in this house, right or wrong, whatever Mama said was so.

"He's a lovely baby, and he's going to look beautiful in your Grandfather Richard's christening dress, I've laid it by all these years."

Thad didn't have to go into the next room to see Edward, sallow and weedy in his crib; he said, mulishly, "I don't see why this one is so special."

"Because it's Edward, and besides, for all you know there may not be any more." She smoothed her cheeks with her two palms, saying, "We can have some of your little friends too, we'll have cold chicken and a ham and sliced roast beef and Papa can order ices from Charleston, you children will all wear white and of course Harry will wear white, he almost always does."

Because he had to, Thad drew in his breath and then began: "Why wasn't he my godfather, Mama?"

"Why dear, I told you, he was just getting started up North, I know he would have loved to, but . . ."

"Why wasn't he Cora's godfather," he said. Her face had already begun to cloud and he continued because he had to draw her on. "Why wasn't he Lila's, or Flo's?"

"He was busy, Thad, I told you." She touched her index fingers to her brows, tracing them back to her temples in uncertain arcs. "He went away, I think he was off in the war."

"Which war, Mama?"

"Mexico, Cuba, I don't know." She drew herself up, firm and unassailable. "Thad, we don't ask questions about these things."

He said, to forearm her: "Well, if he doesn't come I can stand up for him."

"He is coming, Papa is going to wire him and he will come, he may not get here until the last minute, but he will come."

"I could even be Edward's godfather."

She stiffened. "That won't be necessary, Thad."

"I mean, in case he doesn't . . ."

"I *said* he was coming . . . Don't you believe me?"

He couldn't look at her.

She was standing now, her eyes black with fury. "If you can't even believe your own mother, Thad Lyon, you are no son of mine."

She sat down abruptly, holding her head in her hand, engulfing them both in a silence so formidable that in time Thad had to say: "I'm sorry, Mama."

She looked up.

"I wish you really meant that." She was waiting for more, but in time she understood that her son had said all he could say and so she held out her arms to him and big as he was, uncomfortable as it always was, Thad had to go to her and put his head on her shoulder while she put her arms around him.

When Thad went to him, Papa could not or would not help; he only said, "If she wants a party, then we'll have to give a party."

"Papa, she thinks Uncle Harry's going to come and be Edward's godfather."

"She thought he was going to be your godfather too."

"I thought, maybe if you went and talked to her."

Papa was at his desk, surrounded by letters, ledgers, scraps of paper mounting on either side, each covered with figures and the figures themselves seeming to rise, as if they would engulf him soon. Still he was handsome, his hair was as black as it had been the day he was married and his eyes were clear as he looked at Thad now. "Maybe if the party's good enough, it won't matter to her so much when he doesn't come."

Thad shook his head. "If you would just *talk* to her."

"Son, I can't talk to her."

Thad began, "If you can't talk to her, then nobody can." His voice trailed off and he stood, looking into his father's eyes; they looked at each other long after Thad knew he ought to look away.

At last Papa turned back to his desk, quiet and grave. "We'll go ahead with the party, we'll try to have everything just the way she wants it." Even though Thad hadn't spoken, Papa went on, saying, defensively: "Well, at least we have to try."

Flodie was too little to care what was going on but Cora and Lila caught their mother's excitement and it ran in their blood like a fever, sending them to their closets for costumes for the party and then into the recesses of the stables and the attic for bits of wood and broken glass because they were both anxious to make gifts for Uncle Harry; when he came he would be overwhelmed by their tributes, he would look into their bright faces and promise never to go away. Although she was the younger sister, Lila was taller than Cora; her hair and eyes were black, her face was long, just like her father's, and in just a few years she was going to be beautiful, but she was convinced that Uncle Harry would think she was plain and so she pinned all her hopes on the gift she was making; wandering after bedtime, Thad would find her at work on the bedroom floor, gluing glass and dried flowers into a wooden frame. Cora had a round face and a round mouth and stiff little curls, and for two weeks before the christening she flounced in and out of rooms in her party dress, saying to her father, to Thad, who didn't want to listen: "Uncle Harry is going to love me best."

Mama had called in the dressmaker to make her gown, but she would work as long as she had to putting in the hem because her Aunt Florence had taught her to make invisible stitches and she couldn't trust anybody else with this lovely lilac watered silk. She had Biggie take the christening dress away from the laundress and do it up herself, and then Biggie spent the better part of a morning sponging the little satin shoes. Papa was busy too, keeping track of acceptances and arranging for extra help and ordering champagne; he would drive them all to the church himself because he had asked Brewster to spend the morning chipping a swan out of a block of ice. Thad thought he could best protect himself by concentrating on the party, and so he found himself spending hours at the florist with his father, or brooding over the market list with the half-formed conviction that if he saw to it that they ordered just the right amount and kind of food then he could make his uncle come, or at least keep his mother from being too disappointed; he could keep whatever was going to happen from happening, if he could only get it right. Coming into his mother's room without knocking, he heard his father saying, "Lily, please, don't hope for too much." His mother looked up, her face bright with conviction, and said, as if she held all their futures in her hands and could control them: "I will bring him back this time. He will come back."

Mama woke too early on the morning of the christening. She came to Thad's room before six, waking him with a whisper and beckoning him to the kitchen. They tiptoed down the hallway past closed doors, shushing each other as his brother and sisters sighed and rustled in their rooms, and together they crept down the back stairs, gasping at each creaking step. In the kitchen, they ate a secret breakfast in a wash of love; they giggled in the dim morning light, mother and son smiling at each other and mumbling through the crumbs in a closeness which Thad would remember all his life because he was never to feel it again. Her hair was loose around her face and her sleeves were flying; he knew she was already too excited, and by the time she had drunk her coffee she was talking about all the friends who were coming to the party, what they would say when they met Harry after hearing so much about him for all these years. Edward would look just beautiful in Grandfather Richard's christening dress, she would hold him on her lap and let everybody admire him, she would . . .

"Oh Mama," Thad said, "you know how fussy Edward is, he would have a fit."

Angered too quickly, she snapped: "He's a *lovely* baby. You've always had a jealous nature, Thad."

He said, "Yes, Mama," and went and kissed her, but he knew the day was already lost.

They waited as long as they could before they left for the ceremony, and when they did go, Mama refused to trust Brewster or Biggie to know Harry when he came, or to direct him to the church. Lila was bitterly disappointed not to be able to go to the church with them, but even though Cora was the oldest girl and should have been responsible, Cora refused to stay, squinting her eyes and pursing her lips in a beginning tantrum which would damage all of them, and so Mama had to post Lila at the house because she was so dependable. After all, when he came, Lila could get into the carriage with him and come right along to the church, she probably wouldn't miss a thing. When she understood that she had no other recourse Lila said, "Oh well, I can finish my present," and turned to go inside. Saying goodbye, Thad hugged her unexpectedly, and as she struggled to get free, whispered: "When we get back, pretend the present was for her."

16

He went on out to the carriage, where Mama was already waving her hands and talking too fast. Flodie and Cora sat in back, Cora with her lips stuck out and Edward, limp and unwieldy, slipping off her lap. Papa drove slowly, perhaps because this was the first time Mama had been out in months and he wanted her to enjoy it, perhaps because he thought if they poked along, Harry might by some wild mischance be waiting for them at the church. As it was, only the rector was waiting, he had been waiting for some time, so he grew annoyed when Mama took her sweet time, proceeding up the walk with her skirts swaying grandly and her rosy hat bobbing like a great, slow flower. Handsome as she was, she was obviously distracted, and the rector pushed ahead gently, determined to get the ceremony over as quickly as possible for her sake, for all their sakes, looking around with growing impatience for someone to hold the child. So Thad found himself standing at the font after all, acting as a proxy for his uncle, and before he could protest the implications he was forced to accept the unwelcome burden of his brother in his arms, renouncing the devil for him and at the same time forging a bond of responsibility which would trouble him all his life.

Going home, Mama was gay, nodding to other carriages as they passed, perhaps seeing the Lyon family as from the sidewalk: Papa, with his high head and handsome moustache; herself in elegant profile; the children all in white, the snappy horse. Thad tried to tell himself that she understood about Uncle Harry now, she saw the truth at last and would be reconciled, but she was already saying:

"I suppose he got there too late to come along to the church, or that Lila of ours kept him there with her big eyes and her blue bow ribbon. Harry always was sweet with little girls."

Papa said, "Lily, please."

She turned her face to him, with her color too high and her eyes too dark. "Oh Thaddeus, do I look all right?"

Papa said, "Everybody will think you look wonderful."

Lila was hanging in the doorway like an anxious ghost, and as they pulled into the porte cochère she peered over all their heads and then stepped back with a look of misery as she saw that they were exactly the same number as they had been when they started out. Mama seemed not to notice; instead she looked past Lila, as if convinced she would see her brother in the shadows; if he was not there then he must be waiting in the parlor or the music room; he might be asleep somewhere upstairs. She brushed past her daughter and went through the house in a rush, coming back at last to the parlor where the rest of them were waiting, apprehensive but ready to proceed as if they had never really expected Harry anyway and were convinced it would be a better party without him, but were too considerate to say so.

Thad began: "Maybe Edward had better be changed before everybody comes, Mama, he smells terrible."

Papa said, "You won't want him to make his social debut with a handicap like that."

Mama didn't hear. "All right, Lila, where is he?"

Thad began afresh: "Mama, come and look at Brewster's swan."

Lila was saying, "Mama, he never . . . "

"Of course he did, I asked him to come."

Thad said, "He's set it in the middle of a bed of camellias."

"Nobody came, except for the man from the baker."

"How do you know he was from the baker?"

"Mama, he had on white, and he brought . . . "

Mama said, "Harry always wears white."

Because Thad's eyes were on her, Lila proffered the present she had made, saying, "Look, Mama, it's for you."

But Mama pushed it aside, looking around as if she had only to look in the right place to find him. "No."

"Mama?"

She may have understood as well as any of them that it had been foolish to expect him to come, but they were all pressing around her in an anxious cluster, too solicitous, and because she could not let them see her own pain she lashed out instead, and from the maelstrom of her disappointment cried, "He was here, I know he was, and Lila sent him away."

Lila was in tears. "Mama, it's a present."

Lily didn't see; instead she struck out at her most beautiful daughter, crying, "Get out of here, Lila, you are no child of mine," and then with beautiful duplicity turned to greet her first guest.

Thad spun out the day in accumulating bitterness, smiling because his mother said he had to smile, talking to guests because she demanded it, and by the time the day was over he understood that he had been a fool to hope the party was going to help, nothing was going to help. Lila was banished to the bedroom and Cora and Flodie were their most unnatural selves, Flodie grimacing and bobbing in an imitation of Cora, both of them spreading their party skirts.

Clamped in weariness, Papa receded while Mama talked and smiled, turning away from Thad, who was already too fully formed to receive her expectations, and fixing on Edward instead. Dressed in yards of lace, Edward was quiet for once; he sat on Mama's lap while she heaped all her hopes on him, telling everybody: "Blood will tell; Edward is going to be a great judge, perhaps a diplomat. Look at that high forehead, and look, he has the Richard nose . . ." She nodded and smiled the whole afternoon long, recovering herself so beautifully that she was able to say, "It was a lovely party, wasn't it?"

Still, receiving Thad in her room, she said, "And to think Harry would have been here, if Lila hadn't let him get away." She went on, more or less at peace with herself, "It was all that Lila's fault."

Thad started to say: He never, but he knew it was no use; he could not talk to her, he would never be able to talk to her; there was nothing left for him but to escape her, to escape this house and all her visions of the future; he must escape them all no matter what the cost.

LILY

I felt so helpless, Harry just slipped out of my fingers, before I could stop him he kissed me on top of the head and closed the gate. I could hear a carriage and I wanted to open the gate and run out in the road, shouting to him to come back, but I could feel the house rising up behind me and at all the windows, women: Mother, Granny Calhoun, Aunt Florence, holding me back, and I could hear them: My dear, ladies do not raise their voices, and they never go into the road alone. I was helpless, and so *poor;* for all our silks and silver, there were no more men left in that house, and all I could do was stand there inside the garden wall and wait.

Nurse came out to bring me in and when I attached myself to the gate and wouldn't budge Aunt Florence came, cross and overheated, and finally Mother came down herself, still in black although Father had been gone for years; she stooped to put her face at my level and said, You must come in to tea now, and when I said, I have to wait for Harry, she said only, We always have tea at four, standing at her full height in such confidence that I had to follow. If she knew Harry was gone, if she had in fact driven him away, there was no trace of it to be seen on her brow; she sat over the silver service as graciously as if it were any other day; we had to drink from our Minton cups with the same composure, I had to sit there as I did every afternoon with a small pillow on my head, to perfect my carriage: After all, my dear, some day you are going to meet the Queen.

When we had finished tea she took me into the sitting room nearest the road and showed me the scarred panels in the Adam fireplace, they had been ruined for as long as I could remember, but this time she said, Lily, your father took great care to hide his money, and now you see what happened to it; he bought that man to take his place in the War and then the influenza took him. She tried to put her arms around me but I thought only of Harry, and I pulled away. She was saying, You see my dear, you deserve better, but fate has a way.

I would not listen. I do not know to this day what she was trying to tell me, I only knew I had to escape her, as Harry had. I would marry as soon as I was old enough and escape her house, living as I was born to live, I would gather in more sons and servants, more jewelry and pretty things than I would need in a lifetime because I could not bear to be left alone as she was, or as I was that day, bereft and helpless; I would never be helpless again.

For a time even I could not have wished for more; when I was old enough I was much sought after, an ornament to Charleston society; I was presented at the Court of St. James's and when I came home I made the best catch of the season, and then Thaddeus brought me here and built this beautiful house for me; if my life was not yet precisely what I hoped for, we still had time. I meant to make everything perfect inside the house and then open our beautiful rooms to society; our prosperity would fetch Harry, even as he had fled our helplessness. I thought Papa and I would travel, we would visit all the courts of Europe, but then Thad Junior came to keep us here. Then there was Cora, then Lila came, and each time we were glad; then there was Flodie and then Edward, who almost killed me, each one took my strength and weighed me down. Now it is happening to me again. I never wished it but it is happening even so; despite Papa and my sons, despite this house and all the lovely objects I have gathered against such a moment it is happening again and I am helpless, even as I was in the garden so many years ago.

Maybe I can make it not happen this time; if I lace my corsets tight enough perhaps I will not go round in front, and if I do not go round in front then it cannot be so. We may be mistaken, I may be taken with some illness which medicine can cure. I know better. Before I go to bed this time I will have to make Brewster move all the furniture out of the morning room to make another nursery. We will have new curtains and Nurse will come to help me trim the bassinet. I can make Thad Junior climb up to nail the bow, he will be impatient and as soon as he has driven the nail my big boy will be down the ladder and off; I will be alone in the nursery and I will probably cry, I always do, I suppose it is for joy. I know I will be happy about this baby when I see it, I always am, it pleases me first to see that it is in fact alive and then I am delighted that it is just like all the others, our stamp in on them all; for one demented moment I think: I will have a dozen more.

Things are done for me: I am washed and perfumed and put into one of my pretty gowns, my baby is swaddled and set down beside me; for the next two months we live in seclusion, welcoming the family as state visitors. Papa is like a suitor in those weeks, tender and undemanding, it is as if we are courting again. I can imagine that there are just the two of us, we will visit all the courts of Europe without a thought for anybody but ourselves; we can be like twin heads on a coin, remote and fair. I can even pretend that we will never be diminished by children with their desperate, endless needs; I have had enough of children, they fragment the soul, each making off with some piece of the self. My family is descended from the nobility and it surprises me to find that I am trapped in this godforsaken little city, bound by so many children that I will never see Europe again.

Still, when we move out in society we make a handsome crowd. The older children are tall, like their father, but they are all aristocratically pale, like me; they have my nose and my fair brow. My girls will make their debuts here, and in New York; they will certainly ornament the St. Cecilia Ball and I should like them to be presented, as I was, at the Court of St. James's. My handsome sons will go to the University and make distinguished marriages, so that our family will march ahead after all. Thaddeus and I will send out our emissaries to bring luster to our name, and if I must grow old then my children will cherish me and care for me; they will surround me with grandchildren like so many jewels. They have, after all, our example; when the Symphony played here I wore my gown of ivory *peau de soie* and Grandmother Richard's tiara and Papa looked so

21

elegant with the light shining on his moustaches and fire glinting from his diamond studs; we sat in the first box and nobody needed to know any more about us (that Papa may weep when he loses his temper, that my body has begun to change again). Perhaps if we had not gone to New York after all, or if, once there, we had gone on to the opera, but in the end Papa had to take me to New York because he came to me last spring and said, I have a surprise for you, Lily, something wonderful.

Of course I thought we were going to New York, we would leave the children with the nurse and go by ourselves; I began to think what I would wear. Instead he put me in the carriage, and all the children piled in back, they were all shrilling in different keys and I thought: If they could just be quiet for once I would feel more like myself. I should have known not to hope for too much but I was still thinking: If not New York then maybe Washington, or Charleston, he is driving out a ways, we will spread a picnic and he will tell me then. I let the carriage take me along, dreaming until I saw that we were cutting through the woods, going along a sandy track that frightened me, I thought one of the wheels would sink too far and we would heel over and come tumbling out like grasshoppers out of a jar, something bigger would come along and step on us. I closed my eyes and the next thing I knew we had stopped and Papa was helping me down, saying, We will have to walk from here; even though he took my arm the sand sifted into my slippers and made me stumble, in another minute I would fall and the sand would suck me down. The children were wild with suspense and they ran ahead, Thad and Lila first and then Cora, she scolded them and called out for them to wait. Flodie was next and then Edward, who gave up finally and dropped back to attach himself to my skirts, he is my favorite but for a minute I wanted to lift my foot and kick him off. Papa Lyon had me by the elbow, he said, When you see it you will be so pleased; I could not think of anything in this wilderness that would ever please me but he was so excited that I looked up at him and smiled.

Then before I could help myself or stop him he had led me out onto a sandy bank overlooking the river and I looked and looked but all I could see was a rough cabin, it was little more than a shack and I thought some pioneer or some poor Indian would be glad to have it, but that was all I thought. Papa was saying, This is it, Lily, I had it built without your even finding out. I turned to him and said, I see, keeping my voice as still as I could; Edward was hanging heavy on my skirts, weighing me down, and before I could stop myself I pulled my skirts away from him and he fell on his back at once and began to cry. Papa didn't even see, he was so happy, so proud, he said, Don't you want to come inside; I had to get away from Edward for a minute and so I followed him into the big front room. It was two storeys high and rough-beamed, there was a balcony all the way around, that was where the children were going to sleep; there was a kitchen, there were two more rooms, we would have our own private bedroom and outside was a cabin for the cook, I was supposed to be surprised, delighted, but all I could see were raw pine boards and splinters, splinters that would catch in my skirts and hurt the children's hands.

I wanted to say something more to him but all I could say was, What is this? I could hear Cora and Lila in the doorway behind me, they were fighting about whose bed would be next to the balcony stairs, and behind them Edward was still crying but he had damped down to that steady endless muh-muh-muh; Papa turned to me then and when he did I hated his smile, it assumed too much. He said, Lily, I have built the most beautiful house in town for you, but this will be our real home, we can come here every summer and on all the weekends, the children can run wild and you and I can put on old clothes and be ourselves.

What would I have said to him? I don't know; as it was, I was able to throw up my hands and run back outside because Edward was screaming, my big boy Thad had thrown his little brother in the river and then found out he couldn't make him swim; now he was dragging him up the bank and Edward was screaming and Flodie was screaming too. I made Papa take Thad back to the carriage and whip him. I wanted to sit down and decide what I thought but I couldn't, Edward was in my lap and crying, beating my bosom and muddying my dress, Lila and Cora had already forgotten about him and were quarreling again, their voices took me right back to my mother's living room; Edward quieted down a little, he even started to climb down from my lap but then Flodie hissed at him: Baby, crybaby, crybaby, cry, and I thought the noise would kill me before Papa finished and came back.

When he came he had his coat off and his sleeves still rolled up, he was rebuckling his belt. His face was flushed and I thought: He sees how impossible this is. Instead he smoothed his hair and rolled down his sleeves and offered me his arm again, saying. You haven't seen the rest of the house. So I had to go up those raw board steps again, hating it, and I followed him over the raw board floor down the raw board hallway into a raw board room where Papa stopped, saying, See, Lily, two windows, it will be just like living in the woods. The idea made me faint but still I held to his arm and nodded, trying to back out without having to look, but he drew me inside and I looked down before he did and saw the shape on the floor, the flat fur, the evil naked tail, a dead water rat on the floor right where our bed would be. I closed my eyes because I had to shut everything out and when I came to myself we were in the carriage and Papa was holding me; even before I opened my eyes I could hear the children whispering, Edward was mourning me in that miserable wail; I opened my eyes finally and I couldn't help it, I began to cry, I cried and cried until Papa got me home and into bed, I cried until the doctor came, I cried until Papa promised me we would go to New York.

Then in New York this happened to me; we were both dressed to go to the opera but we did not go to the opera; he was so handsome and I so fair.

I want this to be a boy, Thad already wants to fly away and Edward is too delicate to make me proud; this boy will be handsome like Papa, he will dote on me the way Papa does and I will go places on his arm but he will not have the power to change me, the way Papa does. I have had enough of girls. My Cora is a little pig who ate out the middle of my Edward's birthday cake, she got into the pantry and scooped out the soft insides with her hands, gobbling until there was nothing left but a shell. We were all in the sitting room, waiting for Essie to come in with the cake but Biggie came instead, she told us about the poor cake and my baby cried and cried until I thought he would be sick and so I had to make Lila take him up to his room. Cora is tiny for her age, she won't do a thing for me; she has a mouth like a cupid's bow and sometimes I think I would like to cut off all her curls. I depend on Lila, who thinks she is so grand; she is going to grow up to be very beautiful, and even at this age she sails through the music room like the Lady of the Lake; she does as I say but she is impervious, she will not even respond to my Grandmother Richard look, which Papa tells me cuts deeper than any knife. Then there is Flodie, her eyes are stitched on too close together above her nose and I don't know now whether I named her after Aunt Florence because I could see she was born mean, or whether the name has made her mean. No more girls, they will have to grow up to be women, I will be trapped in a household of women; I married to get away from one and will not let that happen to me again.

I think it will be a girl to spite me and I do not see where it will ever end; I look into each baby girl's eyes and see that nothing will be any better for her; I look at each one when she is new and think: You don't know yet, but you will; you may be gifted and sharp, you may even pretend to be a boy for a while, but like it or not you will have to grow into a woman, what's more you have been born a lady and so you will never be free to seek out anything you want. If you want to marry then you will have to sit home and hope for a husband, and if you are fortunate he will come and rescue you, and only in that way can you move from one part of life to the next; if a husband does not come then you will have to live here, in your father's house, for the rest of your life, as I would have lived in my mother's house if Thaddeus had not come to help me escape. You will have to wait but worse, you have to *protect;* you can never go out at night alone for fear, for fear; a man might . . . you are a woman; you know it, the world knows, anybody may come and seek your poor secret which is no secret, some outlaw will take it by force and ruin you, and then you might as well go to the bridge and throw yourself in the river because you are already worse than dead. From the first you will be vulnerable, but if all goes well and you live out your life in safety and you do not have to waste it waiting behind your mother's window, if all goes well and you move on with a man who is both handsome and kind, then you are still no more than a vessel, helpless from the first; you will wait for the next life to inhabit you, for like it or not it will, it will use you and spend you and then cast you off like a shroud, standing aside while you collect yourself again, for you must serve it until it is strong enough to leave you behind for something better, so you are at the mercy of life but you are also at the mercy of death, for death may take your husband, your pillar and your strength, your life and your means of life, and what will happen to you then?

§§§§ §§§§

If Thad hadn't waited with his mother for so many years, with all his hopes spoiled by the expectations which she set up relentlessly, almost as if it was the disappointments she was creating; if his uncle had been clean-shaven when he first saw him, or if he had not been wildeyed and trembling, leading Thad to think: Whiskey, then Thad might have done as his Uncle Harry asked and Harry would have left town without any of the rest even seeing him. If Harry had been taller; if Thad had *liked* him now that he finally saw him, if any one of the elements had been different, he might have stolen into the house to leave the note on his mother's dresser, bringing back the tiara Harry wanted because it had, after all, been Grandmother Richard's, and was therefore rightfully his to sell.

As it was, Thad was coming back from the store in the long twilight of that particular summer, carrying salt for the ice cream maker and already looking forward to one of the festivals the family made for itself all too seldom; Christmas and birthdays came and went with heavy ceremony, leaving him wearied and burdened with remembered unpleasantness, but every once in a while somebody would say, out of a clear sky, Let's make silhouettes, or, Let's make ice cream, and they would all catch fire. Mama would come downstairs; Nell, the baby, would be allowed to stay up way past her bedtime; brothers and sisters would sit down sweetly together, and in the spontaneity of that particular moment they would smile at each other, humming like bees. Thad was already smiling, when he got home with the salt they would start the freezer and they would laugh together, waiting to glut themselves on peach ice cream; when it was all gone they would lie around on the kitchen linoleum, too stuffed to get up; Mama would look down at him with fondness, saying: Get up. Imagine, a grown boy like you. But now there was somebody coming toward him from the corner, they would meet in the shadows in front of the house, and he knew almost at once that it must be his mother's brother; after all, he was in white. Even though Papa had a white linen and Thad himself had a Palm Beach suit, even though Mama still dressed Edward in white on Sundays, in Thad's imagination only one man wore white. As he got closer Thad saw he would have recognized him anyway because of the eyes; perhaps they were set a fraction too close together, like his own, or Edward's, or his sisters' eyes; perhaps they bore the same stamp his mother's did, a faint bewilderment as if he too had been born to palaces, grand rooms which had been denied him or which were already beyond achieving before he was old enough to understand what should have been his birthright. Looking at this face he had never seen before, Thad recognized it immediately; it was as if all his mother's past and future disappointments were visible in her brother's eyes, so that when Uncle Harry said, "I've been watching the house. You're Lily's oldest," Thad answered in an anger that surprised them both: "Well, what if I am?"

"I'm your mother's brother Harry," he said, as if Thad didn't already know.

"Then why don't you go inside and say hello to her?"

His face was pale, his eyes were red-rimmed; Thad would decide it was from drink; he said, "I don't want her to see me now."

"I'll go tell her you're here."

Harry's hand was on his shoulder before he could turn. Up close he seemed a little shabby, and he was so short he had to look up into Thad's eyes. "No. If you would just do me a favor."

"I don't think I can."

"If you'll just go in and get something for me, and leave her this note, so she won't worry?"

"If she thought you'd been here and I'd let you get away . . ."

"She's been keeping it for me."

" . . . she'd kill me."

"Your great-grandmother's tiara, the one with the emerald baguettes."

Thad shrugged off his uncle's hand, saying, "If you want it, you'd better go in and ask for it."

"But it's mine." Harry was reaching for him again. "Once I have the money, once I get a few things straightened out . . ."

Thad stepped out of his reach. "If you want anything from the house you're going to have to talk to Papa about it. If you won't come in now, you're going to have to come around in the morning, just come up to the front door and knock." Later he would tell himself he had only been protecting the family's interests, but he would remember thinking: Now she will have to see him for what he is.

His uncle was looking past him, at the sprawling, generous house. "How many bedrooms do you have?"

"Enough." Thad's voice rose in exasperation. "Are you coming in or not?"

"I'll be back tomorrow," Harry said, and before Thad could stop him he was gone; Thad might have gone after his uncle but Flodie was already on the front porch, calling into the shadows, "Thad? Is that you? Thad?" She must have seen him from the window and so

27

he had to take his bag of salt and go on up the walk, wondering whether he had ruined everything after all, whether Harry would leave town without a trace. If he left, then Thad would have to worry about his mother finding out, she would disown him forever, as she had always threatened to, saying: No child of mine would send him away. My own brother, and you just sent him away.

They made the ice cream, two batches; Thad and Papa took turns cranking and Edward got to lick the dasher, but Thad was too filled with worry to eat, choked by unformed hopes and nameless fears, and although he reached into the freezer in full confidence, scooping out the biggest helping of all, he found he couldn't eat.

Despite Thad's fears Uncle Harry did come the next morning, with two suitcases and twins, Sam and Edna; they were about Edward's age and the girls circled around them as if they were a pair of parrots Papa had brought home from a trip to the tropics, poking them and asking questions with such sharp curiosity that although neither of them would have admitted it later, the twins cried from sheer nervousness. Thad would never find out the truth from his mother, but as he understood it later, Harry had married a frail girl because he wanted her; she had accepted him for romance, but before they had time for any of the plays or parties or trips to Europe Harry had promised her, they were visited with twins, and the minute they were born and he saw there were two of them, the minute the first one cried, Harry left the house because he had never been able to bear responsibility, he was drowning and they were two lead weights; he came back only for the funeral, when some distant, outraged relative of his bride charged him with her death—hadn't he deserted her? Then they thrust the children on him, saying: Here, you take care of them. Now the twins stood in the Lyon hallway, unhappy wraiths, while Uncle Harry waited at the bottom of the stairs for his sister to come down. His suit was fresh this morning, his shirt was starchy and he was smoothly shaved and combed, with his moustache shining and his eyes so clear that, studying him, Thad had to decide his uncle could not have been drinking last night after all, it must have been a trick of the light. Still he had been gone for all those years, without explanation or apology, and so Thad expected his mother to reproach Harry, to hesitate before she put her arms around him, pausing at least long enough to hold him off and say, "Where have you been?" Instead, she fell on him as if she had been starving for him, and Thad and his father exchanged looks: what could they do? Then she turned to Papa and with beautiful ceremony, said, "Thaddeus, this is my brother Harry." Then, as if they had not been standing there together for the past few minutes, Papa stepped forward and shook his hand.

The children were noisy, whirling with excitement, in the next second they would start to yell, tearing through the parlors, and so Mama went back up two steps, standing above them for the moment, to say: "Children, this is your Uncle Harry, who has been gone for so many years."

Thad was aware of Edward pushing past him, crying, "Uncle Harry, Uncle Harry," trying to throw himself around Harry's legs, and although at the time he could not have said why, this troubled Thad more than any of the rest of it, perhaps because he had never seen Edward hug their father with such warmth, or because Edward fought like a small animal for his uncle's attention, pushing past Papa as he had Thad, because Papa was in his way. Uncle Harry scooped him up, laughing, and only Thad seemed to see Sam and Edna, who dwindled, unnoticed, as their father filled the room.

As it turned out the twins were going to spend vacations with the Lyons from now on, what could Harry do, one man alone; in the summers they would go to camp and Papa was going to see that they were enrolled in the appropriate boarding schools. Harry was going to work in Papa's office, Mama wanted him to come and live in the big house with them, but for one reason or another it was settled that he would find himself a room somewhere else in town. They were all sitting around the dinner table, long past dessert; the smaller children had eaten in the pantry and Thad could hear them screaming in the garden, but here was Edward, his eyes dazzled, hanging on his uncle's chair. Remembering the tiara, Thad watched his uncle closely, perhaps waiting for some flaw to reveal itself, some sign of duplicity; then he would pounce, saying, "See, Mama, it was a terrible waste, waiting all those years," he might be able to plead with her to move on to something new. For the moment, however, Uncle Harry was charming; he looked strong and adventurous, and in the failing light his face had a piratical cast; his stories were good and even Papa was smiling now. Still he shimmered in the evening dimness, in the next second he might disappear, and Thad watched with a sense of compression; he swelled in his chair, wanting to strike out, to prevent something, but not knowing what or how. So he had to keep his peace, brooding; he had to wander in the halls the next morning while Mama and Uncle Harry talked in her bedroom and the rest of the family went its way unheeded; Thad saw she barely looked up when Papa came in to say goodbye before he went to work.

They talked on through the morning, Mama on her chaise by the window with Edward on the floor beside her, leaning his cheek on the satin of her robe. Once she spotted Thad through the half-open door and beckoned, but he pretended not to see. After lunch Mama had to rest and Edward came downstairs, bubbling; Thad thought he recognized the look in Edward's eyes and so he said, "What are you so damn pleased about?"

"Uncle Harry is taking me to Charleston."

"*Charleston.*"

"We're going to find Granny Calhoun's jewels."

"Oh come off it, Edward."

Edward's eyes were too bright. "We're going next Monday."

Thad said, gently, "Don't be so sure."

"Half of anything we find is mine."

"I see." Thad was already sorting his thoughts for alternatives. "Except you won't have time."

"Why not?"

"Papa and I are going down to the river for a week." He turned the idea over in his mind; he liked the way it looked and so he embroidered. "We're going to spend the week fishing, we can wear old clothes and never wash our necks."

"I'd rather go to Charleston."

"You can come down to the river camp and fish with Papa and me."

Edward wasn't even listening. "I'm going to sell my half and buy a horse."

"*Edward.*" Thad started forward, he might have shaken his brother, he wanted to do something to bring him back, but his uncle was in the doorway now, and Edward turned away without even seeing Thad's outstretched hand.

"Come along son," Harry was saying. "Let's go for a soda."

Thad tried one last time. "Mama wouldn't . . ."

"We have plans to make."

Harry turned, dapper and confident, and Edward left his brother and followed without question. Thad watched them go with a sense of defeat, even though later that afternoon he had to go down to the ice cream parlor and fetch his little brother, who had finally stopped crying long enough to tell the proprietor who he was. While Edward was dreaming over his soda, Harry had excused himself to talk to somebody in the street; he must have simply forgotten about Edward because he never came back, not the last time he was to forget one of Lily's children, but the last time for a while because they didn't see him for two years, he had just walked out of the ice cream parlor and disappeared from town. Bringing Edward home, Thad would say: "See?" But Edward would refuse to see and Thad himself didn't really see; he would never understand that Uncle Harry wasn't what he thought he was, any more than he was what Edward thought he was; he was not a myth or a scoundrel but only a rather short, neat little man with eyes too close together and an air of impatience, or uncertainty, which would drive him from house to house, city to city for what was left of his life; he would bound and rebound and travel without rest until finally he died in one of the first auto accidents in that city; he was not a villain, as Thad would have it, with suicide his final blow to the family, nor was he a martyr, cut off in the bloom of his youth; he was not anything they thought but only careless, although once he had gone into the skid on the slippery bridge he would let the car go forward with full knowledge and full force of will toward what he hoped would be oblivion, gasping, as the car breached the railing, with a sense of release, almost of relief.

§§§§ §§§§

Thaddeus Lyon's house had six white columns two stories high, there was a mullioned window in the gable above the portico and a stained glass window in the stairwell, and the fluted columns were repeated in the porte cochère; inside there was a bronze statue of one of the Graces on the newel post, her arm was bowed slightly to accommodate a torch with three light globes. It was the proudest house on the street, perhaps in town; at six, Nell was sure it was the most beautiful house in the world. She brooded and mooned over everything that happened there, thinking that just one more touch might make it perfect; if she could just decide what the right thing was and then make it happen, she and her brothers and sisters and Mama and Papa would live in the house in happiness all the rest of their lives. She almost died of delight when the satin portieres in the living room were replaced with wine cut velvet, she stood back and sighed with plea-

31

sure and then she fidgeted until Brewster dusted and replaced the ala-baster urns, leaving the room in gorgeous symmetry. Then she heard Flodie and Edward fighting in the hall outside and knew that would have to be altered too, but when she went to plead with them they only shut her in the closet under the stairs and kept her there for what seemed like an hour, even though she pounded and cried. It was Nell who climbed on Papa's lap and kissed him and whispered that the house wouldn't look right until there was a Pierce Arrow parked under the porte cochère, not only for the spectacle the car would make but also because she understood that the car might make Papa a little happier, so twice enhancing the house. When the last baby died and Mama took to her room it was Nell who planned little parties, drawing Flo and Edward into operas and theatricals, praying for good weather so she could press her big sister Lila to lay an af-ternoon tea party on the lawn; it was Nell who murmured and schemed, dreaming of new ways to lure Mama down. When every-thing was ready she would go to Mama's room and scratch on the door and plead sweetly until Mama sighed and consented, because the handsome house looked its best with Mama sitting under her lap robes in the parlor, Mama in the garden with her skirts spread on rugs and a low table with the silver service right there on the grass; if it hadn't been for the high hedge the whole world passing by would have been able to see what a wonderful family they were.

If Nell had ever achieved what she wanted, it would have been on Mama's birthday, that particular year; she began thinking about it weeks ahead of time, right after Edward's birthday, when Mama came down in a blush-pink velvet peignoir. She had kissed each of them and then, smiling, presided over the cake, teasing Cora and tir-ing only when she remembered what a pity it was Thad couldn't be there, especially since Edward was his favorite. This time Thad would be home, it was the end of May and he had two weeks before he went to Savannah for a summer job in some bank; Thad would be there and Papa would be home from work early, covered with smiles and suffocating with excitement. He had bought Mama an Electric, it had crystal bud vases and was simple enough to be driven by a child, it was already out in the stable, which was now a garage; Brewster had driven it home some time in the night and, taking the younger children out to see it that morning Papa had smoothed one fender absently, saying maybe this would convince Mama it would be fun to get out in the daytime every once in a while. The parlor was already full of yellow roses, Uncle Harry had sent an order to the florist from wherever it was that he was, and Biggie was going to frost the cake in yellow too. For one reason or another Cora and Lila were each secretly working on a satin wrapper for Mama; Nell had wonderingly touched the fabric and then, pledged to silence, did not tell either that the other was sewing and the two garments looked more or less alike; Lila took littler stitches but Cora's was the color of a sunset and Nell, dreaming, picked up the scraps and wished she could make them bloom into roses, fingering them until Cora hissed at her and took them away. Lila said they would even be able to have the cake in the garden this year because there was a soft breeze blowing up from the river and the morning rain had left the garden cool.

Nell had her own plans; she would make a sort of throne for Mama in the garden, a special place for her to sit while they brought the presents and the lighted cake, they would lay everything at her feet while she smiled down on each of them like a lady in a grotto; she would step down off the porch and say, Why, it's beautiful, who did this, and the others would fall back. She would come down and sit in the bower, understanding that it was Nell who had done all this single-handed, she would call Nell to her and pat her cheek and time would end then, with her own face bright, perpetually receiving, and her mother's hand forever stretched out, in an eternal gesture of love. Afterward there would be cake and ice cream in shapes, they would all play like children in the garden, Papa too, and they would already have begun to change but Nell's life would crystallize around that moment, nothing would matter after that.

She began by going to the kitchen: yes, the cake was there, cooling. Once before she was born Cora had stolen a whole birthday cake, Mama never stopped telling about it, she called Cora her little pig, so Nell went next to her big sister Lila and found out where Cora was: off shopping, safely away down town; yes, Lila would let Nell know the minute Cora got back from town. The new Electric was safe in the stable, and Nell satisfied herself that Brewster had polished all the nickel and dusted the tires and even cut flowers to put into the bud vases; when the right time came he would drive it down to the porte cochère and they would lead Mama round from the garden, she would be so happy she would die and then she might even get in and timidly push the lever, taking the children, two by two, for rides around the block. The garden shears were hanging on a nail and so Nell took them around front and attacked the oleander, deciding that she would make her bower there. She would make a niche in the branches and then she would bring out the little gilt three-legged chair with the velvet seat, she would set it in the niche and trim it with greens and surround it with late flowers. The branches were tough, so she had to give up the shears and tie them back instead. She brought some of the potted flowers from the sun room and she was struggling to get the chair out of the house when Flodie found her and said, "What are you trying to do?"

"It's for Mama's birthday."

"That chair? She won't ever sit in that chair."

"She has to, it's her birthday." She had hooked one chair leg over the edge of the rug, and didn't have the strength to get it free. "It's her birthday, Flodie."

Grumbling, Flodie came over to help her. "Oh, all right."

Of course once she saw what Nell was doing Flodie said it wasn't right and had to change it: the oleander wouldn't do, the leaves were messy and the twigs would only get in Mama's hair, so they had to drag the chair down to the trellis and then Nell had to help her bring out the brass table, its top was no bigger than a dictionary but Flo said it would certainly hold all the presents and the tea, they might even be able to move something after Mama opened it, to make room for the cake. When they had finished to Flodie's satisfaction, she brought out a package, something she had made, and about then Edward joined them, he didn't have anything for Mama so Flodie told him he would have to beg a dime from Lila and go off to the store and get something or he would spoil Mama's birthday for sure, and when Nell began crying Flodie said, "Oh, all right, get something for Nelly to give her too." Nell had to go back to the kitchen to be *sure* the cake was all right, Biggie had covered it with pale yellow frosting, there were white candy roses in a circle on the top. It was almost time so she went upstairs without being told and put on her party dress and then, still not satisfied, she went into the front parlor to take some of Uncle Harry's roses; she would twine them around the back of Mama's chair and when Mama noticed them she would be able to say that at least she had done that part all by herself. She had to pull over a chair to reach the top of the pier table where the largest bunch of roses was, and she was so concentrated on collecting the blossoms without overturning the cut glass vase that she was not aware, until she had finished, that Thad and

Cora were quarreling in the music room, too angry to notice her. She thought first: Oh good, Cora won't get the cake. Thad was saying:

"You better stop chasing after him."

"I do as I like and you can't stop me," Cora said.

"But you know what he is. Mama would have a fit."

"I don't care what Mama says."

"What if he won't marry you?"

Cora flipped her curls. "Then I'll chase after somebody who will."

Thad's voice was rising. "You know what you are, Cora? You know what you are?"

"I'm no worse than you are, Thad Lyon, the stories that are going around."

"You watch your mouth."

"You watch out you don't catch something terrible."

Nell took her flowers and ran out of the house.

She was the first to come to the party; the garden was empty and waiting, Brewster had put the wicker chairs in a semicircle around the trellis, the grass was freshly cut and Essie had set the wicker table with a damask cloth, turning the edges under so that they hardly trailed in the grass at all; everything was so nearly perfect that Nell in a moment of fear almost ran out of the garden; instead she had to take her roses and try to make them stay on the chair, she had pulled the heads off without leaving any stem so there was no way to fasten them, and she had to settle for a mound of blossoms on the seat; they already looked a little brown and sad and so finally she took them and hid them under a bush, backing out with her dress stained and her hair snarled just as Mama came down the steps and Nell almost wet her pants right there because she thought all at once that Mama would have seen the ruined roses in the parlor and she would know who had stolen the best of them.

Mama had dressed for her birthday, she was corseted and she had a white lawn dress with full skirts and a wide sash, she had on her leghorn hat with the yellow silk roses, and her hair curled in a little frame over her forehead, Nell could see it like damp feathers under the brim. Papa was in his white linen, he always put on white linen the first of May and wore either that or seersucker through September; his hair was brushed and he was bending over Mama with a careful smile, easing her down the steps so that it looked as if her tiny feet barely touched the ground; Nell thought if he could just get her down this time without jogging her, if he could do it without causing her to gasp or cry out, then everything would be all right so far, she would kiss them all and run her finger around the edge of the yellow cake and everything would begin. Thad and Cora followed, Thad's seersucker was rumpled but his hair was slicked down and in a minute he might even smile; Edward had on his Buster Brown that was too small and Flodie, Flodie must have fussed and fussed until Essie pressed her party dress all over again, it stood out like a ballet skirt; she had on the biggest bow Nell had ever seen and she put her own hand back and remembered she hadn't bothered to have Essie fix her hair. Mama was in the garden now, she came over to the trellis and saw the chair, saying, "Oh, how pretty," and Flodie said, "I did it, Mama, Nelly and I did it," and Mama said, "Oh, my big girls, how beautiful, come here." Then she hugged them both and sat down, already picking at the bow on her first present: the wrapper, from Lila, she held it up to her shoulders and said, "Oh, how beautiful," and next she opened the second wrapper, from Cora, and said, "Oh, how beautiful," and then she opened the two packages from the dry goods store, Edward had bought her a hairbow, from him, and from Nell a bottle of orange blossom perfume; she said, "Oh, just what I wanted," she said they were the most wonderful presents she ever had and kissed the two of them; she loved the satin glasses case, from Flodie, and she kissed Flodie on both cheeks, but the whole time she was looking over their heads as if there was somebody she had expected at the party, some important presence who had not come. Papa gave a big, mysterious smile and said, "There's one more thing, a surprise from me, but not until after the ice cream and cake," and the small children fanned out like runnels in a grass fire, hot and greedy, waiting while Mama blew out the candles and cut the cake.

Of course the first piece was for Thad; he came grudgingly from the porch, where he had been leaning on the rail, but Mama withheld it, saying, "Where's my gift from my big boy Thad?"

Papa said, quickly, "Isn't it enough that he's here?"

"I thought Thad would remember and bring *something*. Did you forget me, Thad?"

His face curdled and finally he said, "You know I could never forget you."

"Well if you never forget me, Thad, how could you forget . . ."

He was still standing in front of her, bound there by her eyes, by the proffered cake; he was not free to go until she had handed it to him but he could hardly bear to stand there either, Nell watched them both in rising discomfort, wishing for the first time that there hadn't been any birthday party, they would all be better off going about their business, with Mama up in her room. She held the plate forward and at the same time offered her cheek so Thad had to bend to kiss her and then she said the best present of all would be if he spent this summer at home, he could help Papa at the office and spend more time with her, and when he pulled back, resisting, she said, well what was the matter, did he hate his home, was he tired of everything they had worked so hard to create; she had one of his hands now and when he pulled away she wouldn't let him go until, desperate for his freedom, he jerked free, saying, too loud, "I've got to go see about the CAR," so that Papa shot him a fierce look to remind him that the Electric was being saved for last and if he gave away that secret, old as he was he would be thrashed; but he wasn't even listening, he didn't even hear Mama calling after him, "Honey, you forgot your *cake.*"

By the time he came back around the house everybody had their cake, Nell and Edward had each gotten a piece with a candy rose; just then Flodie accidentally bumped Edward and his piece fell into the dirt. Even though he was too old for it Edward began to cry, blundering into Thad and sniffling until Thad said, "Sister, stop that." Edward understood that he was calling *him* sister and began crying louder, keeping it up until Thad pushed him away, saying, "Mama's boy," and in a rage at something too complicated to explain or help, pushed him again because he wouldn't stop. Edward ground his fists into his face and went and hid himself in a bush; Nell started to follow but he turned on her and yelped: "Leave me *alone.*"

Above Edward's misery Nell could hear Mama talking to Papa, saying, "You'd think he would have remembered a present, he knew as well as you do what day it was," and Papa was saying, "Lily, don't make too much of it, he's just a boy," but Mama was saying something about "Selfish, all of you; men, they just take you and use you up," but Papa was patting her on the shoulder and trying to shush her, saying, "Oh Lily, just this once . . ."

Nell ran off to the other end of the garden, Thad and Flodie were playing ball; he would hurl the ball hard and fast and she would catch it and return it to him so fast that it made him laugh. He was saying, "Flo, you are as good as a boy." Edward was watching from the steps and Thad whirled suddenly, throwing a hard, unexpected ball that hit Edward in the stomach; he said, "Come on, Sister, catch."

Edward came down, saying, "Don't call me that." His face was all jellied, he looked like he was going to cry again but instead he threw the ball back to Thad underhand, saying again, "Please don't call me that."

Thad's eyes were too bright, he said, "All right, then, come on over here and let's see how good you are."

Edward lined himself up in front of the hibiscus, and when Thad said, "Ready?" he said, "Ready," but he wasn't, because the next ball hit him again and rolled down his front into the dirt. Flodie picked it up and threw it back to Thad who pitched it at Edward, saying, "Come on, Sister, let's make a man of you." Edward missed every time and after a while he was crying and trying not to, his eyes filled so he could hardly see, so that each time the ball would fall from his fingers and Thad would have to walk over and pick it up with great patience and back off and hurl it at Edward's stomach again, saying, finally, "If you don't make a man you'll *never* get out of here." He came over to pick up the ball again and when Edward tried to fall on him and grab him just to make him stop he side-stepped as if Edward had some sickness and Thad couldn't afford to let him get too close or he would catch it too; Thad kept throwing the ball again and again and after a while Edward didn't even try to catch but clamped his knees and hands together and cringed as Thad threw ball and after ball at him; Nell, watching, knew that her day was already lost, she wanted to stop this; the day was gone and she had to stop it before the garden went too, she ran at Thad and clung to his leg, but he only set her behind him and went on throwing the ball. Helpless, she may have seen not just the loss of the garden but the loss of her future, of all their futures, or she may have understood that whatever she was trying to make of her world could never be made in this house, in the garden, anywhere; she may have seen all this or she may only have seen Edward in his misery, Thad in a terrifying, incomprehensible rage; whatever she saw she could no longer tolerate it and she threw herself down in the grass and began to scream.

She kept on screaming until finally Mama had to have Lila come and take her to her room, and before she was borne away Mama had Lila bring her over so she could kiss her sweetly, saying,

"Poor little girl. You almost spoiled Mama's birthday, poor, poor little girl." Of course Mama never used the Electric after that day, she only went out at night when there was somebody to drive her and she could wear her white watered silk and all her jewels, but she liked the wrappers, Cora's a little better than Lila's, even though Lila's was more carefully made, and in the end when she recalled her birthday, despite all their efforts she would only cry because Thad had been there, he was being very *gallant,* he had even pretended to kiss her once for every single year, stopping at twenty, but in the end even though it was her birthday he hadn't thought to bring her a single thing.

LILY

I am so happy; after all these years of everything slipping away from us, it is all starting to come back in. For years we tried but we could never get it *right;* there were nights when Papa would sit by my bed with his head in his hands, he would not let me see him crying but I would cry for him; for years he has sustained this house and all the children and the servants, he holds this whole great establishment together in his hands, and sometimes I wish I could kiss his hair and tell him I will take care of everything but we both know I never can, I have had to lie here in bed and feel everything slipping away. But since the last baby died there have been no more babies and no more losses, we are managing to keep even for a change; until now there have been no new gains, either, but I have hope now, I can feel the air quickening and I believe it is all going to start coming in. For the first time I can number my men and numbering them, I am enriched, I am the great center of the earth.

The first thing is that after all these years of worrying and counting him dead a hundred times, fearing him worse than dead, I have my brother Harry back, and this time he says he is going to settle down for good, he has found a place to live and on Wednesday nights I can look down our table and see him sitting with his dark head bent and I can call him mine. I can count Harry's son Sam, too, I think he already loves me like a mother, children always love me because I always stoop down when I am talking to them, so we are on a level, and I never ever raise my voice. I have Thad back too; he is finished with the University, he is talking about going to that war

39

over there, but it is no war of ours so I will have him stay here, with us. Thad's children will love me too, I will take them up to the attic and show them pictures of Uncle Horatio in his uniform, I will show them his sabre and some of the funny costumes we all used to wear, by then I will be well enough to be downstairs all day. Thad can name his first boy Horatio, after Harry, and the second after Papa, I can be surrounded by babies without needing to *have* babies, and when I am tired of them Thad's wife will take them away. The others will all marry Richardsons or LeFevres or Poulnots, all except Flodie, who is so plain; she can take care of me and the rest of them will move into handsome houses not far from here and bring their families to visit me, so I can count all my men and I can count my girls' husbands, and I can count Edward too; he will make his name in medicine or law but he will never marry, instead he will come home from the hospital or the courts and sit by the bed and hold my hand; Thad may make his conquests and move on, but I will have Edward to sit by the bed and hold my hand.

I have in mind the LeFevre girl for Thad, they can move into the house next to ours, it has been for sale ever since Alton Richardson died and poor Netta had to move away, I have been so afraid the wrong people would buy it. There is already a rooming house on the other side of the block, and if we do not protect ourselves the neighborhood is going to go downhill, we may have tradespeople living right next to us and the next thing any of us know there will be signs on this very street: ROOMS TO LET, or worse. I suppose we could have built on the river the way Papa said, but when I tried to think about it all I could see was jungle, snakes in the parlor and scorpions in our shoes; we would drive all day to get to town and I would feel like white trash, coming in with wrinkled hands and mud on the bottoms of my skirts. Besides, all the best people were building right here, the Richardsons and the Poulnots and the LeFevres, we would go next door to each other's parties, but now Alton has died and poor Netta has had to move away, and Will LeFevre has moved his family to Seminole Acres; he sold to that woman who lets out rooms to just anybody, I hear she takes in all kinds of tripe. Our street is still as lovely as it was the day we came here and Papa carried me up the steps, but the city is just about to catch up with us, somebody has opened a dry goods store not two blocks away and they are blasting for a state road, the Archambaults sold their land for a fortune; next we will have people pulling up under our porte cochère and asking for gasoline, there's no telling where it will all end.

But we protect life inside this house; our lives flow along together toward the future, together we are like a river in the sunlight, dappled and serene, and if a dark bird flies over we are not really threatened because there are too many of us now, one or two may falter or change but our family will not change; all those proud Reynoldses, Calhouns, Richards, the Lyons, all our forebears served kings and gathered wealth, they met and married, lived and died, to create us, and through us this family; we are the embodiment of their trust. Papa and I have taken all these generations into ourselves and now we have passed on the clear brow and handsome nose which stamp all our children and will mark their children's children too, they are our gift to the future, and if I must remind them of this from time to time it seems only right; it is always important to remember who we are. After all, we are one of the best families. I tried to explain this to Papa the other night, it seemed simple enough but he said, People are weak, no matter who they are, you have to expect them to be weak. I said, We are never weak, and when he started to speak I stopped his mouth. I had to will him to belief; when we cease to believe, then we become vulnerable.

I should not have been so upset but it was Wednesday night, and Harry did not come. I was worried to death, he has been here every Wednesday since he came back, I watch from the window and it is a pleasure to see him come around the corner; age and responsibility have not made him stiff as they have Papa, he is supple and jaunty as a boy; he will not jump the gate but he swings into it as if he could if he wanted to, and he always stops in the garden to pick a flower for me; I start downstairs then so I will be at the door to welcome him. He is a delight at dinner, joking with the children and always threatening to sing a naughty song because he knows the very thought will make me gasp and throw up my hands; he likes to laugh at my astonishment, and if he rushes through dinner, if he seems in a hurry to get away, then we are not to be concerned because he is, after all, a very important man.

Still it was Wednesday and Harry did not come; finally Papa came to bring me down to dinner and I said, You don't think something has happened to him. He said, I wouldn't worry, Lily, he may have other things to do. I said of course I was worried, I wouldn't draw a free breath until Harry was safely in the house. Papa knows what an effort it is for me to dress and come down, he suggested that I have a tray sent up but I said not to be absurd, it was Wednesday, Harry would come sooner or later and I wanted to be ready. I had Essie help me into my corsets and I put on my favorite grey silk suit with the black piping around the sleeves and the bottom of the jacket; Papa bought it for me to wear to New York but of course I haven't been out of this city since the last baby died, and I had to wear it somewhere, even though the merest splash of gravy would leave an indelible spot. I did dress slowly, however, to allow a little more time for Harry to get here, but finally I was all dressed and too restless to sit up here in my room so I came down and we sat in the living room and waited, even though Papa said, There's no point in waiting any longer, I think you ought to let Essie start serving before the roast is burned to a crisp.

I said, Papa, it is Wednesday night and we will wait for Harry. Perhaps Lila can play us one of her pieces while we wait.

Lila played the "Nocturne" and the "Moonlight Sonata" and then she asked to be excused. My littlest children are now old enough to eat at the table with us and Edward was already fretting and complaining that he was hungry, but I told him his Uncle Harry would be along soon and the least we could do would be to be polite enough to wait. Cora said she had a beau coming at seven thirty and begged to be allowed to eat early, but I said any man who would not wait was no gentleman. I think she was going to say something ugly but I gave her my Grandmother Richard look and so she turned her back instead and went off in a huff. I told Papa I thought a year or two in a finishing school would not hurt her but he reminded me that she had finished school now, and he said she was after him to let her learn typewriting so she could take a job, he thought it might be a good idea because she is about to die of restlessness. I did not have to remind him that ladies do not work, but even knowing that, he started to pursue it; I didn't want to hear about *that* so I asked him if he would call Harry's hotel, it was pushing at the back of my mind that Harry might be hurt or in danger, perhaps I should have Papa call the police, but then I thought about the embarrassment, the scandal; Essie came in just then to say that Biggie couldn't wait dinner another minute, it would be ruined, and before I could lift my hand Papa said, Very well, you may put it on and call the children.

I was in a rage, as soon as Essie was out of hearing I said,

What will Harry think when he comes and finds we have begun without him?

He said, I tried to tell you, Lily, he won't be here tonight.

I said, You are mistaken.

I am not, I saw him.

If you saw him, why haven't you told me where he is?

He said, I don't think you really want to know.

The children were all gaping so I sent them away and then I had Papa pull the sliding doors to, and then I turned to him, saying, Now tell me where he is.

You don't really want to know. He held out his hands to help me up and lead me into the dining room, but I refused them.

For all I know he is in trouble, or hurt.

Papa saw I was not going to give in so he said, Trouble, yes, but he isn't hurt. He came and put his hands on my arms, saying, Lily, I had business in the waterfront district today, I saw Harry coming out of a place they call Mingo's, he had been drinking, he was already . . .

I cut him off before he could say, Intoxicated. —He must have been there on business too.

I think not, Lily. The woman was no better than a prostitute.

I would not look at him; I said, You are mistaken, Thaddeus.

No, Lily.

I will not hear you speak of such things.

Not even if they are so?

Nothing is so until you give it a name.

I hurried to the dining table so I would not have to hear anything more. The children were waiting in their chairs and as I sat down I made a smile and said, Your Uncle Harry can't be with us tonight, children, he has been detained on important business; Thad Junior was about to speak, I did not like his expression and so I silenced him with my eyes. Naturally all that worry left me exhausted and so I had Papa help me on upstairs before Essie served dessert.

When I was settled in bed I embraced him and said, I shall never forgive Harry for missing dinner.

He said, My dear, you have to be tolerant.

I said, He has no right to disappoint me.

He's a man, Lily, every once in a while a man needs . . .

I could see he was flushed and miserable and I said, quickly, Thaddeus, I will not hear another word.

He was saying, You have to try to understand . . . but I could hear my own voice: Thaddeus, *please.* After all, I didn't want to hear about *that,* and so he turned and went back downstairs. I love him but I will not hear him talk about Harry that way.

NELL

Papa took me to the river, he didn't mean to but I was hiding in the back of the Pierce Arrow, we were playing Hide and Seek; Flodie was It, and I was waiting and waiting for her to come and find me, I think she is jealous because Uncle Harry likes me better than he does her, for all I know she was going to go off and leave me hiding in the Pierce Arrow until I either fell asleep or died from the heat. I kept wanting her to find me, if I came out before she found me then I could tell her and tell her I had won but she would say no, I didn't win, I gave up, and she would win; I was about to get out anyway but then somebody came and got in and started the automobile, I knew it wasn't Brewster because I peeked up and the back of his neck was white, with one of those fine white collars Papa always wears, I could see his black hairs just barely touching it. I folded myself down like an old rug and hid from him, so we were clear out on Center Street before he even knew I was in the car; he was humming all on one note and then I popped up from the back and said, Surprise, Papa; first he jumped, he was embarrassed about the humming, and then he looked tired as if he didn't remember exactly who I was and finally he smiled and said, Why, it's Nell, for a minute you looked just like somebody I once knew. Then he slowed down so I could climb over into the front, after that I sat next to him in the front seat, just as grand as Mama, riding along with my chin out and the wind through my hair. I felt so fine, I have been lots of places with Uncle Harry since he came back this time, but it was the first time I was ever out with Papa all by myself. Nobody else was around, not even Brewster; it was just us two and we just sailed along.

I thought first he was going to take me down town, he would park and take me along to the Daytona Building, we would march right straight through the lobby and up to his office; he would introduce me to all his secretaries and if we ran into anybody in the halls he would say: Doctor (or Judge), I would like you to meet Nell

44

Lyon, she is my youngest, my very best girl. I would get to sit in his desk chair and he might even give me a note pad and an office pencil to take home with me, all those times he took Edward to the office Edward would come home with a whole pile of things, he even let Edward sit in his chair. Once Edward came home with a ruler with black lettering; Papa would find one for me too, or maybe he would give me something none of the others had and then we would go down into the coffee shop together and he would buy me some ice cream; I only wished I was more dressed up, I knew Papa didn't care how I looked but as soon as Mama found out I was down town looking like the ragpicker's daughter, she would have a fit. Then he turned off on the river road so I would never get to see his office after all, maybe there was a big new house waiting for us with an arbor in the front and grass going right down to the river, Papa would let me out of the car and we would walk up and see it together, I would promise not to tell anybody, not even Flo, until he was ready to put Mama in the car and take her out there, he would have the darkies spread flower petals all over the front walk. Or maybe it would be a houseboat, he would name it after me, or maybe it was only a sailboat, I would be the first one in the family to know about it and we would go out for a sail, just Papa and me. It wasn't going to be any of those things, we kept on driving along the river road until we had passed the Yacht Club and the City Boat Club and the houses petered out into shacks and the shacks petered out into just trees and finally I remembered about the cabin, somebody built us a cabin on the river a long time ago but none of us girls ever got to see it, Mama says no lady would go out there, her hair would dry out and the sun would turn her face red and wrinkled just like that. Papa used to take Thad down there to fish before he got too big and then he took Edward but Edward didn't like it, he never caught anything, and finally Edward came back with a fishhook caught in the fat part of his hand, he had to have three stitches so that was the end of that. When Papa gave up on Edward I wanted to tell him I would love to fish, I would cut up fish innards for bait or anything he wanted me to, but I knew it wouldn't do any good because he would only tell me I was too little and besides, the river was a place for men.

But here I was after all, we were on the last road that would take the car and after a while Papa pulled over and we got out, we had to go hushing along on pine needles until finally we came out on

45

the bank, I could see right out over the water and everything was so beautiful that I said, *Daddy,* but when he turned too quickly, saying, *What,* I didn't have any more words to tell him what I meant, that I wanted God to freeze us and the river at that very minute, so he and I would be together out there under the black pines and the live oaks strung with Spanish moss, the river would stand still in front of us for the rest of time; I couldn't say anything, I reached for his hand but he had already started down to the edge, so I only followed him out on the dock. It was getting late, the sky was about to go pink, I thought about Biggie waiting dinner and Mama getting angrier and angrier but I didn't say anything, if she wanted to have Essie whale me then let her have Essie whale me, if that was what I had to pay then I would pay it, here I was with Papa and the whole river in front of us. The water lapped around the dock and if I looked straight out I could pretend we were out there on a boat and the river was standing still while we went by; if I looked back I could see the sawgrass spreading along the bank in both directions, rich as plush and crackling with live things; after a while the tide would come in and the water would almost cover it, if we sat there long enough it would come almost to the top of the dock. I thought for a while I could skate out on the water without even breaking the surface; there were clouds banking far off, they could turn dark and it might rain but if it rained it would rain far off somewhere; where we were, everything was still. Papa had his coat off and his collar was open; he didn't talk and neither did I, I had the idea that as long as I didn't say anything we wouldn't move, we would just sit there forever and look out at the river, the end of the world would find us sitting there. Of course Papa would get up in just another minute but I still think about me and Papa by the river, I have us in a soap bubble; I think when the time comes that my life is absolutely right again, then I will stop time and keep my life the way it is right then, because by that time I will know how to hold it, not in a soap bubble, but in a crystal globe.

Papa stirred, I let out the next breath and after that the sky started going violet, and then it went pink, it was about to go salmon when Papa got up, saying, We'd better get back, the sun is going down.

Can't I see the cabin?

He was still trying to remember who we were, he said, Yes, I think you can.

I've always wanted to see the cabin.

He said, Honey, watch out for snakes.

We went up the steps, there was a lock on the door and he unlocked it and then showed me the way inside; it was dark but after a while we got used to it, and the first thing was that there were dirty glasses and a bottle on the one table, and the floor was smudged with stamped-out cigarettes; I knew Papa would never leave it this way and I said, Somebody has been here, Papa, expecting him to be angry with whoever it was, or at least with me, for marking it.

Instead he was only distracted, running his hand over my hair and saying, I'd say you were right, Edward.

Nell.

Nell.

I was looking at the hallway, it was dark and led somewhere I couldn't see, I didn't want to see where it went and so I began pulling on Papa's hand. They might still be here. We would go into the back room and they would jump out from behind a door.

I said, Papa, what if they're still here.

They aren't here.

We'd better go and tell the sheriff.

He was standing there in the dimness, dreaming. When I pulled on him again he said, It's not important.

Why was I so angry for him? It's your place, they've ruined your place.

It's all right, he said. He was holding something that had belonged to a woman. It was only your brother Thad.

I started to say, Thad wouldn't . . . but how could I know whether Thad would or not? I didn't even want to know, so I said, Papa, we're going to be late for dinner, Biggie will kill us.

Don't you want to see the rest of the cabin?

Next time, Papa. I tried to make him look right at me, so there would be a pledge. Next time.

Instead he said, You're sure you don't want to see the rest?

Mama will have a fit.

He sighed. I suppose you're right. He drew me out the door and locked it behind us, and when he saw how low the sun was he said, I'll tell you what let's do, let's pick up some flowers on the way home, something nice to surprise your Mama with.

I told him that would be fine.

In the car going back he didn't talk and I didn't talk, we both

47

forgot about the flowers and then, when we were back on Center Street, Papa said, How old are you now, and I told him, Ten, and then without explanation or anything he said, Honey, I know you love your Uncle Harry, but I don't want you to pin too much hope on him.

He says I'm his favorite niece.

Papa reached over on the seat and took my hand, saying, Just the same, don't count on him too much.

I was so happy to feel his hand that I said, I won't, Papa.

You have to learn, he said, you just can't count on men.

LILA

I have made my debut. Even though there is a war on I have had to make my debut, Mama has always talked about presenting her daughters to society in her own home with all the brass shining and lights glinting in the crystal chandeliers, but we had to dance in the ballroom at the St. John's Club because by the time Mama was half-way through her list we knew there would not be room for everybody in the house. We had two orchestras and too much champagne and Mrs. Mahittie catered because she does all the best parties, there was a hot buffet at midnight and there were bowls of nuts for the drinkers and little cakes for the old ladies, who all came in their boas and tiaras and stomachers and sat in plush armchairs around the fringes of the floor; Papa kept the orchestra on past one and we all danced until three o'clock in the morning and according to the society page and all those women who telephoned Mama the next morning, it was a great success. It almost killed Mama that my brother Thad insisted on coming to the party in his uniform, but he said every party needs a *memento mori,* it makes everybody have a better time than they are supposed to, and perhaps he was right; that night all the girls looked beautiful and the boys were handsome and the gaiety was touching and a little desperate because we knew a third of the boys would be gone within the year, off to France to join the third who were already there in the blood-soaked mud, yet everybody kept on laughing and whirling the way they must have danced before the Battle of Waterloo; I thought from the first that we should have saved the money and given it to War Relief instead but when I looked at Mama that night I saw her face shone, she was more beautiful than I have ever seen her and I thought perhaps that was why I hadn't been able to refuse.

I would have preferred a year at college, which would have cost Papa about the same and meant so much more to me, I would rather have been left alone and cost him nothing, but I don't have the power Cora does. She is small and capricious, with a cupid's bow mouth and those foolish-looking gilded curls but Cora is the forceful one, she has said no to all the duties of the eldest girl; I am taller and steady, I am supposed to be strong and so I have inherited all of Cora's responsibilities, and that is why I ended up at the St. John's Club instead of Cora, Mama's offering to society, letting Sam Le-Fevre push me around the floor. Sam was my escort because Mama sets great store by appearances, and Sam is a very personable young man; I think she would like me to marry him because Sam is a May-flower descendant and has a beautiful singing voice; there is no need for her to know that he is already an alcoholic who turns ugly after the first three drinks, there is no need for her to know what he said to me the night of the dance, or to see the bruises on my arms which are just now fading out to yellow.

Mama called me in six months ahead and told me I was going to have the finest debut our city had ever seen, she said she waited for me because she has never liked Cora but I know differently; I know Mama had all her plans laid for Cora four years ago and Cora only stopped her by threatening to run away to Atlanta with the mailman the minute the invitations were engraved. I don't know, per-haps she would have been better off with the mailman after all, at least Mama would know where she is at night; the mailman may not be an FFV, like Punk Gresham, but he doesn't have liquor on his breath in the middle of the morning, and he wouldn't take her some of the places Punk and Cora go. Every time Cora goes in to say good night to Mama, Mama says, And who is your escort; Cora leans over her reeking of Fatimas and each time she names Punk it drives an-other nail into Mama's hide. So Mama created this debut partly to spite Cora; she likes to tell me it was always planned for me because I am the most beautiful and I have done the most for the little chil-dren, but if she did it for me at all it was for a more complicated reason; tall as I am I still look the most like her, she was able to look at me in the white gown with the panniers and see her own face where mine should be. Every time I waltzed off with somebody new she would incline her head and fix her eyes on me until I felt them and under their heat I would have to turn and take my partner over to be introduced; then she would smile and lower her lashes and flutter her fan at him as if, by offering myself, the virgin sacrifice, I had somehow redeemed her youth. Now that I am launched, now that I have been introduced to all those weak and foolish young men who used to make dog-eyes at me and push me down in the mud in the second grade, now that the offering is complete I am expected to make the best marriage possible, to a man Mama would have chosen for herself. After that I think I am expected to visit all the capitals of Europe and be photographed in every one, I am supposed to come home and reign over society so that each time I open a hospital or give a ball Mama can look at my picture in the paper and see herself instead. Even though I am to live out my life in this small city, under her mantle, she will write to me on lavender paper, saying, *At last, Lila, I have made you a lady. Look about you and see everything I have done for you,* for there is that, too: having submitted to her will, I am expected to serve her pride, she will be able to say to the world, I have always been a great lady and a perfect mother; now look and see what a great lady my daughter Lila has become. Planning this party, she said to me, Never forget, Lila, you must never forget exactly who you are.

Who am I, after all?

Perhaps foreseeing all she would demand I first said, Mama, we can't afford it, but she only motioned me to sit down, saying, It's vulgar to talk about money, dear.

She kept her eyes on me until I had pulled the slipper chair over to her side and then she handed me a list of two hundred names. I think we will present you at the Christmas season, the poinsettias are so lovely then.

This was in June. But Mama . . .

There are always so many parties, I think we had better open the season with yours.

. . . Papa was sick all winter . . .

People get so jaded by the end of Christmas week.

. . . he still looks so tired . . .

I want them to remember your party for years.

We were in her room, she was out of bed for the afternoon and sitting on the rose velvet chaise with one of her velvet lap robes over her legs, she was looking out the window and buffing her nails; I don't know even now whether she heard me; if she did, then she chose to go on as if I had never spoken. Papa will present you, I can hardly wait to see him in his tailcoat again, it has been such a long time.

She reached for her silver cuticle stick, her head was inclined and she was like an angora kitten, a Dresden ornament, so plump and pretty that I knew there was no point in trying to explain about Papa's land dealings; I still thought I might be able to think of some way to deter her and I said, Mama.

We may have to have it altered, I think your Papa is a little stouter than he used to be.

I thought how harried he looks; when he sits down at our table at night his cheeks are transparent, but he will never trouble Mama with his concerns and so there was no way for me to tell her; instead I said, I don't want a debut, Mama.

Of course you do, you're a Lyon and a lady, Lila, you must be presented to society. I made my debut at the St. Cecilia Ball, my gown was made in Paris and all the best people came, we danced until the morning light; an English earl was my escort, Lila, an English earl, he died at Omdurman.

Can we talk to Papa before we decide?

She had been facing the window with her eyes fixed on our Royal Poinciana; it was so strange and formal, she swiveled at the waist and turned to me with her shoulders set and her head at an elegant angle, it was just as if she was about to bow and begin a dance; she said, Papa knows what is right.

And so Papa has given me my debut, we had guests from Charleston and Savannah, people from Atlanta and Richmond came, there was a moment when I thought Simon Millard would come down from Washington but his mother decided they would have Christmas abroad and after all, I only saw him the one time, at Jeannine Haskell's house last Christmas, so there was no reason for me to hope for him to come. Thad had thought he would be in France by Christmas but the war cheated him and so he had to come home after all; he would sail on New Year's Day and I looked at him in his uniform and wondered if he was going to be killed; he came and cut in on Sam LeFevre, saying, What was he saying to you?

Oh, never mind, Thad. I was blinking fast, trying to smile, but Sam had danced along with me, humming a string of words into my ears, words so vile that I would hear them every night for months; I could feel Thad's arm firm across my back and was happy to have him to be strong; he said:

Let me take him out and thrash him.

It doesn't matter.

I know him, Lila. What did he say?

It's all right, Thad.

I'll kill him.

No, Thad, Mama would die.

He looked around him then, saying, This is all for Mama, isn't it?

A lot of things we do are for Mama, Thad. Over his shoulder I could see Flodie and Edward at the punch table, both cross and surfeited, with the fruit punch and petits fours already going sour in their stomachs; they both looked sallow and exhausted, with frosting smeared on their fingers and dark smudges under their eyes.

Thad was saying, Does she know what she's doing?

I'm not sure what she's doing.

This time I won't be back.

She's our mother, Thad.

Lila, you have to get away. Find a good man and get out of here.

I wanted to tell him about Simon, but I knew what he would say if they met: too sensitive, look at those deep eyes, that uncertain mouth.

He stiffened his arm against my back: Promise.

Could I have promised? I was thinking about our mother, about Cora, whom she still loves best because Cora will defy her, about whatever it was I had been selected to prove in Cora's stead; as it was, Punk cut in, he was only a little drunk and the two of us sailed away to some dark corner where he could crook his arm around my waist and push his wet moustache against my ear until Cora came and found us and led him outside where they could fight in peace. After a while Alden Ford would see them missing and go outside to separate them; of the two, Alden is the gentleman. Cora is engaged to Punk but I think she would like to marry them both; Alden is by far the better man but in the end she will cleave to Punk because the two of them are very much alike. It was, for reasons I cannot completely explain, partly because of Cora and her choices that I could not go into the powder room to rest for a while, but instead had to go back, smiling, to the floor. I could see Mama had been looking for me, craning between waltzing couples; when she saw me she smiled and sat back, her eyes never wavering until I had let Sam LeFevre find me and we began to dance again.

So the two of us whirled, the cream of local society, and Mama was able to sit there in her diamonds with the turquoise *peau de soie* in opposing slashes across her shining bosom, presiding over a party which was, I think, the outward sign or emblem of everything she has ever expected from her life. She had given us a quiet childhood with clean hair ribbons and starched dresses and rides in the wicker pony cart, we were to carry with us memories of afternoons on the lawn under the dappling trees and a home where the silver was always polished and nothing was ever disordered, not even people got out of place; we are to forget all the bitter words we have said to each other over the years and remember instead a series of tableaux: the family around the tree at Christmas time, with all the candles flaming—I in an angel robe, singing, Cora dancing with a Spanish comb in her hair; a party on a velvet lawn which never existed outside our memories, with everybody laughing, and Mama at the center of a smiling group of children all waltzing barefooted in the grass; this particular dance, or party, or sacrificial offering; I could almost hear Mama remembering: It was at the St. John's Club, all the best people came and Lila's escort was a Mayflower descendant, a Mayflower descendant; poor boy, he died somewhere in France.

I changed partners almost as many times as Mama would have wanted me to, I went to the punch table to chatter and giggle with last year's debutantes and I took the time to bend over each of the gallery of old ladies, pressing the hand of each and accepting each one's compliments with my best smile, and after a while I turned to a new partner and felt a firm arm about my waist, I was conscious of the sinew through the black fabric of his coatsleeve, I could imagine the white shirt underneath and beneath that his forearm flexing against me, flat-boned and vital under dark curling hair; I let myself be drawn against his body, feeling the way he moved and taking the measure of his chest, and only then did I look up and see that it was Papa, that he was not only Papa whose presence I had assumed all my life, he was also a man; I saw as well how drawn he looked and understood not only that he was a man but that he was going to die before I wanted him to, he had already begun the process; understanding this, beginning to comprehend his needs, I took Papa's measure and at the same time I comprehended Simon too; I wanted to shield Papa with my own body and restore to him everything he must have lost, I could not supply whatever Mama had failed to give him but I could offer my own strength, I would hold him up with my two arms if I had to, with my bare hands holding his life; just then my brother Thad cut in and Papa turned away without even a word and he went to our mother, bending over and whispering to her. She looked up at him, lifting her arms so he could help her, and although her foot has barely touched the floor for the past six years she rose to him and the two of them stepped out in a waltz, so that, watching, I began to understand what it is she has hoped for all these years. At last she could contemplate her family about her as it should be; with Uncle Harry dead she knew, for once and all, where he was, and for that night, at least, she had the rest of us in sight, Papa manly and attentive, her children all handsome, combed, graceful ornaments to society: Thad was twirling me, Edward propelled little Nelly with a look of dutiful misery and Flodie stood right by the punch bowl in her party dress, thinking God knows what; even Cora was with us now, dressed to the eyes and standing on the arms of not one but two handsome men, and there was Mama at the center of all of us, gleaming like the sun, she could look about at all her faithful, shining planets and know her first satisfaction, without having to know that in the next minute all those lumps of rock and earth would go dark and begin to fall away from her, hurtling out into the unknown and leaving no one and no thing to reflect back her own unavailing light.

§§§§ §§§§

From the beginning Cora had gone places with the two of them and even now, after several years of marriage, she could not have been sure why; she had been so fond of both of them for so many years that on her wedding night it had even come as something of a surprise to her when she and Punk said goodbye to Alden at the entrance to the Hotel Seminole and Punk took her upstairs to the suite he had reserved and they went inside together and closed the door.

She had met Punk Gresham at somebody's party way back before the war, she had gone into his arms to dance without even thinking twice, drawn by the prickly little moustache and the way his raffish grin exposed a triangle of teeth; she had the idea that he stood for everything she wanted: freedom, reckless selfishness, midnight rides in open cars; when she used to come in from an evening with Punk she would see Mama's light still on and Mama, who so seldom came out of her room, would get up and come all the way down the hall to tax her, standing, accusing, in her robe at the top of the stairs. Then Cora, wearing lipstick and colors too bold to become a true lady, would stand on the landing with her compact little body jiggling and she would listen impatiently to her mother's cautions, careless in stance and redolent of the flesh, thinking: When was the last time she spent so much of herself on me? And so she would use Punk to defy Mama, knowing as she did that Punk would never care whether she smoked or drank or went without her girdle, he wouldn't even notice what kind of language she used, while Mama would catch her up on every word, outraged by even the suggestion of anything crude. She would say, Cora, Cora, what are people going to *think* of you," and Cora, outraged, would cry, "I don't *care* what people think," and then before Mama could stop her she would go running out to the car.

Still for all her defiant vulgarity she was her mother's daughter; all her life she would, against her will and sometimes unknowing, find herself drawn in directions her mother wanted her to go, and so perhaps she would not have seen Punk if there had been no Alden Ford, for Alden complemented Punk. If she had cared to look at it, Cora would have had to admit that he offered all those niceties Mama would have said Punk was lacking; he was *gallant* where Punk was brusque and thoughtless; he held doors when Punk forgot his manners, and when Punk's tongue was too sharp and he hurt Cora, Alden was always there to make it up. Everyone said they had been friends for so long that they looked alike and it was true, but Alden's features were finer, his eyes were set deeper than Punk's and he talked with more intelligence; still where Alden was tentative Punk was decisive; Punk had a thick skin while Alden was easily hurt so that Cora was drawn to Punk, finally, because for all his grace Alden was flawed by a vulnerability which irritated her. They had always done everything together, when the time came they went off to war together, and while they were gone Cora loyally wrote to them both. Alden's letters were more romantic, they glowed with a gentle affection, but, reading Punk's splotched and impatient notes ("Alden will tell you about the lousy landscape"), she would remember his body against hers, the hint of cruelty in the way he held her, and she would throw Alden's letter aside to dream about the wedding; after the wedding she would love Punk without restraints. She sent her imagination as far afield as she could make it go, making up new things for them to do and say and always keeping in mind Mama; she would laugh to herself, thinking: Wouldn't Mama have a fit. Still when her imagination failed her she would always take up Alden's letters, which sent her into another kind of reverie, so perhaps even then it might have happened differently.

To the end, she would keep in the back of her mind a snapshot of herself with Punk and Alden, although she had torn it up the minute she saw it, saying, "You know I never looked like that." In the picture Alden and Punk stood on the running board of somebody's Ford with Cora between them, leaning neither to the left nor the right, so that if she wanted to in later years she could tell herself there had been a time when it might have gone either way. The car was pulled up on the sand and the three of them were naked in wool suits with canvas belts and complicated straps; Alden and Punk wore their boaters and beneath their moustaches their teeth showed like white shells for they were laughing, in a time before mortality. They were just back from the war.

She would always remember the night of that day at the beach, or, rather, she would think of that picture as having been taken on one particular day, although it could have been any one of the scores of days they spent on the beach that summer; she would lie on the blanket and look from under her curved arm at first one of her men and then the other. They lay equidistant and she would know before she rolled her head on her arms in feigned sleep that when she turned to Punk she would see only the back of his head, and although she could feel his hand resting on the back of her thigh he would be snoring; she knew equally well that when she rolled her head toward Alden she would find him resting his chin on one fist, looking directly at her with an expression she could not read. Although it could have been any one of a dozen other days she would think of it as the day of the snapshot that she caught Alden watching her and instead of closing her eyes, acknowledged him with a smile.

He said, "Swim?"

She said, "Punk," already knowing that Alden would say, "He's dead to the world." Because he was right she got up, letting Punk's hand slide to the blanket, thinking: Wake up, wake *up*. He only snuffled and turned over in his sleep, spread-eagled on the square that had held the three of them. Alden was on his way into the water and Cora followed, intensely conscious of the salty-sweet warmth of the air and the fragments of light glittering on the water's surface. They swam out to the sand bar without talking and sat there, up to their shoulders in water, looking out to sea until finally Cora giggled, saying, "Punk will wonder where we are."

Alden looked at her. "No he won't."

An undercurrent drew her toward him, she could feel her bottom bumping on the sand and she stood up quickly, breaking free. "He will so," she said and made a brisk flat dive, swimming toward the shore.

The blanket was empty and her mind sorted a half-dozen fears: Punk had left, she would never see him again; he had started out after her and Alden and the undertow had caught him and swept him out to sea. She found him instead at the refreshment pavilion some half-mile down the beach, Cora recognized him at a distance and saw that he was talking to some girl she had never seen before, and when against her will she broke into a run, stumbling over the sand and calling, "Punk, I thought you were lost," he did not turn to acknowledge her.

She could hear her own voice, thin and querulous, calling, "Punk. Punk?"

The girl saw her first and made a show of tapping him on the shoulder and pointing to Cora. Equally elaborately he turned, waved and then turned back to the girl.

Furious, running away, Cora felt the sand trap each foot in turn and she pulled first one and then the other free, aware that her thighs were rubbing together ungracefully and her body was bobbling, out of her control. She slowed to a walk but by this time Punk was thudding after her, and she was surprised by the force with which he took her arm and turned her around.

"If you can't wait to swim with me, sweetheart, we won't go swimming at all."

At home that evening or one of the other evenings she would be aware of the chafe of her pink shoulders inside her summer dress, she would feel the salt accumulated in her hair and she would go to the music room, perhaps to spite her mother, and play the opening of one of the concert pieces she had been forced to learn simply because Lila played so beautifully; then, to prove herself, she would elide into a dance-hall song without a break, pumping her elbows and

57

stamping her foot, conscious of the sound she made increasing, pervading the handsome, dusky room and filtering upstairs. Playing, she was aware of walls rising and mahogany looming and in her mother's room the Eastlake furniture standing in dark walnut ranks, accusing her. There was a slight difference that particular night, although she would not be able to remember for the life of her whether it was the night of the day the snapshot was taken. That night she dreamed at the piano, sliding from Lizst into Debussy; some intimation had seized her so that she was not in the least surprised when she heard the doorbell and looked up to see not Punk standing in the archway but Alden, hesitant in his Palm Beach suit. Behind him in the hall poor Nelly was dipping and grinning, Cora saw she could hardly wait to get upstairs and tell Mama the right one had come for once, and something in her pathetic, barefaced joy so irritated Cora that she gave Nelly a look like a thrown cleaver and then turned on Alden too quickly, saying, "Well?"

"Cora, I want to talk."

Cora could hear Nell overhead now, she imagined Nell's voice and Mama's voice and because Mama would be too pleased she dodged Alden, saying, "Punk will be waiting, I have to get my purse."

He tried to hold her. "Cora."

But she knew what he wanted to say and it was important for her to silence him, for in her cunning greed she knew that so long as there was no declaration between them she could have Punk and keep Alden too; if she married Alden she knew as surely as she stood there that she would lose Punk, and she knew as well that no matter what she did, Alden would be forever faithful; she knew as well that her mother was upstairs in the bedroom, waiting, pleased for once; she could hear Nelly calling, and because she could not bear to answer her mother's summons, she brushed past all of Alden's sweet, unspoken words, and led the way out of her mother's house.

She and Punk set the date later that week, and the wedding was within the month; Cora rushed it so Mama would not have time to make it a family production with too many relatives and fights over the flowers; instead she was married at home, surrounded by her brothers and sisters and a few of Punk's friends who must have seemed a little too loud and too common, because Mama grew faint after only a few minutes and had to be taken upstairs. The wedding was dry because of the new Prohibition law, so no sooner had she cut the cake than Cora mounted to the landing and threw her bouquet so hard it hit Lila right in the face; then she and Punk led their friends back to the tiny apartment, where there was plenty of liquor; it was only one in a long series of times they would drink together over the years. After a while Punk and Cora had Alden drive them to the honeymoon hotel; he would go back to the apartment and wash glasses and empty the ashtrays, so that when they got back, life could go on more or less as it had before.

They fixed up the spare bedroom for Alden, painting it in bachelor brown and hanging curtains in a masculine plaid. The boys were in business and Cora kept house for both of them, welcoming each home from work with a smile and a drink; they did everything together and there was only one door closed to Alden; for the rest it was share and share alike. Cora rejoiced in her riches, spending the days cleaning and polishing, planning little casseroles, beaming over the dinner table as they took turns praising each meal. When the dishes were done it was her pleasure to do a turnabout, rolling her stockings and putting on her best Clara Bow mouth so they could go out together to the only speakeasy in town. Laughing, she would adorn herself with the two of them, wearing them on her arms like fox furs, looking over her shoulder at the other women she saw: *See, I have two.* After Papa died they went around to see Mama every Tuesday, Cora would take a quart of ice cream and put it in dishes for everybody; still laughing, she would look into Mama's fierce, dark eyes and think: Poor Mama, see how much better I have done than you. On the way home she would make Alden put the top down so the whole neighborhood could see them going, trailing a string of giggles behind them in the night. Sometimes one of Cora's friends would say, "He's darling, but how do you put up with him, I mean, every meal, every night?" "Oh," Cora would say, "we couldn't get along without Alden," speaking with the same warmth she would later offer the fox terrier Punk bought for them, never sure whether Alden was friend or possession, even as she could not be sure whether the dog was possession or child.

Without thinking it out, she knew Punk's feelings for Alden must be more complicated and more subtle: Alden was the brains of the business, but he was more; Alden was the family flatterer, the praiser of Cora's cooking, the admirer of each new dress; Alden remembered birthdays and their anniversary, and although Cora may have thought at first that she and Punk were doing Alden a favor, giving him a home without responsibility, she understood after the first quarrel that Alden had a great deal to give them. She never found out what had gone wrong for Punk that particular day but he had come in, and without drawing breath he had begun to snipe: the place looked terrible, what had she been doing all day, and for the first time in their marriage she let herself go, falling into a quarrel so terrible that at first neither of them saw Alden in the door; his hands were moving in distress, he was saying, "Children, children, stop." She saw he would do anything to make them stop.

Punk was behind Cora, rigid and scowling; Alden was in front of her, joking but not joking. "Children, you know how I hate scenes."

She was not finished with Punk but Alden seemed so upset that she let him smooth things over, administering gin like medicine, taking them out to dinner in his anxiety, relaxing at last when they both smiled. From then on she would look to Alden for a way out of any unpleasantness; she understood that he would not tolerate ugliness or disorder and he would take her out in the car and not bring her back until he had made her laugh, he would take them out to dinner, he would take them to Paris or the moon if he had to, to maintain equilibrium.

"Alden, I don't know what we'd do without you."

Alden would blush and say, "You won't have to put up with me much longer," because they all still thought he might be married some day.

But somehow Alden's girls never quite fit in, perhaps because the three of them functioned so neatly as a unit, the boys rakish and manly, Cora playing to them both. They all liked the same things: parties, trips, dinners at the Club, and certain of Alden's money provided the final touches: bracelets for Cora, the fur wrap, the best rooms in the hotel. When she spoke Alden was always there to listen, Alden would always dance with her when Punk was too tired, but when Punk came into his own with a string of wisecracks Alden would recede tactfully. When Alden brought a girl along they would all three bend to her with bright, interested smiles, but by this time they had too much conversation in common, the jokes and allusions were too hard to explain. Cora made quick friends with all the girls, saying, when Alden pressed her about them: "I don't know, Alden, I just don't know," so that under the force of her eyes he would say, finally, "Maybe Maudie (or Jane or Sylvia) isn't exactly what I had in mind."

Cora thought she would have been more generous if even one of them were good enough for Alden, but they all fell short. It was her fault, she thought, for dressing her best and keeping a nice house for him and always being funny and fond; in her generosity she wished sometimes that she were two, so she could marry Alden; it was the least she could do after accustoming him to a certain quality of life so that no other girl seemed good enough, but if she felt a little guilty at tying up his affections in this way she would think, Better to have loved and lost than never to have loved at all: what was it Cyrano wanted? One silken skirt, rustling through his life. While she was still living at home she had found her sister Nelly in a corner weeping over the play; pressed, Nell had told her about the French lady with two lovers and although she had never been much of a reader, Cora had snatched the book from her and read it through because in her heart, she was sure Alden was in love with her.

She would watch him in the kitchen in the mornings, with his face pink from shaving and the sunlight on his dark hair, she would be conscious of the strength in his hands and the muscles moving beneath his coat; she would cherish the idea that he was right there, under her eyes, and that he would probably be in love with her all his life. She was wise enough never to tax him with it, knowing she could keep this romance only so long as she held it at a distance; it was her antidote for Punk's wry ill temper, the embraces which more and more often turned sour even as their bodies met.

So naturally she felt betrayed when he brought Margaret home without prior announcement; she was forced to reexamine all those nuances, those significant looks at the breakfast table, because it was apparent from the way he handed her in the door that Margaret had been in his mind for several weeks; even as he had flashed a kiss across her cheek on his way out that morning he had known he would bring Margaret home tonight. He presented her to Cora more gently than he had any of the others, perhaps asking her forgiveness even as he willed her to accept this one because she was special; quiet and plain as she was, she meant more than all of the flappers and debutantes and girlish schoolteachers he had paraded through their lives so far. Cora could not be sure what moved her that night but she set out the best dinner she had ever cooked, she deferred to

Margaret and she condescended to Margaret, she made Alden stop and tell Margaret the complete history of every allusion any of them made and she herself gave a painstaking explanation of every one of their jokes; she was so sweet and obliging that even Punk was disturbed by it; after dinner, when they were sitting around drinking watered bootleg whiskey, and Cora launched into a minute description of her breakfast preparations for Alden, Punk snapped:

"For God's *sake,* Cora, will you stop?"

She let her eyes cloud over too fast. "I was only . . . I thought Margaret ought to know how Alden likes his eggs."

"Well you don't have to stampede her."

"It's all right," Margaret said, already puzzled. She was looking from one to the other. "It's all right."

Punk was saying, "She can't leave anybody alone for a minute."

Alden was shifting in his seat, lifting one hand as if he could spread his palm like a policeman and make them stop.

Cora could hear her voice rising, tremulous. "I don't know what you mean."

". . . won't give Alden a minute to himself."

"Punk, please . . ."

Alden said, desperately, "Hey, how about a movie?"

". . . think if he'd let her, she'd go in and wipe his ass."

"Punk!"

Margaret was already on her feet, looking miserable. She tugged at Alden and they stood together, saying, "Better go."

Cora was crying; she saw over her handkerchief that Alden was lingering only for her sake, and knowing how much it hurt him to see her this way she said, gallantly, "We're no fun, Alden. Why don't you two go on?"

She knew well how much he hated disorder and it satisfied her to watch the two of them flee.

The fight after they left was not nearly as bad as she would let Alden think it had been. She and Punk squabbled until they were both tired of it and then went into the kitchen and finished a quart of ice cream between them, wondering what the fuss had been about, and after that they went to bed and made love, with Cora slipping out of bed the minute Punk dropped off to sleep. She put on an old bathrobe and went out into the living room to keep vigil, huddling and shrinking the minute she heard Alden at the door. She saw him hesitate in the doorway, standing with the light behind him, and she made a small sound.

"Cora?"

"Don't turn on the light."

Alden said, "Are you all right?"

She sniffled. "Don't worry about a thing, I'm fine."

He went on too quickly. "How did you like Margaret?"

"Oh, she's lovely." Cora gave a sharp little cry. "Oh!"

"He didn't hurt you, did he?"

"Of course not."

"We were—thinking about getting married."

"How wonderful. I hope . . ." She was sniffling again. "I just hope you have a better . . ."

"You and Punk and I have a wonderful time."

"The three of us."

He drew back. "You don't think Margaret and I would . . ."

"Fight? Every married couple fights."

"No," Alden said firmly, "I wouldn't want it to be like that."

"Oh Alden, I don't know what we'll do without you."

He had his arm around her shoulder. "It's all right, Cora, it's all right."

"But when you marry Margaret . . ."

"I only said I was thinking about it," he said, tightening his arm. "I didn't say I was going to do it any time soon."

"I know it's selfish, but I'm glad." She could hear her voice lift. "When it does happen, Punk and I are going to give you a swell reception. We'll do it up brown at the St. John's Club."

When he saw she felt better he giggled with relief; they raided the icebox together, sitting down to tremendous sandwiches in the early dawn.

A few months later, when she was feeling stronger about it, Cora would say, "If you're going to marry Margaret, Alden, you'd better go ahead and marry Margaret. My best dress is getting wrinkled with age."

"I don't know . . ."

"You don't know what you're missing," Cora said, but as it turned out he never did marry Margaret; the moment had passed, and so she still had both of them.

She should have known she could count on Mama to try to ruin it; everything she did seemed cheap when Mama looked at it. Cora was only trying to be nice, Alden and Punk had a Rotary meeting one Tuesday night and Cora took the ice cream over to Mama's all by herself, already pleased by her own generosity. The two of them sat in Mama's room talking about nothing until the shadows gathered and Mama said, out of the midst of them:

"Why are you always afraid to come and see me by yourself?"

"What?"

"Don't you want to talk to me?"

"Of course I do, Mama, I love talking to you."

Mama seemed to take on mass; soft as she was in her pastel bedjacket, she looked strangely threatening, so that Cora watched her in a sweet dread which fulfilled itself as Mama said, "You're afraid I'll say something about your two men."

Cora swallowed, saying, "Why Mama, I don't know what you mean."

"Two men." Mama regarded her with a grave, nearsighted gaze. "I'm your mother and I love you, I have to tell you what I think."

"You mean you think I'm . . ."

"What else could I think? Two men, in that tiny little place. Two men."

"But I'm not, Mama, I'm *not*."

"Then why are you crying?"

"Oh Mama," Cora said, helpless, "you always think the worst of me."

Mama said, "I only know what I see," overriding her denials with her eyes closed and her soft hands flat on the comforter, fixing Cora at last with a loving, unrelenting stare: "Appearances."

Cora was sobbing, in a rage at herself for being so easily hurt. "But we can't just get *rid* of Alden."

"Then you'd better have a baby," Mama said.

"Oh, *Mama*." She wheeled and ran, with the next words fully formed and ringing in her head, so that she could never be sure she hadn't shouted, from the hall, "Oh Mama, go to *hell*."

Cora cried all the way home, seeing all the streets and houses, her whole life distorted by tears, and by the time Punk and Alden came home she was inconsolable, not because she set store by anything Mama said but because Mama could make her beautiful, comfortable life look so shabby; when Punk took her to bed she was still sobbing, perhaps because she understood now that although she had

64

always been faithful to each of her men, saving her body for Punk and certain of her hopes for Alden, she had never been able to love either of them exclusively and so perhaps would never love any man with purity, no matter how long she lived. Lying awake that night, with her eyes fixed on the dark ceiling, she vowed to put the whole thing out of her mind, but even though she willed otherwise she may have known that she would all her life end by reaping the seed Mama had planted. So it happened that some weeks later, in a resentful acquiescence for what she would always pretend were reasons other than her mother's, she touched Punk in the night and opened the question, saying with trepidation: "Punk, what if we had a baby?" Because it was the first time, he hugged her and laughed, saying, "Don't be ridiculous," and she was able to put it out of her mind for the time being.

LILY

The house used to be full of people all of the time, sometimes I used to think it was no better than the County Orphanage, with some child crying all the time, and now I can't even get anybody to come and bring me a cup of tea. Biggie is still in the kitchen, her cooking is worse than ever and Flodie says she wants more money; I say we can always find somebody else and then Flodie gets on her bulldog look and tries to tell me there isn't anybody else. So we still have Biggie, for better or worse, but Brewster has been gone for so long that I can't be sure whether he quit or got cut in a fight and went to jail or Papa caught him stealing and had to let him go; Essie is gone too, I think she ran off with the iceman, you can't count on them, or maybe they told me she got cut, some buck just left her in an alleyway to bleed out her life and Papa had to go down and identify her, and now I sit up here all by myself and ring and ring and not one living soul will take a minute to come on up and see what I want. Brewster is long gone, Essie is God knows where, Cora is married to that cheapjack and Thad has run off to New York to make his fortune and now even Papa has deserted me, I am alone in all my rooms and I don't remember when Papa went, or how it happened to me, this place is like a tomb and the only good thing that has come out of it is that I can go out into the halls without being bowled over by somebody going somewhere, and when I am up to it I can go down into the parlor and sit, without having to worry about some strange young man or heedless child blundering in and seeing me without my corset and my jewels; I sit among my things and try to call up pictures of my life around me, life the way it ought to be.

Sometimes when I am sitting there alone Edward comes; he does not see that there are times when I prefer to be surrounded by my things, for they alone are constant. The chandelier from Bavaria never changes, the silver candelabra still shine underneath the dust, but when I look at Edward, I can see that everything is slipping away; he is still my dearest child, but where is the promise that used to make him shine in my eyes? He is little more than a boy but his hair lies flat and dead across the top of his head, his suit is always rumpled; he tries to straighten up so he will look like Papa but when I look into his eyes there is nobody there. I want to take him by the shoulders and shake him back to life, but instead he sits, and I sit, and when I try to find out why he isn't at the University, when I suggest that it is not too late for him to go into medicine, or law, he says, What kind of flowers did we have at Lila's debut party? I have to stop and try to remember; we talk and soon we are reliving all those good moments, wandering in all those old rooms, and we have to be content with that. I look to Edward but I have to wonder if there is any hope for him, and I have already lost hope for poor little Flo; she is not really ugly, no child of mine is ugly, but she has an ugly expression, you would think she never had a pleasant thought in her life and now what is more she has gone to work down town in an office, I tell her I never thought any daughter of mine would have to work but she won't listen, she only says we need the money and that is so preposterous that I scold her and send her out of my sight. She isn't going to make a good marriage, either; when she catches a beau she drags him in here like a cat that has got a mouse and is going to maul it to death and then wonders why it won't play. Nell has qualities, but she mopes around the house all day, bringing trays, and she doesn't want to talk about her debut, or where all the nice boys have gone; the town will be empty soon, they are all slipping away like so many grains of sand; the last time I remember seeing a face I liked was at Lila's wedding, and I told Nell so at the time but she missed her chance, so if it is all slipping away she is letting it slip away.

It was a beautiful wedding, we had it in Washington, because Simon's family has always been prominent there; I would have liked to have it here, so all of our friends could come, but of course it was more important to have my Lila launched in Washington; I thought my other girls might find some attractive young men, friends of Simon's, for I do agree the pickings are much better in a big city like that than they are down here, and if Nell hadn't been such a fool it might have worked out that way. At first Papa said he didn't know how we were going to do it, but when I said we had to do it, I knew he would want it for Lila's sake, why then of course he did. At first Lila cried and threatened to elope, but I told her we were going to have a big wedding because she was a Lyon and it was expected, and when the day came I'm sure even she had to admit it was worth all the trouble and expense, my dress came from Paris and so did hers, the wedding was in the National Cathedral and the reception was at the Wardman Park Hotel.

It was lovely seeing the family all together, all except for Thad, and all of us looking so fine, even Cora looked like a lady, she had on a pastel for a change, even if it was too short and it did have too much fringe; Flodie had an egret plume and a bandeau that hid her squint and Nell looked like a fairy princess in pink. I wore my écru from Paris and Papa looked handsomer than he ever has in his morning coat, I could see us both standing there together and for once it was the way I had always expected us to look, wearing our children like a diadem. When you are young you never think about your body failing or your cheeks going flat like tired old kid gloves, you never think you will take hold of your husband's arm for support and find that even though he looks substantial and prosperous, with a figure to be proud of, his substance is all gone so that it is like holding on to a stick and what is worse he is trembling; I said, Papa, you are trembling, don't be nervous it is only Lila getting married, and he said, I'm not nervous, Lily, it's just that I'm so very tired; I don't know why but I was frightened for him, I wanted to take both his arms in my two hands and hold him until he stopped trembling but just then he lifted his shoulders and became himself once more, making a beautiful bow because Mrs. Millard had come over to us, she has not lost *her* substance, and we turned to her, both smiling, both gracious. She said, Your daughter looks lovely. I said, Your son is very handsome, I know he will take good care of her, and for one moment she looked distracted; instead of a simple yes, which was all on earth I expected, she said, I have hopes for them; I said, Of *course,* but she didn't seem to be listening. Then over her shoulder I saw Nell dancing with a fair-haired young man, he had a profile like something off a temple and I said, Who is that young man dancing with my daughter, and her mind came back from wherever it had been wandering and she told me it was Simon's best friend, Theron Renault. We watched them dancing, she said, Don't they make a handsome couple; I said they certainly did; Mrs. Millard said he would make somebody a good catch, and I said he certainly looked as if he would, and we watched the two of them dancing until a famous judge came up to pay his compliments to Mrs. Millard and then I turned back to Papa and he was gone.

He didn't come back until the reception was almost over, and I found out afterward that he had been feeling so ill that he had to go and lie down but he wouldn't tell me because he knew I would worry, he crept away because he would rather die than have anything happen in front of his guests. I found out afterward, from Nell, because the minute I missed Papa I looked around for Nell and she was gone too, when she saw him go she ran after him. So Nell left the party before she'd had a chance to make any kind of impression on that Renault boy, by the time she came back he was with some Washington belle with a candy smile and an expensive dress and she never saw him again. If only Cora had gone, it would have saved us a lot of grief, Nell could have stayed with the boy and we might have been spared the embarrassment, Cora would not have had the time to make a spectacle of herself. As it was any fool could see wild horses could not have dragged her away from the party, Punk brought a flask and even though we had prewar champagne, Papa had paid the world to get it, it was not good enough for our Cora. Cora preferred to drink out of the flask, it was racier, I could see her going off behind the portieres with Punk and some friend of Simon's I didn't like, they would all three come back giggling and I could see how flushed Cora was, like the day she ate all of Edward's cake, except that day she was sick as a dog and it served her right; that day it was only in front of the family.

But here we were surrounded by the cream of Washington society, with some of Papa's and my best friends mixing with them; here we were with all the family together for once, except of course for Thad, and my girl Cora came up to her sister Lila with her hair gone frizzy and whiskey on her breath and she tried to hug Lila, pulling so Lila had to bend her head down, Cora crushed that lovely veil and smeared lipstick on her sister's cheek. She said, I just wanted to wish you all the best, Lil, but what she meant was: I have always hated you. My own daughter. I must say Lila was the perfect lady, she said, Thank you, Cora, and tried to straighten her veil. But Cora would not leave it at that, her voice got too loud and she said, Nothing but the best for our princess, she was still smiling, a poison smile, and Lila said, Yes, Yes, Corry, thank you, and tried to turn away, but Cora put a hand on her arm and pulled her around so she would have to listen and then she said, If you expect the best you are bound to be disappointed, except that before "disappointed" she used a word I have never heard used in my presence; I have never been so humiliated, she let all those people see that she and Lila do not always get along and what is worse she let them see she is not always happy, it was inexcusable. A lady does not have troubles; if she does then they are her own business, she keeps from the world; it is important to go ahead as if nothing is ever wrong, the least of my children know that.

Of course as if she had not already done enough Cora said something else, whispering and shaking her head, but I think Lila was so dazzled by her own happiness that day that she never even heard; if she did hear she didn't care, she only went to the grand staircase to throw her bouquet, for Lila has breeding and shows it, for all her airs she is the most like me. I could see her looking around for her pretty sister Nell and I was looking for her too; she finally had to throw it to Flodie, it was embarrassing, the poor girl was just like a fish snapping at a fly. Papa was back at the party by then, he put his arms around Lila with a look that almost broke my heart and then my most beautiful daughter pecked me on the cheek and she was gone.

My feelings were about to get the better of me so I turned on Nell, I had to say something, I said, You let that Renault boy slip right through your fingers, where were you, and I think she would have been just as happy for us to squabble about that but she was looking at me with that lopsided, abject expression that means something is wrong so I closed my fingers on her wrist, I had my thumbnail through the aperture in her sixteen-button glove and I said, Why did you leave the party. At first she wouldn't answer and finally she told me she had to, she wasn't feeling well, but she has never been able to lie to me and so finally she had to tell me she had followed Papa up to the suite because she saw him leaving and he didn't look well. When she got there he was lying down all by himself with the shades down and the lights out, she was frightened and went for the house doctor, she wanted to come and get me too but Papa wouldn't let her, he had the doctor give him something so he could come back to the reception and before they came down he tried to make her promise not to tell me about it at all. Of course she had to, and although I will never forgive him for hiding the truth from me, I understand what he was trying to do and I admire him for that because the Lyons, like the Richards and the Calhouns, know what is right: If you are not well enough to carry out a social duty you must first of all hide it from your guests, and if you are not well enough to stay at the party then you must leave someone else to carry on; Papa knew how upset I would be; one of us had to stay there to entertain the guests and so he simply slipped away and left me to carry on which is exactly what I did. When we were alone in our room that night I looked at Papa standing there so frail-looking in his shirtsleeves and for the first and last time I cried and cried until he hugged me and promised everything was going to be all right. He put me to bed and had the doctor come and give me something because I have been frail for such a long time and the trip and the excitement of the wedding and all that standing at the reception was just too much for me.

Of course everything was not all right, Papa has gone, and I don't even know when or how it happened, I only know that the time came when even though he was right here in my room, smiling and touching my hand, a part of him was already stealing away; each day he was a little *less* but we would not talk about it for so long as we did not mention it, it could not be so. Then one night he did not come at all and the girls tried to tell me he was on a business trip, and finally Nell broke down and cried and said our Papa was in the hospital but would not tell me why, and I when I began to rage and cry for him the doctor came and gave me something, I will never forgive them because when I came to myself again Papa was gone, absolutely gone, and what's more Thad had come and gone and I don't even remember what I said to him; I woke up one morning to find everything and everybody gone and I have not been myself for one minute since; it is just slipping away, everything is slipping away, and nothing I can say or do will make it stop, so I know I must have got it wrong somewhere along the way; if I didn't get it wrong then why have I lost Papa, why am I losing my children, wherein have I failed that I should be left here in loneliness and want?

NELL

Papa is dead. He stepped off a street corner down town, he must have been dreaming, and someone came along and hit him with a truck. He died in my arms that very night; for once I had his complete attention and I looked at him and vowed that when I have a man like Papa I will take better care of him than our family has, I will love him more than life and never let him out of my sight. The doctor says it is a mercy, his heart would have killed him within the year and Papa knew it, they both knew it would have cost him so much pain and grief that in the end he would have despaired; the doctor tries to tell me this was better; we knew he was sick, he worked too hard and when he came home he spent most of the time sleeping upstairs in Lila's old room but he was here, we still had him, and now that he is gone it's as if the blood or center is gone from the house, there is nobody left to stand between us and whatever may happen, there is no real reason for me to want to stay. If it weren't for Mama I'd pack up now and go out looking for the blood, or heart, or whatever it is we are missing, I'd get a job in one city and if I didn't find it there I would go on to the next and the next, I'd keep going on and on until I found the man I need and then I'd marry him, I would keep his house and he would be the heart, or center, but I am caught here; when Mama got so bad I looked to Cora for help, but she has Punk, and Flodie has her job, much as Edward loves Mama he can't take care of her, I thought: Somebody has to, and so here I am.

Poor Mama cries all the time, she has not been herself for a long time and when Papa was killed we had to keep her deaf and blind with drugs so she wouldn't fly into fragments and hurt all of us; when Thad came for the funeral he went to her, she spoke to him but she may not even have known who he was; after he had gone she came up through the layers of drugs and reproached us all: Thad, where was my boy Thad? Half the time she loses track of who she is or *when* she is, she rings for Essie and then rails at me when nobody comes; she cries for Papa and can't remember from one minute to the next where he's gone, or if she does remember, she never remembers for long; she will ask me why we are alone for so many days at a stretch, sometimes she cries so hard I want to hold her shoulders to stop them from shaking, I hug her and pat her and when she's better she will look me in the eye and ask: Where has it all gone?

I know, or think I know it's all out there, I could find it or at least my part of it if only I could leave the house, but we can't afford a nurse right now and Mama can't be left alone. Besides, no nurse alive would understand her or put up with her; she sits there and talks about people who have been dead for years and then she complains because not one of them has been to call since Papa went away, and then she wants to know where he has gone. Sometimes she takes me for Cora even though Cora hasn't lived at home for years; she says, You are running with the wrong crowd, if you want to make a decent marriage you are going to have to stop being seen everywhere with boys who are no better than common trash. Then in the next breath she knows I'm Nell and begins to berate me for staying around the house all the time, she says I have been indoors for so long that I look like a mushroom, my face is all white and drawn, and there is no way for me to explain without hurting her that I am here for her sake. If I had my way I would be out of this house like an arrow shot from a drawn bow; as if she knows what I am thinking she smiles in blind forgiveness and I am struck with remorse. She scolds me for not being happier and then with a sweet smile she begins to talk about giving a series of little luncheons for me, we'll have all her friends with their daughters, ten at a time, so I'll know all the right people, and when they are making lists for the big parties they'll all remember Lily Lyon's youngest daughter, and that they had a lovely time at a luncheon in Lily's beautiful home. Fortunately by the time she has figured out that we will have fruit salad and chicken in patty shells she has forgotten what we are going to have it *for,* and then I can go down to the kitchen and bring up our sandwiches and soup and we have our lunch on trays right here in her room, just the way we always have.

When everybody lived at home she had more to think about, but now the others are gone, Edward and Flo are gone all day and there is nobody around but me, I am left alone in Mama's consciousness and sometimes it's almost too much to bear. I never know what I will find when I come in; sometimes she's sitting on the chaise by the window with the daylight in her hair and her face untroubled and sweet, she greets me with such patience that I want to hug her, but there are other times when she is upset and I can't reach her, she seems to be a little girl lost in a garden, looking for someone, or else

72

she is a debutante, or a bride, and there are other times when she is gripped in a vision too dark for me to see, she *wants,* she is insatiable; I have no idea what, or why, I only know she wants. Some days she calls me in and tells me secretly that she has always wondered if poor Flo is really her daughter, the white laundress was having a baby around the same time and she thinks there must have been some terrible mistake, and when she sees how that upsets me she will backtrack and say, I didn't really mean it, Lila, your sister Flodie is just one of those unfortunates, Saturday's child. Then she will start talking about how it is Flodie's job to earn enough for my debut party, Lila's was only a rehearsal for the party she and Papa will give for me, and the only way I can make her let go for even a minute is to ask her about all the silver and fine china in her mother's house in Charleston all those years ago, it was lost in the War long before Mama was even born, but she can number all the pieces as her mother numbered them to her. Before he died Papa looked up into my eyes and said, Your life will be better, and I don't know to this minute whether he was promising me or trying to make *me* promise; if he was promising, I wonder how he knew?

§§§§ §§§§

Although he could not let himself believe it, Edward grew up with the suspicion that he had been born too late for the true life of the family; the others had skimmed off the cream—the money, Mama's youth, the best of Papa's strength, leaving behind a life which flowed along drably, marred by hard places which stuck up like rocks: tightened circumstances, short tempers, the residue of old quarrels lying in the corners of all the rooms. The house was almost deserted now, all the ornaments were dimmed with dust, and because he could not accept this as the present Edward chose to dwell in his mother's vision of the past, the two of them talking endlessly, weaving pictures in loving complicity, until in time her memories became his memories. He assumed the house of the early days as he assumed her memories, raising about him the freshly painted columns and shining mullioned windows, all the undimmed marble and alabaster and rich Oriental rugs, seeing it in this way even as he brushed flaking paint from his coat sleeve or caught his toe in a hole long since worn in the Kashmir summer rug. When she was not too bewildered

73

or troubled in her mind she would be waiting in the parlor when he came home from work, her hair curling loosely around her face, her body soft in the dressing gown but her features clean and pure as the profiles on Granny Calhoun's cameos, but even as they bowed their heads and murmured over the silver service, Edward was troubled by discrepancies. When Mama spoke of lovely parties in the garden he remembered the lawn as hot and seedy, his brothers and sisters quarreling, himself miserable in white linen knickers which had once belonged to Thad and already bound him between the legs. He was troubled by the recent memory of Thad at Papa's funeral, planting both hands on the casket and leaning over it to say: "Edward, we have got to get you out of here," of himself answering, frightened because it was not a promise but a threat: "Anything you say."

". . . the garden," Mama was saying. She looked at him sharply. "Edward, why do you look so hangdog?"

"The garden," he said quickly; if he was not careful, recollection would betray him, and he would feel himself at the border of the lawn again, light-footed and timid in his linen suit, he would see his brother Thad throwing, he would feel the ball in his stomach like a rock; if he could not stop the process he would smother in his own regrets, and if his memories started to go then the imagined present would have to go too, he would see the house dimmed by time or Mama weak and querulous; she was about to remind him that it was time for her enema, she was about to reproach him for failing at the University, and because he had to forestall the present at all costs he said, finally, "Thad has a job for me. In New York," and in all his reconstructions of what followed, would try to convince himself she had kissed him and said Godspeed.

He went to New York because he thought it would be easier.

Coming to the door, Thad looked not like their father but like somebody's father, disproportionately weary and trim in pinstriped trousers with his black suspenders crossing a starchy shirt; Edward could see his suit coat carefully folded over a chair, and his tie folded over that. Thad looked at him for a minute without saying anything, as if noting Edward's clothes, his expression, the fact that there had apparently been no changes, turning away even as he said, "Hello, Edward," and went back to his newspapers on the couch.

Edward said, to his back, "Hello, Thad," and, still holding his suitcases, stood at the edge of the carpet.

"The bedroom on the left is for you," Thad said, from the shelter of his paper. "When you're settled in the job you'll want to find a place of your own."

"Everybody sends their love."

"Good."

Edward stood in the doorway, thinking: This is *hard,* and when it became apparent his brother wasn't going to say any more he crossed to the hall and opened a door.

Thad's paper crackled. "The *other* door."

Slumping, Edward turned, thinking: Of course.

Perhaps because he had grown up surrounded, overwhelmed by their mother's bric-a-brac and heavy mirrors and urns and fringed throws and ornate candelabra, Thad had always hated ornament, and so the room he had prepared for his brother was spare, with nothing more than a studio bed, a dresser and a lamp. There was a maroon carpet and the window was covered by colorless monkscloth. Depressed, Edward unpacked quickly, looking at his shirts and underwear with dissatisfaction as he laid them away in the drawers. He would have liked to lie on his back on the studio bed, closing his eyes to the room; he would have crossed his feet and folded his arms under his head and passed the evening that way, but he knew he had to go out and face Thad and so he ran a brush across his head and then went to the door, turning to look at the miserable little room, already wondering if he had made a mistake. He had in his billfold a collection of pictures: Mama, with her first baby, holding Thad at arm's length and regarding him, herself exquisite in profile and his Grandmother Richard in profile behind her, looking over her shoulder with an expression both fixed and stern; Cora and Lila dressed for a party; a girl at the beach, he had never known her very well but she was the only girl who had ever given him her picture. He took them out without even having to look at them and propped them against the mirror. Then, satisfied, he left the room.

He had to stand for too long in the severe living room, waiting once more for Thad to acknowledge him, and when Thad did look up he seemed surprised all over again: What are you doing here? Thad's eyes were expressionless and under his stare Edward could feel his feet moving in an inadvertent shuffle; Thad was so much older that they might as well have grown up in different households, nothing had been the same for him and so Edward had always looked to Thad as a grown-up, an extension of Papa, something like an uncle; if he was a brother at all then he was the stern older brother, the standard against which Edward would always be measured, the model son in whose wake it would be Edward's fate to follow and perpetually fall short, so that perhaps his mother had been trying to protect him when she kept him a baby for so long. Thad had never been affectionate, he had hardly noticed Edward at all. Shifting in accumulating misery, Edward thought perhaps he would go back to his room and begin to pack, he could sneak out after it got dark, leaving a single word on a torn envelope: *Sorry*. If he did not ship out on a freighter that very night he would take the first bus home and fling himself on the street car and not open his eyes until they got to the corner of Palm and Verona; then he would slip down the darkened street, going to earth in the bushes outside the house where he was born. He might spend the rest of his life there, he would feed on glimpses of his sisters, coming and going, and at night he would yearn outside their lighted window, watching as they sat with heads bent in the glow of glass-shaded lamps; at that distance every detail of the setting would appear faultless, their lives as perfect and inviolable as life conducted inside a picture frame; from time to time Mama might even come down and join them and he could watch without having to listen to anything she said, he could memorize for all time the details of his mother's elegant face; he faltered, he would have fled right then except that his brother sat up, saying abruptly:

"'d you hear the one about the midget that married the epileptic?"

"No."

Thad got up, smoothing his shirt, and he looked at Edward with a wink, saying, "He had to hire four bellhops to hold her down," and he followed that with a crash of hard, mechanical laughter, barely noticing that Edward could manage only a forced smile. Then he hit Edward on the shoulder. "Good to have you here, let's go out and eat."

They went to Thad's club, which looked very much like his living room: leather furniture, group photographs in black frames; the only difference was that the rugs were better and the walls were paneled instead of a dull Bronx cream. The waiter brought drinks in coffee cups; Edward abandoned his quickly but Thad took three in a row, downing them automatically, so Edward knew without having to be told that he always took three, no more, no less. He would not drink wine with dinner and he didn't take anything afterward.

76

"Look," he said as if Edward had protested, "Tomorrow is a working day." At the table he offered Edward the best he had, tips on the market, inside stories about goings-on at the office, a blow-by-blow of his conversation with an important investor; when he had finished he produced that hard laugh again, letting Edward know that although he had missed the point the whole thing was important to Thad; he made a smile. "Another thing," Thad said as they left the table. He drew Edward into an alcove, giving him perhaps his greatest confidence: "I'm not putting my eggs in one basket, and neither should you. I'm buying gold."

On the street, Edward had a sense of his brother looking up from time to time, as if surprised to find somebody with him; he was not annoyed, only surprised, and in a rush of hospitality he stopped at a speakeasy where they each had to have one drink, even though tomorrow was a working day. Then, sitting down with Edward on his leather couch, Thad began to brief him.

"You can go in with me tomorrow, since it's the first day, but after that it will look better if you get there by yourself. You're not expected to talk to me during business hours unless it's on business, and it's better if you can find things out on your own. If they keep you on it has to be on your own merits, not because you're somebody's brother. If you're good and you can prove it, you may end up in the Brussels office; I have too many interests here but you have time for the Continent, you're still a kid." He said, as if presenting a gift, "You can go a long way if you'll just buckle down."

Getting into his pajamas, Edward was first tremendously relieved to be free of his brother's concentration and then struck with chagrin because he didn't remember saying anything to Thad all evening, he was uncertain of the sound of his own voice. If he had been as quiet as he feared then he hadn't thanked him; Thad would hold it against him, Thad might be regretting his kindness even now. He started toward the door to rectify things, remembered he was in his pajamas and retreated to change, tucking in his shirt-tail and deciding, at the last minute, that he shouldn't go so far as to put on a tie. He crossed the hall, calling:

"Thad?"

He had to wait for a long time, he was about to decide Thad was asleep and give it up, but then he heard Thad saying, wearily, "Come in."

He was sitting on the bed, still dressed but with his tie and shoes off now; the paper was on the bed beside him, opened once again to the late stock quotations. The page was marked in several different colors of lead; in places Thad's markings had left holes. The bed lamp locked Thad in a small circle of light, so that Edward had to speak from the darkness:

"I wanted to thank you."

"Don't thank me, I just didn't want you on my neck later."

"What?"

Thad said, almost grimly, "I want you to be self-supporting, not like that bunch down there."

"I am, I mean, I was."

"No you weren't and they aren't either, I have to send Flo a hundred every month just to keep food in the house."

"I didn't know."

"I wanted to get you out before they pulled you down. Three women." His voice was edged with pain. "Three women, with nothing to their names but that old house."

Edward set his lips. "Papa left them well provided for."

Thad was shaking his head. "Papa didn't have it, she used him up, they used him up, when he went all he had left was a little land."

Edward's voice was unsteady and a little shrill. "I wish you wouldn't talk like that."

"They can't help it, they're just women, but I have hopes for you."

"I guess I'd better go to bed." Edward backed out quickly because he didn't want to have to hear any more.

Thad had a man, a small, disapproving Filipino who cooked for Thad and Edward, exquisite little meals which always left Edward hungry, served so beautifully that he was made too nervous to eat. He made the beds and straightened the apartment and to Edward's unending despair laid out their clothes each night, so both gentlemen would be prepared for the coming day. He always did it while they were at dinner, which meant there was no way to forestall him, and Edward could imagine his distaste as he fingered the cheap shirts, the shabby underwear; Edward's black pinstripe was spared because he had only the one suit, but he imagined that one of these nights Thad's man would come out and make him stand while he went over the suit jacket and trousers with a whisk broom, picking off stray hairs with the implication that there were too many of them, because Edward was already beginning to go bald. After the first week Edward would come in, more often than not, to find the table set for one because Thad was at the club for dinner or dining with a woman. He had explained with great patience that he could take Edward to the club as his guest only once, and it was much too soon to propose him for membership; if he was going to a party he would explain that Edward was not yet ready to meet these particular people, and so Edward had to eat at home. He begged to be allowed to go out for a sandwich, he would rather not have eaten at all, but Thad insisted the Filipino had to earn his salary, and so Edward had to sit down each night at the small table, waiting only for the moment when the finger bowl came and he would be free to escape those cold, critical eyes. Even then, retreating to his bedroom, he would be conscious of Thad's man in the apartment, reading or listening to the radio in a cubicle somewhere behind the kitchen, in a territory Edward hadn't been able to bring himself to explore. He could not seek his comfort in the living room or shuffle out into the kitchen for an apple because Thad's man would be in the doorway in the next minute, buttoning his starched white jacket and asking if Edward wanted some cocoa or something to drink; he was not empowered to answer the door and although he leaped every time the phone rang, he knew Thad's man would answer the phone and it would never be for him. He hated the idea of being waited on and he was puzzled by it, since this servant was so obviously his superior; he would look up from his dinner occasionally, thinking: He ought to be in the office instead of me.

Edward knew from the first day that it was going to be too hard; under Thad's instructions he put himself forward that morning, volunteering for some special assignment, and when he saw what he would be expected to do he receded, content to spend the hours at his desk doing some small clerical task. Seeing Thad from a distance, he had reason to wonder whether he was at fault for not being like Thad or, more complicated, whether at heart he already knew he did not want to be like Thad. He watched his brother go about his business with his eyes alert and his expression closed, and on the few nights they were at home together Thad's face would be equally closed; he woke that way and went to sleep that way, feeding on figures and creating his successes step by step. He explained to Edward that he never considered a single success reason enough to stop or even let down, it was important to go on to the next thing; when he was with Edward he talked only business and laughed only at his own jokes and Edward, considering him over the edge of his newspaper, thought: Thad is a machine.

When the Filipino finally had a night out Edward moved into the living room and spread out with his shoes off, liberated; tonight at least he would not have to listen to Thad's criticism—yes, he had let an opportunity slip by today, yes, he knew Lang thought he was a dead weight and if he did not begin to do his share he would have to be let go, but tonight at least he would not have to hear about it, he would not be subject to Thad's daily review of his failures, or suggestions about how to improve his state; for the time being he could forget about making his way in life, he could even forget about being waited on; if he wanted a sandwich he could go out in the kitchen and make a sandwich and devour it in silence, standing up; he could even answer the phone. The first call was a wrong number, the second was a girl; when she heard Edward's voice she brightened, saying, "Thad?"

"No. This is his brother."

"Of course not Thad."

"Can I help you?" He was already thinking he would keep her talking; on the phone he could be witty and glamorous, she would end by saying she was glad she had gotten him instead of Thad, she would give him her name and phone number and eventually he would take her out. "I'm Thad's brother Edward. From down South."

"Isn't that funny," she said. "He never talked about you. Well, goodbye, Edward."

"Is there any message?"

"No message. He'll know who called."

He did, too. Edward waited up and when Thad finally came in, looking rumpled and sated, he accused him: "Somebody called."

"A girl."

Edward said, "A girl. She says you never even mentioned you had a brother."

"Marietta Sterling," Thad said. "It just goes to show."

"Show what?"

Thad sat down and took off his shoes, turning to Edward with an instructive look which he had begun to recognize. "It's never too early to start worrying about what kind of connections you make. I used to see that girl when I first got to New York and thought I had nothing to lose, and now she won't give me a moment's peace."

"If you're tired of her I'd be glad to . . ."

"I never got tired of her, she's pretty and I still like her—I was too damn stupid to know that even in the beginning you can't afford to get involved."

"But if she was pretty and you liked her."

"Now I stick to the kind of girl who wants a good time with no questions asked. It's much, much easier."

Edward said, "Wait. If she was . . . What's the *matter* with her?"

Thad set both of his shoes on the floor, side by side, brushing the uppers with the soles of his socks. He looked up and when he spoke it was in a tone Mama often used; Mama would have said, Well you know, she's not our *kind,* her people are just . . . Thad would have been enraged by the comparison; still he said, with the identical measure of pride and calculation, "She would not make a suitable wife, she would have been an embarrassment to me."

"That's heartless."

Thad looked up in quick anger. "What do you think you know?"

Edward heard himself saying, "You don't have a drop of blood left in you."

"Oh hell, Edward, I just can't afford to take chances, and neither can you, if we take chances we're going to end up just like Papa did."

"There was nothing the matter with Papa."

"He was a desperate, desperate man. We had to have the parties and the cars and all that help, she needed so much and he had to keep ahead of her, he worked all his life to keep one step ahead of her, so she'd never find out how little we had. But the worst thing . . ." Thad's head was lowered, his face dark as he said, "I think she knew."

Edward lifted one hand, trying to stop him.

"She knew and she kept on asking anyway."

"You're talking about our *mother.*"

Thad said, "Oh, you poor bastard."

"She's our mother and she loves us . . ."

"We all danced her dance, Edward."

". . . everybody said what a wonderful family we were."

Thad stood, boring in as if trying to administer a dose of medicine which would cure Edward for once and all; "She used him, Edward, she used us all."

"*Stop it!*" If he had been at home Edward would have run out into the street, if he had been stronger he would have killed Thad if he had to, anything to sto ʰ ʰs voice; as it was he fled to his room, locking the door on his brother, and in tears he said in a desperate whisper, "That's not true, it's just not true."

When he was pressed about why he left New York so quickly, right when he was doing so well, Edward would not think of his own conscious choice to fail but rather that he did not want to be like Thad, he never wanted to be like Thad, and he would say only that he'd had to leave, Thad had said something unforgivable.

FLODIE

I tried to warn her, I said, Nell, I know you want to go to all the parties, but why can't you go with Jerry Little, his family has lived here forever, they were charter members of the St. John's Club and besides he's dying to take you out.

But she wouldn't listen, she only said, Jerry Little is made out of library paste. Oh Flodie, leave me alone.

Then I said, Nell, remember Uncle Harry. You have to look out for men with smoky eyes.

Nell only said, Don't you dare say a word about Uncle Harry.

He'll do you just like Uncle Harry did us, you just wait and see.

Don't talk to me about Uncle Harry, Nelly said; she just didn't want to hear.

So I couldn't stop her, there couldn't anybody stop her, she was bound to go out with Cleve Lothrop even though we didn't have a blind rabbit's idea who he was or who his people were, maybe it came from being cooped up here ever since she finished school; well, *somebody* had to stay in and take care of Mama, and it was my place to go out and work, I was the one that had a job. Then after Edward got back he would sit with Mama in the evenings, Nell would just barely stay around until dinner was off the table and then she would be out of here like a shot, she would go down to the drug store with one of her girl friends and they would sit in a booth and giggle and wait for something to happen until it began to get dark and she would have to come home.

Well I suppose it was all she ever had on her mind, she has talked about getting married ever since I can remember, she used to make me put on one of Papa's hats and we would play bride and groom, she would fall in love every year from about the third grade, she used to spend every living minute talking to me about Sammy or Jimmy or whoever it was, did I see the way he smiled, did she ought to send a note, but if I pushed her up to where she had to talk to one of them she would just curl up and die. After a while she got to spending her money on those pretty nightgowns, she would go in front of the mirror the minute she got up to see if she still looked pretty, did the material wrinkle or get stringy; she used to practice rubbing night cream into her face so it wouldn't show and she tried all different ways of doing her hair so she would not have to go to bed in curlers on the honeymoon, she talked about boys and she dreamed about boys, she did everything but catch one and I think if Judas Iscariot himself had come in here and asked her to go out with him she would have looked him in the face and gone all squashy, she would have gotten her coat and waved byebye to us all without a second thought.

With Papa gone I thought Edward would be the man, he knew as well as I did that Cleve was no good and he would put his foot down and forbid her to go out with him for once and all. We were all together in the parlor after dinner, Mama was even well enough to be down for the evening, maybe we would settle Cleve Lothrop before all the Christmas parties began and Nelly got too thick with him; I looked at Edward hard and I said, Edward, we haven't heard from you.

Then I waited but all he did was look up at Nell with that damn weak apologetic smile and say, Honey, you know you have to be careful of strangers from out of town. He might as well of said, Honey, watch out you don't get too much fresh air . . . or something less.

He's not a stranger, she said, He was Thad's best friend at the University.

I could see Edward had already backed down so I said, fast, So he says, but how much stock can you put in that?

Well, if only we had called Thad right then and there to check; I tried, I said to Edward, Let's call Thad, you can do it, and he said he didn't necessarily want to talk to Thad right then, why didn't I, and I said, All right, but then I got to thinking how much money it would cost and what if Thad said Cleve Lothrop was absolutely his best friend, that would only make it worse, so we never did get around to it. Well, even if we had called him, and Thad had told us everything we now know, Nell was so set on Cleve Lothrop I don't think she would have budged an inch.

She was saying, If I can't see Cleve any more I won't go out at all.

Our Mama wasn't listening until just then, she looked pretty as a picture with her fur lap robe and the grey velvet dressing gown I gave her for Christmas this year, she was watching the fire with that sweet face. She must have been hearing in some part of her mind because she roused herself, saying, Why you *have* to go, Nelly, the Lyon girls always go to all the parties, why you girls ought to be making your debuts this season, I just don't understand why Papa hasn't . . .

There was a little silence while Edward looked at his hands and nobody else reminded her that we didn't even have Papa any more; we all hung there for a minute and then I had to go over and pat Mama on the knee and tell her what she always tells us. Mama, you know Thad Lyon's girls don't need debut parties, everybody in town *knows* who they are.

Mama only gave that sweet smile she used when she wasn't going to listen, much less budge: Nelly, everybody would miss you, if you weren't at all the parties, people would think there was something wrong with you.

Nell cut her eyes at me and Edward; she had us. Then make Flodie and Edward leave me alone.

So we did, and she went ahead, she took him to all the best parties even though he was never on the debutante list, she would just walk in on his arm and nobody would say anything because she was a Lyon, she cut Jerry Little and Addison Richardson and even the Barnard boy, who had been to Law School at the University of Virginia and would be important in the State Legislature very soon; she cut all the nice boys from good families, boys I would have given my eye teeth to dance with, she would throw away her dance card as soon as she got inside the door, she would hang on to Cleve until I wanted to rage and scream at her. I tried to warn her, Lord knows, but he filled her eyes so she was blind to the rest of us; she would have followed him anywhere, him with no more to his name than the white suit he stood up in and a handsome face and lashes like silky black caterpillars tracking across his cheeks, she followed him the way she used to follow Papa or Uncle Harry; all she ever wanted out of life was just one man who would let her follow him and if he turned around for one minute and gave his attention to her and her alone then that was all she ever wanted, it was all she ever cared about.

I think Nell knew all about Cleve, I think that in her secret self she had looked at him head-on and knew he would cause her grief, but while she had him she would *have* him, so she set her heart anyway and went right straight ahead.

There were plenty of signs and reasons not to trust him, we never even knew what kind of work he did. He just came to the house one day and said he knew Thad, and expected us to take him in. All Nell had to do was take one look at the outline he made in the doorway, tall and good-looking, and the village idiot could have seen she didn't care who he was or where he came from, he was looking at her, right at *her,* and she had been waiting around for him for years with her hands folded and her eyes full of dreams. I got in from work that night, I was tired and hot and cross and I knew something was wrong, I could hear Mama upstairs ringing her bell and when I went up she asked me to take her tray and where was my sister, she hadn't seen her for hours and when she rang for her medicine Sister didn't even holler up to say why she didn't come. I could see she was upset so I went downstairs looking in all the parlors, I called and called. Finally I went out back, I thought maybe she had gone off somewhere but the car was still there, I was thinking up all the things I was going to say to her when I came around the corner and there she was sitting with this man under the live oak, right where the laundress used to put her tubs. Lord he was handsome, he jumped up like a real gentleman when she introduced us and for one minute he looked right straight through to my brains.

I pushed at my hair but I knew it was no good, it was the end of the day and I just looked frazzled, so I tried to make it up with a smile, maybe he would think at least I had a pretty face; I said, How do you do?

Well he was polite enough to make you throw up but after that first look his eyes just flicked right off me, so I thought: Well brother, if you don't have the time of day for me I don't have the time of day for you. I never talked much to Cleve, I was only alone with him the one time, at Clara Richmond's tea dance, but I already knew all about him, I knew exactly what to expect right from the beginning because when I looked into his eyes I saw Uncle Harry, they both had that same slow, smoky look.

Once when Mama was little Uncle Harry went out in the garden and played hide and seek with her, they each had a turn, the first time he was easy to find, and then she had a turn and then he hid again. She counted to a hundred and then she went to look for him, she looked for him for hours, if she didn't find him soon she would never see him again, he would be lost somewhere in the shrubbery for the rest of their lives. She hunted and cried, she even dug, and finally it got dark and she had to go inside with her pretty white lawn dress all ripped and muddy around the bottom; she went in, sobbing, and there he was reading in the parlor, he had been there all the time. Of course he was sorry, he laughed and hugged her until she stopped; she used to say that made up for everything, but I wonder. When we went out to play she would say, You always stay where somebody else can see you, if you don't some stranger is going to come along and steal you, but I'm not sure that's exactly what she meant. Uncle Harry was careless of her, he was careless of everybody, and I think that's what she was trying to tell us: Don't you ever cause anybody that kind of grief.

When Uncle Harry was sixteen he used to skin off his clothes and swim out to the ships moored in Charleston Harbor. Mama always said our great uncle Horatio that he was named for had to swim out with secret messages during the Blockade, but he was a grown man at the time, it was for the honor and glory of the Confederacy and not just to make you swallow your heart; Uncle Harry would just dive off the seawall on the Battery in broad daylight, any time he felt like it; he would swim and float, swim and float, and when he reached a ship he would bang on the hull until somebody noticed and they hauled him up. He was very pretty then, like one of those boys in Italian paintings, with too many black curls and lips as red as a poison flower, and Mama said they would always pound him on the back and give him money or something to drink because nobody else in town was crazy enough to risk his neck like that. Mama would stand on the Battery with the nurse and look out over the water and cry because she never knew whether she saw his head bobbing or only thought she did, or whether he would ever come back. When he did come, grinning in the prow of some ship's dinghy, our grandmother would plead with him, but his father was dead and there was nobody left to make him keep his promises. When he was eighteen he refused to go to Sewannee or the Citadel, he said he was going to be a harbor pilot instead, out there on his own boat with three days' growth of whiskers and a cap on one side of his head; naturally our grandmother said that was not a fit occupation for a gentleman, she would see to it that he never got his papers, and so Uncle Harry never did anything, except stay out too late and sleep late and sit around in the afternoons in his beautiful white suit. Then one day he kissed Mama at the gate and told her to wait right there, he'd be right back, and then she didn't see him again for years. She used to mourn and watch for him from the upstairs window; she would go out on the Battery and strain to see beyond the water, maybe a boat would come in and he would be standing in the prow. Our grandmother even hired a man from Richmond to go up North and look for him, but of course he didn't want to be found. Then he came back again out of the blue when she was grown and married, I remember we all danced around him in the front hall, and even after he left Sam and Edna, just dumped them, and went away again, Mama would tell my brothers: You must grow up to be like your Uncle Harry, he is a prince among men, people can always tell a gentleman by the way he keeps himself.

I don't know, even when he came back for good I kept my distance, but Nell, Nell always grasps at straws and tries to build something out of them, she never seemed to mind when he walked out, right in the middle of playing with her; she would sit with that same blind smile Mama had and wait for him to come back. She could sit and listen to his stories and never care when he walked out without finishing but I am not that kind, I would rather not hear any stories at all. I guess he saw I wasn't so easy, he came around one day and took me to Parnell's for a soda, just me, and he almost won me. Then he said, I'll be right back, honey, and went out to talk to somebody in the street. When I finished and went out to look for him he was gone, he had forgotten all about me and I had to find my way back home alone; by the time I got there I was crying so hard Mama had to put me to bed for the rest of the day and he never came in to see me, not even once.

There was something ugly in him that liked to raise your hopes; I remember overhearing Mama saying to Papa, I think Harry is settling down at last, and that night the police came. Uncle Harry was the first person in our city to be killed in an automobile, he had been drinking and his car ran right off the bridge into the river; maybe he even did it on purpose, but Mother and Nelly and the others all cried buckets all the same. When they dragged for him they found a woman too, Thad told me, some cheap whore still plastered to him like a sign reading: SHAME; the thing is, he *wanted* you to expect too much from him and as soon as you thought you could count on something he would turn around and betray you, just like that. I could look into Cleve Lothrop's eyes and see that he was the same man, and when I looked at Nelly I knew she would make the same kind of damn fool of herself over him; I wanted to get back at Uncle Harry for everything he did to all of us, one way was to stop Cleve Lothrop before he ever got started and I almost did it, too, it was at Clara Richmond's tea dance that last Christmas season we had before the Crash.

I had to go with Jerry Little, he had to take me because Nelly couldn't see him for Cleve; I wasn't even second best, I was a way for Jerry to get a minute of her time because if nothing else he would be going and coming in the same car and if nothing else she would have to say, Yes, Jerry, or, No, Jerry, and hello and goodbye. He should have known he was no prize either, it was like dancing with a stick; I had to look over his shoulder and watch Nell dancing with Cleve Lothrop like her life depended on it, I had on my grey ankle-straps and my wonderful silver-beaded dress and I don't remember ever *feeling* better, I felt beautiful, I could feel my whole body all at once, the skin moving under the beads, the blood, the bones, everything right down to the nerves, but there I was with Jerry Little, what a waste.

They had draped the house with ropes of oleander greens, the leaves were shiny and beautiful and at dusk Mrs. Richmond had the darkies light about a hundred candles, we simpered along with teas and petits fours until the candles were lit and then Mr. Richmond had them bring in a big bowl of champagne punch; I thought it was ersatz, made up in somebody's back room somewhere, but Nell still swears it was Mr. Richmond's private stock, from before the war. We were all dancing and whirling from too much champagne, it was far and away the best party of the season, and we would all arrive jaded and too late for poor little Sally Master's deb dance that same night. Mr. Richmond came and took Jerry away, he had some joke to tell him in the pantry, and I danced with one boy and then another, drunk on air, so that I don't know how I ended up out on the porch with Cleve, he was sitting on the railing with his pale hair parted low and falling so that it almost hid one of his smoky eyes, his hair was silvery, so was my dress, I was every inch alive, for what? Jerry Little? I don't know; when I try to think about it everything blurs.

If I remember right, Cleve looked at me and said, You don't like me, do you, and then I think he pulled me or else I fell against him so he more or less had to catch me, it must have been the ersatz champagne. I looked him right in the eye and said, I like you, I just don't trust you, but I let him kiss me all the same.

We kissed too much, but it was all in Nell's interest, and then I pulled away to get my breath and there was Clara Richmond, looking shocked and foolish and dumpy in all those egret feathers and that silly dress with flying panels of *crepe de chine;* I turned to Cleve and slapped him hard and then I went to find my sister, I had to explain that I had done it all for her. She was in front of the mirror, the Richmonds had lights all around the mirror in their downstairs powder room so you could sit there and powder yourself and imagine you were getting ready to go on stage. Nelly seemed all taken up with her own face, I had to yell to make her listen, but finally she said, Yes?

I said, I always had my suspicions about him, Nelly, and now I know for sure.

She still wouldn't turn around. Her face in the mirror had a tired look, all those parties had left us all exhausted, she said, What?

Cleve, he's unfaithful, we were out there alone on the porch and he tried to, he tried to.

She said, It doesn't matter.

I had to keep trying, saying, But Nelly, you can't trust him out of your sight.

Well I thought that would do it, but she only said, Flodie, that's enough.

But Nelly, you can't *marry* somebody like that.

I don't want to hear any more about it.

You have to.

But she only kept working on her hair, working on her hair.

I was angry by then, I took her by the shoulder and turned her around, I looked her in the eye and I said to her, You have to do something.

Then she said the strangest thing: What does it matter to you what I make my life out of? Why can't you let me be? She was crying and her eyes were so bright with pain that it made me ashamed, so I went out and we never mentioned it again.

Well she went ahead and married him and it happened, I can

only thank God Mama was beyond caring by the time it did; Mama has always been a great lady, she wears a size four-and-a-half shoe and her bare foot has never touched the floor; she deserves better for her children and I'm just glad she wasn't there to see, I don't think she knows yet that Nell is married, and if you ask me, it's just as well. It was such a *puny* wedding, not like the ones our family used to have; Mama was too sick to be downstairs and Cleve's people never even sent a note. Everybody except Nelly cried; she never batted an eye, she just stood up there in the right-hand parlor and promised to follow that man anywhere, her foot was twitching, she could hardly wait to be shut of all of us. She gave herself to Cleve Lothrop's keeping, there he was with no past and no future and she was ready to settle for that one minute; maybe she even knew more or less what was going to happen but she set her heart anyway, and went ahead.

The hand-wrought silver and the Minton with the blue border went to Cora and the alabaster urns were supposed to go to Lila, if she ever sends for them, so we didn't lose too much after all, we only lost the clock. After the honeymoon, Cleve Lothrop brought our sister back to the house and piled all those wedding presents in the car, all the silver and china and crystal and the stocks Thad had given them, along with our great-grandfather's enameled Florentine clock, and he said, I'm going to New Orleans now, honey, I have an import-export business that I want to start, I'll send for you as soon as I find us a place. Then he drove off and we haven't seen or heard from him in these three years, not since the photograph postcard he sent on their first anniversary. On the back is a picture of Cleve taken somewhere in the tropics, he is wearing the same white suit and posing on an elephant and he has scribbled on the back: Thinking of you. C. Somebody told us he was wanted by the Government on three counts and I heard somewhere else that he was already married, with a flock of children with that same flat silver hair, but do you think any of that gets through to Nell? When I try to talk to her about it she won't listen, and that picture postcard means more to her than anything that has happened to any of us since.

What did she get out of it after all? Even after everything, her eyes glaze over with his image, and every once in a while I will come into a room and surprise her looking at his photograph. It's not what Cleve did to her that bothers me, it's that she looks up from the picture and I think she has just now hidden a smile.

CORA

What hurt most was that Punk thought I wanted it; who knows, maybe I did, but I don't think I did. I waited until I had to and then when I told him: yes, I was certain, no, I was sorry, there was no mistake, he looked at me and yelled, I hope you're satisfied, and then he stamped out and banged the door. I had to get Alden to take me down to the Seminole for dinner to cheer me up, I had to dance too close to him, playing we were lovers, because he didn't know the truth yet and I could let him smell my hair and pretend I was the same old Cora, but even though it didn't show, Punk already knew the truth and I knew it too, I was grotesquely changed and there was nothing any of us could do or say to stop it, it was going to get worse. God knows it was the last thing I had in mind, Punk and I promised each other we would never, no matter what Mama said; if I did then I would go to bloat like all those dumb girls I went to school with, I would never be any fun any more and neither of us wanted that; my waistline would go and my brains along with it, I would have to wear dowdy dresses and sit on the porch with the rest of them while all the smart girls kept on being taken out to dinner every night, tucking their skirts up in their underpants so they could dance on top of the bar. I would have to rock and watch the children's heads bobbing in the grass and I wouldn't much care which one was mine, it wouldn't much matter what the child was like, it was having one at all, they will change you when you don't want to be changed, they will come out and bump into time and start it toppling downhill, they grow taller and taller and they mark you off like ugly little yardsticks, one year older, one year less.

Well when we got back from dinner Punk was home and I guess he was sorry, he had stuck flowers around in all the jelly glasses and on the couch was a baby doll along with the biggest ugliest pink teddy I have ever seen in my life so naturally I broke down and sobbed on Alden's shoulder, he had to know what was the matter and it all came out and he backed off with the saddest look I have ever seen, saying, Why, that's wonderful, my best to both of you. Then we couldn't think of anything to say for a while until finally Punk said, Well, I guess we'll have to look for a bigger place, a house with a yard, and Alden looked at us both and didn't say anything, I could see he was thinking he would probably have to move, he was waiting for one of us to beg him not to and I thought we would all choke on the silence, it got so thick.

He was waiting, maybe he wanted one of us to touch his arm and say we would all go on just the way we always had, the three of us but with the baby, but I wasn't sure; I didn't know what kind of a baby it was going to be or how we would feel about it or what kind of a family it would make out of us so I couldn't promise him anything; he might even hate babies and then he would learn to hate us too, and God only knew how we were going to feel. But I couldn't tell him it was going to be different either, because I didn't know how I would get through being pregnant and everything without him, so we would have to put off talking about it until we had to, I don't think Punk or I could bear to do without him, not then, not on top of everything else. I had to let him know so I said, Oh Alden, you will have to help us decide what to name it, and Punk gave that needle laugh of his and said, Gee, maybe we ought to name it Alden. Then I said if we did that we would have to name it after all three of us, which would sound pretty funny, no matter whether it was a boy or a girl. Then Punk brought out a bottle he had been saving and the three of us finished it that night.

Alden said he hoped it would be a girl, she would look just like me and when she got bigger he would take her everywhere, Punk said it had better be a boy. It was going to be a famous quarterback for the University, we would get fifty-yard-line seats for all the games. I said if it was a girl we would get to go to all the games anyway because she was going to be the most beautiful girl in the state if I had anything to do with it, I would spend a fortune on her clothes and every year the fraternities would elect her Homecoming Queen, we would get to sit on the fifty-yard-line anyway, and at half time she would come up and kiss her father on the cheek. I thought if it was a girl I would do my best to bring her up to be smarter than I have been, if she got married at all it would be to somebody rich, who treated her like a queen, she would wear all the most beautiful clothes; she wouldn't have a worry in the world, instead she would be a great success and at least I would have that to go on, that wouldn't be so bad.

Still I felt terrible every morning, Punk stopped treating me like *me,* instead he was reverent half the time and mad at me the other half, he would either hand me out of bed like somebody unloading eggs or else he would slap me on the haunch and say, well, how's it cookin' with you? He loves me, I think he was proud, but after I told him I wouldn't be able to go to Homecoming this year on account of the baby he stalked out and he wouldn't talk to me for two days; he was mad because we hardly ever had dessert any more, I was trying so hard to keep my figure, and when I said we would never be able to go anywhere without finding somebody to keep the baby he got furious, it was like *I* had done it to *him*. He was like that the whole time, up and down, but at least he understood if I decided to let the house go for a day; he didn't care if I just sat around and watched my ankles swell, but Alden, Alden would come in and if everything wasn't neat and wonderful the way he thinks it ought to be, he wouldn't exactly say anything, but he would let me know. He would stand there for a minute and suffer and then he would say, Get your things on, Cora, we're eating out tonight, so I would have to dress up and that would make me feel better, and we could turn our backs on the house. Maybe Alden understood after all; I know he understood part of it better than Punk because Punk kept on bringing home baby clothes and tacky little toys but Alden would always bring roses, he brought me pretty little presents, like earrings or perfume.

Naturally I didn't want to tell Mama until I began to show; one thing, if you don't talk about it and nobody notices, then it doesn't seem too real, you can even forget about it off and on. Besides, I knew what Mama would do when she found out, she would sit up there in the bed and she wouldn't say anything, really, except maybe that it was about time, but her eyes would say, Ha, you think you are so wonderful, but you see you are no better off than I am after all. It was worse; Mama is crazy as a jaybird half the time now, she goes out in the hall in the nighttime and says terrible things to my sisters, and even though she claims to be too weak to set her foot on the floor they have even found her in the back yard in the middle of the night; once she got as far as the corner, she was right out in the street and it's a wonder she wasn't run over by a car. I put it off and put it off and finally I had to go in and tell her, I had on one of those terrible old dresses with the big bow on the front, it's supposed to take away attention, but Mama looked at that silly bow like she could see straight through it and me too, she was looking right into the center of things and she said, Well, Lila, you are going to lose both of them, and I never did know whether she meant Punk and Alden or Punk and the baby or Alden and the baby, or if she

93

knew what she was saying, or if she knew something I didn't, how she knew, or if she even knew it was me. At the time I was scared, mad, I wanted to yell, What do you know, you've never been able to hang on to anything in your entire life, but after all she was my mother, by the time I got my mouth open she had already forgotten what she was saying, she was looking at me with this perfectly beautiful smile. Then I felt bad for all the things I had been thinking about her and to make it up I said, Mama, if it's a girl, we'll name it Lily, after you.

So she made me swallow down the knife she had sent up through me, and it stayed there; I was already afraid we were going to lose Alden, maybe even before the baby came, because everything was a mess and Alden hated mess, Punk and I were fighting half the time and Alden would do anything not to have to watch us fight. He was going out with Margaret Alcott again, she has never been a patch on me but that summer I could feel myself getting uglier and uglier while we all watched, I had to hide a lot so Alden wouldn't see me cry, and I think he ran away to Margaret's because she has big feet but her hair is always smooth, he knew her house would always be small and neat and quiet; Alden has never been able to stand upset or mess.

Lord knows there was plenty of it, at the end Punk and I would sit around the kitchen table and half the time we would eat our dinner out of cans; Alden would come back late and find us sitting up over highballs and he would fairly reek of peace and quiet, you just knew Margaret Alcott had smoothed his hair and served him some neat little piece of chicken with parsley on the top, it would be on her best china and there would be about eight peas laid out like checkers on the plate.

Right at the end I used to run out of the house because I couldn't stand it; I would go and sit with Mama. We have never been friends, half the time I sat right there and she didn't even see me, but I was big and broody, I was getting scared, who wouldn't, and I knew she would never tell me anything but I thought I might catch something off her, some knowledge I needed; she had gone through it all those times and she was still alive. I came back from the house one night and Punk was tight, I guess because I forgot to leave him any dinner, he had this big old ugly lady there, he said, This is Malva Johnson, from the office, when you get home from the hospital she is going to take care of the baby and we are going to get out of here, we are going off to Charleston to get back our wits, and I looked at her, she looked mean, I thought I couldn't leave because I would have to feed the baby, Mama has always fed all our babies and if I didn't do it too I would never be able to look her in the eye; besides, this Malva Johnson had on oxfords and an ugly old brown dress, she looked so *mean,* I said, Oh Punk, I could never do that, and then I cried and wouldn't talk to him until he had sent her away. He called a taxi and then nobody said anything until it came and he put Malva Johnson in it; then he came back in like he wanted to hit me, he was furious, and he said, You are going to let this thing turn us into prisoners, we will never have another free minute. I said, Punk, it's our *baby,* and he said, It's nothing but a ball and chain around our necks, and of course by the time Alden got back we were in the middle of another fight. He just stood in the doorway, clearing his throat; I could see his eyes were begging us to stop it, and when I looked at him I started crying, I ran and hid in the bed and I stayed there for the next three days until the pains started and they had to take me to the hospital.

Did I want it or not? Maybe I did after all, I have been so depressed ever since it happened, when the boys aren't here to bring me drinks or fool around and make me laugh, I just cry and cry. But maybe I never did want it, because it turned out something in my body, or maybe only all our bad thoughts had gotten to it and it was a girl, beautiful, but it was born dead. The funny thing was Punk took it even harder than I did, I never knew until I saw his face that he had really wanted it after all, he had wanted it all along.

When I was well enough to talk he and Alden came, but Punk came in first, he said, Cora, I love you, I will never put you through that again.

I didn't have to feel to know I was flat again, my cheeks were thin and our freedom was still safe; I was sad too, I hurt, and I understood what Punk was trying to say. I said, Oh honey, if you want it, we can try again.

Then he put his head down on the covers, he was crying, he said, Oh Cora, I don't know, I just don't know.

The door was open a crack, I could see Alden in the hallway, I was thinking our lives could go back to what they were; I wanted Punk to stop crying so I said, Honey, just as soon as I am better we are going off to New York for a while. Just think, we aren't tied down any more, we can go anywhere we want.

He said, into my front, I thought we could name her after my mother.

I know, honey, I know.

I had my hand on his head but I could still see Alden and it was not that I have ever really wanted Alden, although I have thought about wanting Alden, but rather I could never go it alone with Punk, and because I could not bear to lose anything more I said, Oh Punk, it hurt, it hurt, and then he looked up at me, saying:

I will never put you through that again.

So we made a pact. And thinking it out, about marriage or the purpose of marriage, if marriage has a purpose, maybe even though she is crazy, Mama is right about one thing; when I was well enough I went to her, I didn't know whether she was listening or how much she understood, but she was my mother and I had to tell her all about it, I said we had lost the baby and for a minute or two she didn't say anything, she just kept stroking her rings, and then her eyes cleared, she looked right at me and she said: I love you, Cora, but it's a judgment upon you, it's a judgment upon us all, and as she spoke the world shifted just a little, it shook me; who was I to say she was wrong?

§§§§ §§§§

In her last weeks in the house Mama was a constant source of pain and anxiety to Nell, who changed her gown and her soiled sheets several times each day and bowed her head under the torrential flow of Mama's life, which came forth in incessant, soft words of bitterness and regret; it was as if Mama's body and brain were both emptying themselves at once so that she could go on to the next thing with her mind void and her body an empty vessel; she would continue, purified. She had, however, written *finis* at a time when her life was not yet ready to end and so it became impossible for all of them; the pain and inconvenience spilled over into Flodie's life as Mama's demands interrupted her meals and her cries shredded the night, stealing hours of Flodie's sleep, so that she was forced to recognize at last what Nell had been trying to tell her for so many months, she began to share her sister's desperation. Edward was no help at all, he fled the house as soon as it got light, and when one of the girls would go to him and say,"We have to *do* something," he would refuse to listen; instead he would draw himself up with some of Mama's old stern-ness and reproach her: "You are talking about our *mother.*" When Flodie first broached the idea of a rest home, or a sanitarium, he wouldn't hear of it; he turned pale and his fingers clinched as if he saw a part of his own life being taken away. He said, "But Mama has always lived here," preferring not to know that Flodie answered, in the grim stillness of her mind: Well she can't live here any more. By this time Nell was taut and desperate, and because she could feel her own skin being drawn so tight that she thought she was going to split in a minute like a tomato in a flame, spewing innards every-where, Flodie ignored Edward and went ahead, deciding finally that they had neither the money nor the strength to maintain Mama at home; they would have to find a place for her.

Edward charged her later with going ahead without even bother-ing to consult their older brother who was, after all, the head of the family now, even though he had chosen to make his life way up there in New York. She would never tell him that she had called Thad, begging him to come down and help her, not to take over or even share the physical business of finding a place for Mama or moving her, but only to assume part of the simple weight of the decision. He said, "I can't leave town now, Flo, I've got something important going here, but I want you to do what you think is best," and then he sent too much money because he knew as well as she did that he should have come.

Cora was the worst; she flew at Nell, saying, "You're just heart-less, you're terrible, I'd have Mama at my house if I weren't still sick from losing the baby and all," and when Nell tried to answer and couldn't because she was crying, Cora went into Mama's room and she didn't say anything, she just pressed her forehead against Mama's hand and cried for a few minutes until Mama, rising to the occasion as she sometimes did, put her other hand on Cora's hair, saying, from an unexpected calm, "It's all right, Cora, there will be other ba-bies, you just wait and see." Cora got up, crying, "Oh, *Mama,*" and hurried out; she didn't even speak to her sisters again until the next Tuesday when she came back with the ritual quart of ice cream which she and Mama consumed as if nothing had happened and nothing were going to happen, although Mama must have known that Nell had spent the week packing her things, and Cora had already made plans to be in Atlanta on business with Punk and Alden on the day when Mama was finally moved. "What good would it do for me to be there," Cora said later, refusing to go and visit, "poor Mama doesn't even know where she is." Then she would always add: "And a good thing, too," so that Nell and Flodie, trapped together in mingled guilt and relief, found they had very little to say to her.

There was nothing they could say to Edward. He said, over and over, "There is nothing the matter with our mother," and, "You don't understand, this is our *mother*," and once the decision was made he fled the house because he didn't have the strength to fight them and he could not bear to look Mama in the face; he would call Flodie every night about the same time and plead; she would hold the receiver away from her ear so Nell could hear his querulous, unending whine and then she would say, "I'm sorry, Edward, our minds are made up," and then she would hang up on him. Once Mama was in the hospital, Edward came back and collected his things and told them he was going to leave the house forever, saying he would never spend another night there as long as any of them lived.

The girls used to go see Mama quite often, they could always count on finding her looking clean and pretty, and it was a great source of comfort to them that even though she was delighted to have company she seldom recognized either of them, or if she did, she would recognize one but not the other; perhaps because she could not assimilate the present she always chose to recognize them in the past, so that she might say to Nell, one time: "What ever happened to that boy you used to go with, you know, the handsome one with the silver hair," and another time she would say to Flodie: "Florence, don't squint like that, you know it makes you look mean," but in all the years that she lived and they continued to go and visit her, she never once reproached either of her girls for the fact that she was there.

II
Lila

LILA

I first dreamed about the child in the field early in our marriage, when we were so sure there would never be a child; Simon was the child then, I would have to love him and listen to him: Yes, yes, Simon. Yes; I would have to hold him because his mother never had, in my mind she has always just gone around a corner, trailing watered silk; Simon had grown up alone and so the vacuum around him was bigger than the vacuum around me—we were young, we both thought I could help him fill it, he would need everything I could give. We were too young to see that what needed doing, he would have to do for himself, and so we were hopeful and happy, understanding too late that I could do nothing for him and Simon, Simon was flawed and in the end he could not act to save himself.

Simon's mother would have wanted us to go on the Grand Tour, but he had his way for once and instead we were at Sea Island on our honeymoon, in an old frame hotel with porches all the way around and split bamboo shades in all the bedrooms; it rained that afternoon and I remember lying with my eyes closed and listening to the thunder, the blowing rain; I smiled and smiled. I lay with Simon and thought about all those afternoons when I hid on our second floor screen porch at home, damp but protected, looking out at the rain; Daddy's pride dictated the six white columns on the front of our house but Mama wanted comfort and so behind the columns, marring their sweep, was the second floor porch with its rusty black screens. When it began to rain and the house got too full I used to run away from my steaming, squabbling brothers and sisters and the mud tracks on the Orientals and the smell of wet dog fur and go upstairs to be alone; I would hide in the big wicker chair hugging my knees under my chin and listening to them call: Lila, Lila. Lila this, Lila that, Lila come help me untie my shoe; I would hide from them and laugh; I couldn't wait to be alone, one of the reasons I got married was to live in a house where I could have my own room and nobody would ever again come whining after me to tie his shoe. I was lying on the bed after Simon left my body, I lay flat under the damp sheets smelling the summer rain and I must have drifted off; when I woke he was not beside me, he was sitting in the chair by the window with his head down and his hands clamped tight between his knees, he was trembling and I went to him, saying, Simon, are you in pain? but he only looked up at me with his beautiful face drained and white and said, I can't. I hugged his head, saying, Simon, Simon, what's the matter, what's the matter? but he only said I just can't, and there was no way I could make him explain so I drew him back to bed and held him; after a while the rain stopped and he slept for a while and by suppertime he was all right.

At least he seemed all right, he was the Simon I married, graceful, reckless; after dinner he took me to the band concert and we sat on the grass without touching, playing a game. I was the reticent maiden and he was the dashing stranger—could I, would I, would I let him touch my hand? Oh, sir . . . We played the game for the better part of an hour and finally Simon, confident of winning, reached for my hand and I gave him an evil smile and then pulled away with an offended little cry. He winked, meaning: Your point, but somebody else had seen our tableau and taken us at face value, one of the town gallants came over and said, Miss, is this man bothering you? Oh no, I said, he is my husband, but thank you for your kindness all the same, and Simon bowed, hiding laughter. I appreciate your attention, sir, it's nice to know my wife would be taken care of if I should ever have to leave her alone in your beautiful little town. Alone. Was he warning me? I don't think so, I don't think that at the time he knew any more than I did, we were both hostage to the future: vulnerable, hopeful, fettered and blind. I looked at him quickly, he was lithe, laughing so that I had to laugh too; we went, like children, for an ice cream and then we went back to the hotel, joyful in the soft night air; we slipped into sleep like children, and for the first time I had the dream.

I was in white muslin with a heavy skirt, the kind of dress Mama used to wear, and I was sitting in a field with soft grass spreading all around to a distant ring of trees. The air was still and the clear, brilliant sky cupped over the field so that I was sealed in safety and peace, with the child playing in the flower-studded grass several yards away. The child could have been either a girl or a boy in a little white dress, with its own gold head drooping like a chrysanthemum. I should have been watching the child but in my dream I toyed with daisies until a flicker made me look up. The child started to its feet and began to run toward me with a bright smile and both arms wide, and before I could get up or cry out a chasm opened between us, splitting that beautiful, grassy field, but the child didn't see and only kept running, smiling, until I woke with my whole body pulsing and fear thundering in my head. I know I cried out but if I did, Simon didn't hear: he lay still beside me, sleeping on. I shook him awake and made him hold me but he drifted away again with his arms loose around me. I didn't sleep again until dawn, but when I did it was a heavy, harmless sleep empty of dreams. Simon woke me with lunch, saying, What happened last night? Something . . . but he didn't really want me to tell him, and in the safe daylight I didn't want to because the outlines were fading and I was afraid words would renew it and make it come true.

We ate and then I made him lie down next to me, we talked for hours; I remember asking all about his childhood and his whole life since then, had he ever loved anyone before me, had he ever been this happy before, what was the happiest day of his life until now, what was the worst thing he ever did. He laughed and tried to answer and then couldn't understand why I was furious at him for not asking the same questions about me; didn't he care? If he loved me, why shouldn't he be obsessed by my past as I was by his? He said, I love you, but I'm not built that way, and so I forgave him and for his penance made him answer all my questions all over again. He balked at childhood; he hated his own and so didn't want to hear about mine; it was his own fault, he thought, that his childhood had been so miserable, he had failed either himself or his mother and if he was forced to examine it he might be forced to recognize and exhibit for the rest of his life some unforgivable flaw, he might . . .

Don't. I kissed his mouth to stop it. We'll be better than your parents. Wait.

But he didn't want that either, children looked at you and saw the truth, they knew you were no better than they were, never would be, but they would pretend you were stronger than they so they could use you; they would take from you strength you didn't have to give, until they sucked you dry, and then they would abandon you, leaving behind only hollow bones. What did I know about children? That my brothers and sisters fought all the time, they would come into my room and spoil my things, eating up my time . . .

He didn't want them and just then it seemed easy and so I told him he would be my child and I would be his child, we would belong to each other forever with nobody in between. We pledged, laughing, yet later after Simon went out to walk by the water, I sat in the chintz-covered hotel chair and hugged my knees and thought about what he had made me promise, fighting back uneasiness: was it guilt? fear? If he wanted no children we would have no children, maybe that would keep him safe; I couldn't place my own uneasiness; knowing I had already promised, did I want them after all? If that was so, then it would explain the dream.

Maybe if his mother had let him work, but he was a gentleman, and what could a gentleman do? Maybe if she had lost all their money when everybody else did, and Simon had *had* to work; if I had been able to be with him every living minute, or if I had laughed in the face of his fear and started giving him children that same day, filling his house and his life with children, crowding out his fear; if he had been stronger or I had been better; if.

I had feared his mother; at the wedding she was monumental in blue satin that crossed and recrossed her bosom, with her handsome head pure as a stern figurehead, rising from her collar of diamonds. Facing her over the champagne fountain I had blushed and smiled and thought: She is going to devour us. She would furnish an apartment right next to hers and come around in the mornings when Simon wasn't there, pointing out that my choice in draperies was a little gauche, that *she* was always corseted and fully dressed by breakfast-time; she would want us with her every minute, and when we weren't with her, she would expect reports . . .

Instead she gave one enormous party in our honor when we came home to Washington—I remember standing in front of a fire-place banked with yellow roses—and then she simply forgot us. We lived in the same building, in an apartment at the far end, but we hardly saw her. Left to ourselves, Simon and I feasted on being together until even I had to admit I was bored and then we began to wander, to galleries, to parties, but all that took up only so many hours; for the rest we wandered around the apartment, bumping into each other and trying to keep one step ahead of the maid because she had work to do, and we were in the way.

Simon did have work, but nothing he wanted to do. He was the perfect gentleman, good at so many sports that he could have taught sailing or played polo professionally or coached tennis champions; I would have been proud of him, too, but his mother meant to see that he lived like a gentleman. She had even manufactured a gentleman's work for him, setting it out like a chore, so that he would never take any pleasure in it, but instead would want to put if off forever, adding guilt to boredom and restlessness. She was descended from a Dutchman named Melyn, the patroon of Staten Island, and Simon, who had studied history at Princeton, was to do a genealogy and then write a history. She had specified nothing about our apartment except that the small room next to our bedroom would be Simon's study; when we moved in she had already paneled that room in oak with built-in shelves and a rolltop desk and an opulent leather swivel chair; she had stacked his shelves with all the books he would need and filled his drawers with quires of paper: manila, tissue, bond; she had put out a gold monogrammed pen and pencil set and a silver pipe rack and a Sheffield humidor, placed so he could reach them without looking up from the document she had made her wedding present to us; she had paid too much for it and stuck it neatly into one corner of a leather blotter tooled with Simon's initials: a disintegrating letter, signed with the Dutchman's name. When we came in, giggling and still glowing from the sun at Sea Island, Simon cursed and stuffed the document into a drawer, but in all his worst times the Dutchman would rise up to accuse him; I would find him sitting in the grey light of late afternoon with Melyn's scrawl in front of him, he would be riffling the pages of one of his mother's source books in a patient hopelessness.

He had a job for a while, but because he was his mother's son he couldn't start at the bottom, they put him in an office with a carpet and nothing to do, and when he resigned they all wished him the best of luck. He tried other firms but all his best plans fell through and finally we decided he would not be free to think about something new until he got the Dutchman off his desk. So he would get out all the books and the tin box full of family records and stare at them until he was sick of them and then he would put them away and all his devils would gather and start closing in. For a while he was able to stave them off by writing poetry, but when the first poem was published his mother said, Oh darling, that's wonderful, passing on immediately to something else. He must have written three dozen poems in the months before he showed her the magazine, I thought they were beautiful, but when he sat down after that nothing would come. He thought she would be pleased by certain investments he made for us, but of course we lost that money in the Crash; I will say she never mentioned it, she never mentioned any failure, afterward, but she never acknowledged even the potential for success.

I even went to her once, before I knew better; she was sitting at a little inlaid writing table in the morning room, with the sunlight behind her; she had never cut her hair and it swept up from her face, catching the light; she could have been painted there. When I came in she looked up and said, Yes, Lila, as coldly as if I had been the maid coming in to get the orders for the day.

I said, You. We kept up the fiction that I called her Emma, but I could never bring myself to use her name.

Yes.

If you would only believe in him.

She turned to marble as I watched. When he has accomplished something, I will believe in him.

He tries.

That is not enough.

If she had been willing, could she have helped? Maybe nobody could have, but I didn't see, or want to see; he loved me and I loved him and the fear didn't come on him all at once, it came so gradually that for the first few years it was easy to pretend it didn't exist; for the most part we were happy, and when I dreamed again about the child in the field I kept it from Simon because I thought it was he who was running into the chasm, I still didn't know how the dream ended, but being forewarned, prepared by the dream, I might be able to stop him. When his devils were at a distance Simon could do anything, he was handsome and confident and it wasn't until I woke one early dawn to find him gone and the bed saturated with his cold night sweat that I realized what a long way he had come. I found him sitting on the caned toilet cover, hugging himself and rocking; I said, Simon, Simon, let me help; he rocked, saying, I couldn't make it without you, and when I said, I know, he said, If I couldn't go out any more, you'd take care of me? I promised and he said, If I went to bed and never got up you'd take care of me? I promised and he said, If I just sat here, you'd take care of me?

I'd take care of you and put you to bed and then I would stay there forever and take care of you.

He said, I knew you would, and let me lead him back to bed. He slept until nearly suppertime and when he got up he was almost himself again, although by that time neither of us knew exactly what that meant; from then on we would laugh and joke when he was himself and at night we would lie down together and I would fight sleep in a fury of planning, marshaling parties and projects and excursions, anything to keep his devils at bay.

As we got older he seemed to need me more and more. Once I had to go into the city alone at midnight because he called; he was sitting in his club and there was something lurking just outside the lighted windows, he didn't know what it was or why he was so frightened, he could only tell me that when his friends left after dinner, excusing themselves one by one, he couldn't bring himself to get up and go with them, and when it came near closing time he knew I would have to come down and help him, he couldn't come home by himself; he was all right, rather, he would be all right so long as he didn't have to go outside alone. Another time I had to drive to the marina and talk to the salesman from the marine outfitting company; Simon wasn't sure why but he knew if he had to do it his face would start twitching, his voice would go out of control and he would fly into a million pieces; there was nothing wrong with him, he just . . .

I wanted to get help, but part of my pledge to take care of him involved never telling anybody else; if we kept it between us, it might not be real. He said it wasn't anything a doctor could see or touch, if he needed anything maybe it was an exorcist, or a priest, but so long as he did not believe in God no priest could help him; I thought in my darkest moments about calling in an alienist, but I had promised, and I knew what his mother would do: she would reproach us both with Bedlam, thinking that would bring him to his senses, and he would look into her eyes and fly apart before either of us could stop him; he knew better than I did what she thought about madness, or the hint of madness, she would rather see him dead. Instead of asking for help I had to be strong for him, and so I did everything I could: I met people for him, I made telephone calls for him, I tried to fill every minute of his life so there would be no time or room for his devils and in a final crafty despair I conceived the child for him, thinking: At least he will know this part of him is going to go on and on, hiding my own selfish happiness with the thought that his mother might at least say he had done this one thing right, but when I was

107

sure and went to him, he dropped his head between his knees, saying, My God, what are we going to do, and I knew I had lost him at last.

Of course his mother was delighted, but terribly sorry it was only a girl; Simon said she came once while I was still unconscious, looked briefly into the nursery window and told him she was sorry she couldn't linger, but she had things to do. She had enrolled the baby in Sarah Lawrence, that was her present to us, if Simon had fathered a poor little woman to make her way in this world then the least she could do would be to give it some small advantage at the start.

I was in bed in the hospital for two weeks, I was supposed to be resting but instead I worried about Simon: would he eat the food the maid brought him even though I wasn't there to smile uncertainly and distract him with questions and watch every bite he took, would he have the sense to go to the club and get friends to help him fill the vacant time with talk or would he pace the apartment after the maid went home, restless in the moonlight and afraid without knowing why. Each day he brought magazines and flowers; he would settle on the edge of the one chair and try to talk to me even though I could see that his devils were gaining on him; he wasn't eating, I don't know whether he slept at all, there were blue shadows in his cheeks. He would go to the nursery window before he came to my room and then he would try to talk about the baby as if he really believed she was a person and he could love her, but if he began to shake I had to lie where I was, still too weak to get up and comfort him, and I knew he could not love the baby because she already used too much of me.

The last day they let me get up long enough to dress to go home and then I had to lie on the bed again, waiting for Simon to settle the bills and come; I had on my French blue crepe with matching suede gloves but Simon had brought any old shoes and any old hat; I had to wear the shoes but I was already so tired from being up that I stuffed the hat in the suitcase and crawled back in bed. When Simon came I wanted to cry because he was shaken, worried; could he get the bookkeeping taken care of, how could he get us both into the cab without hurting me, could he get us home in one piece?

I said, They're bringing the baby in just a minute.

He couldn't smile.

Now there are two of us to love you. Simon?

He was by the window with his forehead pressed against the

frame so that I could hardly hear him saying, Two to take care of, and I can't even take care of myself.

The nurse came in with a pitcher of formula, and when she saw Simon, set it down and hurried out again.

I had to help him, I said, You're going to have two Lilas, we can call her Lila Lyon Millard.

Mother.

All right. I would do anything to help him. Lila Melyn.

Still he pressed his forehead against the wood; the nurse brought the wheelchair and put my suitcase on the back of it, tactfully pretending not to notice; she helped me down from the bed, patting my wrap around me and setting a vase of roses between my feet, and when everything else was ready she brought the baby, clean and swaddled in the pink blanket Simon had brought, and set her in my arms with such a decisive thump that I looked down at the package, amazed, and then took hold because it made such a neat fit. She was bright, cheery, saying, It's time, and when Simon finally looked up she ignored the red crease the wood had made in his forehead and said firmly, Let's go. He smiled unevenly as the nurse pushed off and he followed us down the hall; I looked at him and thought perhaps it was going to be all right, but when we got down to the emergency ramp Simon had forgotten to hold the cab and he was frantic; the baby in my arms was already too heavy, she had changed my body so that I could not get out of the chair and fend for him; I thought wildly of setting her down or giving her back to the nurse so I could take care of Simon and in the next second I held her twice as tight, already taken by remorse. There was a practical nurse waiting at the apartment; Simon's mother had laid in all the necessary supplies and turned our bedroom into a sort of bower where the baby and I would stay for the next six weeks; Simon was to sleep in his study and come and visit us in the afternoons and again after dinner. She left word that she herself would wait until Sunday to come because she didn't want to tire me with too many visitors too soon. I remember crying for no reason and then the day blurred so I don't remember much except that tired as I was, I couldn't sleep that night, and when I did I dreamed about the child in the field and woke remembering that I had wanted to put my baby down; in my remorse I thought I would have to sacrifice everything to protect her simply because I could never be sure I wanted her. Then she must be the child in the field; I would have to love her and take care of her and for Simon's sake pretend I didn't really love her, or: I would have to take care of her and pretend to love her more because I didn't really love her, only Simon—I have never, never known, I only know that my life with the child has been hard because I have never seen my feelings clear; I have had to juggle her and Simon, Simon and her for so long that I can't be sure which of them I have to protect or which of them I have to hurt for the sake of the other, whether if I had sacrificed the child at the outset I could have saved Simon or whether he was already so nearly lost that I should have let him slip away so I could save the child. At any rate he is gone, gone despite all my bright patience, despite the equilibrium I tried to reach, hurting the child to prove to him that he is the most loved; he's gone and I understand that he is not the child in the field and never was, and neither is Lila Melyn; I am both the mother and the child, I can neither help nor be helped, I can only compose myself and wait for the chasm to open.

EDWARD

Lord knows I don't like to go to the hospital, but every once in a while something happens and I have to go; first I make sure she knows me and then I say, and then I have to sit in that pretty room that is costing us so much money and wait for her to say what she is thinking, although half the time I don't know whether what she thinks and what she says have anything to do with each other, any more than her beautiful face and that lacy gown have anything to do with what's going on inside. Still she is my mother, and so I had to go and tell her about Vivian, and if I knew a way to make Vivian go with me I would take her out and say, See, Mama, see, because I would like Mama to admit for once that I have done the right thing. Of course she never would. She looks at me and she doesn't see me, she sees what she expects of me. She would never really notice that I am short and not all that good-looking, she would never see how remarkable it is that a pretty woman like Vivian finds me attractive. Instead she would look at me and see the last of the Lyons, and then she would look at Vivian and say, This is all very well, Edward, but is she really good enough for you?

She hates me; no matter what I do or say it is a disappointment to her. She says I am her favorite, blessed boy but at the same time she is looking me up and down, ripping my clothes to ribbons with her eyes and I see that she believes I put her there. She holds out her arms, she may even smile but her chin is too high and I know what she is thinking. It was Flodie and Nell who packed her off to the hospital so fast you would have thought it was contagious, they could hardly wait to be rid of her. They did it without even consulting me and when I found out I told them it was a sin, there was nothing in the world the matter with her, and when they would not back down I packed my bags and I never spent another night under their roof; I have told Mama this over and over, but when I go to see her she holds out her arms and looks at me with a little flicker, it glows at the back of her eyes like the tip of a poker, and I know whatever she says, no matter what I do, she is going to hate me because she is still convinced it is all my fault.

I hate going out there because it is never the same twice in a row. Half the time she says, Oh, I thought you might be Thad; either that or she pretends not to recognize me, and then when she finally gets it straight she says, Edward, Oh, it's you, Edward, and I can see that knife point hanging somewhere at the back of her eyes. Then she asks me about Papa, and I lie to her, and after a while she says, I hoped you would be in New York on business, or else in Washington, getting your credentials, when she knows perfectly well I work down at the pharmacy, and I was lucky to get that, what with the Depression going on. Either that or she says, Edward, Edward, what are you doing home from the University, when she knows as well as I do that I never went to the University. Then I give her the candy. I get it cut-rate because of working at the pharmacy, and then she remembers and asks me how things are going at the pharmacy, and then before I can answer her, she says, You know you are lowering yourself. She says I am playing false to my heritage, and I feel terrible because I remember how she would never allow us to associate with anybody whose parents were in trade; it wasn't that they weren't every bit as good as we were, it was just that we were a little different; After all, she would say, water seeks its own level. Now she asks me when I am going to find something better, I have to live up to the other men in the family, but if I ask her which ones she will say, Well, Harry. She has forgotten about the gambling parlor; I found a tin box in her closet, stuffed full of Uncle Harry's receipts, but when I mentioned it to her she would always say she didn't want to talk about it, or else she would say, Those were hard times for everybody, Edward, and besides, your Uncle Harry never really had anything to do with it, he was only helping a poor widow take care of her affairs. I knew as well as she did that he ran a gambling parlor, he did a lot of other things you wouldn't be proud of, but all she would say was, Poor Harry, he never got over the war, but I could never get her to say which war.

Why won't she say, Poor Edward, the Depression? Doesn't she think I would like to be a professor, or a stockbroker, bringing up a beautiful family in our old house? Lord knows I am trying to please her, I live out half my life trying to please her, I am doing the best I can. I have hung on to all the shreds and tatters, trying to keep as much of our old life in one piece as I can manage, when I left home for good I took all the family photographs and some of Mama's best things; my room at Mrs. Peebles's is as much like our old home as I can make it, I have the cotton lace coverlet on the bed and the Dresden pair on Mama's knickknack shelf, I live as graciously as I can, but when I visit Mama all she does is press me about Flodie and Nell and how often do we use the silver and the double damask tablecloth. I have tried hard to let her believe everything is just the same, and bad as things are I have never, ever taken a job where I could not wear a coat and tie, but all she sees is that I am in trade, and if that isn't enough to hurt me she says, If you really loved me, you would get me out of here. Then I have to hug her and promise to come and get her the minute the doctor says she is well enough, and while I have my arms still around her she says, This is all your fault, Edward, you are no child of mine. Doesn't she know I would like nothing better? Vivian and I could find a bigger place, we would go out there in a taxi and bring her home, her room would be just like it was in the old house, silk drapes and pretty pink walls. But no matter what I do or say to Mama, it goes wrong and she is disappointed in me; you would think she sat out there with nothing to do but be disappointed in me. I took her wonderful news, about getting married to a beautiful woman, and even that turned out to be wrong; when I broke the news all she could find in her heart to say was: Counterfeit gold, I can tell from her picture, that pretty hair is counterfeit gold.

Well, to tell the truth, Vivian did come in to buy something for her hair, she had the baby with her, propped on her hip, she told me later that she had to take him everywhere because she was more or less alone in town, her husband was dead and she didn't have anybody to leave him with. I don't know what she was living on. All I know is, after I wrapped the peroxide she went over to the counter and looked at all the pictures of sundaes and things and then she sat down and I could see that she had her stockings rolled. I got behind the counter and asked her could I help her, but I could see that she didn't have any more money, she'd had to squeeze out the last two pennies for the peroxide as it was. Still she propped the baby up so his arms were more or less folded on the counter and she said, This is Terence. Say hello to the gentleman, Terence, and maybe he'll give you a nice Coke. I knew she couldn't afford any Coke but she was so pretty that I looked in the back to be sure the pharmacist didn't see me, and then I drew her a Coke. Well, as it turned out he did see me, there he was in the doorway with his eyes on the cash register so I made a big show of taking the nickel out of my pocket and putting it in the till. Then I put the Coke down for the baby but she took it and started drinking it, and he began to whine. She clucked and said, Poor baby, so I had to draw another Coke for him. When I gave it to him he put his mouth on my hand and wouldn't let go, and she looked up at me with those blue eyes, just as big as his, and said, I think he likes you, and I smiled and said, That's good.

I would like Mama to know she wasn't fast, there was nothing forward about her, but Mama is too much of a lady to say what she suspects, which means there is no way for me to deny it. She didn't even tell me her name that night, she told me the next time, it is Vivian Furnald, and she came four or five times more before she would sit down for more time than it took to drink the Coke. She came one Saturday while the pharmacist was on his dinner hour and I gave her the Cokes and then I gave the baby a dish of chocolate ice cream, I thought, That will keep her for a while. It did, too, because she had to hold him on her lap while he jabbed at it with his spoon and by the time he was done he had it all over the counter and himself and then he squirmed around to hug her and got it all over her dress. I had to get her a rag to clean it and she said, Oh dear, I can't go home all wet like this, and I said why didn't she sit and talk for a while, business was slow anyway, and she said she guessed she might as well, so we talked until her dress dried out. I can never really remember what we talked about, except what we liked to listen to on the radio, and whether we would rather have a Chevy or a Studebaker, but it didn't matter anyway, I would say something and she would start talking and I would just sit there and look at her, that thin, pretty face and that light gold hair, I would think how she made my sisters look like big old lumps by comparison, and how it would be if we had a big wedding, Mama would come home for all the parties and even Thad would come down, he and all my sisters would throw rice on us as we ran out between the columns and down the steps.

I used to come out from behind the counter and sit next to her while we talked, it didn't matter what we said because I would look at that white profile, like one of Mama's Dresden pair, I would look at her and I would think all these things. Mama would say Vivian saw a good thing and set her cap for me, but that wasn't the way it was. I did all the wishing, *me,* and I kept quiet about it all for the longest time because I was frightened of scaring her off. It was three or four weeks before she would come in the drugstore late enough so I could get off work and walk her home, and even when I walked her home she would have me carry the baby because he was heavy, I couldn't even hold her hand, so it wasn't at all like Mama thought.

It turned out she was staying with her in-laws, they had about a dozen children and when we would come up outside the house we would see light coming out of every window, and there was always somebody yelling inside. I could see why Vivian took the baby with her when she went out nights, she used to take him to the public library and when she had the money she would take him to the movies, unless it was gangsters he would cuddle down in the seat next to her and go right to sleep; if it was gangsters she would usually have to hold him on her lap and give him candy so he wouldn't be scared and start to cry. The poor kid didn't have any money, she wanted to get a job but she couldn't even trust her in-laws to take care of Terence while she was working, they would leave the screen door open all the time and they'd just as soon let him crawl out in the street and get run over by a car. There was a night job open at the rubber factory, they had told her she could have it, but she couldn't trust her in-laws with Terence, there wasn't a soul living she could trust. I wanted to take her and hug her and say, You can trust me, Vivian, but I have been by myself for so long that my arms wouldn't move and my voice stopped in my throat so I shuffled around a little and the next time she came in I got a dish of ice cream for Terence and I made her a banana split, with four kinds of syrup instead of three. She ate it like she hadn't had anything since lunch, and then she looked at me and smiled. She had on a skimpy little dress and the curl had fallen out of her hair, there was a speck of chocolate on her chin but she looked to me like that picture of Ophelia or whoever it was, the Lady of Shalott, that Nelly used to have in one of her favorite books.

I would like to explain to Mama that if it was up to Vivian, it could have gone on like that, just us in the drugstore with nothing beyond, but I was tired of waiting, all I have ever done is wait, and so when it happened, it happened because of me. I would look at her sitting next to me at the counter and I would think, We could be sitting together on Mama's love seat; I would have her put on a silk dressing gown and pour tea for me when I came in from work and then she would put her white arms up and pull me down to her. I would be wrapped in silk, I would take care of her and she could take care of me, we would take care of each other for the rest of our lives. I kept seeing her at the drugstore and walking her home like that, her and Terence, and the whole time we went along I would be dreaming, I was dying to put down the baby so I could kiss her but I couldn't, she would be worried to death he was going to crawl out into the street. At first I thought she might come one night without him, but when I asked her she kept saying she didn't have anybody to leave him with, so I knew I would have to figure it out for us, I would have to have a right, or an excuse. So I went over to the house while Flodie was at work and I didn't even tell Nell what I was doing, I just kissed her and went on up to Mama's room. I went through all the bits and pieces in her dresser, she had most of her jewelry with her at the hospital, in her little velvet chest, but I finally found one of her old dinner rings, it wasn't worth much, but there were two chip diamonds in the setting and it was the best I could do; I could already see Vivian's hand with the ring on, long and white and lying across my arm, with the diamonds on her finger glinting fire. The next time she came into the drugstore I said, I have something to ask you, and after work we walked out together, with me carrying Terence. When we got in front of her house I made her hold Terence for a minute while I got the ring out and then I showed it to her, saying, Vivian, I love you, and she said, Oh, Edward, what does this mean? So I said, It means I love you, I want to marry you, and she thought for a minute and said, All right, Edward, and so we were engaged. She set Terence down for a minute and let me kiss her, she wrapped around me like a flame.

I hate going to the hospital. I should have known what it was going to be like, but I was so excited I didn't even think about that, all I thought was I had to tell Mama I was engaged. It should have been easy but the nurse said Mama wasn't too good that day, and when I went in the room she was sitting up there in the bed as pretty as ever but she wouldn't talk to me until finally I got out the picture and I put it in her hands and got close to her, so I was almost shouting:

Mama, I'm engaged.

Then she looked at Vivian's picture and said, Counterfeit gold.

I said, Mama, I'm getting married.

But she wasn't really listening; she dropped the picture on the covers and then she hooked all her fingers on my arm and drew me close so my face was almost touching hers and she said, If you really loved me, Edward, you would get me out of here.

I said, I do love you, Mama, I want you to come home for my wedding.

She said, What wedding?

Mine, Mama, mine and Vivian's. If I had stopped right there it might have been all right but I had to keep on talking, I had to try and tell her, I told her how poor Vivian was, how beautiful she was, how I loved her, I even loved Terence, and that was my mistake.

She said, Terence?

I said, The baby.

Whose baby?

Vivian's baby, she's a widow.

You are marrying Vivian.

Yes, Mama.

She got tall in the bed and she said, You can't marry her, Edward, she has been *used*.

Mama!

Used. Used, used, used. The word faded off until it wasn't a word any more, she was wandering and I sat with her fingers on my arm, waiting for her to come back, and when she finally did she had forgotten all about Vivian, she said, If you really loved me, you would get me out of here.

I do, Mama, I do.

Then go and get my coat out of the closet.

I thought I might as well, we could keep her home until after the wedding, Nell could take care of her, and so I went to the closet, but there was nothing in there except some old negligees and a bed jacket I remembered from one Christmas years ago; I turned to her and I said, Mama?

She saw as well as I did that the closet was empty but she said, Coat, Edward, my coat, coat, coat; she had Vivian's picture in her hands, she was crumpling it without even looking at it, she was ripping it to bits, she was saying coat, coat, coat, over and over until it stopped being a word, it was just sound, her voice went on and on like there was no end to it, and nothing I could do or say would make it stop; the nurses ran in, the doctor came, finally they gave her a shot and I knew it was all right for me to leave her now, she couldn't see me any more because her eyes were closed.

The doctor took me out in the hall, saying, Well, that's it for another couple of months, I'm sorry it had to happen while you were here. So I knew she was never going to get better and come home, she was just as bad as she was when they took her off, and I could whistle myself blue and she would never be well enough to come to my wedding, I might as well turn my back and walk out.

Well, I thought the best thing I could do under the circumstances was to make the wedding quiet, so Vivian and Terence and I went down to City Hall without even telling my sisters, somebody in the office stood up for us and when it was over we went down to the drugstore and the pharmacist came out front for once and made us both a double chocolate nut sundae, with a dish of vanilla for Terence and Cokes for all. I thought she would find some place to leave Terence for a couple of days at least but she didn't trust her in-laws and there wasn't anybody else. I'll admit my room wasn't the best place in the world for us to set up housekeeping, and as it was the honeymoon had to wait until I found us a place because there was only the one room and the first night we had to keep Terence in the bed with us because it was a new place for him, and he was scared. When we came in the room and Vivian put her bags down she said, Well, I'll be able to get the night job at the factory now. I said, Vivian, I don't want you to work, I want to protect you, but she brushed me aside and looked around my room, passing off my pictures and the coverlet and Mama's knickknack shelf with the Dresden pair with total scorn, it was as if she didn't even see them, and she said, When I get the job, we'll be able to afford a decent place. Well I don't care, she's mine now, and as soon as we get everything right we will be happy forever, but I am bothered about Mama, what am I going to do the next time I have to go see her? As long as I could plan for her, it was all right to go out there, but if I go out there now she is going to smell Vivian on my flesh, she is going to look into my eyes and see that I know she will never get out of that place, she is never, ever going to get well, and she will think that it is all my fault, everything is all my fault.

LILA MELYN

Daddy is gone, Mother says he is dead now and I am supposed to pray that he is somewhere he can rest at last, but my Grandmother says he is living with the angels, they have taken him up there to straighten him out. I don't know where he's gone, he's just gone and our apartment is gone and all our furniture is gone, Mother only let me keep my best dolls and my clothes and now we are on a train going South because she says home is the best place for us. My home is on Connecticut Avenue, I've never lived anywhere else but maybe Mother is right, after everything we don't want to go back there. I went to the bathroom Thanksgiving night, I ate too much when we went to the Shoreham with Grandmother and I thought I was going to throw up. When I got to the bathroom there was already light coming out from under the door and when nobody came out I knocked and knocked until Mother finally heard me and came out of the bedroom with her hair down and made me go to Grandmother's while the men came and opened the bathroom door. Grandmother had her hair down too and I was surprised because it isn't white all over the way it looks in the daytime, the end of the coil is black mixed with grey; everything on her was hanging down, she had on a blue silk robe with dragons and she took my shoulder so hard that I thought she was mad at me and she made me go lie down in the guest room with my eyes closed even though I knew I couldn't go to sleep because I still might throw up and she would kill me if it happened on her sheets.

I don't know why she had to be so ugly to me that night when she was no nice at the Shoreham in the afternoon. She had on all her pearls at the Shoreham, her front was up high in her dress and she was full of smiles, I had on my port wine velvet dress with the organdie pinafore and I got to sit next to her. We sat and looked at the light coming in the long windows and Mother and Grandmother were

118

the only ones that said anything, Grandmother even said she thought I was going to grow out of it and be a very handsome woman, but that was before Daddy ran out and her mouth got tight, like it was all my fault.

Maybe Mother knew ahead of time, because going over in the cab she told me twice not to bother Daddy with anything today, he had a bad night, and I was supposed to be especially nice to Grandmother and help take her mind off Daddy. Daddy sat and looked out the window like he didn't even hear, while Mother told me not to ask him a lot of questions at dinner or spill my water or tilt back in my chair because it made him nervous, and if Grandmother started to talk to Daddy about the work he wasn't doing on the family history I was supposed to get up and put my arms around her and start telling her all about my accordion lessons even though they tell me over and over never to interrupt. When we got there and got our coats off Mother looked into the dining room and said, She's already there, she's got the table closest to the string trio, and Daddy said, I'm not up to it, and when Mother took his arm and said, Simon, he said, I mean, not yet, tell her I've taken Little Lila for a look at the park.

So Daddy and I went out on a balcony and looked down at the park, it was nothing much, just the rocks, and cars going along the road underneath a bunch of dead trees. In summertime you can look out over the green tops of the trees and you think you could jump out and walk along the top of the leaves without falling through but it was almost winter and there wasn't any pretending anything because you could see tree bones with the hard ground underneath and everything was grey. I didn't have my coat and I was cold but Daddy didn't notice, only leaned against the rail and looked out until I thought he was going to freeze that way and I didn't mind because I never got to go anywhere with him alone except by accident, like this. He stood and looked out at the dead trees and *looked* out at the dead trees and finally he turned without saying anything and went back inside, he went through the door first instead of holding it for me the way he always does, so I think he forgot I was there, and when we finally got to the door of the dining room he started mumbling, I think he said something about this being an important day, maybe he said he loved me, I don't know. Then he saw Grandmother in her pearls and his hands started flapping at his coat pockets and up to his face until finally I caught one and said, Daddy? and started to lead him into the dining room because I knew if I didn't we would never get in there to the table and I was partly scared for what Grandmother would say and partly I was getting very hungry. I took his hand and he looked down at me for the only time that day and said, You're a very good girl, and got himself together and pretended to be leading me. When we got to the table I said to Grandmother, Daddy had to take me outside for some fresh air, I thought I was going to throw up, and she said, We never talk about *that,* Lila Melyn, especially not at the table.

After she got us in our chairs Grandmother nodded to the string trio and they played "Liebestraum," her favorite, and then she did most of the talking, questions, with Mother doing the next most, answering, and when she didn't answer they would both stare at me until I said something, even though Grandmother kept saying, Simon? and, Don't you think so, Simon, and, Simon, I was asking *you.* Daddy didn't eat, either, we had pink sherbet on our fruit cups to start and he wasn't going to touch his but he never even thought to ask me if I wanted it. His face is always blue-white after he shaves but that day it looked grey and his mouth kept going funny, he made me a doll out of his napkin and when it accidentally fell on the floor he yelled at me, so maybe the whole thing was my fault after all, but he was just so sad and quiet that I had to keep bothering him and bothering him, I thought I would do anything to make him smile even once.

After the fruit cup we had a fish course and then the turkey came, everybody kept on chewing but the only person that ever seemed to swallow anything was me, they all sat and chewed on one side of their mouth and then the other and watched me so I had to sit there and stuff it down until I felt like a turkey too, I just wanted to go somewhere and split and let everything out. Grandmother said it certainly did her heart good to see a child eat like that and Mother said yes, it was remarkable, wasn't it, but of course everything was so good, wasn't it, Simon, and Daddy put his head against his fist and looked out the window until Grandmother stripped her voice to a sharp edge and said, Every year I think something will have changed, and Daddy said the only thing I can be really sure he said that day, Nothing changes, and then my elbow went funny and the water rolled all the way across the table and into his lap and he said, Oh my God, and got up so fast his chair would have fallen over if Mother hadn't stopped it, and he ran out with his hands stuffed up against his mouth. I thought maybe he was going to throw up but I knew he couldn't, he hadn't eaten anything. Mother ran out after him and I wanted to go too, I thought it might be my fault, I thought it *was* my fault, for spilling the water, I wanted to run out and tell him how sorry I was and make him forgive me but Grandmother was still sitting, she put her hand on my arm and said, Ladies never leave the table until they are excused, so we had to keep on sitting there smiling and have our ice cream and Indian corn pudding and wait for the after-dinner mints, I was supposed to put the leftovers in my pocket for later, and then I had to wait until Grandmother had her demitasse and then the string trio played "Mexicali Rose," which is supposed to be my favorite, so we had to stay there and listen to that, so by the time we finally got out of there the sun was going down like a ball of blood.

I tried to be quiet while we went back up Connecticut Avenue in Grandmother's car, she even let me sit in the jump seat so I could see where we had been, but the sun had turned everything orange and it scared me so I kept talking about my accordion lessons and did she think I could ever have a dog until finally Grandmother put her hand down on my arm and said, That's *enough*. What I really wanted to do was ask Grandmother why Daddy looked so funny and what was wrong but she was so stern with me that I guess she already thought whatever happened was really my fault and maybe it was. If it wasn't, he would have said something to me before he went, he was lying down when I got home, Mother looked dead tired and wouldn't let me talk to him, and he wasn't up by my bedtime so I never saw him, he must have thought it was my fault too or he would have found some way to tell me goodbye.

So I didn't get to see him again, I had to stay at Grandmother's all night and when I got home Daddy was gone and Monday they made me stay home with the maid while they all went to the funeral, Grandmother said there wasn't any point in my having to go through all that and besides, I would only be a distraction. Then Mother said I had to stay at Grandmother's for a while because she was going to be breaking up housekeeping, I knew better but I started crying because all I could think of was her going around with an axe, going after Daddy's things. What she meant was selling all the furniture, but I didn't want to think about *that,* either, it was too terrible, all our chairs would go out on trucks and we would never sit in them again. I finally had to go back to pick up the things I wanted to take with me and the front room and the dining room were already bare, the floors were shiny and there was nothing left in there but the sun, I rattled around on the wood and didn't know what to say until finally Mother took my hand and said, I kept the best pieces, they are sending them down by Express. We went past Daddy's study and there was nothing left in there but empty shelves and a packing crate, Grandmother was sending all of his books off to some museum. Mother was backed into my room by then, her clothes were stuffed in with mine and her makeup and her stomach medicine were all over my dresser with the flowered skirt. She fluttered around and tried to smile while I was picking out what I wanted to take, she said we had to travel light but there would be a whole new life when we get there, I am supposed to have a room of my own and right outside the window is the mulberry tree, my Uncle Thad used to sneak out the window at night and skin all the way to the ground.

Mother has her head against the train window, she looks sick, it might be her stomach again or else she feels bad because she thinks it is all her fault. I want to tell her it's not, it's mine, but if I do she might get mad at me and put me off the train somewhere in South Carolina so instead of telling her, I keep asking her things like, Will there be anybody to play with, and she says Yes, of course, our neighborhood has always been full of hundreds and hundreds of children, all the Barnards and the Richmonds and the LeFevres, and when I ask, Is anybody going to meet us, she says Of course, my favorite sisters, your Aunt Flodie and your Aunt Nell. I made a mistake, though, just now I said, Are we ever going back to Connecticut Avenue, and she has put her head back on the seat and closed her eyes, but I can't be sure if she is crying; if she is crying, there is nothing in the world I can do to make her stop.

§§§§ §§§§

When they were both in the sixth grade Mo used to walk Lila home from school every day and Flodie would follow along, wincing at the atrocity, for using his love to its full advantage Lila had her way with him, pushing Morris into rose bushes or trying to trip him in front of the other boys, who already despised him; she would grimace at them over Mo's head, trying to make them laugh. She would hit him on the head with her lunch box more often than not and because he loved her Mo would permit it, so that their progress went: step, bash, step, *bash,* step. "Lila, Lila," BASH. Each day Mo declared himself in renewed hope and Lila accepted and Flodie's heart rose anew. Flodie promoted Morris even in his darkest hours; she would carry notes for him and act as decoy, delaying Lila with some cock-and-bull story until Morris caught up with them. He would stand there all red in the face from running and trying not to puff; Flodie would feign surprise: "Oh, Morris, it's you." Lila would sigh heavily. "Oh. Morris. It's you." Mo would take Lila's books and they would start off, Lila first, Mo walking with his shoulders slightly hunched and Flodie following in an unconscious crouch because sooner or later Lila would grow impatient and her arm would describe its fatal arc, and whether or not they knew it they were all poised, waiting for that inevitable clank. Still Mo persisted and Flodie lingered, thinking that eventually he would give up on Lila, or she would have done with him and he would turn away from her and discover Flodie herself, as if for the first time. Instead he made of Flodie a monument to all his remembered embarrassments and so did his best to avoid her.

Trapped waiting for the train, Flodie could not stop thinking about Morris; it seemed to her that Lila had used him up very quickly, she had used up a whole string of boys, spoiling things with them so badly that they would never come around again even though Flodie and Nell were still at home, fresh-faced and anxious, and now Flodie couldn't help wondering what she had done to Simon. According to the note Simon had killed himself so Lila could have her freedom, and remembering the lunch box, Flodie thought she knew precisely what he meant. She had used up young men like so many handkerchiefs and then gone off to Washington without a backward look because she was heedless, Flodie thought; she didn't give a damn about the people she left behind.

When Flodie ran into Mo on the street she would pat her hair and create a smile but he always said, even before he said hello, "How's Lila?" The smile would dissolve and Flodie would have to say, "Fine," adding, in inadvertent bitterness: "Living high off the hog up there in Washington." She wanted to ask Mo about himself but she was never quick enough; as soon as he had satisfied himself about Lila he would flee and Flodie would have to go back to her office, thinking: It was that damn lunch box, Lila was beautiful and she ruined it, she ruined it for all the rest of us.

Now Lila was getting off the train; she wore grey for mourning, crepe trimmed in platinum fur, and the child was with her, awkward in a pink coat that was already too small, her pale ankles huge and ridiculous in thin white socks which had worked down into the heels of her Mary Janes. Flodie studied them both as they came onto the platform, thinking: It's just like Mo and the lunch box, she's made the child look this way because it loves her, what is she going to do to us? She hung back, fretting, until Nell rushed past her and threw herself on Lila, already in tears. For one uncertain moment Lila's face softened, in another minute she might even let herself go, but she seemed to catch sight of Flodie over Nell's shoulder, recognizing her as she would an old adversary, and she drew herself up, touching Nell on the cheek as she pulled away.

"Flo," she said, and then, because Flodie seemed to be waiting she said, "This is Little Lila," pushing the child forward with too much force and saying in a funny, strangled tone, "Isn't she *huge?*"

"Hello, baby."

The child scraped at the back of one leg with the other shoe and tried to look smaller; Lila gave her another push, saying, "Honey, say he*llo.*"

Flodie was sure she recognized the look in the child's eyes: just what you would expect.

"Hello, baby." Nell got on her knees to the child, saying defensively, "She has very good features."

Lila swayed slightly and then pulled herself together, saying, "She takes after Simon's mother, she's got those big mule bones."

Flodie thought: And Simon not even cold in his grave. "Nelly, you take Little Lila and get her a Coke."

Lila watched the child go off down the platform with her aunt and then, unexpectedly, put her weight on Flodie. "All those sad mule relatives, blaming me."

"Honey, don't take it out on the child."

"You don't understand."

"Lila, honey, you're upset." Flodie put an arm around her shoulder. "What you need is a good rest."

"If I rest I'll have to think."

But Flodie wouldn't listen; instead she said, "Besides, you don't look well." It was true; she looked at Lila squarely, wondering just when she had passed her in height. "You can't run around as if nothing's happened."

"Oh Flodie," Lila said. Then, "Dammit, *dammit.*" She pressed her grey gloves to her mouth and ran.

She came out of the ladies' room pale and angry, and when Flodie offered her an arm to lean on she accepted it, and Flodie understood this was not only grief or fatigue or strain; she was in fact sick. "Let's get you home to bed."

"I'm not sick."

"We'll take care of the baby while you rest."

The child rode up front with her aunts, she told them all about her school and her accordion lessons and the pony she was going to get when she got back to Washington; Flodie, at the wheel, said, "Who says you're going back to that old Washington?" Depressed, the child fell silent and so Flodie had to distract her with promises; they would get her some of Aunt Flodie's polish and paint her nails, as soon as there was time they would take her down to the beauty parlor for a nice permanent; there was a tiny lick of malice at the back of her mind: *that* would show Lila, who should have done more for the child herself.

Lila lay in the back and didn't talk at all.

When they got to the house they sent Little Lila out to explore the yard and then helped their sister inside. She wavered in the hallway, looking into the two sitting rooms with an air of faint puzzlement, as if she found everything shabby and diminished, and was going to accuse them in another minute; Flodie fought back anger, thinking: She didn't have to stay here and take care of Mama, *she* didn't have to hold everything together with her two bare hands. They got her up the stairs before she could notice anything worse, and they hurried her down the hall, but when they got her into Mama's room she looked around with weary incomprehension, saying, "Everything looks so *sad*."

Flodie snapped: "You don't know what it's been *like*."

Nell was unzipping her dress, helping her out of it. "Come on, honey, you'd better get yourself to bed."

Remorseful, Flodie turned back the quilted satin cover. "We thought you'd want to be in Mama's room." She looked around in a glow of accomplishment; all the curtains and covers were clean and she had even resurrected Mama's lap board for her. Flodie had put restful peach bulbs in all the lamps and there were glads in a vase by the bed.

Nell said gently, "I don't think you're going to be warm enough in just that little gown."

Lila was quick and anxious: "It's only for today."

"All you've been through," Flodie said, "You're going to have to take it easy."

Nell said, "I'm going to go and get my robe."

Flodie unpacked Lila's dresses and began to hang them up for her, noting the tailoring, the labels, thinking: Lila has always had everything. She always will. Lila tried to stop her but Flodie drew her over to the bed and made her lie down.

"You have to get your rest."

"I don't want to rest."

Flodie saw that she fell back in spite of herself; that was Alençon lace on the gown. "You look terrible."

Lila tried to rise again but fell back, catching at her side. "It's my stomach, just this little thing . . . "

Nell came back with the robe, white chenille, lumpy and reminiscent of heavy winter colds. "Just slip into this."

Lila struck out at it, crying, "Take it away."

"You'll catch your death."

"Don't make me wear that ugly old thing." Lila tried to get up, she was furious, but she couldn't seem to pull herself together to fight them, as she would have in the old days. "Please."

Nell looked at Flodie and then she set the robe aside and covered Lila with the quilt instead. "You just rest, we don't want to do anything to make you tired."

"I want to see the baby."

"Not now, Lila." Flodie switched off the bedside lamp, leaving her sister in the shaded glow of late afternoon. "She'll only make you tired."

"I have to tell her . . ."

"You just rest."

". . . what we're doing here."

Flodie closed the door on her.

When the baby came inside, looking for her mother, they hushed her with a piece of cake, saying, "Don't go in now, honey, you'll only make her cross."

Nell saw that she was about to cry and would have given in and let her see her mother, if she needed it that much, but Flodie hissed, "I said, not *now,*" and so the child wandered the house instead, drifting from room to room and trying to put herself at ease about the huge, marching pieces of furniture and the ominous shadows in the big parlors and the dining room. At suppertime the sisters started turning out lights and the child withdrew from the shadows of the formal rooms to the safety of the chintzy family living room, underneath the stairs. They put her in the overstuffed chair by the radio and the three of them made a picnic on hamburgers and ice cream and Malomars and Lila Melyn unwound a little, telling about the cookies she used to make with the maid at home and the tissue paper stained-glass she used to make with Mother—well, once, when she was getting over the flu. At first glance her face was like a pudding, white, with features a little like Lila's, but heavy and unformed. Sitting there in the smocked dress with her heavy arms hanging out of the tiny puffed sleeves, she was somehow a reproach to Flodie: if Lila's life in Washington had been so wonderful, would her child look like this? If Lila were as cruel as Flodie thought, why was the baby crying for her now?

"There there," Flodie said awkwardly, and when the baby still yearned toward the stairs Flodie sent Nell for her Hit Parade Song Book and they sat on the couch with the baby between them, teaching her all the words to the "Three Little Fishies," until finally she began to forget her mother and smile for once, for heaven's sake. By the child's bedtime Flodie had decided Lila had made her this way on purpose because the baby loved her, she was going to use her up just like she had Mo and probably Simon and all those forgotten beaux; if the baby was huge and funny-looking it was because Lila had always been beautiful and cruel. Now Lila was alone upstairs, sick; Flodie would have to call Morris and tell him, not knowing as she did so whether it was for Lila's sake, to take her mind off it, or if seeing Lila lying there would somehow recompense Mo for all the petty tortures he had suffered at her hands.

"I know how you used to feel about her, Mo, so I wanted you to be the first to know."

"Well yes." He was hanging on the line; he might have been thinking of a way to end the conversation or rather of something more to say; was he really all that interested in Lila, Flodie wondered, or was he enjoying talking to her?

"I'm calling all her friends, the company will do her good."

"I'll try to get by," he said dutifully.

She persisted. "Just a little hello, a couple of magazines."

"Don't count on me, Flodie, I . . ."

"I'll tell her," Flodie said quickly. "She'll be expecting you."

He came the next night after all, and Flodie was glad she had gone ahead and dressed and fixed her hair, even though she had thought as she did so what a damn fool she would look, sitting around all by herself in her rust-colored wool with the matching shoes. She was on her way up with a tray when he rang.

"It's terrible," Flodie said in a hushed whisper, "the doctor says she can't eat a thing but milk toast and poached eggs."

"Maybe I ought to come back another time." Mo was already backing toward the door so Flodie turned to the stairs, calling, "Lila, company," and he had to follow her after all.

For one reason or another she hadn't told Lila he was coming, perhaps so she wouldn't get her hopes up, or get overexcited; whatever the reason, Lila wasn't prepared and so she looked like the wrath of God when Mo first saw her, lying back in Nell's old bathrobe with her hair stringing down and not a stitch of color on her mouth. She sat up, chagrined, and scrabbled for her makeup. Seeing her off guard curled the edges of Flodie's heart in a way she wouldn't have expected, but even so she could not forget the lunch box; if Lila wanted to hit Morris with that lunch box now she would have to get up out of bed in that awful robe and stand on the flowered boudoir chair. But in the next second she was finished with her makeup and was as beautiful as ever, the exiled princess with long hands and a luminous face. She made a gesture and without thinking Flodie obeyed, setting down the tray like a servant who can be dismissed, while her sister and Mo looked at each other with such concentration that they might as well have been alone. For reasons of his own Morris had never married, and the idea of this man alone with Lila in their mother's bedroom struck Flodie as not quite right; she lingered in the doorway, she owed it to them both.

"Oh, Morris. It's you."

"You look swell, Lila."

"I wish I did." She lifted the napkin off her plate. "Flodie, what *is* this stuff."

"I guess you could say it was milk toast. Doctor's orders."

"He didn't say I had to *starve* to death."

"I know a chili place we can go when you get well." Mo seemed surprised that he cared and he backtracked quickly, "I mean, when the doctor says."

Flodie was quick. "Not for a while, Morris."

Lila's voice wavered. "There's nothing the matter with me."

"I was sorry to hear about Simon," Mo said.

"It was over a long time ago." Lila pushed at the soggy toast in her dish, and when she looked up her voice was sharp. "Flodie, when I'm finished I'll *call* you."

"I can't let you get too tired."

Lila's voice went up. "I'm *not* too tired. Ever since I got here you've been trying to . . ." Her voice broke and she put a quick hand to her face, dismayed to feel tears.

"You'd better come along now," Flodie said to Mo. He looked stricken, he looked as if he wanted to sit down on the bed and pull her together with his own two hands, and Flodie knew she had to protect her sister from any unnecessary strain. "She tires so easily."

"I *don't* tire easily," Lila said tremulously, and then, in a fury at her own weakness, she turned her head to one side.

"We'd better go, Mo." Flodie added, *sotto voce,* "I don't know how she made it home."

At first he was going to go off without even saying hello to Nell but Flodie said, "Oh don't go, you have to see Little Lila, she's the image of her mother, poor little thing."

He was looking back up the stairs. "She seems so weak."

"I could see your visit perked her up, it perked her right up."

"I should have gone in alone."

"Maybe tomorrow," Flodie promised him. "And later on you can take her in the garden, or maybe even out in the car, the fresh air will be good for her."

"I really can't stay."

"Look," Flodie said, "Nelly's made supper for us."

The plates were already on the table, and they had a good time despite all their worries about poor Lila; they closed the door so the noise wouldn't bother her, and when supper was over some more of Lila's friends came by, all the people Flodie had called so they would know she was home. The Mastertons brought flowers and the Cranes had some Harvey's Bristol Cream, and Flodie had to tell them it wouldn't be good for Lila to have any more company but she wished they would stay for a while anyway, it would be a shame for them to go off without even a drink. They all said hello to Mo and it was like the old days, when the Lyons had the most popular house in town; later they rolled back the shag rug and everybody danced. They tried to keep it down but even so, Lila heard and came prowling in her nightgown, like a ghost; Flodie found her at the top of the stairs, clinging to the railing, she must have called and called before Flodie heard and went to her because she was chilled through.

"Lila, you're going to catch your death."

"Who's down there?"

"Just the Mastertons, and the Cranes. The Cranes brought some Harvey's Bristol Cream."

"Help me down, I want to see them."

"It's past midnight, honey, and besides, you're not yourself."

"But they all came hours ago. Why didn't you come up and *tell* me?"

Flodie was trying to draw her back to her room. "You're not up to a lot of excitement right now, we'll have plenty of parties when you get well."

"Flodie, please, I want to see them now."

"You aren't up to company, honey, just look at those big black circles, and besides, your hair is a mess." Flodie pulled back the covers and helped Lila in. "Now don't cry."

"I'm not crying," Lila said fiercely.

"Your face will get all blotchy. I'm going right down and send them all home so you can get some rest."

The doctor came back the next day and prescribed something for Lila's nerves. He was alone with her and Flodie couldn't be sure what he'd told Lila but she was morbidly depressed all day, Flodie had to send the baby in to try and cheer her up. She had put some lipstick on her and just a little rouge and she and Nell had worked on Shirley Temple curls and taught her a little song so she could give a show. Flodie gave her a push and then stood in the doorway behind her, the proud impresario, but before the baby could start singing Lila said:

"Lipstick. Oh, Flodie, how could you?"

By that time the baby had started, " 'Down by the river in an itty bitty pool . . . ' Mama, what's the matter?"

Flodie patted the child on the shoulders. "She's just a little tired, honey, try 'Whispering.' "

Lila's voice cut between them. *"Don't.* Don't you dare, Lila Millard, you take yourself out of here and wash that junk off your face. Out, get *out."*

The baby ran out of the room, crying, and Flodie turned on her sister. "Why do you have to treat her so mean?"

130

"Look what you did to her, all that lipstick, it's so *cheap.*"

"You hurt her, Lila . . ."

". . . you take everything you touch and make it cheap . . ."

"You've hurt people all your life."

Lila couldn't say any more, she only threw a bun at Flodie and started crying because she didn't have the strength to hit her mark.

"You're sick, Lila, you ought to go to the hospital, where they could take real care of you . . ."

"There's nothing the matter with me." Lila drew herself up, scared and angry. "Nothing. Now leave me alone."

". . . hospital, with milk toast, and thin soup."

Lila looked at Flodie hard. "I see. I know what you're trying to do."

"We're trying to get you well, that's all."

"You're going to starve me, so I never feel any better, and keep me in bed until I lose all my strength. Oh Flodie, this place is like a tomb." She fell silent then, considering, and then took her comb and mirror and tried to put herself to rights. When she had her lipstick on she said, "You'd better send Little Lila back, I have to see her."

"She'll be all right."

"I have to apologize, I have to explain." Lila rose on one elbow and then fell back saying weakly, "Flodie, please."

"She'll be all right," Flodie said, closing the door on her. "You just get some rest."

LILA

I had delusions, I thought I was going to get well, until Cora came; she came in here and saw me in the bed and I could see her thinking: My God, look at her, and she's three years younger than me. She came in here with Punk and Alden at least three weeks after she found out I was here, I can imagine her telephoning Flodie, asking, Are you sure it's all right for us to come around, wanting to be told it certainly was not, so she wouldn't have to go through with it. I think she knows what she is doing: why should we have to sit here and look at each other getting old? But she did it, she put herself together and came; she was fully armed, she had on a jersey dress and silk hose and a lot of jewelry, colored rhinestones, and all that perfume she has to wear to keep from being just anybody; she even had on one of those terrible furs with the minks eating each other's tails, she had them running around her shoulders as if they could guard her and make her strong; she had on too much makeup and she looked tacky, tacky; she used to be a very pretty girl and just looking at her made me feel like I was already run into the ground; when Flodie puts makeup on the baby I look at her and see Cora and not one of them can understand why it makes me cry.

So Cora came, she and Punk and Alden brought flowers and a five-pound box of candy which Flodie took away before I could even break the cellophane. First Cora pulled the drapes back to let in more light and then she looked at my face and closed the drapes again, and then she lit on the end of the bed as if she would fly off if I made one move to touch her, and she had a cigarette and went on about all the parties she and Punk and Alden have been to for about the last ten years, and then she told me about the Cadillac Punk and Alden have bought her and how they are all going to drive it to New York together in the spring; if she could just tell me enough things then I wouldn't have to open my mouth and tell her anything she might not want to hear. Punk sat in the corner chair and sulked, I could see he could hardly tolerate the ten minutes he was forced to spend in here with me, but after all, he is the loving brother-in-law. Cora presents him at family parties and pushes him forward so everybody will have the impression that he always does the right thing; she buys gifts for everybody at Christmas and puts cards on them with his name and opens his gifts from everybody and writes his thank-you notes along with hers: Punk just loves his tie. She props him in a corner at the requisite family gatherings, she would like to be able to smile for him but she can't manage that; she makes him polite for us, and now she was making him visit the sick, I could see he could hardly wait to get out of this place and get a drink. Punk has always hated the Lyons, and I think I understand it; he has to lash out when he is forced to meet us, needling us because something has made him afraid and he has to keep it at bay. He thinks he must protect Cora or she will catch some family weakness, she will contract it like polio and once she does she will begin to drag him down.

Alden was quiet, I think he was embarrassed by the two of them, he is too decent for them and yet he is blind to that; he hasn't got anybody else and so they are his sun, his moon, all the family he has. He kissed me on the cheek when he came in and cracked one of his jokes and then went to sit in the corner next to Punk; he looked

132

at his hands like the obedient footman, waiting to be called. I could see how hard it was on all of them; Cora teetered and fluttered and tried to sneak a look at me without me seeing and then she tried not to look at me because it depressed her, sickness has always depressed her; she is terrified that she may come down with something and have to think about dying, and when she couldn't stand another minute of it she patted my hand without getting too close and she said she absolutely had to go, if she didn't get Punk and Alden to their tennis game they would be cross with her, and then she swept up her two men and left without even closing the door behind her and she hasn't been back since. She won't be back, if she can help it; even if she wanted to come Punk wouldn't let her, I remind them all of where it's going to end.

Edward comes faithfully, but he is never enough. Every once in a while I ask about Punk and Cora and he looks at me and shrugs. They live in different neighborhoods, they might as well be in different worlds. If they are related by blood my brothers and sisters are separated by time, by distance, or concerns; they all get together at Thanksgiving and Christmas in a ritual way, but then they simply forget each other until next time, it's as if none of the bonds or responsibilities exist. I asked Cora about Edward once, couldn't Punk find something decent for him, and she was furious, saying: What am I supposed to do? It's his life. Thinking back on Simon, I wonder if she may not be right; I loved him, I turned my heart inside out for him and in the end I couldn't even save his life, any more than my brothers and sisters are going to be able to save mine. Oh Cora, I hoped for more, I wanted more for all of us.

I don't know what's happening to me. I knew I was sick, but I thought once Simon was gone the strain, the suspense would be over and I would get better; I knew it was sad, bringing his daughter to this, but I thought that would get better too, or at least we would get used to it, but I get weaker and crosser, and when I look at Lila Melyn I know I'm not the only one who cries every night; I want to hug her and promise we will get out of this house and get her old life back but we both know it's hopelessly gone.

I hurt people now, I hurt Flodie when she will let me, I hurt Nell even though I would rather die than hurt her, I even hurt Mo; when he looks at me his eyes cloud over and I can't decide whether he thinks I am going to die and is trying to keep it from me, or whether he's brooding, wondering if I am lying here gathering up the strength to hurt him again, and before I can make up my mind he kisses me too sweetly and hurries out so that I have to lie alone in the darkness feeling the tears glaze over my face; after a while it will be so hard I will never be able to use it again. Worst of all I hurt Lila Melyn; I make her cry and her aunts feel so bad about it that they treat her like a baby and so she lisps and stumbles the way she did when she was half this age and then she looks at me in a terrible guilt; I am hurt to see her changed and her aunts keep on trying to change her, thinking it will make me love her more, she comes in and I say awful things to her, humming and choking on my tears. Maybe Cora is right, when we're together we destroy each other; I look into all their faces and think if we could just be on our own and free of each other's weaknesses we all might have a chance. But I am sick and weak now, all the strings running from my mind to my mouth and my hands have gotten mixed up with all the other strings, so that I mean one thing and do another, nothing comes out right, and if I love my daughter more than life and want to save her, there is no way for me to tell her and no way to get us out of here in one piece. Sometimes I think if only I could have something besides eggs and milk toast and those damn cup custards, if only I could get my strength then I might be able to get up and get out, to stop being the monster I'm turning into; then I think that until I can get out of this house I'll never be able to get my strength. One day Flodie will come in with one of those trays and I'll knock her down and take her clothes and run away, I'll go off somewhere and have a big dinner and when I come back I will be myself again, smiling and strong. I'll come in the door and pick up Lila Melyn and hug her and say, We're going to have things our way now that your mother's better, honey, we're going to have things our way from now on.

CORA

I could see what Lila thought of me and Lord knows I wanted to say something to make her feel better, but she looked so godawful that I knew Punk was going to have a fit in another minute if I didn't get us out of there; he would start sniping, kidding Lila about how even the finest swans come crawling back when somebody steps on their tail feathers, or else he would get grinny, the way he does when he just can't stand it, he would wink at my sick sister and try to haul her out of bed, saying, Come on, honey, let's us go off somewhere and neck, and then on the way home we would have to talk about how lucky we are not to be sick or tied down like poor Lil, why that child alone is a millstone big enough to sink a yacht; then Punk would make a silence too big for Alden and me together to be able to fill it and I would know that he was thinking about the child, a child, any child, because all our lives it has always been true that no matter how much I have, Lila will have just one thing more, so that even when I think I have everything, I am forced to want.

I should have been special, after all, I was the oldest girl, but I was too little and then Lila came along and she was tall; I was pretty but Lila was beautiful, Papa would put his arms around us, me first, he would squeeze me because I was his muffin and his honeybun but when he turned to Lila his face would change; he thought she was beautiful, I could never see it but I think I knew what he saw, she could look at you with her black hair down and that look she always had, you had the idea she could see things you would never see. Now some of it has changed, I am pretty and she is still beautiful but there is a touch of time on her face, it is going to push her past me so that she will age before I age, she will die before I die but I know that if she is so old then I am still three years older, and when she dies she will stay this same age, thirty-whatever-it-is, she may even still be beautiful at the end and everybody will remember her that way, of course later they will even build it up in their minds. Since I am going to keep right on living I'll get older, I'll age right on past her, so she will win out on that one too. But if she dies then I know I will have to die, sooner or later; I just know she is going to go out like a lady with that quiet face, maybe even some beautiful last words for us to remember, and when my time comes they are going to have to drag me off kicking and screaming and goddamn Lila will still be one ahead of me.

Well we had to get out of that room, we had to go fast but I thought I had an idea that would make it better, maybe after Lila went I could take on that Lila Melyn and raise her up like one of my own. I could buy her all those clothes and give lots of parties for her when she got bigger, she would be invited back to all the biggest parties and we would be invited to sit at the parents' tables, we could watch them all and gossip about them and have a drink or two to make the time slide by. Of course we would want to send her to a good college, maybe the University and she could pledge Tri Delt and maybe she would be Homecoming Queen; we would send her through college without even touching Simon's money, and when she got married we could use it for the fanciest wedding this town has ever seen, we would invite all our friends, Punk's and mine, and by that time half the town would have forgotten she wasn't really mine, she would be pretty and popular and we would get credit for all of that and nobody would ever forget that Cora and Punk Gresham gave the fanciest party this old town has ever seen. I thought I could promise Lila that at least, so she could rest easy about the baby's future, but then of course the baby came in with that big bottom and those big cow eyes, she had a glass of warm milk for her mama and I had to look at her all over again. Well any fool could see it would never work, she is so huge and big-boned and sad that it's just impossible and so I didn't say anything because I don't like to make promises I think I won't be able to keep. I knew I would do it if Lila came out and asked me but we have never been real close and I knew she wouldn't ask me, not even if she thought it was the best thing for all of us and in a way, that was a relief; you can depend on somebody who has pride. Well there we were; even in the bed like that, Lila still looked beautiful, even if she is dying or whatever it is, and that child was so bumpy and plain that she was an insult to both of us, I wanted to hit her with a stick and turn her into something else but I knew I couldn't and so instead I looked around at my two men and I patted the baby on one of those fat shoulders and told my sister it was time for us to go.

§§§§ §§§§

It was partly the restricted diet and partly being in bed so much, perhaps it had to do with the stomach thing, whatever it was; whatever it was, Lila seemed to grow weaker, not better, despite all the days in bed and medicines and boring foods; she would cry every whipstitch now, and when anybody came near she would lash out with all her wits, aiming to cut to the bone, but her brains seemed to be ebbing with her strength and it never came out the way she had intended; she would make the baby cry and she would cry too, saying, "That's not what I meant to say." Then Flodie would take the child away and Lila would say the most terrible things but Flodie let her, saying,

"Now honey, don't get upset, Mo's coming tonight, you want to see Mo, don't you?"

And Lila would nod because it was understood that if she did not behave herself she would get too tired, and if she got too tired, Flodie wouldn't let Mo come up at all.

Even with Lila sick in bed, the house was happier than it had been in some time. Flodie and Nell hummed around the kitchen, Flodie making a lunch for the baby to take to school, bustling and sending the child off just like the mother in all the advertisements because she thought it would be good practice. Despite what everybody thought, she was going to get married one of these days, and leave this house for good. In the evenings Lila's friends still came, the ones she hadn't driven away, and Flodie spent some of her money on new jewelry and little scarves to pep up her outfits; they hadn't had so much company since they were girls.

Most often Morris came, at first he spent most of his time in Lila's room but as time wore on he would come down, shaking his head, and sit in the family living room with Nell and Flodie until Flodie said for heaven's sake Nell, it wouldn't hurt to take the baby out for a soda or something when Mo came around. She dressed for those evenings in a fever, thinking: Maybe this is it, it's way past time for me to have my chance. After a while she kept the Mastertons and Kyle Hinney and the rest from seeing Lila, saying, "We don't want to use her up," but she sent Mo to Lila's room because she counted on it. Besides, she knew if Mo couldn't see Lila, he wouldn't come; more: she hoped Lila would turn on Mo one night, hurting him, and say the one thing that would free him for her for once and all; he would come downstairs with anger in his eyes, saying, My God, Flodie, and she would say, I know. Then she would pull him to her, just to calm him down, but they would end by kissing and his hands would begin to travel and she would be halfway there. Lila had more than a life before this happened, she was even rich, Flodie thought grimly; now it's my turn.

Gaunt and weak as she was, Lila still drew Mo; no matter how well Flodie entertained him in the parlor, he always pulled away from her to say, "Lila's waiting," and no matter what she said or did, he would disengage himself, leaving her to cool while he straightened his tie and slicked back his hair. Then they would tiptoe up to Lila's room and Flodie would linger in the doorway to make sure he didn't tire her. Even when Lila didn't want to talk he would sit by the bed and hold her hand until finally Flodie cleared her throat and then, when he didn't even hear her, would have to say, "Morris. Mor-*ris.*" Even without talking Lila could hold him, and no matter how cross or slatternly she looked in the daytime, no matter how ordinary she seemed to Flodie, she would be powdered and combed by the time Mo came; she gleamed at him like a pale flame. Flodie would have to come and stand by his chair finally, watching until he was so uncomfortable that he would have to give Lila a brief kiss and disengage her fingers so he could leave the room.

If Flodie had stayed with them that last evening, if she hadn't given in to the urge to go and take down her hair and get into something more comfortable, it might have gone along smoothly, Mo might still be coming around, he might have seen through Lila and married Flodie in the end, not because she had plotted but because it was bound to work out that way. As it was she made a mistake that night, leaving them alone; she had made a worse mistake that same morning: she and Lila had a fight. Lila was lying there, weak and feverish with rage, and Flodie knew full well she couldn't help it; Flodie had the advantage, she had her health and strength, but she had within herself years of accumulated rage and so although she knew better, could have *been* better, she let it happen anyway.

Lila began it by fretting over her breakfast tray, to which Flodie had added some forbidden orange juice and a rose; she pushed it away with fierce impatience, as if she wished it was Flodie she had within the power of her hands. "Flodie, the doctor never told you to *starve* me to death."

Flodie resettled the tray with too much force. "Doctor's orders."

"You want me to starve and die of boredom too." Lila's voice rose, thin and helpless, and then in anger at her own weakness she lifted both hands and tilted the tray on the floor.

Flodie watched it go, numbering all the other trays she had fixed and toiled upstairs with and then carried away, all the uneaten Cream of Wheat, all the dirty dishes, and now the broken china, the ruined rug, and she swept down on her sister, pinning her to the bed and crying out: "Damn you, Lila, you lie down and do like I tell you or you aren't going to last much longer, you won't last out the week."

"You're trying to kill me," Lila said, furious, and then her eyes cleared as she read Flodie's expression: I won't have to. "Oh." She raked her fingers down her face. "You had to let me know."

Flodie was busy picking up the dishes, stabbing at the rug with Lila's napkin, smoothing the bedcovers. "We have to work hard to get you better."

Lila's voice was thin. "You've always hated me, so you had to let me know."

Flodie made a face to greet her with. "We're only trying to get you better," she said doggedly, adding, before she could stop herself, "Honey, you look terrible."

"That's it." Lila was laughing now, or crying, one. "You're trying to get even."

All the weeks, the years piled in on Flodie, her face cracked and she heard herself saying, "That's a goddam lie, but if I was, it would serve you right." As soon as she said it Flodie tried to swallow it back, she wanted to stuff the words back in her mouth and jam a cork in on top of them to keep them down, but it was already too late; she moved forward to put her arms around her sister but Lila pulled away, saying, with a wintry gleam in her eyes:

"It's all right, Flodie. So would I, if I were you."

"Now honey." In a panic Flodie fooled with the bedcovers, tried to touch her sister's hair. "You just relax honey, you just forget everything and try to get some rest."

So it began with that mistake, and that evening she left them alone together and that was another mistake, for all she knew he'd gotten in the bed with Lila before he helped her dress and they went off. But Flodie had to take the chance because before she let him go up to see Lila, she and Mo had gone farther than ever on the couch, Nell and the baby were at the movies, they wouldn't be back until late so she and Mo would have the house to themselves and at that moment, everything had seemed very close. They were on the couch together and Mo wouldn't have gotten upstairs to see Lila at all that night except that Flodie remembered the ridges along her back where the girdle cut her, and the bra, she thought about making a smooth line for Mo's hand and she excused herself, thinking: My peasant dress, I will look better in my peasant dress, saying to Mo, just to get rid of him, "Why don't you go up and tell Lila 'lo." Then she went to her room and took a bubble bath and changed every stitch she'd had on.

When she came back they were gone, both gone, Mo was gone and Lila's silver-grey crepe dress was gone from the back of the closet and Flodie didn't see either of them again until well after midnight when Mo carried her in and laid her on the bed and helped Flodie unbuckle her silver evening shoes. By the time they got back Flodie had control of herself, she didn't say anything to Mo except:

"I was worried to death about you."

"She said she was so hungry." Now that Lila was out of his hands and stretched out on the bed he turned his back on her. His face was charged with blood and his look was one Flodie recognized from childhood, he would hate the foolishness that led him to his own betrayal. "She just begged and begged."

Flodie didn't listen to him at first, she put a pillow under Lila's head and made sure she was comfortable; Lila's face was dead white and although Flodie wouldn't put it into words she had a suspicion that her sister was bleeding, seeping somewhere inside.

"She said she was starving, she wanted to go out and raise some hell."

"Later, Mo. Right now I have to call the doctor."

"You do that." He followed her down to the living room without a backward look for Lila, and he sat on the sofa while Flodie telephoned. He followed her to the kitchen while she made coffee, he was pink and so full of his story that Flodie knew she had to let him get it out.

"Tell me about it, I have to be able to tell the doctor if there's anything she ate that she shouldn't have, I have to tell him what she had."

"I'll tell you what she had," Mo said. "She had a hell of a lot to drink."

As it turned out they had started at the chili place with two big bowls and crackers and raisin pie and Lila had thanked him for getting her out; it was like a rescue, the princess from the tower, and then in the next minute she had turned ugly for no reason at all, she wouldn't smile and she wouldn't dance and she wouldn't do anything he wanted her to do, she sat there with this godawful bleak look and when he tried to make her talk she snapped at him. By the time they got to the Mirobar she was feeling bad; she wanted to dance, she made him take her out there on the floor even though they both knew he was holding her up because she wouldn't have the strength to stand there by herself. Then they went back to the table and she began to drink some more, she wouldn't slow down on the highballs when he begged her to, they seemed to give her some unexpected strength because she started talking about train tickets and hotel reservations and getting out of this dried-up old town.

"How could you, Mo, when she knew she was sick . . ."

"She said I had to, and then when she started talking about the trains and everything I tried to quiet her down, I said, I love you, Lila, but you know you're too sick to leave town, it was the first time I'd said anything about her being sick at all and she said, well . . ."

"What did she say?"

"Never mind what she said." There was a look of pain in Mo's eyes, he was tired, duped; Flodie could almost see the lunch box coming down: CLANK. "Then she passed out and I brought her home."

"Well it's no more than I would have expected."

The doctor came in just then and while Flodie was in the front hall with him, Mo got up and in the next minute he was in the doorway, making his escape.

"See you tomorrow," Flodie said quickly, as if that would work.

"See you," Mo said but he wouldn't look at her, he was finished with Lila, he was finished with all of them.

When he was through with Lila the doctor came down and talked to Flodie for several minutes, she tried to offer him some coffee but he wouldn't take any, he told her goodbye quickly and went off. She left one light on for Nelly and the baby and went up to Lila's room, looking down at her sister with such complicated emotions that finally she had to cover her eyes with her hand and turn and find her way to bed.

When she went in the next morning Lila was sitting up in bed as if nothing had happened, but it had; it had drained her face and lined her mouth, making her look diminished and mean, she looked terrible.

"The doctor thinks you ought to go into the hospital."

"It won't do any good."

"He thinks you ought to go anyway."

Lila set her jaw. "I don't want to go."

She looked so terrible that Flodie wanted to hug her, she wanted to do anything to make her feel better. She said, without conviction, "They could take better care of you."

Lila looked at her with tears in her eyes. "Flodie, why do you hate me?"

141

"Honey, I don't hate you, I—love you."

"You've never loved me; I don't know, why should you?"

Flodie said, slowly, "If you thought I hated you, why did you come back?"

"Don't you know? There wasn't any money, I didn't have anywhere else to go."

"Oh Lila." Flodie put her arms around her sister and buried her face in her neck.

"It's not your fault." Lila's arms were light as sticks around Flodie's back. "I knew there was nothing for me here." She let her sister hide her face for a minute longer and then put her aside. "Flodie, promise me I won't have to go to the hospital. Not yet."

"The doctor says . . ."

"I know, but let me do it my way."

Flodie couldn't bear to look at her another minute and so she excused herself, muttering, and went downstairs to make a tray. She brought it upstairs and set it on her sister's lap, watching as Lila lifted the covers on all the bland dishes with an expression bordering on despair. "Eat up, honey, Mo will be back tonight, you want to be up to seeing him."

Lila's eyes were direct. "No he won't."

"Well what if he isn't," Flodie said, trying to hide her bitterness. "Listen, you have to take care of yourself, you have to eat."

Lila was considering. "Yes."

"The Cream of Wheat first, and then . . ."

"Flodie, listen. I want a sandwich for lunch, I want fruit and a salad, and I want you to get on the phone and tell the Mastertons and the Langs I want to see them tonight, and maybe the Coles can come tomorrow night . . ."

"Honey, you're supposed to take it easy, you're supposed to rest." Even as she protested, Flodie looked into her sister's eyes and understood.

Lila was smiling now. "And in the meantime, I'd like something decent for breakfast, kippers, I think, you can send Lila Melyn down to Crane's before she goes to school . . ."

Flodie knew what Lila wanted to do and weighed it for only a second, for in spite of everything they were still close, they had always been too close, and Flodie, in this final act of love and vengeance, would help Lila do what she intended. She said, in complicity, "I'll call the baby."

"Well hurry up."

At the door she turned back as if to say something and saw that Lila had pulled the sheet up over her face.

LILA MELYN

My room isn't like Mother said it was going to be at all, the rug is all worn out and you can't bounce on the bed like she used to because some of the springs are broken and you would stab yourself to death. There's nobody to play with, nobody at all, every house on this street except this one is a boarding house or has doctor's offices or something and there are no kids, there isn't even any mulberry tree. They took me to see the school where I'm supposed to go after New Year's and I hate it, all there was was about twelve kids with scabs and Band-aids playing in this grey sand that turns your ankles grey, at home we used to have a cement playground with swings and in the winter lots of snow, it never snows down here. When we got in here Mother took one look at the living room and cried so I thought she would change her mind and we wouldn't have to stay here, but then she got sick and we have to stay here at least until she gets better, the only thing is she isn't getting better fast enough, I have tried everything.

I thought first if she had to eat a quart of ice cream every night that would make her strong, I fussed until Aunt Nell promised to walk me down to the drugstore right after supper, we went out and she even bought an extra cone for her and one for me. When we brought the ice cream in to Mother she took her hand off from over her eyes and sat up and smiled at us, and she thanked us for the ice cream and started to eat, I was already thinking Look at her, she's better, but then she stopped all of a sudden, she said I'm sorry, it gives me a terrible headache, and she began to cry. The next minute Aunt Flodie sailed in with her big voice and said what were we trying to do with Lila, kill her, and so Aunt Nell and I had to take the rest of it downstairs and finish it ourselves. Another time I thought maybe if we opened the windows and let some sun in for once she would get better, but Mother closed her eyes and hid her head until we shut the windows and the shades and the curtains and it got pinky dark in there again, just like it always was. I kept on making things for her, pictures and a pencil holder out of nail polish and a toilet-paper roll, I even made a pin out of soup alphabet, you paste the letters on a piece of wood that spells the person's name, but when I took it in I was in such a hurry that I bumped her, getting up on the bed, and she couldn't look at it, she only cried so I had to cry too and then she said she was worry and I went to find Aunt Flodie, I didn't like Aunt Flodie at first; when she hugs you she is hard in front and she always gets lipstick on you, but right now I am always glad to see her because she is bigger than Mother and her voice is strong, her fingers could go right through your arm if she wanted them to.

I thought Mother would get all right for Christmas, she even promised me she would and I wrote a letter to Santa Claus to make sure. It was silly because I know there isn't one, Daddy got drunk and told me when I was little, but I wrote the letter anyway and left it propped up on Aunt Nell's dresser where she would find it and take it in to cheer up Mother. I said I had been good all year, how could I write about what happened to Daddy? I said I had been good all year and I wouldn't ask for any toys, I wouldn't ask for anything except for Mother to be well and come downstairs for Christmas dinner, and if it wasn't too much trouble an angora sweater like Aunt Flodie has. Mother never let on she read it but I know she had because we were sitting in her room one night after supper, she was trying to play Fish with me, and she said, I don't think you would look well in angora, Lila Melyn, it would only make you look fat. So I knew she knew, she couldn't get out and buy me anything but she might get Aunt Flodie to, since there were no kids to play with and no mulberry tree and I had to do something, and at least she would come down for Christmas dinner, that wasn't too much to ask, and if she only got down there and ate some of the turkey and things it would make her stronger, she would start looking like herself again and everything would be all right. I really did want the sweater; Aunt Flodie's is pink, when she puts it on with her pearl choker she looks like a glamour girl.

I didn't ask for anything else for Christmas, I thought I would get a lot of things anyway because I always do; I made presents for everybody out of beads and nail polish and cardboard I found around the house and I waited for Christmas because Mother was going to come down and all that dinner would make her strong, being in clothes instead of that nightgown would make her strong so she would get well and pack us up and take us both back to Washington where we belong. I made a Christmas list: Mother, Grand-mother, all the aunts and uncles and Terence, and I ducked my head when Uncle Edward would ask what was Santa Claus going to bring me and I thought about getting out of this place and back home where they don't have sandy grass at Christmas time, they have snow, I would wear my angora sweater on the train. Aunt Flodie even took my measurements, she said it was for a jacket, so I knew everything was going to be all right.

Christmas Eve Aunt Flodie let me come along to get the tree, she said I'm sorry, honey, we can't get the kind with the short needles, that's only in the North, and then she told me about how when she was little the big kids would stay up with Grandmama and Grand-papa and decorate the tree on Christmas Eve and the little kids, which I guess was Aunt Flodie and Aunt Nell and Uncle Edward, would lie in the bed and watch for Santa Claus and try to stay awake but they never made it, they were always asleep when he finally came. They would come running down in the morning and every-thing would be there, the big tree, the presents, everything, and the house would be full of smells. After the tree we had to get a lot of stuff at the market because Uncle Edward was coming along with Vivian and Terence, he's supposed to be my step-cousin and they all said I was going to like him a lot right off; we had to get ready for Uncle Punk and Aunt Cora and Uncle Alden too, Aunt Flodie says the Lyons are a close family and we spend Christmas together every year, she said it was so nice this year because we were going to have a child in the house again, I thought she must mean Terence instead of me because my name is not Lyon, it's Millard.

I never said anything to Mother about coming down for dinner, not to her face, but I went in that night while Aunt Flodie and Aunt Nell were down setting the table, I got out her jewelry and her un-derwear and a dress and her tan snakeskin shoes and laid them out on her chair and while I was in her dresser I just sort of looked to see if there were any boxes with paper and ribbon, something she might be hiding from me, but I decided she had hidden everything very, very well because I couldn't even find a dime store bag. After I finished laying everything out for her I said, Mother, we're going to have chestnuts in the stuffing, and she looked like she was about to cry. Instead she said, Honey, I wish we were going to have a better Christmas, but I do have one good surprise for you, and I told her I don't need any surprises, I just want you to get well, but I was thinking about the sweater too. Aunt Flodie and Aunt Nell let me stay up real, real late, they even let me help decorate the tree, I never had a little one that stood on a table before, it looked small and mean and there were too many decorations because Aunt Flodie and Aunt Nell had everything that used to go on the big tree, there were about four boxes and they were trying to make it all fit on all at once. So we stuck things on the tree until finally even Aunt Flodie had to admit we weren't going to get any more of it on and then she dragged the box with the rest of the glass Santas and bead chains away and stuck it in the closet under the stairs. Then she said I had better get on up to my room or else I was going to miss seeing Santa Claus go past the moon in his sleigh and so I had to kiss them and then I went up-stairs, I couldn't stop thinking about the silver tree Grandmother puts up in her front room, she always decorates it with blue balls and blue lights, and there are jewels in the star. Then when I was in bed in the dark with my eyes shut so it was twice as dark I thought about this other thing that if only it would happen, we would all be sitting around under the tree with our presents and suddenly Daddy would come in because everything that happened at Thanksgiving was dif-ferent from what everybody thought it was, he had been kidnapped, he had amnesia, they had a funeral for somebody else and all of that was only a mistake. If Mother wasn't up yet he would go upstairs and pick her up and carry her down in her nightgown, she would be saying Oh Simon, the way she used to, and the three of us would stand in the doorway and say Merry Christmas everybody, goodbye, and then we would just march out and go home. It made me feel partly good to think about it and partly bad, like I used to feel when I would tell a fib and Grandmother would stand there and look right through me. So I thought about the sweater instead, maybe mine would be blue, which is supposed to be my best color, and maybe Aunt Cora and Uncle Punk would get me a string of real pearls be-cause they are rich enough to, they have two Cadillacs.

It wasn't light yet when I woke up so I stayed in bed until I couldn't stand it. I thought I would go into the living room and there would be a pile of presents under the tree, like we have in Washing-ton, but there wasn't much, only a couple of boxes that you didn't even want to shake, and tacked up on the fireplace was one of those red net stockings you get in the dime store with everything wrapped ahead of time, I guess it was supposed to be for me. Nobody was up yet so I turned on the tree lights and sat down and opened the stocking and ate all the candy, I don't know why it made me so sad. Then I waited until I heard this light padding upstairs, that was Mother going to the bathroom, and I went and got out the calendar I made for her, it was on a cardboard with a manger scene pasted up top for decoration, I punched holes in the edges and wound it all with wool and then I made a cord for a pencil with a wool bow on it so she would be able to mark off the days. I took it up and tapped and went in, thinking she would be sitting up in a good bed jacket and she would look strong and wonderful because she always does on Christmas, she would have a big box on the bed, the angora sweater, and she would smile like the sun.

Her eyes were open but she was still just lying there, and then when she saw me she pulled herself up and said Merry Christmas, darling, get me my lipstick, and I got it and the bed jacket I wanted her to have, she put them on and looked better right away, just like I knew she would. She took the calendar and unwrapped it and then she hugged me, saying, It's beautiful, honey, I love it and I know your daddy would too, he would be very proud of you. Then she had me go into her dresser, she got upset because I couldn't find what she wanted right off but I got to the bottom of her jewel box and there was a little leather box with a pattern on it in gold, I took it over to the bed and she held me close and said, Lila Melyn, I couldn't go out to shop for you but this is the best present I could ever give you, I want you to wear it and think about me and your Daddy for the rest of your life; I held my breath while she opened the box but what it was, it was only her engagement ring with the cat's eye diamond in it, she stopped wearing it after we lost Daddy and I thought it was lost too. I said, I couldn't take it, it's too beautiful, and she pushed it at me and I said But Mother, it's yours, and she only said, It's yours now, whatever happens I love you, I heard your aunts up so you better go down and get breakfast, I bet they have some real nice things for you, and then she rolled over and wouldn't look at me. I put the ring on my middle finger and stuck the calendar up on the dresser mirror where she could see it from the bed and went on downstairs.

Aunt Flodie and Aunt Nell were down there in their bathrobes with those lapel pins made out of Christmas balls, they had their hair all combed and lipstick on. I wanted to give them their presents but Aunt Flodie said Not yet, honey, first we have to eat, did you find the stocking Santa Claus left for you? I had to make my face change so they would think I was glad, I said yes I did and Aunt Flodie said, And he got in here even though there isn't any chimney in the living room, imagine that. Then we ate and after that we went in to the tree, there were the same four boxes, they all said Little Lila from Santa on the tags or Love from Santa Claus and I had to open them very slowly because Aunt Flodie and Aunt Nell were watching with their mouths open, I don't know what they expected from me; I knew none of them were big enough to be the sweater so I thought either they would bring it down afterward or maybe Aunt Cora and Uncle Punk were the ones that were going to give it to me after all, since they are the rich ones in the family, either that or I would go up to get dressed and it would be lying on my bed with a tag in Aunt Flodie's hand: Love from Santa Claus. So I opened the presents, there was an old, old book of Grimm's Fairy Tales with Aunt Nell's name on it from when she was little and a watercolor set and some bath salts and a slip, there was a box with a sign on it saying Little Lila from Mama, Aunt Nell had written the card so I couldn't tell them I already had my real present; I don't know why but I didn't want to tell them, it was something between Mother and me, so I opened the box and it was a new nightgown, pink flannel with bunches of cherries all over it, and I thanked Aunt Flodie because I knew who picked it out. After that I got my present from Grandmother, it was only an envelope which is why I didn't see it under the tree. She has given me my own pony but she is keeping it at some stables in Warrenton, Virginia and every time I come up to visit her she will drive me down to the stables and I can ride it whenever I want. Aunt Flodie and Aunt Nell kissed me and said they loved their note pads I made with the leftover yarn but they were still watching me, I said Thank you for everything and they said, You mean, thank Santa Claus and I sighed and said, Thank Santa Claus and then they both sighed too because whatever it was I was supposed to do about everything, I hadn't done it enough. Then Aunt Flodie gave me a pink package that gurgled, toilet water, and said, Here, honey, I want you to take this present up to your mama, it's from you. She already had her present from me, but this box was all wrapped with silver ribbon and a paper rose so I had to take it up. Mother's tray was on the bedside table and I could see she was sleeping so I set it down and left. When I got downstairs Aunt Flodie said, Well, how did she like it? and I said, She liked it just fine. Then I had to go up and put on my wine-colored velvet dress with the organdie pinafore, it's getting small so there are little white gaps between some of the buttons on the front, you can see them through the pinafore.

Aunt Cora and Uncle Punk and Uncle Alden came early, about a half-hour before they were supposed to come, Uncle Punk was carrying a pile of boxes so I thought maybe they had gotten me the sweater after all, but when I opened them it was a kitchen set, a pink toy stove and an icebox and a sink to match, they were all made out of tin and when you opened the icebox there were cardboard boxes of pretend food inside, I used to have one like it when I was six except that mine was white. They were waiting too, so I had to go around and kiss them all and say thank you but I could see Uncle Punk making a face behind my back, I heard Aunt Flodie talking to Aunt Cora in the doorway: The least you could do . . . Christmas day . . . but I didn't care, I didn't want to hear so I got down off Uncle Alden's lap and went over and pretended to play with the stove. About then Uncle Edward came in with Vivian and Terence, who had on a suit and a felt hat, and Aunt Cora and Uncle Punk and Uncle Alden gave them their presents and left before they even opened them, it turned out they were going to the St. John's Club for Christmas dinner, they weren't going to eat with us after all. Uncle Punk was going *pstpst* and pulling at Aunt Cora but she took her time, she said it was very sad but she said, We thought it would be better with Lila so sick and all; then Aunt Nell said Shh the child and then Uncle Edward came over and gave me a Merry Christmas kiss, his face is always a little wet and cold. Then he said he didn't have a real present for me. I should go out and buy something for myself, and he gave me a half-dollar. Vivian brought a present though, a box of stationery with violets, she said, It's to write all your thank-you notes.

So there were only six of us at the table, Aunt Flodie had Matty take off the extra plates. We had fish chowder and I had to sit next to Terence, who is sickly looking and kept showing off his new watch; Aunt Nell was on my other side, but she had to keep jumping up to see about the oyster dressing, which she always makes separate, and her orange-and-raisin sauce. Aunt Flodie kept talking to Uncle Edward and then Uncle Edward would say, Don't you think so, Vivian, leaning his head around until Vivian answered him and then turning back to Aunt Flodie to make sure she heard. I sat there remembering the turkey from Thanksgiving and after a while everything I had in my stomach started to rise into my mouth, I thought I

149

was going to have to get out in a hurry but I couldn't ask to be excused because Aunt Flodie and Uncle Edward were having a fight. He said, Mama always had rice and potatoes *and* sweet potatoes, and she said, We are having *exactly* what Mama used to have, and he said, We are not, it's not the same, nothing's the same. Then Aunt Flodie said, I'd like to see you do half as well on what I've got, and Vivian said, If he had half what you've got he wouldn't have to work in that stinking market, and then everybody got quiet at once because there was a sound in the hall. All my food went down in my throat and I said Mother, oh Mother, because she was hanging on the doorway, swaying, she was like a white statue draped on the dining room arch and then Uncle Edward said My God, she looks just like Mama, standing there.

I thought, Maybe we will be out of here by New Year's but then I saw that she had on Aunt Nell's old bathrobe instead of her silver dress that I love and besides her hands were grey, right down to the nails. Aunt Flodie said, Lila, you shouldn't, but she only pulled herself up and came over to the table and said, I'm tired of being stuck up there, I'm going to have a decent meal for once, and then she came and stood next to me until they had Matty set a place for her. I kept telling myself it didn't matter about the sweater, it didn't matter about anything, she was going to get well and we were going to get out of here and go back to Washington so I could ride my pony any time; then I guess I looked at her close and saw that she was too thin to go anywhere, she was so pale I could see right through her skin; she was weak, I wanted to do something to make her strong and so I said, My sweater, as rude as I could, You knew I wanted a blue angora sweater, thinking her voice would get big the way it used to when I did something terrible; if she got mad enough at me it would make her strong, she would get twice as tall the way she always did and then she would yell at me. I could hear Aunt Nell murmuring to Vivian, Poor child, too much Christmas, and then Aunt Flodie had her nails in my wrist, she dragged me out into the hall and punched me right in the arm before she sent me to my room without dessert, I didn't care, I was so glad to get away from that horrible table but then I looked back through the arch at Mother, she hadn't moved, she hadn't even heard, and I began to cry because it is all gone now, she can't even make me feel bad any more, so I know she will never be able to do anything to make us feel good. I don't know what I am going to do, she can't even help herself.

III

Lila Melyn

§§§§ §§§§

Orphaned, Lila's child was not out of place in the house because despite all of Papa Lyon's hopes the house had a history of orphans: a cousin of Papa's once, in 1900; Uncle Harry's children until finally they got too big to care. Dark and pinched, still bewildered by their many losses, they came for the holidays, sharing gifts prepared for the Lyon children and racing the others down on Christmas morning to sit between Nell and Flodie under the swelling tree which filled the hall; they knew better than anybody that they didn't belong but they had to pretend they had a place there, picking up the accents of the others and snuggling between the two youngest Lyon girls. Like the other children they itched, they squirmed, they sighed heavily and wriggled, they could hardly stand it; they could all have been painted there in the hallway, a white-gowned garland around a tree thick with candles, apples, stars, ornaments and dipping strings of silvered beads which repeated the circle of children and spiralled up into the stairwell, mounting the tallest tree Papa Lyon could find, so that for the day at least Harry's children could be like all the other children, with a father, a mother, everything the ordinary child expects. Papa used to distribute gifts in his smoking jacket and that year's new pair of slippers and Mama would come down for the day in one of her velvet dressing gowns, she would eat breakfast with the rest of them, right down to the last sweet roll, and she would even accept the candy and Christmas cookies which the children proffered throughout the morning, all dipping and wheeling like attentive birds, each one prancing or sulking or trying to stroke her cheek because they were all desperate to be noticed.

While the presents were opened and discarded Mama would sit in a reclining chair with Edward on her lap and the others gathered about her as if for a portrait. All of their ends were already implicit, if not defined, but nobody chose to see it then; they would have to go through this Christmas, they would have to go through with every Christmas as gallantly as if, hoping for the best, they were justified in expecting it because some day it would be delivered to them, even as Mama said; the children could imagine that if not this Christmas, then some Christmas soon all their wants would be satisfied. For the moment everything appeared complete and Harry's children were able to pretend that the tree, all the largesse, the very parents were for them.

So there were always orphans at Christmas, but by the time Lila Melyn was orphaned, the Christmas tree had shrunk, even as life in the house had shrunk, and if there was an orphan now it would not be just a Christmas orphan, in the house for a few days to make the Lyon children feel blessed and generous, but an orphan who would wander in pain, surprising ghosts in hallways all year round. Dying, Lila had no time for trivia, and so for the last months of her mother's life Lila Melyn mourned in waistless dresses with lots of tucks and smocking, so that at eleven she had to go out with her fat thighs showing and her white arms hanging out of incongruous puffed sleeves; her shoes were too tight and the black patent leather straps cut into her ankles, anchoring shrinking socks. Still she had no sense of herself as ugly, she knew her dresses were too tight across the shoulders, she was always pulling loose at the seams and being scolded for it; she would be fifteen before she realized that not everybody wore underpants with sagging elastic, not everybody had to keep hitching and tugging and holding the tired waistbands with rusting safety pins. When her mother died it seemed appropriate that her own seams should part, her underpants should droop; she would seek out corners in big chairs and window seats and she would settle in and weep all over, chewing on her hem and poking angrily at the flat, fat pillows which had begun to show in the top of her dress. In time it would come to her that she would be too large all her life, trying to hide herself in the corners of unyielding houses; she remembered being six or seven and bony and having a mother and a father and she hated this house and her tight clothes and all her flesh.

Flodie hated it too; looking like that, the child was an affront to her, an affront to all of them, it was as if Flodie herself were insufficient as a guardian; more: so long as the child moped around the house like a huge, regretful spook then Lila was still there too, and Flodie would have to conduct her days in the shadow of her beautiful older sister. If she was going to marry and make her escape from this house she couldn't have the child hanging around with those big fat legs sticking out, she was an embarrassment to them all.

The first thing she did was to take Little Lila down to Lerner's and get her something decent for a change, starting with a brassiere. At first the child was dumb with humiliation but Flodie explained they weren't trying to make her look bigger, it would make her seem smaller in a way, and by the time they got to picking out the plaid skirts with matching pullovers she had begun to smile. They got her a yellow cardigan to go with both outfits and some thick white socks and a pair of oxfords with fringed leather flaps and then they went and got the permanent; Flodie wasn't so sure she looked that much better but at least she looked *different*. What's more, the child was pleased; if she pulled the front of her pullover away from her stomach and then put the cardigan around her shoulders, she could pretend the body wasn't there or if it was there then maybe it wasn't so pillowy and revolting; if she squinted down at herself in just the right way she could be a set of clothes going somewhere, just as good as anybody else.

"Oh Aunt Flodie, I look like the high school girls."

It fascinated Flodie that the child didn't seem to notice how fat she was; she was smiling and for once she didn't look so much like a weeping pig. Flodie said, in a burst of generosity, "May be we can get you a coat with a fur collar next winter."

"Oh Aunt Flodie, you're so wonderful."

"No I'm not."

Flodie only did it because she couldn't stand to see the child dragging around the house with her face swollen and her eyes all red another living minute, that and she secretly knew it would kill Lila to see the permanent. What did Lila know. The child had moved forward, trying to hug her, but like all the rest of her physical motions the hug went wrong; Flodie turned her a perfumed cheek and left the room.

Alone in front of the mirror, Lila Melyn turned once more, looking over her shoulder to see that despite the enormous size of the cardigan it did not hang loose, the way she had hoped it would, so she could pretend to be almost any size underneath; instead it rode up over her round bottom and instead of seeing a single smooth, deceptive line when she looked behind her she saw her sweater caught in the fold where her skirt band cut into her middle, it would creep back in there no matter how many times she pulled it out; she would never look right no matter what she did and if she didn't look right she would have to spend the rest of her life alone in this big old house; she heard her breath rattling out in a thick, inadvertent sigh. She was going to Aunt Cora's for dinner that night, and she thought maybe they would ask her to come and live with them, or else she might end up with Uncle Edward and Vivian, maybe Terence would change and they could be best friends. Maybe she had a real brother somewhere, a long-lost big brother who would come for her, they would get a house and she would stay home and make cookies for him. If she had to go on living here maybe a boy would come to the house and they wouldn't know who he was but he would get sick right there in the doorway so Aunt Flodie would have to bring him in; Lila Melyn would bring him soup and sherbet and sit by his bedside, when he got better they would talk and talk. Maybe her father was not dead after all, but being held captive somewhere, either that or he was sick somewhere; he would get well and come and find her; he would stalk into this house, bigger than ever, and he would enfold her like a poultice, drawing out all the pain. She could not know how it would end, she could only hope; she had been born hollow, even her bones were empty and she would spend what was left of her childhood trying to stuff them with dreams, mooning and nibbling cake or peanut-butter cookies, trailing crumbs in that sad old house; she had to believe it was going to end *right,* because whether it did or not she had to continue, and so she pulled at the sweater once more and left the mirror.

Aunt Cora picked her up in front of the house, saying in a mixture of guilt and mechanical politeness, "I would have had you over sooner, honey, but with your Momma and everything . . ." and when Lila was unable to reply she clamped her spiky little shoe on the accelerator and from then on was so busy driving that they didn't have to talk. Nobody was home so Aunt Cora took her all around, showing her the house, Uncle Alden had helped them buy it, this was his room and this other room was the guest room; it had flowered wallpaper and a quilted satin spread with matching curtains. Shifting tentatively on the pale blue rug, the child thought maybe her aunt was trying to think of a way to ask her to come and stay with them, but then Aunt Cora opened the cedar closet with a flourish, saying: "And they gave it to me for my birthday," and she brought forth the silver fox. Lila had to think this could be a beginning so she said,

"Oh, Aunt Cora, it's beautiful," and her aunt went on to bring out the rest of her wardrobe, linens and crepe dresses with beaded bibs and all the suits, each with its own hat in a round box, and because it was expected, Lila murmured and touched the clothes; Aunt Cora had so many *things* that Lila could hear herself crying out, Oh Daddy, because all her own rooms were empty and it was more than she could understand.

They ate in the kitchen, Uncle Punk complaining because there wasn't enough room at this little table, Uncle Alden touching her hand but unable to find anything to say. At first they were all so uncomfortable that they were very polite.

Aunt Cora said, "I bet you're having lots of fun with your aunts."

Lila knew she was supposed to say yes so she said yes.

"And just think, your Momma and I went to the same school you're going to."

Lila could hear herself chewing and chewing; she wouldn't remember what they were eating, only that it never got small enough to swallow, no matter how hard she chewed. Uncle Punk muttered something to Uncle Alden and then snickered until Aunt Cora hissed at him. After a while Uncle Alden asked her what she wanted to be when she grew up and she said she thought a nurse. Uncle Punk said, "I thought you were going to grow up to be Lana Turner," and then he put his finger where her ribs should be and laughed.

Aunt Cora said, *"Punk."*

Uncle Alden said, "Maybe we ought to get a puppy."

Aunt Cora said, "It could be your dog." Her face was close to Lila's now, her lipstick was bright but her mouth was uncertain and when Lila didn't say anything, she said, "Wouldn't you like that?"

At least she would have a dog. "I guess so."

"Of course we would have to keep him here for you but every time you came over you could take him out on a leash."

Uncle Punk said, "Ruff ruff ruff." He giggled and poked her in the ribs and kept on saying "Ruff ruff ruff" until she began to cry and Aunt Cora shushed him. They were having poker guests after dinner and Aunt Cora gave her an extra piece of cake in a napkin and drove her home.

Aunt Flodie met them at the door, asking too quickly whether she had a good time, so Lila had to say yes and Aunt Cora was already saying, "We just had a wonderful time," clacking back down the steps in obvious haste, leaving Aunt Flodie to heave a sigh and say, "Well don't just stand there, baby, come on in."

At Uncle Edward's, everybody was always very nice to her. Uncle Edward would put her and Terence in the living room and when they wouldn't play he would take Terence on his lap and try and tell them about how he and Lila's mother used to ride their ponies right where the Federal building was now, and Lila, looking around the tiny room, would try to think about spreading trees and fail; it never mattered because Uncle Edward would keep on talking anyway, telling about the beautiful birthday parties and all the fun they had at the camp, but by that time Terence would have turned his triangular face to Lila with a look of such malice that Edward, seeing, would have to let him down. He would go off to the kitchen and after a while Vivian would call them to the table. Everything that Vivian made was sweet: the creamed chicken and the Jello salad and the yams with marshmallows were all too sweet and Lila gulped them down in helpless speed, desperate to fill herself. Vivian would pile her plate, saying, with rancor, "My, I wish Terence had your appetite."

Uncle Edward would say, "I remember Biggie in the kitchen, why, the meals we used to put away . . ."

Vivian's voice was like the food, too sweet. "Lila, honey, have you had enough bread pudding?"

". . . the funny thing was, we never got fat . . ."

"How about some leftover biscuits?"

Lila knew she ought to stop but Vivian had already put two biscuits on the edge of her dessert plate, and she was nudging the grape conserve over until the cut-glass dish clinked against Lila's plate.

Edward looked down, mystified, at the pot his own stomach made, hanging from his skinny ribs. ". . . it didn't matter how much we ate."

Terence was hanging on the back of his chair, scrawny and resentful. "Edward, it's time for me to go to the movies."

"But Lila hasn't finished."

Embarrassed, Lila looked down at her plate. Even if she hurried it would take too long, she would sit there with crumbs falling out of her mouth while they all watched and watched.

Terence whined; he always whined. "Edward."

"Edward, you promised the child."

Sighing, Edward got up. "Honey, if you'll excuse me . . ."

Lila's mouth was full but she tried to smile, and when he got up she got up too, wiping her hands on her front and thinking maybe she could get away, but then she stopped where she stood because Vivian was looking at her sharply, saying, "You just sit there and finish up, honey, I don't mind," so she had to sit down hopelessly in front of the food she no longer wanted, knowing Vivian would not let her leave the table until she had finished the extra bread pudding and the biscuits and the conserve, and then she would have to go out and try and help in the kitchen while Vivian moved around her, quick as a wasp, flashing dishes in and out of the soapy water and whipping the towel out of Lila's inept hands because she would never ever be able to get all the wet spots off the plates. She would keep on going to Uncle Edward's for as long as she could stand it and then she would accept but develop a stomach ache when it came time for her to go and then, to her Aunt Flo's exasperation, she wouldn't accept at all but would linger in the hallways while Flodie got ready for her dates. Then Flodie's date would come and take her away, leaving Lila to hang around the house with her Aunt Nell; she would want to reach out for her aunt and try to talk to her but Nell seemed to drift, right then she wasn't real, and every once in a while Nell would come to herself and reach out to Lila but each time their voices and their hands would fail and so for the most part they were solitary, the two of them revolving slowly, like isolated spheres.

Watching, waiting for solutions, Flodie thought of the child as a millstone; if she could just get the baby settled at Cora's or at Edward's; if her Grandmother Millard had not died so cavalierly, or if, dying, she had left more money . . . but there was Lila Melyn when they got up in the morning, there she was when Flodie came home from work, there she was when Flodie got ready to go out, lurking in the hallway with that great moon face, distracting Flodie in front of all her dates. Her whole life had been filled with obstacles, first her sister Lila, who was too beautiful and used up all the men, then Mama, weighing on them like an anchor or a cross, and now it was the baby, holding her; she couldn't just pick up and leave it all, she couldn't just walk out and say Goodbye, don't look for me; there had to be a right reason. If she got married then she could leave Nell and the baby with a high heart and a clear conscience; she had to get married soon, if she didn't get married soon she would be stuck here, she would have to spend the rest of her days going in and out of this old house.

159

It may have been apparent to everybody but Flodie that she was trying too hard; she was afraid each new man would escape because eventually each one did, fleeing her bright anxiety. Plotting, she thought it was because of the baby, floating in the shadows, it was enough to put off any man, but all of her plans for Lila Melyn seemed to come to nothing. When she suggested something to Cora, a dinner, a trip, Cora would shake her bright fingernails and find some excuse, and when the child did go she would come back pink and miserable, probably because of Punk. Vivian still invited her, but the child preferred to go down to the street car stop to talk to her Uncle Edward; Flodie came along one late afternoon and saw the two of them for the first time from a distance, Edward pacing, silent and distracted, Lila Melyn talking to his back. Then finally Flodie came upon the baby in a sepia twilight, hugging a pillow in the shelter of the old wing chair, and she sighed and spoke to her, saying with great patience, "All right, you can come in and watch me dress."

Usually Flodie dressed and made herself up with ritual care because it was important, but tonight it didn't matter so much, it was only Ranny from the office. Still, tightening the straps on her brassiere so she would come out in points, Flodie thought the evening was in the future and anything could happen; Ranny was from the hill section and beneath her, but he might bring along some tall, hitherto undiscovered friend, or Ranny himself might reveal hidden depths or some rich lineage which he had concealed because he wanted her to like him for himself. He was already here, waiting in the chintzy room behind the formal parlors, he would be sitting with his hands growing too big for his lap and all his hair tortured forward to cover his bald spot. Spreading pancake makeup on her face and neck, Flodie thought maybe he was taller than she remembered, maybe he would take her to the Seminole hotel, he would grow romantic under the soft lights in the Mirobar, he would take her hands and say . . .

"Aunt Flodie, can I try on your earrings?"

"Get off the bed, honey, you're wrinkling my dress."

"I'm sorry. What pretty shoes!"

"Why don't you go and find my toilet water? I think I left it on the basin."

"I'll be right back."

"Take your time."

While she was gone Flodie worked on her mouth, it was a good dark shade that made her lips shine and Flodie knew that while she had never been as pretty as the others she had the fullest mouth, and if any boy had had the sense to look past the obstacles, she would have been married years ago. The child was back in a second, too soon; Flodie took a dab of cotton and sprinkled it with Trailing Arbutus and then, conscious of the baby's overwhelming admiration, she tucked it into the crevice in her brassiere. She checked to be sure everything was perfect and slipped into her dress, sitting down quickly because she didn't want the baby to say anything until she had combed out her pincurls and they had the full effect. Little Lila was on the bed now, all ungainly thighs and rumpled plaid skirt; her eyes looked about to run molasses and Flodie understood that she was tickled to death to be there, simply to be asked:

"Well, how do I look?" Flodie stood, looking over her shoulder at the mirror to see if her seams were straight and said, "Oh dammit," because there was a split big enough to drive a truck through right where the pleats joined the yoke over the hips.

Little Lila was stiff with sympathy. "Maybe I could sew it up for you."

"I'm going to have to change every *stitch.*"

"I could get some pins . . ."

Flodie had the dress over her shoulders, it was stuck and she could hear the silk splitting. "Not now."

"It would only take a minute."

With her head freed and the dress still hanging from her arms, Flodie turned on the girl, saying crossly: "I said, not *now.*"

Lila stood for a moment longer and then with a sigh went on down the hall and knocked at her Aunt Nell's door but if Aunt Nell was there, she was either asleep or not answering; from there she went down to the kitchen and took some cake from the huge refrigerator and then even though she had been scolded for it before, she went into the living room to have a quick look at Aunt Flodie's date; she would be gone before he knew it, she would take the cake up to her room even though she wasn't allowed to have food upstairs because of roaches, and she would eat it while she listened to the radio.

He was small and something of a disappointment; he didn't look glamorous enough for Aunt Flodie, he was almost as round as Lila herself and he looked nervous, matching up the knuckles of his two hands with such concentration that she came too far into the room and he saw her.

"Is that cake?"

He was an old man, at least forty, but there was something young about him, an open look; if she squinted her eyes he could be almost any age and she could say, "Want some?" He nodded and so she went in and sat next to him on the couch and they divided the cake.

"Are you Flo's little sister?"

"I wish I was. How old do you think I am?"

He spoke gravely, through the cake. "Oh, fifteen at least."

It was the Lerner's outfit, it had to be, either that or he was fooling, but even if he was, she couldn't stop smiling. "I'm going on twelve. She's my aunt. My mother died and I have to live here."

He finished the cake. "You have very pretty hair. My name is Randolph but you can call me Ranny, everybody does."

"My name is Lila Melyn Millard, I'm the biggest kid in the class."

He said, kindly, "So was I when I was twelve."

She wanted to be polite but he was too round and little; she couldn't believe it. "You're just saying that."

"Some people get their growth early; the boys will catch up and pass you, wait and see."

"Well Ran," Flodie said, from the door. She had on a different dress and different shoes and her hair looked a little uneven, as if she had tried on too many dresses before she decided on this one, and her curls were beyond repair.

"Are you ready?"

Her voice rose in exasperation. "Don't I *look* ready?"

"See you next time," Ranny said to Lila.

In the doorway Flodie was astounded to hear herself saying, "What makes you think there's going to *be* a next time," and then she covered her mouth because she had never in her life talked to a man that way. She saw that in some mysterious way she had attacked Lila Melyn too, the child's mouth had gone soft and she said: "Aunt *Flodie.*"

"You get yourself to bed."

But there was a next time; Flodie was surprised to find that her acerbity drew this man, when all her soft romantic hints had driven other men away. She dressed for this second date all by herself, faintly annoyed because Lila did not come in to badger her and trot back and forth with hose and earrings and admire every stitch as she put it on. When she came downstairs Lila was in the parlor with Ranny; she hardly looked up as Flodie came in.

"Look, Ranny brought his class picture, he really was the biggest one."

Flodie said drily, "That's wonderful," and Ranny got up suddenly, coming over to take her hand.

Lila said, "Don't forget your picture."

"You can keep it, honey, with my compliments."

"Oh Ranny." Lila grinned all over; she grinned until she embarrassed them all, ungainly in her naked, awkward love.

Even though they all knew it wasn't true, it looked as if Ranny were courting Lila as well as her aunt; he always brought some little gift for her and one school vacation he invited her to come on down to the Daytona Building for lunch with him and her Aunt Flo. She went down on the street car in her brown plaid skirt and slipover with the yellow cardigan, she had a pair of saddle shoes by this time, she had even whitened the edges of the soles but despite all this, despite the Coty's Natural she had put on her mouth she was brought up short at the office door, overwhelmed by the clatter of too many typewriters, a little frightened at seeing her aunt out of context; at home Aunt Flo had presence, she was strong and important, but here Lila could hardly pick her out; she finally saw her in the far corner, just another frowzle-headed girl chewing a rubber band and typing fast; she had one earring off so she could answer the telephone, and she had a pencil behind the other ear. Rapt, Lila watched for a while, willing her aunt to look up and see her, but finally she had to advance, saying, "Aunt Flo?"

"Dammit." Flodie struck three keys too hard and looked up; her face was shiny and her lipstick had worn off from the middle outward as if her mouth were wearing out along with the typewriter ribbon as she clacked relentlessly, pushed by the machine.

"I'm sorry, Aunt Flodie. It's lunch time."

"I have to finish this letter," she said, and didn't look up again.

Even though Aunt Flodie ignored her, everybody else was watching and Lila could feel her hands and feet getting bigger, in a minute her hands would raise from her sides and she would float like a Mickey Mouse balloon with cardboard feet; just then Ranny came out of the men's room, all combed and polished, and said, "Hello, Lila," and big as she was he sat her up on a desk and introduced her to everybody as his best girl.

Lila heard an acid voice saying, "Well, can you tear yourself away?" If she had a minute alone with Aunt Flodie she was going to try to think of some way to ask her please not to treat Ranny that way. Then went through the cafeteria line in a solemn progress with Ranny heaping things on Lila's tray in friendly extravagance, piling on biscuits with honey and Swiss steak and Jello and chiffon pie, and during lunch he talked almost exclusively to her while Aunt Flodie tapped her nails on the table and got up to talk to somebody across the room; a couple of girls insisted on coming over and when Ranny said, "And this is Flodie's niece," they said, "Is that your niece, Florence, I never knew you had a niece," and Flodie had to try to smile and say, "She's my oldest sister's child." Lila was faintly troubled because this wasn't precisely true but she was pleased enough to be sitting there between the two of them, with Ranny bending over her in all kindness, offering her his own piece of nesselrode pie. After lunch Aunt Flodie gave her a fifty cent piece, maybe because she had spent so much time away from the table they'd hardly had time to talk. Lila stood for a long time after the elevator doors closed on them, sending them up with a little prayer that Aunt Flodie would be nice to Ranny because she herself loved him and everything might come out all right for once, she would die if everything didn't come out all right.

If Lila was in love with Ranny, Flodie treated him indifferently, partly because she was irritated by the baby's devotion and partly out of a weary sense of inevitability because she had hoped for more for herself but she knew, without admitting it, how this courtship would end: it didn't matter how badly she treated Ranny, he kept coming back; the worse she treated him, the more often he came to seek her out. She would make him wait longer and longer before she came downstairs and each time they went out she would make him take her to the most expensive places and perhaps because she didn't seem to care at all he was more and more persistent and made more and more of an effort to please her; as he did so, Flodie remembered a lesson she should have learned from her dead sister Lila years ago; thinking of the lunch box, she began to treat him terribly, leading him on to a certain point and then squashing him, confident that he would return so she could attack again, and in some complicated way, attacking, she could begin to get even for all the years. Sometimes she would make him wait hours for her to come down and sometimes she would come down and tell him she didn't feel like going out, and sometimes she wouldn't come down at all.

Lila feasted on his visits; she would be downstairs an hour before he was expected and always opened the door before he knocked. They would sit down with fudge or cookies she had made and talk about their favorite radio programs or how they both hated Phys Ed. After a while Lila thought she would make him something, when she gave it to him he would know how she felt about him, so she began knitting a scarf. She would sit down with her knitting every time he came; he teased her about it, knowing perfectly well that the long colorless strip she was working on would be a muffler for him. Lila loved him very much but she was realistic enough to know that if she was going to keep him, it would be through her aunt, and so she would sit there loving him and agonizing because Aunt Flodie was taking too long to dress again; she would begin making excuses for her: she worked so hard, that was why she was sometimes late or cross, Ranny didn't mind, did he, and then she would hold her breath until he said: "Of course not, she's worth waiting for." In between their dates Lila would follow Aunt Flodie everywhere, saying Ranny this and Ranny that, lobbying for him until Aunt Flodie would turn on her in impatience, saying, "Stop *advertising,* I know you think he hung the moon." Lila would withdraw for the time being, satisfied that she was making an impression, and when the time looked right she would begin again.

It was natural that Ranny should come one night with flowers, for Lila, and with a jeweler's box, which he turned over to her as if bestowing a charge. He was so excited that his skin looked too tight.

"These are for your Aunt Flo."

Lila stopped stroking her flowers long enough to look into the box.

"Oh Ranny, earrings. They're just beautiful."

"Ask her if she'll wear them. For me."

"Of course she will."

"Tell her if she does it will mean something special."

She ran all the way upstairs, sketching entire futures for them all; Aunt Flodie would fall in love with the earrings and she would have to love Ranny too; she would put them on and they would get married and Ranny would live in the big house with them; Lila wouldn't exactly have a mother and a father, it would be better, because she and Ranny would always be best friends, they would have so much to do together that she wouldn't have time to eat so much; they would all be happy together and she would be thin again.

"Oh Aunt Flodie, Aunt Flodie, look what Ranny brought."

"Oh," Flodie said negligently, looking into the box. "He always has had terrible taste."

Lila was looking at her with big dog eyes. "If you wear them it will mean something special."

"Well they're not my style."

Lila was all exposed, mulish pain. "All you have to do is wear them once."

"Well I don't like them," Flodie said in rising anger.

"You'll hurt his feelings. Please." Lila was still proffering the box, she was pleading for all their lives.

But Flodie wouldn't take them; she only said, as if justifying something to herself, "I've been in this house long enough."

"Aunt Flodie, *please.*"

"They're perfectly hideous," Flodie said, and knowing by now what would happen next she allowed herself one final gesture, taking the box from the baby and hurling it into the trash. When she left the room Lila was sobbing, fishing the earrings out and laying them on the dresser, side by side; not understanding, she would probably cherish them in Flodie's stead, and end by putting them on.

Driven to it by this final injury, Ranny ended his torment by proposing that night, as Flodie had known he would, and since he had proposed, then Flodie had to accept him; even though he was small and inept and beneath them all socially, she liked him fairly well and he loved her, at the time it looked like it was going to be the best she could do; now at least she could make good her escape. They came back from the Mirobar engaged, and when Ranny begged her to wake Little Lila so they could tell her all about it, Flodie went up without hesitation and got her out of bed. She came down in her nightie, laughing and gargling her delighted disbelief.

"I thought you would never . . . it's just wonderful. Oh Aunt Flodie, isn't it *wonderful?*"

Ranny was beaming. "We're getting married at Christmas."

"You can take the scarf on your honeymoon, and Aunt Flodie, I'll make something for you."

"That's real sweet, honey."

"And when you get back we can have a party every night."

Ranny was laughing. "Not *every* night."

Flodie understood; Lila was pleading with her whole body, trying to hug them both at once. "You're going to be with your Aunt Nell now," she said firmly, adding, "but you'll come and see us real often."

Ranny had his arms around Lila so he couldn't see her face and he echoed, "Real often, OK?"

Flodie was saying, "I guess we'd better wake up Nell and break the news."

Lila's face was muffled against his side and she hadn't answered so Ranny squeezed her again. "OK?"

"OK," she said, and Ranny would think she was crying because she was so happy for them; Flodie was relieved that she was taking it all right; after all, she still had her arms around them and so they stood, tableau, with Lila between them, huge and tearful, remaining not because she was happy but because she had to, soaking in the temporary warmth, understanding now that the sum total of her life might well be unrequited love.

EDWARD

I hate going down town any more, I will put it off as long as I can because I am almost alone in this terrible dead city and when I go out the only people on the street are old and dried-up or else those girls with the bombshell breasts that aim right at you, and only sometimes clumps of sailors from the Base; the way I stick out, you would think I was the last man on earth who still got on the street car in his business suit and rode down town to the bank in the middle of the day. The worse thing is the way the women look at me, if the women are looking at me; I may be a little thin on top but I don't look all that old and still I know they are either thinking, Too bad, too late, or else in another minute one of them is going to come up and pound on my chest and shout right into my face: Slacker, why aren't you in the war. God knows I would like to be in the war, I would have run away to the last one but I was only twelve and besides I knew how much Mama needed me; now I have responsibilities, Vivian, the girls, my hernia, and to tell the truth it would be much easier to forget them all and run away to the front than it is to have to sit on that damn streetcar and think about what people are thinking about me, what Thad is thinking about me, what he has always thought; I will never forget how he came home that first time in the puttees, that uniform, he clanked in just like a man, he almost *was* a man and I knew from the way he looked at me just what he was thinking: Even if you were old enough you wouldn't go, you will never go. He may have thought he was very brave but I remember our mother, too: Thad, you know you are running away to play soldier, you are running away from everything that is dear to you. After he left she let me sit on the end of her chaise while she had her tea, she gave me chocolate cookies and told me being in the service was going to coarsen Thad, it always did coarsen a man, but all I know is that he went on to Chateau Thierry, or maybe it was Meuse Argonne, and whatever he did there freed him so that he never had to do what she said again.

After Thad left all his girls came around to pump my sisters for details, but when one of his letters came nobody had a chance to read it because Mama would take it to bed with her. On those days she would come down for dinner; she liked to sit there at the end of the table and feed the letter to us, bit by bit; we would each have to find the right thing to say to please her and then she would tell us one more thing. Those nights she wore her hair combed high in front but instead of having the back coiled up with pins she would have tied a ribbon around it and the tail of soft hair would hang over one shoulder like a Gibson girl's; after she finished with Thad she would begin to talk about our Grandfather Richard who held the city of Charleston together while the Yankees were in the harbor, and Great-uncle Horatio, who swam out to the boats with secret messages, and what Uncle Harry must have done in the Spanish American War; it was like going along a portrait gallery with her and I could see them, I could see Thad, I could see all the men in our family in gold lace and epaulets, ribbons and cockades, stretching all the way back to the beginning, looking proudly out at me from their heavy frames; Mama could always make things sound the way they ought to be, and there was no point in her knowing Thad wrote Papa at the office almost every week and told him more, or that I had heard all the things she said to Thad right before he left or worse, that he knew I had heard, and what he said to me.

If I heard, it wasn't my fault, it wasn't my fault they talked at all; he came home for Lila's debut wearing the uniform, he walked in the afternoon of the party and Mama had so much on her mind with flowers and champagne and the caterers and all my sisters' gowns that there wasn't time for her to talk to him, and that night she had to see everybody at the dance, she had to sit next to Papa and accept everybody's compliments and smile and smile; she had to keep everything perfect, all her sons and daughters, she had to see them all doing exactly what she wanted and so there wasn't time for her to talk to him but it was in the back of her mind, she saved it up and then next morning when she was ready to talk he was still asleep; we had all stayed up too late and danced too long and we were tired, she was tired, when I went in with her lunch she said she hadn't slept a wink, the skin around her eyes was blue and I could imagine her sitting up in the night, spinning out the party in her mind, what everybody said, what everybody wore, coming finally to Thad and the uniform and spinning them into a circle she would have to go round and round, planning what she would say when he came, and then waiting for it to be morning so he would come and then waiting for him and *waiting* for him, so that when I came in she snapped: Where is your brother, and when I said he was still asleep she said, Why hasn't he been in to explain himself; I said I would go and wake him up but she said oh no, thank you, she would wait. When he finally did get up it was late afternoon and she knew the minute he sat up on the edge of the bed because she sent Nelly for him and sent down word to Biggie to make up a tray. I had to take the tray up, there were two cups, one for her and one for Thad, and I still thought it was going to be all right and I might even be able to go in and have tea with them but the door was closed and the two of them were in there, she was crying like I have never heard her and she said he was selfish, selfish; then Thad said something, I would rather not know what, and she called out after him, she said he was a coward and she said one last thing I didn't hear but I would never be able to make him believe I hadn't heard because he bumped into me on his way out and I couldn't look any way but guilty, not for overhearing but for them having to say those things and for me being in Thad's way when he was in such a hurry to get out of there, for me being there at all.

I knew I was supposed to go in to Mama and be her sweet boy and make her feel better but Thad's face was so terrible that I had to put down the tray and follow him downstairs saying Wait, Thad, wait, I had to keep on trying to talk to him even though I knew what he would probably say; when I got to the bottom of the stairs he was in front of the hall mirror, fastening that high collar, and I couldn't think of any other way to begin so I said, I didn't hear anything and besides, you know she didn't mean it, and he said, without even looking at me, You will never get out of here, you are trapped for the rest of your life. I said, I am not, I'll go with you, and he said, You're only a baby, and I said, I could lie about it, I could be a bugler or a drummer boy, and he said, You poor simp there aren't any more drummer boys, only people who are going to die, and I said, I don't want you to die; then he looked over my head, up the stairs and said, I don't know but what I'd rather. I could see it all over him, his face was like one of those dead faces struck on a medal and I thought I would give anything to look like that, to be able to say something like that. Then I saw he meant it and I thought I would do anything to stop him, and so I tried to grab his wrist, saying, I'll go anyway, I'll come after you. Then he took his arm away and he finally looked at me, so coldly that I didn't want to face him, and he said: You wouldn't make it, Sister, you wouldn't even make it off the boat.

I heard Mama calling and I turned my back on Thad and went on upstairs to her, her face was as smooth as ever and she asked me where was the tea tray. When I brought it in she said, Your brother has turned his back on us, and then I got to drink Thad's cup of tea and she brushed my hair back and said at least I would be true to my heritage, in her heart of hearts I had always been her favorite. After a while she said the war was going to turn Thad into an animal, and if he was going to slough off his birthright like that then he deserved whatever he was going to get; she ran her fingers down my jaw and let me eat every cookie on the plate, she has never been so fond, but I could only think of Thad somewhere downstairs, getting ready to go; I knew now what he thought of me and I had his place, I was drinking his tea but it was bitter, bitter, I wanted to put down my cup and run downstairs and beg him to change his mind but Mama had her head inclined, she was talking, by the time she finally let me go it was too late; I ran downstairs but I knew he was already gone and after that I never saw him again until after Papa died.

So I was responsible, he had left the house with everything gone sour and nothing mended and I was going to have to think about him all through the war, I had to answer the door every time the bell rang because if somebody else went it would turn out to be bad news, if I didn't go to the mailbox first somebody else would sort the letters and it might be bad news; I had to be the first to see the paper and the first to answer the phone because if I didn't, if I let my attention waver for a minute, Thad would be killed in the war and it would be all my fault. I did the best I could, I ran myself ragged keeping track and Mama never even saw; she went on just like there was nothing needing mending, nothing had ever happened between her and Thad. She had the gall to come down to dinner that same night, painted and smiling as if none of those hard things had been said, she sat there in her best watered silk as if nothing had happened. We knew Thad had gone down to the Daytona building to tell Papa goodbye, he had caught the train on out without saying another word to Mama, but she sat there at the foot of the table and said, as if it had been her idea in the first place: Children, I have something to tell you. Your brother Thad has gone to be a soldier of his country, he is going to make us proud.

After the war he didn't even come back to see her, so Papa died without Thad and Mama mending anything, and after the funeral he went in to see Mama for five minutes but when he came out I could see from his face that she may not have even known him, or if she had, they hadn't mended anything; now she is in the hospital with nothing mended, and even so she talks about Thad the way she talks about Uncle Harry, you would think he had hung the moon, and she has never once acknowledged what I was trying to do all those months while Thad was off in France, she never saw.

Well, he is too old to go to this one, he went to the Army and the Navy and the Air Corps all three, I don't know what he thinks he is trying to get away from this time but even with all his money and his influential friends, nobody would take him, so at least there's that. At least I could get in if I wanted to, I'm almost sure, but I'm not careless and selfish the way Thad was, I know I have my duties here. I went down, the sergeant said they would take anything that moves, but after the examination it was the same thing all over again: my feet, my stomach, the hernia. Still, my boss has a connection in the O.S.S., I think Papa's friend Judge Teter has pull with the Army and somebody I knew from school is the executive officer out there at the Navy base, I could get one of them to fix it up, I could be out of town in the time it takes somebody to turn around and say, Why aren't you in the war. If I pulled the right strings I could probably get a desk job in Washington or maybe London, I could go off and see what was left of the world but I'm not like Thad, I see my responsibilities; I have Vivian and my sisters to protect, I have to carry on the family name.

God knows I wanted to go, I even went out to tell Mama I was going, but frail as she is, it was poor Mama who put everything into place. She was well enough to go to the solarium so I sat her down on the wicker chaise with the plants all around and we sat there with the sun streaming in while I tried to explain. I told her everything, even how it would be good for Vivian and me, I said this war wasn't a game, I could do more than Thad had ever done, and I couldn't be sure whether she heard me because all she said in between was whatever happened to Brewster, why didn't he come back to us, did some young buck cut his heart out in an alley or was he in jail and then the fog went across her eyes and when it passed she looked out at me as if she had been listening all along: Remember, Edward, you are the last living receptacle of the family name, and I don't know now whether she had only given up on Thad getting married or whether it was deeper and she understood, finally, that Thad had given us all up and so finally discounted him, turning to me at last; whatever it was, she had put the weight of all our lives directly on my shoulders and I knew I could not go where I might be hurt or killed, at least not yet, because all our past was in my hands.

Still, there was no point in my staying, either, because Vivian will not understand. She says we love each other too much to put a child between us, we owe it to Terence, she is too nervous, we don't have enough money; she never says the same thing but she always says something, so I had thought the war might make the difference. I would come back in my uniform and Vivian would be so glad to see me that we would have a child and he could carry it all for a change: the house, my sisters, the family name. I had to stop in the house on the way home, I had a bunch of Mama's lace collars for Nell to mend. I looked up the stairs, listening for all our old voices, and I touched the statue of Truth or Hope or whoever it was, half the bulbs have burned out in her torch; I looked beyond into the parlor, thinking: I am the receptacle of the family name but my God I have to get out of here. Then I saw Lila Melyn, poor old thing with that huge bottom, Mama's only grandchild, and I thought: Dear God, maybe Mama is right, it's up to me. Nell came around the corner like a spook and said, Is there anything you want, Edward? I handed her the collars and then before I knew it I was saying, I came for Great Uncle Horatio's sword.

So I thought I would force the issue, I took the sword home and laid it across the mantel, thinking at least Vivian would see my point about the family honor, but she didn't, she only saw that the sword handle was crushing one of her crocheted doilies and she said, What in God's name is that? I said, Vivian, I have to go and do my part, and she said, Please get that thing out of here before Terence comes in and hurts himself. I said, Vivian, it's our country, I have to go, but she didn't cry, she only turned that kitty-cat face to me and said, Why Edward, what would I do without a man around the house? I tried to explain, saying, This is important to me, it's important to all of us, but she wouldn't listen, she said, Who would I have to carry in the groceries? I was full to choking, I was up to *here* and I said, Vivian, you're being selfish, and she said, You're the one who is selfish, all you think about is what you want, and I said, Do you think I *want* to go? Then I had to look away fast because I wasn't sure.

By that time she had gone cold, she said, You don't want it, Edward, sleeping in strange places, eating bad food; Edward, who would take care of you? She flicked the gold cord on the sword handle, saying, What would you do without your things? Lord, she knows me, I was already thinking about the dangers, but I had to stand up to her and yell: Vivian I have to go, and that very second she changed tack, saying, softly, Don't desert me now. Then she touched me in a way that made me think I was the one who had it wrong, I had started back end to; I would plant our family name like a flag and then I would never have to worry about Mama or the house or my sisters ever again, I could go off to Washington or London without another backward look; if I had to wait for that then I would wait for that, it was just a matter of time. But it's hard, hard going down town on the streetcar and going out to see Mama and going back to the house and so far nothing has happened with Vivian, and the war hasn't happened to me either because I have my responsibilities and the hernia, if I didn't have the hernia dear God I would have to go.

NELL

Here we are alone, the two of us, and I don't mind, the baby is much sweeter than poor Flo even when she was at her best, and with her here at least I have something to do. Even if I didn't have her, I couldn't leave. What would I do? If I closed up the house and took off for a war plant in Savannah or Atlanta or found an apartment somewhere else, Cleve might come, he would find the house dark and there wouldn't be a soul around who remembered me, or could tell him where I'd gone. I have to stay here so he will know where to find me and besides, one of us has to stay, for so long as there is one of us living here we can keep the house alive. But it must be sad for the baby, with no place but here and nobody but me, it makes me sad to see her; when I was her age there were plenty of people to talk to and fight with, no matter what time of the day or night you came in there were lights and voices somewhere in the house. But when Lila Melyn comes in from school in the afternoons I have to hurry down and try to be everybody and fill her up with cookies or cake or cream cheese and crackers and anything else I can find to stuff up the corners of her heart; if I'm not right here, if I am read-ing and don't hear her, or if I am out shopping and come in late I will find her in our front hall, she will have her hands on the hall table and she will be looking at herself in our hall mirror; when she sees me she goes all red and awkward, not because I have caught her looking but because she knows I know what she sees.

When I was her age I used to come down and watch my two big sisters, they would be in front of the mirror too, but there would be somebody else laughing in the kitchen and I could hear Edward and Flodie fighting off somewhere, somebody would be playing the radio and there would be voices in every part of the house; my sisters would both look wonderful in their pretty dresses, Cora the magazine flapper with her knees showing and that tight red mouth, and Lila dark and beautiful, both of them bright-eyed and dangerous, with young men sitting in the parlor in three-piece suits just waiting to be hurt. I would be able to stand there for just so long, watching with my heart swelling and the inside of my mouth wet, and finally Cora would throw down her comb and say, Well, what are *you* staring at, but Lila never minded, she hardly even noticed until one time toward the end when she was going to meet Simon she turned and touched my cheek, saying, Just wait, honey, your time will come. We stood in the hall with the house spreading around us and she believed what she was saying and I believed her; we were still rich then, we still had Daddy and most of us were still living in the house, and there was no reason for any one of us to think that life would change, or my time would not come, so I would stand there every night and watch my sisters and ache with waiting. I should have known even so that my time was not going to come, or if it did come it was not going to be anything I had expected; if it hadn't been Papa dying or

Mama failing or any of the rest of it then it would have been something else because I am me, I have never been anybody else; I came too late and by the time I was old enough everything was used up.

Well I waited, but by the time I was old enough all the young men were gone, maybe the war had swept them all away: I waited past waiting, my time came too late and went so fast that I wasn't able to keep anything of it but this one memory of Cleve: he is standing in our front doorway with the sun bright behind him, his shape fills my eyes and because nothing has happened yet I can hope for anything. I knew about him, I knew more about him than I would admit to Flodie even now, but out of all my time, the months with Cleve are all I want to remember. He left me waiting, either that or I am waiting again, it's hard to say where waiting begins or ends, but if he doesn't come soon he won't know me; I can see in the mirror that I'm losing substance, my bones are all showing, they're ugly, and when he does come I'll be so thin I'll frighten him away— why not, why should I expect any better? The baby doesn't know it yet but she's a lot like me, she came too late and it's all gone now, the house is empty and there's nobody else for her but me. I want it to be better for her but everything seems to be getting *less* and I don't know what there is left for any of us to hope for.

The baby turns from the mirror with those sad child eyes and I have to say, I like your hair that way, or, That skirt looks good on you, honey, because she is only a child and still hopeful and I'm scared to death I'm going to slip and tell her something she doesn't want to know. We go into the kitchen and I open Cokes for both of us and then we talk about whether blue would be better with her face and whether the black skirt really makes her look smaller; I try to suggest as gently as I can that she ought to be doing exercises, maybe we can both give up desserts for a couple of weeks. She hates being plump but she keeps putting on more and more flesh to protect herself, and I am trying to think of a way to tell her that when her time does come she may find herself trapped in there, so deep inside that nobody will see her at all.

She doesn't want to listen and so she asks what it used to be like here when I was her age, is it true that Uncle Thad had a huge row with Mama and left forever, and after we have gossiped for a while she asks me if it's true what Edward and Flodie say, was our mother the most beautiful woman in the world; I try to answer truthfully, but what can I say? I tell her I think *she* has the most beautiful mother

175

anybody ever had and we have to go on quickly; she isn't sure what she wants to know but I know what I don't want to tell her. I will tell her about the pony cart and the games in the stable and everything we had on the table for all our Sunday dinners, I'll tell her about all of Cora's young men and what I wore to every single one of Mama's birthday parties so I won't have to tell her about any of the rest of it, not even about being too late. Edward was meant to be the baby and I was just too late; when I was little and used to go in to her, Mama would only look at me and cry, or she would smile and hold our her arms for me to come to her, I would get up on the bed and try to hug her and accidentally bump her and she would cry; once when she still went out I remember everybody was in the car, Flo and Edward were fighting and Papa wasn't noticing who was there and who wasn't but Mama saw me, I know she saw me running out of the house with my sashes streaming, crying, Wait, wait, but she let him drive off without me; I think she heard me sobbing but she let them drive off without me all the same. I think she loved me, I think she still loves me but she has always made me feel sorry for things; I had to be sorry she was so frail and I had to be sorry for making her cry and I had to be sorry life in the house had changed; when there were no more young men waiting in the parlor and no clusters of florists' boxes coming to the house it was somehow my fault, and when she called for Thad or asked for Papa and neither of them came, that was my fault; it is my fault she is in that place and now I am alone, the only person left who will take care of this poor fat child and I know that is my fault too but at least the baby is sweet, she doesn't charge me with it, she doesn't ask me to explain; Mama would look at me with those sweet grey eyes and she wouldn't let me rest until I had explained.

Mama used to ask Flodie and me about the boyfriends and the parties, why weren't there more young men, why weren't there as many dances as there used to be; our sisters were gone and she was sick by then and we would have to make up stories to please her because if we didn't she would cry. We still had a few invitations, people who remembered Papa or people who had us around for Lila's sake; there were a few young men left and some of them came around, but if somebody came who worked with his hands we would have to lie about it; he had to be in business, or a lawyer; Mama would look into our eyes and say, Where are the Breaults and the LeFevres, whatever happened to the Poindexter boy? It never bothered Flodie, she would lie and smile, smile and lie, but I knew what Mama wanted, I knew my own hopes, and when I thought about Thad and Papa and all those men in books, and all the beautiful boys who had died in the war, then the ones who were left all seemed shabby to me; they used to make me sad. One of them would come and sit in our parlor and look at his hands; I would see dirt in the cracks of his knuckles and that would make me sad, or we would go out together and he would forget himself, beginning not with flowers or with words but with his hands, and that would make me sad. I thought sooner or later I would find somebody better, somebody with Papa's gallantry or Thad's looks; I looked into each one's face and I was disappointed and so I waited, for most of my life I waited. Mama got worse and worse and I was left alone with her so much that there was no more time for the young men who did come, there was only time for waiting; she would wake me in the night and I would have to go and sit in her room, and while she talked I would wait, or think about waiting, and then she began to wander in the night; some nights I would lie awake until it got light, wondering when I was going to have to get up and go after her, and other nights I would close my eyes tight and gather myself in on myself, thinking if I could only concentrate I might be able to make out the face of the man I wanted, if that came clear then maybe Mama would stay in bed that night, at least, or I would be so concentrated that I wouldn't hear and somebody else would have to get up and go to her. Nobody ever did. In the end I always heard and I always had to go, and then one night I found her out back in her bare feet, she said, I left my hat in the carriage after we came back from the LeFevre wedding, I wanted to be sure it was all right. I said, Why Mama, you know perfectly well your hat is in the closet, I put it away as soon as we got home, and she said, I wanted it to stay in the carriage, but she let me take her back to her room.

But she wouldn't go to sleep; instead she told me all about her debut, again, and the Court of St. James's, again, and how all my older sisters were disappointments because they had settled for less than they were born to, and she had saved her best for me. She said, I think it would be nice if your wedding didn't come for at least a year after you make your debut, people get jaded if you invite them too often, and I want them to talk about your wedding for years to come. Your sister Lila went and got married off there in Washington, where we hardly knew a soul, but I want all Papa's and my friends to come and see you in your pretty lace gown, we'll have the reception here, just family and close friends, and then give a big supper dance for everybody else, we can have it at the St. John's Club.

I said, All right, Mama, thinking she would go on about the dresses, but instead she said, When you get married you are going to live in the old Burlington house, right down on the river, Papa still holds the second mortgage and I think that would be the best place for you to entertain our friends; I know you young people like evenings to yourselves, so you can have all my friends around in the afternoons, for tea, my present to you will be a silver service, and I think it would be nice if you had at least one daughter, you could name her after me. I said, That would be lovely, Mama, praying that would end it, but there was no stopping her, she said, Your sister's wedding was lovely, but I had no real part in it, why some of our friends never even sent wedding gifts, why should they, when it all happened so far away? This time we're going to do it all right here, we will drape the downstairs with ropes of greens and I think I will have Granny Calhoun's standing candelabra sent from Charleston, and if you like I'll have Papa propose your young man for the St. John's Club, after all, I want him to move freely among all our friends . . . Her eyes were deep, almost black, she had her hand on my arm and her fingers were hurting me, I wanted to say, What candelabra, what young man; Mama, don't you know there isn't any Papa, there isn't even any *money* any more; I was angry at her for all that, but I could never, ever tell her, I had to try and bring her back and I heard my own voice, screaming, *What friends.*

Then she drew herself up in her nightgown, saying, Why, all our friends, Papa's and mine, and I couldn't bear to look at her another minute, I raked my fingers across my face and ran away. The next morning Cleve came; I don't know who sent him or why but I knew he had been sent to me, I looked at him there in the doorway and I thought: Whoever you are, I am going to marry you. I'll admit it, I would have let him have anything he wanted right from the beginning, but he took his time, when we finally went down to park by the river it was me that unbuttoned the top button, I was the one who helped him disentangle my arms from the sleeves of my dress; I was frightened, I was sad, I knew it was wrong but it was my last chance, my only chance, he was good to me and he was so beautiful, and besides . . . I lay next to him and when we looked up and saw it was

178

beginning to get light I said, Now you're going to have to marry me. First he smiled and patted me, saying, You don't know what you're saying, honey, just calm down. Then after I began to fight and cry he smoothed my shoulder, he hugged me and said, Anything, sweetheart, if you'll just shut up. Then he helped me dress and after we were both dressed he hugged me again, saying, If you want it that badly, honey, I'll marry you, and even now I don't know, I can't be sure whether he meant: Want me, Cleve, or: Want to get away. Flodie doesn't know this but I could never pin him down on anything, where he came from, or who he was, and I heard later that he'd already had a wife back in New Orleans, he may even have been married twice before with no thought of a divorce, so why shouldn't he say he'd marry me, why shouldn't he go through with it? After all, it made me happy, and what did he have to lose?

Flodie had a fit but she made a good show of it, it was either that or have me run away to Valdosta or someplace worse, so she gave in gracefully, she hired the caterer and invited the family and covered the dining room table with a double damask cloth so we'd have a place to display the gifts. Thad couldn't come so he sent a check, but the others were all there, everybody but Mama, she was too sick, she was raving, and I couldn't bear to have her see my wedding, not with that other wedding filling her mind; instead I had to stand up there next to Cleve all by myself, Edward offered but it was grudging, and besides I didn't want it, his own weakness would ooze out from him and spread until it overshadowed any future I might have. I chose to stand up there alone; Cleve hugged me and whispered, I love you, honey, but don't expect too much, and I said, I love you too, and I don't expect anything at all. I suppose he knew and I knew it wouldn't work, he didn't have the slightest intention but I had to have him, I had to have something to go on or at least look back on and so we were married, for as long as it lasted, right here in this house; we made our pledges and kissed and then turned around to greet the few people who had come. Cora was crying because she thought it was the thing to do and even Flodie looked soft and pink, she said, Well, honey, it's not my idea of a good match but I want to wish you the best of luck. She brought rice from the kitchen at the last minute so everybody would have something to throw. We all had ersatz champagne and I could see Cleve beginning to fidget, he looked like he couldn't stand another minute of it and so

I threw my flowers into Flodie's face, Edward said something I couldn't make out and Cleve and I began running, we kept on running right straight out of that house.

We were supposed to stay two weeks at the hotel but the bill came to more than we had expected and so we left after ten days, but I already felt like I'd been married a hundred years, I had it all stored up and I knew I could live on it if I had to, I could live on it for as long as I had to; I can still see the way his hair fell, I can feel his eyes on me, I can feel his strong back under my fingers, and when it looks as if there is nothing else I can remember the time we spent in the hotel, stringing minute to minute and dwelling on every minute until Cleve fills my days. I used to tidy up the hotel room every morning, thinking about the home I would make for him if he would ever let me; I may have known he was already slipping away but for the time being I could put my arms around him, or stand with him at the window, the two of us with our heads pressed together; we would look out at that tacky little city and Cleve would say something, it was never anything important, but I will always remember our two skulls touching, flesh and hair, and the vibration of Cleve's voice coming through the bone.

At the end of ten days he took me home and that was it; I took his hand and dug my fingers in, whispering, Let me go with you, and he said, I can't, honey, I'll send for you, and that was all. At first I thought I might have his baby, I kept thinking it long after there was any reason, I would tell myself: It's going to happen anyway, my body has made a mistake. There was no mistake, I had had all I was going to have and there was no reason to expect any more, but I have never been able to stop thinking that life will change or Cleve will change, he'll come back or send for me; it's not so much that he has to as that I have to think he will. Once I thought I might go and look for him; even if it didn't do any good at least I would be *looking* for him, but Mama needed me, she got a lot worse while I was away with Cleve, and when I came back after all, she wouldn't let me out of her sight. Then Lila came back with the baby and she needed me, she needed all the help she could get, so there was that, and then Lila Melyn needed me, and so I'm still here, it seems more or less appropriate that she is all the baby I will ever have. Still I can't stop looking out of windows; the war has changed everything outside this house so gravely that while I am no different the light inside the house is different, and I keep seeing new possibilities. The war may send Cleve down here and he will have to come to me after all, then he will be mine; either that or he will die in the war and they'll find my name somewhere on his person and so they will notify me, and he will be mine after all; for once I will know where he is. In the meantime the baby and I sit in here waiting, even though there is nobody else for me. The last war took my generation of young men and this one is eating all the young men who might love this fat little girl so there may not be anybody for her either, but at least we are company for each other, I have somebody to hug and she has somebody to hug her, and together we are keeping my father's house alive; if there is never going to be anything else for us, we can take some pride in that.

LILA MELYN

I went to the door and there was some woman I had never seen before, she had on a tweed suit and one of those hats with a bird on it, she was on her way from somewhere to somewhere else but there was something about her, some particular curve of eyebrow to nose, so I wasn't really surprised when she stepped right on into the hall as if she belonged here, saying, I'm your cousin Edna, you must be Lila Melyn. She looked like all my aunts except that her eyes were pale, like Uncle Harry's; he looks out of all his pictures as if he never saw a thing. She was already in the front sitting room, the one where the pier table was before Edward took it, and she said, Oh, where's the pier table, and then, almost as if I had something to do with it: Where is everybody? Where has everybody gone?

I said, They're all out at the hospital seeing Grandmother Lyon, and she said, Dearest Mama, I'd give anything to see her face again. I said, Aunt Flodie says she gets too excited, they probably wouldn't let you in; she said, It's all right, I only have an hour. My aunts won't even let *me* see her, they want me to remember her from the pastel on the piano, so I thought it was probably just as well. She was saying, I suppose Cora is out there too, and when I told her Aunt Cora was off in Savannah she just went on without hearing: Cora and I were like sisters, she was my best friend. I had never heard Aunt Cora say one word about Cousin Edna one way or the other but I said, I just know she'd love to see you, they'll be back Saturday. She just shook her head, saying, I have to get my train.

I offered her some sherry but she said she didn't want to be any trouble, and then she went on paddling through all the rooms and touching everything, she talked about Thad and Cora and the rest as if they were right there with her and I could see it didn't really matter whether she saw any of them or not, she was getting what she wanted out of the house and she would take it away with her and feed on it on the train. She went through the music room into the dining room where we hardly ever eat now, she touched the backs of all the chairs and said, Sam and I used to sit here, with Nell and Flodie, Edward sat on the end next to Mama, he used to pick the middles out of his biscuits and throw the rest away. She looked at the chandelier, we have lost some of the prisms and some of the rest are cracked but she said, You know, it's hardly changed, it's hardly changed at all.

I said, Edward says it's all gone downhill.

Who?

I mean, my Uncle Edward.

She wasn't really noticing but I felt guilty anyway, he always makes me feel guilty; his hands are cold and damp and I have never been able to call him Uncle so in the beginning I didn't call him anything and then Vivian seemed to want me to call her Vivian so it was going to be all right for me to say Edward, but most of the time I don't call him anything. Aunt Flodie is after me to call her Flo, she keeps saying: After all, you call Vivian Vivian and she's not even a member of the family. That's the whole thing of course, but there's no way for me to make her understand.

We were in the kitchen now, she could see the filmy glass on all the cabinets we hardly ever open, she must have seen the corner where Aunt Nell and I eat all our meals on the checkered oilcloth but she said, It doesn't change; you know, the most important thing in the world used to be that it never changed. Our father would take us off to one place after another but it didn't really matter because we knew we would come back here in the end and it would be the same, he would drop us in the front hall and everybody would look up from whatever they were doing and then move over to make room for us, there were always plenty of people here, it made us feel so *rich*. You're so lucky, growing up in this house.

I said, Yes Ma'am.

You know, I was an orphan too.

I said I knew and she said, Your mother was very beautiful.

She pulled out one of the painted chairs and sat down without seeming to notice the honey smear on the oilcloth; I got us two Cokes, I wiped the rust off mine with my hand and then I saw I had better get her a glass. She was saying, Everybody was always so happy here, you all had everything. I put the glass down in front of her, one of those plaid jelly glasses with the Scotties, the way she took it up you would have thought it was the Waterford. She said, You know, this was all the family we ever had; when Mama smiled at me I could store it up and live on it for months. Sam and I used to sit around at school and talk about what everybody was doing that very minute, and when it got too hard we would sit down and write to every one of them, I remember Nell used to be so good about answering. We would start packing for the holidays weeks ahead, we were always scared to death our father would decide to take us off to New York or some place else instead. He never did, he never really took us anywhere that mattered, but I used to think he never would stop dragging us from pillar to post when all we ever wanted was to come here and be like you all.

When she said that I looked behind me to see if my aunts had come in but they hadn't; she meant me. She was saying, We used to come down on the train all by ourselves and Papa Lyon would be waiting at the station with everything on his car polished like a diamond, you could see how proud he was, he would have Edward sitting in front next to him. We never had a Thanksgiving dinner without Mama's orange-cranberry relish, she would come down and make it special the day before, and nobody was allowed to watch; we would starve ourselves for the big dinner and the game was not to look at the food until Mama lifted the first fork. Afterward we were all too stuffed to move, we would lie around on rugs with our feet up, feeling rich. Papa used to tell ghost stories until somebody got scared and started to cry and then he would have to get down and wrestle with whoever it was and the rest of us would pile on until Mama sent down word to be quiet; sometimes she would come to the head of the stairs and pretend to be mad but Sam and I used to laugh and laugh because we were home, this has always been home to us; Mama used to take me aside and tell me my father was better than any of us, he was going to make us proud some day; it's the only time I know she has ever been wrong.

She was quiet for a minute and then she looked at me, I think she finally really saw me, and she said: You don't look at all like your mother.

I said, I know. I take after my father's side.

Yes, she said. Sam and I didn't get to the wedding, it was going to be too hard.

She stopped then, she let her hands drop and I thought she wanted something from me. There was a ring on her left hand so I said, Do you have any children?

She said, No, I'm not even married, I mean, I was for a minute, but he was killed at Tarawa, I'm going to Camp Pendleton to join the Women's Marines. Funny, all I ever wanted was a home like this, I was going to have nine kids.

She got up and I followed her back into the parlor; she tried her voice in a couple of the rooms but it was late afternoon and dead quiet, the shadows were brown and so heavy that neither of us could say anything. She went to the hall and squatted in front of the book-cases and slid back the glass doors; all my aunts and uncles have left their old books behind and she took them out one by one and touched each of them, I couldn't tell if it was the stories she was trying to touch or the people who owned the books; for a minute her eyes changed and I thought whichever it was, she almost had it. Then she got up, saying, Where is everybody, but there was no answer I could give her. She ended up in front of the hall table, looking into the mirror, saying, I never thought I would come back like this, so many years after, and find everybody gone. I said, I'm sorry, you just picked the wrong time, and she said, No. You know, the rest of them, but I couldn't see what she was seeing in the mirror because the house has always been empty to me.

§§§§ §§§§

At that particular point in his life Thad went to elaborate expedients to keep from having to go home; he used to linger at his club until he understood that the few people left there in late evening were as desperate as he. When his last acquaintance had gone home he would cast about him to find only other solitaries with nobody to go to; some were only blind bores who would try to corner him so they could unfold the same old stories, but there were others: colliding with Thad, a man would look out at him with eyes so pale that there need be no words spoken; their globes of loneliness would ring against each other and there was nothing either of them could say. If he took his time at the office he could make that last until eight o'clock, but eventually he would find himself staring at an empty desk-top, and it would be time for him to go. He could walk for a while and then he would go to dinner somewhere, with a woman or without her, and then on to the theater or a movie, since his club was like a ghost ship to him now; if he gave in and went there he might find himself cut loose with the rest of them, drifting in loneliness for all eternity.

Sometimes he could persuade his date to come to his place for the night; then he would be able to wake up in a jumble of hose and garter belts and powder on the basin, he would have somebody to talk to at breakfast for a change. Ten years ago it had been much easier, girls from good schools and rich families would come home with him, covered in embarrassed giggles; some would even spend the night, because at that point Thad had not yet solidified, he still looked like any other man, open to the future, which meant each girl in turn would sleep with him because she was convinced he was going to marry her. Now Thad was older; his jaw had set and so had his habits, and the last of the old girls had given up on him. The women he knew now were just as pretty, but they were hasty WACS with tireless smiles and tight uniform blouses, or graceful ladies of good breeding who had, in every case, something to lose. If Thad had changed, so had his women; their hopes and needs had changed, and now if a woman sought him out it was not because he might marry her but because he would not. These women took him on their own terms, so that more likely than not he would end up at a place his partner had chosen: her apartment, if her husband was away in Italy or the Pacific, or in a hotel room if he was not; she always, whoever she was, seemed to have something she had to do in the morning: report back to the base, get up with the children, so Thad would have to leave her bed and dress once more, and go back to his place alone. He would take his time about laying out his underwear and shirt and socks for the morning, and then he would lie stiffly in bed and court sleep, surrounded by his clothes and the evening papers and his chair and his desk and his dresser, and beyond those barricades, all his empty rooms.

The mornings weren't so bad. He would make himself get up at seven so he could devote the right amount of time to his breakfast and the newspaper; his man had gone some years before, he had made enough money in Thad's service to go back to the Philippines and get married; for all Thad knew he was hiding out in the hills now with the Huk, or maybe that neat, precise body had been split by a bayonet, and all those mornings of exquisitely laid breakfasts and rooms tidied almost to the point of reproach had gone for nothing after all. Thad still missed him, not because they ever talked but because he was a second living presence in the house; in bed at night, Thad had been able to imagine he heard the Filipino's radio filtering in from the tiny maid's room at the back of the apartment; he could think about the little man sitting on the narrow bed, solemnly sponging his black suit; now he thought dimly about getting a dog or a cat, but it would just be one more thing to take care of, he wouldn't be free to pick up and go whenever he wanted to. Now, at least, he could count on using up a certain amount of time each morning making his own breakfast; because he was a precise man he had the same thing every day, and it took him exactly the same number of minutes to make his egg and toast and eat and finish his first cup of coffee and clear up after himself. The maid would be in later but he always liked to leave his dishes rinsed and stacked on the left side of the sink. Then he would take a second cup of coffee into the living room with his newspaper, he could make it last until quarter of eight; he would look at the stock quotations one last time and then it would be time to go to work, where he would be gripped by routine and it would be dinnertime before he looked around and saw that everybody else had gone.

On weekends his resources were stretched to the limit; he would have to sleep late with grim concentration, surfacing and submerging several times because he knew when he finally did wake it would be to an empty weekend with the market closed; even granting dinner and the theater, there was too much time to fill and if he managed Saturday there was still the long, blank Sunday morning, when time after time he found himself forced, unwilling, into all the Sundays of his childhood, remembering them whole: best clothes, church, a Sunday dinner so stultifying that there was no need to worry about filling the rest of the day, a house crowded with family; he had spent many Sundays in a tiny oven of a room in the attic, courting solitude. From his childhood the business at church had meant nothing to Thad, it meant nothing now but at the same time he was conscious of an absence, a void he might never be able to fill. At first he had assumed it was ritual he missed, and had tried to assemble a congregation of three to go with him to the golf course every Sunday morning, or a handful of friends who might want to put on their Sunday best and gather at the same country inn every week for a pious dinner amid the whale oil lanterns and the hobnail glass, but the war had dissipated the faithful, some of them were dead, and even at the beginning none of them had wanted to commit themselves to the same thing Sunday after Sunday like that; after all, they had their lives. For a month or two after Pearl Harbor the war had seemed to Thad like an expedient; he remembered going everywhere in a press, a vise of other bodies, moving with such purpose that time almost disappeared, but when he went to the Army this time he was told he wasn't fit, and by the time he had gone down his list of possibilities, from desk jobs in Washington to the Coast Guard, he was almost overwhelmed by a sense that because of some inner flaw he was destined to go the rest of his way alone.

Now Thad spun out his weeks as best he could and on Sundays gave as much time as possible to *The Times,* and when he had finally used that up he would put on his coat and have his midday dinner out, eating too much almost as a matter of duty, and then he would walk exactly the same distance into Central Park, returning to his apartment at last in mid-afternoon with the weekend almost over, and the worst part of Sunday safely past. He never wasted his time with the radio but on Sunday nights he always made himself an open-faced sandwich and sat down with Jack Benny; when the program was over he could allow himself to begin to think about the next day's work. Even with the radio, Sunday was a time of dense silence for Thad, when the phone never rang and even the doormen and elevator boys in his building seemed to drop from sight; often it was some time Monday morning before he had a chance to try his own voice.

Unwitting, too young to have planned it even if he had known, Phillip Crossen blundered into Thad's Sunday silence; he had been instructed to present himself at the office on Monday morning, but he had already spent an appalling first Saturday in Manhattan; he woke on Sunday to a flutter of panic and regret and he was at Thad's door before noon, apologizing and stretching his neck against his collar and trying not to gulp. Thad was in shirtsleeves but the shirt was fresh, and alone as he was he had his shoes tied and his suspenders tight and he was wearing a tie; he looked over the silver rim of his glasses in amazement, and when he finally understood that this boy, whoever he was, had come to see him, he stepped back and let him come inside. A stiff, unaccustomed host, Thad tried to bundle up the newspapers, at the same time proffering a Martini, a sandwich, eggs and bacon, coffee: coffee, finally, and when the pot was ready the two of them sat in Thad's sparse living room with peanut butter and Rye-Krisp and talked until Thad realized the light in the room was turning grey and this Sunday, at least, was almost gone; it was because of this, as much as anything else, that Thad was so kind to Phillip in his first year in the office. Phillip had been sent by Thad's cousin Sam Richard, he was the son of a friend whom Sam owed a favor, he had just finished college and was ready to begin. Phillip said, self-deprecatingly, "Sam said tell you I was good at figures," but as he said it he fixed Thad with his eyes and Thad saw he was ambitious too; Phillip had a weak heart and would never be drafted, much less killed in any war, which made him an ideal trainee, and although Thad had vowed, after his failure with Edward, never to invest his time in training anyone, this young man faced him with concentration and respect, and despite himself, Thad nodded, agreeing to help him any way he could. There was more: Thad looked into his eyes and saw that for the moment, at least, his time was as empty as Thad's own.

Beginning the next day, Phillip would sit out the war in the brokerage, and when such of the other young men as returned did return, they would find Phillip Crossen a partner; they would face him with a certain resentment which he would meet with helpless embarrassment: They wouldn't take me in the service; don't you think I *wanted* to go? By this time Thad would have detached his life from Phillip's, or Phillip's life from his, he would be sitting in the front office as remote as ever, but the others coming back would see the brass plate on Phillip's desk, they would look at him and think: You had a head start, it was easy enough for you. They would assume some advantage for Phillip even though they could not be sure Thad had helped him, or if so, how; they had no way of knowing that the new partner had fought his way, surviving every trial or ordeal Thad Lyon could devise, that he would have made it in spite of Thad, if that had been necessary, because he was as ambitious as the best of them and had as his great advantage time; he used it remorselessly

188

while the rest of them saw hundreds of thousands of their best hours swept away by the war.

Pleased as he was to have Phillip in the office, Thad could not accept him at once, and so he had heaped work on him from the beginning, riding him mercilessly in the course of business, sending him off on half-wits' errands and impossible interviews because he had accepted Edward into his life too readily, without knowing whether he was equal to the trials and so had been, if not surprised, bitterly disappointed to find that his brother was as weak and foolish as any of the Lyon girls. Phillip proved to be different; Phillip was able and strong, he would come back from each impossible task with the job accomplished, smiling with mixed satisfaction and curiosity because he understood Thad was putting him through all the stages of an important game, but he didn't recognize the game. He did as he was told and came back each time, smiling, until finally Thad understood that this boy was not going to disappoint him, he would never disappoint him and so he would have to make room for him in his life.

Thad was at dinner with Carlotta Baron one Friday; she was one of his favorite companions because she never asked him to think beyond the evening's pleasure, she never asked any questions or made any demands, and she liked him for most of the same reasons. Thad had ordered quickly because they always had the same thing when they came here, and now they had the paper on the table between them, trying to decide between a play and a movie; it was important for them to spend a few minutes mulling over the choices because that was what they always did, even as Carlotta always paused for a second in front of the mirror, drawing in her bare stomach and smothing it with one hand before she got into bed with him. But tonight Carlotta looked up from the paper, saying, "Well, who's this?"

Surprised, Thad lifted his head to find Phillip standing at a corner of the table; he had his briefcase open and in a minute he was going to prop it on the cloth and start rummaging.

"I finished those estimates you wanted," he said.

"So soon?"

"I stayed on until I finished." Seeing Thad's expression, he closed the briefcase, but he was still lingering, not knowing whether to sit down. "I thought you would want to see them as soon as possible."

Thad said, drily, "I didn't think it would be *this* soon," but he was trying not to smile. It was what he would have done at that age.

Carlotta touched Thad's arm. "Oh Thad, *do* let him sit down."

It was what Thad wanted to do. "Carlotta, this is Phillip Crossen, our leading light. Phillip, I'd like you to meet Mrs. Baron, she's an old friend."

Phillip was pulling out a chair, delighted, and Thad found he was pleased to have him there, and equally pleased that the boy had sense enough to finish his drink and excuse himself when their dinners came. Carlotta wouldn't be able to stay with Thad tonight; one of her daughters was home from school for the weekend, she was going to meet them here and Carlotta would have to play mother for the next three days, so Thad was going to have to satisfy himself with the next few minutes' talk. Carlotta gave her best: more about a friend whose head was crowded with messages from drowned sailors, telling about ships in danger and shipmates in distress; she went on to divert him with the anatomy of somebody else's affair with a marimba player, and even though he knew it would probably bore her Thad offered in return his opinions on that day's trading. She listened, not minding that the details were so dull, and because their hands were touching on the banquette, because they were such old friends Thad said, finally, "Well, what do you think of him?"

"He adores you."

"Don't be ridiculous. He's ambitious, and I know something he wants to learn."

"You must be very proud of him."

Thad said, grudgingly, "He's learning."

"Well I think he's done you a world of good."

Thad was too proud to think of it quite that way, but he did have to admit the boy was a pleasure to work with: Phillip was ready to learn and well worth any time invested in him. Working late, Thad was pleased to see Phillip bent over a pile of papers at the far end of the office, engrossed; they never spoke in these periods, they usually left separately; it was enough for Thad to know that he was not the only one pressed by the importance of what they were doing. At first he assumed that after Phillip had learned all he could teach him they would be finished with each other; after all, business was business. Instead, to his surprise, Phillip still chose to seek him out. The boy was alone in the city and so far he had been too busy to develop any life outside the office; his hours were even more empty than Thad's. He never pushed himself but Thad knew that when he himself didn't have a date with the WAC major or Carlotta or one of the others he could always stop at Phillip's desk and suggest that they pick up a sandwich somewhere after work. Thad's Sundays remained as empty as ever but they never seemed empty now; for years he had known that nobody, not anybody, would drop by but now there was at least one person somewhere else in the city who was lonely enough to call or perhaps even to drop in for a drink.

There seemed to be more work than ever and Phillip began to appear every Saturday morning with a full briefcase. He was sensitive to Thad's routines; he didn't need to be told when Thad had plans for the day, he would set down the briefcase and go, but if Thad greeted him at the door with a certain bleak look of impending weariness then Phillip knew at once that his weekend was empty. He would wait until Thad said, "Sit down, won't you, this will take a while." Instead of sitting down he would say, "Mind if I make a sandwich?" Thad would nod, already preoccupied, and Phillip would head for the kitchen, spreading out slices of bread and slapping on lunch meat and mayonnaise while Thad went through that day's sheaf of papers. Each time he came back with a plate of sandwiches, Thad would look up as if surprised to find him still there, even more surprised when he said, "I made one for you." By that time Thad would have found some point he didn't approve and they would have to hash it over, finishing the sandwiches and beginning to talk almost like old friends. In time Thad understood that while he had fought shy of entanglements all his life, this boy had been transformed somewhere along the way from pupil to friend; Phillip no longer had anything to gain from him and still they were going to be friends. Thad thought eventually he was going to have to cast around for a suitable girl for him, Phil was too lonely, but most of his friends' daughters seemed too shallow or were already married or had gone off to work on a military base halfway across the world; Thad didn't totally understand it, but it seemed that the war had dislocated these girls in such a way that they felt the only way to do something about it was to rip themselves out of context to begin somewhere else. He would have to ask Carlotta to work on it but in the meantime it was pleasant to have Phillip to go on the Friday night rounds with him and Carlotta, or to talk business, or just to talk.

At first Thad only listened, as Phillip described in all the ways he knew the shape of his own father's failure, but then to his surprise Thad heard himself telling the boy about the old house, which had always seemed too full, and then about his own father who had died trying to maintain the family's sense of plenitude, and finally about Edward, who was such a failure; Phillip would listen and together they would begin to sort details, Phillip saying, "He had to be a failure, he's never been anything but your shadow," and Thad saying, "I suppose you're right. I suppose it could be my fault."

"You set a hard pace."

Looking at this boy, who was like a brother, or a son, Thad would say, "You manage to keep up."

Phillip shrugged. "I'm not one of that family."

Although his routines never varied, nothing was going to remain the same for Thad. He was conscious of deaths: the son of an old friend, burned alive on Okinawa; the brightest of the young men in the firm, drowned in his ship in the Coral Sea. Several young women had simply disappeared from his life, plummeting out of existence, and no matter where he went to eat these days he had to wait, and when he was seated the service was always poor; when he brushed her hair back he saw new lines in Carlotta's forehead, and when Thad went into the kitchen after one of Phillip's visits now he always found the bread wrapper crumbled any old way instead of folded, and mayonnaise smeared on the sink.

Phillip was late for their date with Carlotta one Friday; she and Thad sat at their table for the better part of an hour, she tapping her nails on her purse and he drawing with his fork, making a deep groove in the tablecloth; at eight they went ahead and ordered anyway, and at nine they went on to the movie without him, telling each other that Phillip would be sorry to have missed *that* one; in bed later they agreed it had been rather a treat to be alone together that way, there were so many things one couldn't say in front of the young.

Phillip came near noon the next day, putting down his briefcase and heading for the kitchen without the usual pause to await Thad's diffident "Sit down." When they were settled with the papers and their sandwiches, Phillip said, "I'm sorry I missed out last night."

"It's all right, we gave you ten minutes and then went on ahead."

"Leona had to go to Ridgefield to see her parents, she talked me into it at the last minute and there wasn't time to call."

"Leona?"

192

Phillip was still looking directly at him but even so Thad saw him begin to withdraw: "Somebody I've met."

"Good," Thad said, trying to sound businesslike. "It's time you met some of the right girls."

Phillip's hands were moving in different directions.

"Why don't you bring her along with Carlotta and me next Friday, we'd like to meet her too."

Phillip's face was in the grip of a funny, inadvertent grimace. It crossed Thad's mind that she was probably not one of the right girls.

Thad said, "Carlotta and I would love to meet her."

He managed, finally: "I don't think she's ready for Mrs. Baron yet; she's shy."

"Well," Thad said. "When she is."

"Look, Thad, if those figures are all right—I guess I'd better go."

Thad looked up, surprised.

"I mean, she's waiting downstairs."

Thad heard himself snap: "Well for God's sake, bring her up."

She was no better or worse than dozens of the girls Thad had slept with; she was short and high-breasted, jiggling in a printed jersey dress and when she turned to move *The Times* from the chair Thad had offered, he saw that she had added to her leg makeup two meticulously drawn lines, seams; she was vivacious, she was nervous, she was very pleased to meet him and even before she spoke Thad watched her with a twinge because he knew he ought to like her for the boy's sake but he knew as well that she was not good enough for Phil, she couldn't even come near being good enough for him but at the same time she was pretty and sweet enough to slip tendrils about him and pull him down. Thad suggested lunch in the ladies' dining room of the Union League Club but they both wore looks of chagrin and he had to agree that it was such a nice day it would be fun to do something outdoors. They ended by going around Manhattan on an excursion boat, the boy with his arm around the girl and Thad already growing uncomfortable on the wooden seat, out of place in his three-piece suit; Phil and the girl went aft to hang over the railing but Thad stayed where he was, feeling the grit forming a greasy film over his face.

Despite his misgivings Phillip agreed to bring Leona along with Thad and Carlotta Friday night; the girl wore white and they went

193

dancing, and in bed afterward, Carlotta said, "Thad, I think she's lovely."

"Oh, Carlotta, wait a minute, a girl like that could ruin his career."

"She's pretty, Thad, and she's going to learn."

His voice was flat and miserable. "It's not enough."

He could feel Carlotta turning to face him. "Why on earth not?"

"I don't know." Thad heard himself sounding crosser than he had intended. "She's just not good enough."

Carlotta settled back, content to forget it. "Well I think she's adorable."

Thad heard himself crying out: "She's all wrong!"

"I see." Carlotta paused, thinking, and then her voice took on a new note. "I see."

"Carlotta."

He was conscious of the length of Carlotta, stiffening beside him; she was withdrawing even as she said, "Well Thad, all these years. You certainly had me fooled."

At first he did not know what she meant and then he had to pretend he didn't know; if he thought it out he could not bear it. He pretended not to know and she was willing to pretend that she had never said it, but it lay in the bed between them, it cooled his ardor, it followed him home and stayed with him so that, even though she called that same night to apologize, begging him to come back, he was not able, even on his loneliest nights, ever to call her again.

Phillip came as usual the next morning, blundering in with his briefcase as usual, coming back from Thad's kitchen with more sandwiches than they could ever eat together and settling himself in Thad's favorite spot on the couch with his usual engaging grin.

"You were right," he said. "Mrs. Baron was wonderful, and Leona wasn't embarrassed at all, she says tell you she had a perfect time."

Looking at the papers Phillip had brought, Thad was strangely irritated to see that despite the girl and the late night Phillip's figures were exactly as they should be, there was nothing reflected in them, nothing had changed. He said, after too long a pause, "I'm glad."

"I. She." Phillip went on, embarrassed but determined to get it out. "She likes you very much too."

"Uh. Good."

"She says it's hard to get to know you but it's, well, worth it."

"Mustard," Thad said, getting up hastily because he couldn't bear another minute. "You forgot the mustard, Phil."

In the kitchen, he stood for several minutes with his hands on the sink, touching tentatively and then digging at Carlotta's words, prying them up like a scab. When the wound was exposed he was able to turn finally and look through the doorway at that relaxed, un-witting boy, thinking that if he continued to see Phillip then others might take Phillip for a homosexual, he himself would be taken for a homosexual; he could haul himself into bed with woman after woman and still be taken for a homosexual, and damaged, so, he would lose his only friendship; or he could hope to marry Phillip off and pray that he and Phillip's wife would get along and know that they wouldn't and so lose the friendship anyway; no matter how it ended, he knew it would have to end; it would be best to cut it off now and spare both of them. He went back into the living room, thinking it would kill him, but because he had to protect himself, perhaps to protect them both, he cleared his throat, saying, "That girl, Phillip, she really won't do."

When they had played their scene, when Phil was gone, he went back into the kitchen to clean up, noting automatically that all the bread was gone, when Phil knew he needed it for Sunday morning toast; he crumpled the wrapper and began to wipe away the spilled mayonnaise, thinking: Oh, well. He wrapped the lunch meat with a sigh, because, after all, he had never been able to bear disorder, or inconvenience; he wiped the already spotless counter, thinking, to console himself, that perhaps he did not have the stamina or the heart to keep another living person in his life, not even to assuage his terrible loneliness.

FLODIE

Well, we are going to have to do something about her soon, the plain truth is that her body is growing up too fast for the rest of her, either that or she is hiding when she's around us; she has always had those big legs and that big bottom, there is still too much of everything but it is all going into the right place all up and down her, she is not shaped like a woman but like one of those big old statues of a woman, huge all over, and half the time she still acts like a little girl. I suppose it's our fault for not having parties and things for her so

195

she would have some friends her own age, but heaven knows Randolph and I are not set up for it, our place is too small, and Cora is so busy entertaining for all those friends of hers from the club and having poker nights and bridge lunches that it wouldn't occur to her to do something for the baby, the thought wouldn't enter her head, she fobs her off with lunches at Walgreen's and family dinner twice a year. So here she is, almost fifteen, and all she does is go to school and then come home and mope around with Nelly, I don't know what the two of them do with their time, except maybe sit around and talk about people who are either gone or dead; then when she does get invited out, and Ranny and I take her over to Cora's, she won't sit up straight and talk like everybody else, she keeps her head down and answers questions in that polite little voice as if she were eight years old and three feet tall.

You would think she would want to sit up there and be treated just like anybody else but the first chance she gets she leaves the table and when it's time to go home you have to go and hunt for her. She is always curled up in a chair at the opposite end of the house with all of Cora's *House Beautifuls,* either that or she's staring out the window or trying to make up to that smelly old fox terrier; the way Cora makes over that dog you would think it was the Prince of Wales; the last time we were there Maurice bit Lila Melyn, she didn't want us to see it but Cora caught her holding her arm and made her take her hand away, so it came out. I made Ranny go right up into their bathroom and get the Band-aids and some iodine, he thought we ought to have a rabies test but all Cora could think of to say was, Well, you must have been doing something to make him bite you, I thought she was going to shake her to find out what it was. Punk came stamping down, I don't know what he was thinking but I saw the way he looked at the baby, with a sort of added spite; she may not know about her body yet, but Punk knows; I saw the way he looked at her when we first came in.

It was a horrible evening anyway, Cora called up and said, We'll make it special, just family, and she had roasted a turkey because that's easy and then tried to fancy it up with supermarket rolls and that bing cherry salad of hers. It didn't matter, as soon as she said just family I knew she would ring in Edward even though she knows I can't stand the sight of Vivian with that dyed hair, she's ten years older than I am but she keeps it a sort of reddish gold; she would ring in Edward and Vivian and get us all over with at once, she would get everybody in and out without having to cook her quiche lorraine or invite anybody else, like the Farmers or the Galantins, we have never met any of their friends from the bridge group or the poker circle or that new Hacienda Club and the worst thing is she has us over in a lump and then she tries to dress it up by bringing out the crystal and the best china and the double damask tablecloth with Mama's napkins, with the Italian monograms.

You would think after all the times Randolph and I have had her and Punk over for dinner and put up with Punk the way he gets; we only have a tiny place but we don't have them all by themselves or with family either, we have them with somebody that matters, like Ranny's boss or our friends the Nevilsons, who will probably be members of the St. John's Club before the year is out; you would think after all the times we have had them over Cora could put herself out a little bit for us. You'd think she could bear to have us in with some of their real friends, but maybe she's afraid her friends are going to like me and Ranny better than they do her and Punk; Punk certainly never adds anything, he just sits around and drinks too much and then he insults somebody and goes upstairs to sleep. Maybe we just aren't good enough for Cora, I'll admit poor Ranny doesn't have a very important job but we both do our best to live decently, Mama would be proud of us, but Cora, well, all I know is, after all the trouble I've gone to she still just lumps us in with the rest of the family, even though Edward and Vivian never have them for anything but those tacky suppers, she has to twist Punk's arm to make him go, and except for Christmas when we all bring something, Nelly never has them over at all. I can almost hear Cora after the door shuts behind us: Well, *that's* over for a while; every time I vow I'm never going back but she calls up again every time and I accept her every time, thinking she might have some real people in with us for a change, she might even give us some real food.

She said, Of course you'll pick up the baby, Nelly has a cold and can't come, and I said, Of course. Nelly hates these things and she'll use any excuse not to go to Cora's, even though she hasn't got any more social life than you could put in your eye with a dropper, so Ranny and I went around and Lila Melyn came out; she had on one of those horrible pleated skirts and a big old sweater, she was trying to pull it away from her front and her back all at once so you would think it was just a bag and underneath it she was no bigger than anybody else; her feet looked like gunboats in those saddle shoes and in spite of everything she looked older, like a real person; she came down and got in the car and I said, Why, honey, you look all grown up. Ranny said, Hello, glamorous, but she just ducked her head and got in back, she seemed to lose all the affection she had for poor Randolph the minute we got back from our honeymoon.

She got in the back and Ranny said a couple more things to her, nothing you could really use to get a conversation going, and after that it was dead quiet in the car, it made me nervous; I said, I suppose it would be a lot more fun for you, being with people your own age, but you'll just have to put up with us, and she said, I like to put up with you, but none of us could think of anything to say after that; sometimes I think Randolph and I are running out of things to say to each other, and that's one more reason I wish we had a bigger social circle, we would have plenty to keep track of and swap notes over if we just belonged to one of Cora's clubs; the way it is now we have our dinner and do the dishes and turn on the news right away before the silence has a chance to fall.

Punk was out on the front steps before we got out of the car, I suppose Cora was right behind him pushing because we hadn't any of us seen the inside of that house for six months and she wanted to make a good job of it and send us away satisfied; Alden was in the background, smiling, I don't know why he puts up with them, oh yes I do know, but still; anyway Punk was propping up his smile and then he noticed the baby, I could see his eyes go all up and down her, he couldn't stop himself, he sort of patted her when she came in and said, Well, if it isn't Two Ton Tessie, because he has never been able to be kind. She was trying to hide herself all over at once and I could hear Cora saying, Hush, Punk, that's only baby fat and she'll grow out of it before you know it, and behind them both Alden said, I think she looks wonderful. If we could hire that man to be her daddy for a while she wouldn't always look that way, like something terrible has just happened and it's all her fault.

When we all got out on the sun porch Lila Melyn had a quick Coke to be polite and then asked if she could take Maurice out for a walk, she is always trying to make up to him even though he hates everybody but Punk and Cora; they treat him just like a baby but he's worse than a baby, he's so spoiled. Edward and Vivian came late, I could see Vivian was put out because it turned out Lila Melyn was there and they hadn't asked Terence, but Cora just twirled her fingers and said, Oh well, we didn't think he would have any fun.

Vivian was all full of a beach house she had just been looking at, if we all went in on it we could rent it for the summer and take turns, and when that didn't work out Cora said maybe it was time for us to go in and eat, so we took our highballs in to the table and Cora brought the turkey on, it was lukewarm, I think she must have finished cooking it about two and then just let it sit around. But we had baked Alaska for dessert. Cora said it was something special for Lila Melyn but I knew better, I knew she had something on her mind, no sooner did she get the coffee on the table than she said, Punk and I have been thinking, and I knew before she said anything else it was about Mama, she had even gone to all the trouble of going out to the State Hospital to investigate. She said it was in all our best interest but I could not believe my ears, I said, You wouldn't do that to *Mama,* and then Punk said: She's costing us a fortune, and she doesn't even know where she is.

I said, *We* know where she is, we have to go and visit her.

Punk said, Well, the point is, it doesn't make any difference to her any more.

Edward was yipping, Stop it, I thought he was going to cry.

Alden doesn't really have any part in it but he said, If money is the problem I'd be glad to help; I honestly thought Punk was going to turn around and hit him but all he said was, It wouldn't be a drop in the bucket, Alden, but thanks anyway.

Edward said, But she's our *mother.* Then Cora turned around and used Mama on him the way she always does, she said: Mama always said you shouldn't send good money after bad, and besides, you don't any of you pay half what Punky and I do; then poor old Edward said, Heaven knows we want to, Cora, if you don't think we're giving enough maybe we could . . . but Vivian had him by the elbow, I could see her digging in with all her nails.

Cora said, It's just a terrible drain on all of us.

She looked the perfect Christian martyr and it was more than I could stand, I got up and looked her in the eye, I said, Cora Gresham, you know damn well Thad is paying two-thirds of it, he always has.

Well he can afford it.

Besides, I said, Thad would have a fit.

Cora said, We thought we would move her and *then* tell him.

Well Vivian had to get into it, with that stupid Little Woman smile, she batted her blue eyes and said, I think it's a good idea.

Then Edward said, I don't care what you say, I won't hear of it, and his voice was breaking, I knew I had to do something fast. Cora was saying, Why, she's out of her head most of the time, they have to keep somebody with her every minute and costs are going up, and Punk was saying over and over it was for her own good; in another minute Vivian was going to chime in, It's for her own good, and there was old Cora, pink and pious, saying, Yes, Edward, it's for her sake really, they have to keep a catheter in her day and night, and all those drains; out of the tail of my eye I saw Little Lila leaving the table with her face all screwed up but I didn't pay much mind because now I knew what I had to do. I said, Where's the telephone, Cora, I'm not going to do a thing until we talk to Thad.

She said, We can't talk to Thad, he'd have a fit.

I said, Yes, I know.

Edward chimed in, We're not going to do anything without Thad, and Cora turned on him, this time I thought *she* was going to cry, she said, But he isn't down here, he doesn't know what it's *like*. I said, Neither do you, you hardly ever go and see her except when you have to, and she said, You know that isn't fair, I go every free minute I get. Cora knew she was licked but she kept on anyway, she said, I thought we would get her all settled and then tell Thad. So I looked her in the eye and said: If you make one move toward that State Hospital, I will get Thad down here so fast you won't have time to defend yourself. I could hear Edward echoing, That's right; then Punk stamped off to his room with a bottle of Scotch and that was that. We were all crumpling up our napkins and thinking about getting out but Alden can't stand scenes so he pulled himself together and asked if we wouldn't like some brandy, Edward said he thought he needed some so there was nothing Cora could do but offer us more coffee and so we had to sit around and be polite, which is the last thing I wanted to do; I wanted to get out of there while we were still ahead, I thought I would say the baby looked tired and it was way past her bedtime, but when I looked around for Lila Melyn she was off somewhere and so I had to sit there and sip my cold coffee and make kissyface smiles at Vivian, who is sucking our brother Edward dry just like a vampire bat. I got up as soon as it was decent, I nodded to Randolph and we all went out on the sun porch; it turned out the dog had bitten Lila Melyn so we put on the iodine and took her home.

LILA MELYN

I'm so happy, all the kids are coming over here now, the girls and I do lots of things together and I think Richie likes me. Aunt Nell says she wishes she could give a real old party for me, a dance with an orchestra like they used to have, but we don't have the wherewithal and even if we did it wouldn't be right with the war still on. Besides, she says, You young people aren't like us, you can sit and listen to those records by the hour and never once get bored. I suppose you even sneak a smoke. I never answer that one because she might forbid me or something; it makes me feel like a grown up person for a change, instead of a bumbly little kid. We both know she will never give a dance or anything so Aunt Nell doesn't sit around making a lot of dumb promises, like Aunt Cora; instead she says, You can have your friends in here for Cokes and records, honey, I'll stay out of the way and not embarrass you. I say, You don't embarrass me, Aunt Nell, but we both know how nervous the kids make her, she doesn't have anything to talk about with them, and the first time the girls came in after school Barbie hardly waited until Aunt Nell got out of the room before she whispered, Gee, Lil, your aunt looks like a spook, and Arlene and Betty started to laugh, I wanted to push her and make her take it back but they are the only friends I have. Then we met the boys and we needed a place to have a party, Aunt Nell said we could come here and they decided she wasn't so bad after all.

The thing is Barbie said she would like to have it at her house but her mother is too nervous, she hates any kind of noise, and Betty said she would like to give it except her living room is too small and besides, every time somebody comes over her father comes in and sits on the sofa and cracks jokes with this gimlet look until whoever it is gets so nervous that they go home. So I asked Aunt Nell if we could have it here. She said, You can have everybody over, just remember I'm in the house, and don't do anything to make me ashamed of you. I promised we wouldn't and then she said, You look real pretty in that sweater, honey, it picks up the color of your eyes, and her own eyes were so soft that I thought I would promise her anything in the world just to make her happy. She was as excited as I was, she said, It's so good you are going to be popular after all, and then she looked at me with that sad smile we are both used to and said, Have fun. I said, Don't worry, we will.

I got in with Barbie and Betty this winter, it was a new school for me, too many buildings and people I didn't know and for the first half of the year the only person that would talk to me was this girl with a leg brace; the bell would ring and everybody would thunder off to the next class and we would be left behind because she was lame and I was scared; then she got into the school band, the striped uniform trousers are going to cover the brace, so even she had someplace to go and something to do, so that left me. I used to hold my books tight and pretend to be thinking about something, I kept my head down but underneath my eyelashes I would watch, I watched all the girls going places in clumps, they all had sweaters that matched; I watched the cheerleaders and the football boys, I watched all the ones that had boyfriends, hanging on to them, and I watched the boys, I watched them all until my eyes got wet and my mouth watered, I wanted to break out of myself somehow and yell Hey look, I'm in here, but there was no way to prove it to any of them. So I had to hang around and watch, I could have done nothing but watch all year long except Betty sat next to me in algebra, we had been in there about six months when she gave me the elbow, saying, Hey, and pushed her notebook in front of me, if you looked at the drawing one way it was somebody with bags under their eyes and a beard but another way it was a woman, you know; I put a hat with a veil on it and handed it back to her and she started to laugh so we got sent out in the hall together and then at lunchtime I met Barbie and Barbie's little sister Arlene. We used to sit up on the bleachers together and eat our lunch out of papers bags, Barbie was always accusing Betty of sitting so the boys could see up her skirt but she would only laugh and spread her feet. I didn't say anything because I wanted them to get used to me, if they just got used to me they might not notice what I look like and somebody might get to like me for once; they were all complaining one day about not having any place to smoke so I said why didn't they come over to my house after school, Betty looked at Barbie and Barbie said Why not, so they came.

The thing is, it's nice to have somebody coming over for a change, and now I have these girls to do things with, it beats coming home every afternoon and hanging around with nothing to do but finish my homework and talk to Aunt Nell. Barbie wears her lipstick too thick and Betty likes those Lana Turner sweaters, all they ever talk about is boys but that's fine with me, I would like to have nothing to talk about but boys and besides, they are the first real friends I have ever had. Aunt Flo came over one afternoon when they were here, we were all spread out in the kitchen and Aunt Nell was upstairs somewhere hiding, I asked Aunt Flodie to come on and sit down with us and have a Coke but she said she had too much to do; I followed her out in the front hall to say goodbye and she said, I'm not sure I like your friends, honey. I said, They're in my class at school. She said, I want you to have friends, honey, and then she bent her head closer and whispered, But aren't those three a little *cheap?* I said Oh Aunt Flodie, don't be a snob, and then I was amazed at myself for saying it and she was amazed too but she was just a little embarrassed because we both knew I was probably right. She got pink and ducked her head, saying, Just remember, honey, behave, and I said I would and then she left.

After that we met the boys; spring baseball practice started and we decided we would go down and hang around the field until something happened, we hung around for about a week waiting for somebody on the team to notice us and ask us to ride home after the practice game. That never worked out but there were these other boys on the edge of the field, it turned out to be Rich and Jimmie and them, they would horse around and make fun of the pitcher until finally Coach had to yell, You guys beat it, and they would go Huh-huh-huh-HAW-HAW, the Woody Woodpecker thing, and drop back so he couldn't get at them. But he couldn't make them go away either; finally they kept on drifting and we kept on drifting until pretty soon we were standing more or less in the same place and Betty said, too loud, Oh DEAR, I've lost my comb, who has a comb, and Peter took out his, he has this big pompadour, and Jimmie said, I wouldn't use that thing, it has grease all over it. Betty laughed and took it anyway and pretty soon we were all talking, or Barbie and Betty and Arlene were, I couldn't think of anything to say, I was just having fun standing there with all those boys. Then it was all set for a party Friday night, it was only where were we going to have it, and everybody started looking at me. It was the first chance I ever had so I said sure, and they have been coming around here ever since. Friday Betty took me aside and gave me the flashlight, she said, We might want to play this game, you know, the one you catch necking is It. I said I didn't know if it was right to, and she said, You are going to have to face it, Lips, you aren't going to make it on your looks alone, and I thought about it for a minute and then I had to say, I guess you're right.

So we have all the parties here, Barbie and Betty and Barbie's sister and me. Aunt Nell puts out potato chips and then kisses me and goes upstairs before everybody comes; the boys come and we have Cokes and play records and after a while somebody has to keep the record player going while we have the games. If one of the guys had a car we could all go to the movies or do something different, I keep trying to think of other things but Betty says if we don't keep doing like we're doing the boys will get tired of us and that will be the end of that. I know the main reason everybody likes me is because I have them over and nobody comes down to ask what we are doing, but I think Richie is beginning to really like me, so I don't care.

There are five boys, Jimmie and Alfred and Richie and Peter and George, and Richie is the only one I ever kiss; when we are playing Flashlight the others switch around but I am always Richie's partner, and if it is Post Office or one of those I always ask for him and he always asks for me; if Alfred and Barbie go out for a walk, then Richie walks with me, we go along in the dark for blocks and blocks sometimes, he has his arm around my waist, we bump but his arm seems to fit and it doesn't matter if we don't really have too much to say to each other because I fit him and he fits me. Peter goes to the Y to lift weights, he is terribly interested in building his body and we all think he is the cutest but he never seems to pick any one of us in particular, instead he comes and plays the game with whoever turns out to be his partner. Jimmie told Barbie that Peter says the whole thing is disgusting, that Betty and Barbie and Arlene and I are disgusting because we give these parties and he gets all dressed up to come over here and have a good time and then all we want to do is turn off the lights and neck. Well he comes over anyway, no matter what he says, and he may mind but none of the others mind it, I can tell; the girls all say Aunt Nell is *neat* for letting us have the parties here and when everybody goes home I clean off the smudgy lipstick and go up to her room; she asks me how the party was and I say Oh, fine, and she takes my face in her hands and says, I love you, honey, I'm glad you're having a good time, I was so afraid you would never have a good time.

I guess Aunt Nell would be bothered if she knew there's not so much party to our party any more, everybody comes in and they are all already furry, thinking about what we are going to do, we have some Cokes and the boys eat all the potato chips, Jimmy or somebody makes about one joke and then everybody pairs off, there is a little bit of talk but we're mostly sitting around in the dark, necking, there's usually one person left over to run the record player until finally Peter jumps up from whoever he has been with, he says something I can't hear, Ow, and runs out of the room but I don't pay too much attention because I can feel myself changing, I get closer to Richie, I would never do anything I shouldn't, at least I don't think I would, but I love to be close to him, it's the first time I've had somebody all to myself like that and I think I never want to let him go; he says if my Aunt Nell will ever let me we will got out on a date all by ourselves, he'll make his father give him the car and we can really have some fun.

§§§§ §§§§

Nell was in her room hiding from the young people when the phone rang; Spike Jones almost drowned it out and for some reason she couldn't understand Nell was frantic with fear that the children wouldn't hear over the music and it would just keep on ringing until whoever it was quit and hung up. It never occurred to her to go herself; to answer it, she would have to venture out of her room, and even if she was very quiet they would hear her footsteps coming downstairs and through the hall; they would all stir like animals surprised in cages and in a flurry they would all stop doing whatever it was they were doing and fold their hands in their laps in quick impersonations: polite youngsters at a birthday party, so that by the time she reached the living room, where the phone was, they would be bobbing and smiling: Hello Mrs. Lothrop, Hello Ma'am, Hi Aunt Nell I was just about to get the phone. Bending to answer it, she would be sure she heard a stifled snicker not because they disliked her in any particular way but simply because they were young and she was getting old. When she took the message, whatever it was, they would all be watching to see how she took it and afterward she would have to face their curiosity, saying, Having a good time, children? and they would all say, Oh, yes Ma'am, watching without expression and waiting for her to leave. So she had to let the phone go, although her heart was thudding in a void of expectancy; the phone never rang this late and she thought she would die unless somebody answered soon and came and told her what she thought she already knew. It stopped finally, and after a long lapse Lila Melyn came up to her room with her hair frowzled and her lipstick smudged, a fact Nell noted with some part of her mind just before Lila spoke and her own thin covering flew apart and she began to tremble. Lila said, "It's a telegram for you, it's Cleve."

Not knowing what she expected, Nell said, "I knew it was."

"No. He's all right. He wants you come to Washington." Huge in her own hope, Lila Melyn looked at her aunt, and they began to giggle and hug each other, both trembling until they threatened to shake the room. The girl was sobbing, delighted; finally she wiped her eyes and said, "I wrote down the message, it says where you're supposed to meet him. I'd better go tell the kids they have to go home."

"Oh no," Nell said fondly, "I want you to go on with your party."

"I couldn't now." Lila was trying to pull herself together; her face was bright. "Besides, we've got a lot to do."

They were up most of the night, Lila taking over and telephoning the Atlantic Coast Line for reservations, going through their closets for the right things for Nell to wear and impatient at the poverty in each; they both had quantities of Cora's castoffs pushed up to the far end of the rack, but Cora's taste ran to flounces and sequins and Lila threw aside dress after dress, disgusted to think how much they must have cost. Feverish, she even went through her mother's things, saying, "We could take that one up, or you could put a peplum on this one," and Nell heard her own voice break as she saw her dead sister's silver-grey crepe and cried out: "No." Finally they decided she would have to wear her tweed suit but with a blouse Cora had given Lila Melyn last Christmas, it had never looked right on her because of the ruffles but the jabot would fill out Nell's thin chest. Decisive for once, Nell said at four that the two of them would have to get some sleep, and so she turned in the heavy silence of her niece's sleep; she was unable to think but she was unable to sleep either, except for a desperate hour or two well after the sun came up and she heard the first car going down the street outside; she woke at ten, frantic with haste, and found that Lila Melyn had been up long before her, she had already washed her face and was down in the kitchen, frying something and calling: "You'd better hurry up if you want to eat."

Nell was all packed, bathed and dressed before she looked at Lila Melyn, still potting around in her bathrobe, and said, "Oh Lord, honey, you're supposed to be in school."

"It doesn't matter."

"But you're going to be all *alone.*"

Lila said quickly, "You'd better hurry."

"There's no hurry." Nell set her mouth. "I've got a couple of hours before the trains leaves, I've got to settle this before I go."

The girl was looming in her bathrobe, bulky and uncomfortable. "I wish you wouldn't bother."

"I can't go off and leave you all alone." Nell was already ticking the others off on her fingers, rehearsing the phone calls, bracing herself against Flodie's waspishness, Cora's querulous tone. She took a deep breath. "How would you like to stay with your Aunt Cora for a while?"

Lila's back was to her but her shoulders were slanted, mulish. "No."

"It would only be for a couple of days, that's not so bad."

"It would be terrible for *her.*"

Nell's hands fluttered in her uncertainty. "Maybe you would be better off at Edward's."

Lila still had her back turned. "There isn't room."

"You could sleep on the sofa."

"Edward sleeps on the sofa."

"Oh honey," Nell said. She was about to cry.

Lila turned, anxious to release her. "I'll tell you what, I'll get Arlene and Barbie to come and stay with me."

"Their mother wouldn't hear of it."

Lila kept herself from saying: Their mother wouldn't care. Instead she said, "We'd get along just fine."

"I'm sorry, honey, it isn't proper."

"Then I'll just take care of myself."

"No." Distraught, Nell touched the jabot. "I can't leave until it's settled."

Lila Melyn loomed tall in her bathrobe; she had both fists on her hips, almost adult in her impatience. "I don't see why."

"Because nobody goes off and leaves a girl your age alone in a house this size."

"Oh for Pete's sake."

Nell lifted her chin. "I'm not going until you're taken care of, if we can't get you taken care of then I'm . . . " her voice wavered, ". . . not going."

"All right." Lila's big face was composed in a puzzling serenity. "If that's the problem, Aunt Flodie will do it."

"I can't ask her to do that, she has a full-time job."

"She'll do it." Lila said. "She still feels guilty about me."

Nell shot her niece a quick look but she was too rushed to pursue it; through all the preparations she had dwelled on the clothes and the packing and the logistics alone, but now Cleve was beginning to crowd into her mind. And so she called Flo at the office, saying first, "Cleve wants me," and then, over Flodie's gargled surprise, "Cleve wants me and I can't leave Lila Melyn."

"I can't talk now, I'm at the office."

"I have to go this afternoon."

"Honey, I have people *here.*"

Nell swallowed hard and pressed on. "I thought maybe you could come here and stay with Little Lila."

"Oh," Flodie said, terse and wary.

Lila was at Nell's elbow, hissing, "Tell her it's only for a couple of days."

Nell repeated, "It's only for a couple of days."

"Oh." Flodie's voice lifted with relief. "Well sure, I'd be glad to. I'll come right on over after work." She hesitated. "Would you like Randolph to take some time off and get you down to the train?"

"Thank you, I can take a taxi to the train."

"Well have fun," Flodie said.

"I'll take care of the grocery order and the laundry . . ."

"Don't you worry about a thing. Just have fun."

"And Lila has a party I'd hate to have her miss . . ."

"You just have fun. And hurry back, hear?"

Nell let the phone drop into place. "I will."

Lila insisted on riding down with her in the cab, she kept Nell occupied with her chatter, suggesting places she and Cleve could go on a second honeymoon, speculating on whether he had gotten rich in the years since Nell last saw him, whether he had been a prisoner of war and was coming back to her sick and diminished but blazing with love; Lila thought he might have been off on a secret government mission, which accounted for the long years' silence, she wondered whether he had gotten bald or grown a beard; she went on in mounting excitement until finally Nell, stifling, had to put her own hands on Lila's, saying, "Calm down, honey, you're getting too excited over nothing."

"It is *not* nothing, he's back, he's come back after all these years."

"Wait and see, honey." Nell could hear her own breath, quick and uneven, "Calm down and let's just wait and see."

They went through the station in a great rush, Lila grappling Nell's bag through the crowd and jerking it away from any boy in uniform who might make a pass at helping her, running with it until they reached the platform and she put it on the train. She pushed it ahead of her, stumbling through the crowded day coaches in determined haste until finally she found her aunt a seat, blocking the aisle until Nell settled herself, glowering at anybody who threatened to sit down next to her aunt before she had taken off her hat and folded her coat and put it on the luggage rack. When Nell had smoothed her hair and wedged her purse between herself and the armrest Lila hugged her and then hurried off the train; Nell's eyes filled to see the child's hips bumping the plush seats as she threaded her way down the aisle, but in the next moment she was conscious of movement outside the window and looked out to see the girl's anxious, loving grimace just below. Nell wanted to put her head back and close her eyes but Lila stayed and so they had to mouth senseless farewell messages through the glass right up to the minute the train started and then they both had to wave and blow kisses until finally Nell was able to settle back in her seat with the goodbyes over because at last Lila was out of sight; she would not know that behind her on the platform the girl, watching the racketing cars, burst into tears, sobbing as if she would never see Nell again, as if her own life had ended with the departure of that particular train.

The soldier who had taken the seat beside Nell was a sweet boy who tried to make conversation until finally he saw that he was only embarrassing her; she was too preoccupied to make sense and wanted nothing more than to put her head back and close her eyes. She held herself stiffly against the plush and tried to call up all her memories of Cleve but nothing came; instead she was aware of the boy beside her sighing, fidgeting with a cigarette, clearing his throat wistfully as if to rouse her and finally riffling the pages of a book. When the sandwich man came she had to talk; she pretended to be waked by his call but her eyes flicked open too quickly and the boy next to her said, "What's yours," and she responded, automatically, "Chicken," so they were dinner companions after all, and they had to talk.

He was on his way to New York to be shipped out. He said, "Where are you headed?" and when she said, "Washington," he wanted to know if she was meeting somebody and she hesitated for several seconds before she was able to say, "My husband." He said, "That's good. How long since you've seen him?" There was another long pause as she tried not to count: eighteen years; finally she said, "Years," driven to a protective lie: "He's been a prisoner." The boy said, "That's rough. You must have missed him a lot." By that time night had fallen and the boy was drowsy; in the next second he dropped off, leaving Nell alone to answer that last difficult question. It was difficult, too, because she understood now that while she had thought of nothing but Cleve for years it was of Cleve abstracted, she had not so much missed him as cherished him, or the idea of him, for all these years, holding it unchanged because it was Cleve unchanged she had loved, the idea of Cleve unchanging. By now the boy was sound asleep with his head jiggling against the back of the seat and bobbing closer and closer to Nell's shoulder; she made a ball of her coat and put it between her and the window, laying her head on it, and at last she was alone with Cleve, or the idea of Cleve. She had held it for so long that it took several hours riding into the descending night, a gradual separation from her home and a determined erasure of that last flash of Lila's twisting face to enable her to fix on Cleve, to try and bring him back. When she saw Cleve at the hotel, she thought, she would run into his arms quickly, so neither would have to see how the other had changed or aged; once their bodies fused they would not have to look too closely, and they would never be separated again. Even here, anticipating their meeting, she could not make Cleve's remembered face seem real; when she tried to think what he really looked like, what his voice sounded like and what he had been to her, she was distracted by thoughts of Lila and an awareness of the sleeping boy next to her; his head bobbed closer and closer to her shoulder and she had to work hard to bring Cleve's face into focus. When it finally did come clear she squinted her eyes and writhed in her seat because he was as beautiful as she had always remembered but the memory came at the same time as the knowledge of the other wives, his own betrayal; not precisely betrayal: desertion, so that she could no longer separate her happiness with him from remembered pain, and she grew stiffer and stiffer in her seat, aching, until finally the sleeping boy's head dropped on her shoulder and she couldn't think about Cleve any more because she was more or less pillowing this soldier she had never seen before, and she couldn't decide what to do. Was he really asleep, or taking some kind of advantage of the night and pretended sleep? Should she wake him, and if she woke him, what could she say? Excuse me, but your head . . . Perhaps she could jostle her shoulder and he would snort and move away from her without waking up; maybe if she coughed. But if she coughed and he lifted his head and apologized then she would be alone with Cleve again, and while her body warmed at the idea she could not divorce the reunion from the remembered separation and so she didn't cough or shrug but instead sat up a little straighter, so the boy's head would rest more securely; she sat there with her back straight and her ankles swelling until finally the sun rose outside the window and the boy snuffled and twisted and woke up without even knowing the greying little woman next to him had lifted her shoulders and sustained him through the worst part of the night.

Outside Washington, Nell went to the ladies' room and made a desperate toilette, lifting her unsure hand to make a neat mouth, knowing perfectly well that she was working against eighteen years; bracing herself against the motion of the car she ran a lead pencil across her eyebrows and then she murmured over her hair, combing and combing and finally jamming on her hat with a little sigh of resignation; no matter what she did she was still only Nell and he would still be Cleve so she couldn't hope for much. There were no cabs at the station and she arrived at the hotel two hours late and almost sobbing with distress; she stood in the lobby for the better part of an hour, pressing herself into a niche with a scraggly potted palm because she needed to see Cleve before he saw her, she had to be able to gauge his feelings and then compose her face. Waiting, she saw that all the other women in the lobby were years younger than she was, that the uniformed presences were really only boys, that these were all children trying to find each other; the place was so crowded, laced with meetings and assignations, that it occurred to Nell that Cleve might have another woman or all his women waiting for him; if she recognized even one of them and that one was younger or even a trace more sure than she was, then she would slip from behind her palm tree and get away without ever letting Cleve know she had even come. Frightened, she searched one face after another, looking at several shattered bodies and ruined faces with a certain lift of hope: if he had come back to her damaged, then there would be something she could do for him. Once she started after a man who might have been Cleve; he turned and smiled and she fell back with a little mutter of distress because she understood that if he or any other man were too kind to her she might let herself dissolve against the proffered arm and go wherever he wanted. Waiting for Cleve, she saw that some of the people there were waiting for people who would never come, and, looking down at her own brown-spotted hands, feeling the way her bones had yielded and her soft flesh hung, she found herself thinking: perhaps it would be better if Cleve never came. Then she fled the thought because she couldn't bear it, running across the lobby and almost suffocating in the minutes it took the desk clerk to get around to her. Hounded, she whispered:

"Are there any messages for Mrs. Lothrop, Mrs. Cleve Lothrop."

After several intolerable seconds of rummaging, the clerk said, "He left yesterday. Here's a note."

> *Darling,*
> *Called away. I kept the room for you. Will telephone tonight at eight.*

He does love me, Nell thought, and in her weakness and fatigue began to cry.

The minute the bellhop left her alone in Cleve's room she put her face against the bedspread; she went through the empty drawers and took a deep breath in the closet door, thinking to find some trace of Cleve, a single silver-blond hair, some vestigial smell, but there was nothing but a box of chocolates on the dresser, tied with a red ribbon, and propped on the bow was another note:

> *Dearest. Love, Cleve.*

so that in her morass of exhaustion and suspense Nell found herself wondering if he even remembered her Christian name. She might have left then but she had to lie down for a minute, just to get her breath, and because she could not bring herself to consider or to plan she flung herself into sleep.

Cleve's call woke her; it was dark.

"Nell? Is that you, Nell?"

"Cleve, is that really you?"

"Of course it is."

"Oh Cleve." After all these years.

"Well, honey, how are you?"

"I'm fine." I had to wait so long.

"It's so good to hear your voice."

Too long. She was trying to make something of the man at the other end of the phone but his voice was metallic and abstracted, sifted through hundreds of miles of wire, and she couldn't think of anything she wanted to tell him. "Where are you?"

There was a pause. Finally Cleve said, "Well, that's what I was calling about. I'm—in New York."

"New York."

"I thought I'd be finished tonight, but there's been a mix-up here."

"I see."

"Tell you what, honey, why don't you come on up?"

Another train ride, another desperate wait. "Come?"

"I have to go on up to Canada for a while, you could come with me."

"I can't."

"I'll meet you in Grand Central in the morning."

She had ridden all night and waited too hard and he had not come, he might never come. "I don't know."

He was getting impatient. "We'll have a wonderful time."

She held the receiver away from her ear and looked at it for a minute; she tried to call up Cleve's face but all she could see was Lila Melyn on the platform, puffy and deserted.

"Nell?"

"I'm sorry," she said at last. "I can't."

"Oh for God's sake."

"I have responsibilities now."

"It's only for a week."

She thought: Exactly. "I'm sorry, Cleve, I have to look after my niece."

There was another pause; she could almost hear him casting around for the right thing to say. "But I love you."

She could see the girl clearly, her mouth loose, her lipstick fuzzed. "I love you too, Cleve, but I have things to do at home."

After he hung up on her she threw herself on the bed and cried as if it were the end of everything. Then, washing her face, patting the skin around her eyes back into place, she decided that it wasn't, because now at least her past with Cleve had crystallized, so that no matter what happened from now on it would always remain intact for her to look at, frozen in time.

LILY

Papa, Papa, where are you, I need you to come and take care of me, I need for us to be in Mother's rose garden before the beginning, if there are no beginnings left, what is left to hope? Mother says I will be the queen of society when we are married and you take me where we are going, it won't be a really big wedding but we will have everything perfect, it will be the most exquisite wedding Charleston has ever seen and when you take me South to live I will be the greatest lady in our new city, an ornament to society, Papa, you and I will be most admired. I will, too; I would, but all the babies, I had to stay in so much and now the babies are gone, I have been left to wait in this place until you have the new house ready and in the meantime these terrible people come to visit me, middle-class to their shoes, with their faces so striped with apologies that I can't even tell what they look like. In spite of everything they call me Mama, and when they are gone the nurse tries to tell me they are the spit and image of me; they are nothing I ever hoped for, why should they look like me? That Florence is nothing more than a silly little secretary, her eyes have always been too close together and I would never have her to any party of mine except as a little charity, she looks as if she has never had a sweet moment in her life, and Cora, Cora is a forward little flapper, she is hard, hard; you would think she had covered herself over with nail polish, it would take a chisel to crack her shell. I used to think that Edward was mine but if he was he would have given us an heir, and besides, he is so sad now and craven, craven; he has given up wanting anything and his hair goes in three strips across the top; I think now he must have been Nurse's child, she got herself in trouble and had the baby in secret and then she crept into my room and left him in the bed while I was asleep; maybe she took away my boy, the one with the fine high forehead who looked just like Harry and was going to give me grandsons; Edward says to me, Well at least I have Terence, and I say, Terence does not bear the family name; he says, We had it changed, Mama, I thought you wanted it; I say, I never wanted anything, he's not fit to carry any name at all. Last time Edward came I said to him, If you are my son then you will get me out of here, but all he did was cut his eyes and start going on about dead holidays in the old house and that party we gave Lila all those years ago, he wouldn't listen to me, he didn't even want to listen; he was building his own picture and trying to make me look but all I could see was the open door behind him with all those terrible people with their uniforms and tubes and drains, squeaking by on rubber shoes, I put out my hand and said, Stop it, Edward, stop; he said, I can't; I said, Then you aren't going to take me home? He said, Oh Mama, I can't, and I said, Don't you dare call me Mama, you get out of here you little man, you are no true son of mine.

My true children are Thad and Lila, but Thad is gone and may never forgive me and I have only Lila; Lila is the most beautiful, she will be even more beautiful than I; I have given her everything, I have even given her a stronger name than mine, my name is helpless but hers has authority; she will cut smoothly through life, she will take her proper place in society, she will charm all the crowned heads of Europe, she could have charmed all the crowned heads of Europe but she has buried herself in Washington with that poor doomstruck boy, such a good family and what a pity, and now they tell me over and over that my true daughter Lila is dead. I don't know why they have to keep telling me things like that, I don't know why the nurse has to come and tell me, week after week: Mrs. Lyon. Miss Lily. I'm sorry; Miss Lily, your children are here. These are not my true children, we found them under cabbages and had to take them in. Don't bother me with them any more, just let me know when my son Thad comes, why doesn't he come?

He looked so much like Harry; Harry was with me in the garden that last time, right before he left; I was crying like a child, I was a child and I held onto his waist and cried and cried until he tried to put me away, saying, Oh Lily, just let go, stop crying and let go of me. I said Harry, Harry, I can't, you're going to leave me, you're going to leave me and our mother too and he said Hurry up and kiss me goodbye, Lily, it's way past time. He stood away from me and he was everything our family has ever stood for, tall and handsome, witty and fine, I thought if only I could keep him there we would all be perfect and nothing would ever change, but he was already slipping away from me, I could hear a woman's voice outside the gate, calling, and my handsome brother Harry tucked a rose in my sash and before I could reach out to keep him he had run away, they have all run away; Harry came back to me all those years later but he was not the same, his absence changed both of us, and life has never been the same. I remember Thad in my doorway one afternoon; he looked like Harry, he always has; I said, Gentlemen do not take jobs as day laborers, your Uncle Harry never forgot himself, he wore a clean white suit every day right up to the day of his death; then Thad turned on me and spoke to me in a tone Harry would never have dreamed of using with a lady. I will not be your toy doll, Mama, and besides, you know as well as I did Harry was a rotter. *Thad!* He even hated himself, that's why he drove off that bridge. I said, You call him Uncle Harry, Thaddeus Lyon, you show some respect for the dead. Mama, he committed suicide. I had to shut him out, I said, Don't be ridiculous, no Richard would ever do that, it isn't in our character. If you don't believe me, ask Papa, he'll tell you. I said, Your Papa would never say a thing like that. Mama, he was there when they fished him out. Stop it. I was screaming at him, I screamed, Stop it, stop it, stop it; weak as I was I got up out of the bed and I tried to slap him, saying, Thad, you are a nasty liar; big as he was he had tears in his eyes, he said, Oh Mama, can't I make you *see,* but I let go of him and lifted my elbow so he could help me back to bed; he laid his forehead against my shoulder for a second, I hugged him and we both scrabbled like dogs, trying to bury the words and forget; we almost did, too, but he had to bring home that girl, he brought her up to my room and had her wait outside the door, I heard her whisper: Thad, calling, just like that woman who tried to ruin Harry, calling for him from the shadows outside our garden gate.

Papa wanted me to like the girl, I think her name was Alicia, Thad met her at the University and I knew at once that she was not a lady, she was studying to be a doctor and no lady would dream of doing what she had to do: handling bodies, looking at bare limbs, she would pull Thad into a tangle of limbs, he would forget his honor and all the things of the spirit in that tangle of bare limbs; well he came to me, he said, I want you to like her, Mama, and I put one hand across my forehead and said, Very well, Thad, bring her in; I could see his eyes, I knew he wanted me to be kind, he was praying for me to be kind but I had too well in mind what he had tried to do to Harry, he had tried to destroy the memory of Harry, so how could I be kind to this cheap girl he'd brought in off the streets, I said, I'm so sorry, I'd like to take your hands, but I can't help thinking of all they've had to do and as I said it I saw Thad's face, it closed to me forever in the second before he turned and left the room. As it turned out he soon finished with that girl, or it finished, so I needn't have worried because she was not good enough for him; still I would have done it, I was sorry afterward but I had to do it because of Harry, I hurt Thad to save Harry's memory but then when I looked back I saw I had lost Thad; he was finished with me and he never came to my room alone until that last day, I think Papa sent him, he made him come because he thought Thad might be killed in France and he was not free to go until he had come to make that last attempt to make it right. He came in to say goodbye and we tried to say the right things to each other but everything I said hurt him, and when I saw I had lost him I said, At least you can kiss me goodbye, and he put his mouth on my forehead but that wasn't any kiss, and he wouldn't let me pull his head to my bosom, the way we used to make up in the old days; instead he said, I have to go now, and you are only trying to pull me down. So it was Thad for Harry, I gave up one for the other and now when I think how much they looked alike I am sorry, for it was Harry who ran away and it was Thad who remained constant after all, he vowed never to forgive me and he has not forgiven me to this day. Did I make a mistake in letting Thad go for Harry, should I have let Harry go for Thad? I can keep Harry's memory but Thad might as well be dead to me, he is doing well somewhere but he never writes and he never comes.

He never comes even when I need him, I need him to give me grandsons to carry on the line but in his rage he has cut himself off from the family and he will refuse to do God's duty, he will not honor his mother and he has refused to carry on the family name; oh Papa, I have let Thad go for Harry and now there is nothing left. If I could make him come there might still be time, if he would forgive me than we would still have a chance to continue, I could take his face in my two hands and say: I hurt you, Thad, you must forgive me, and then we would embrace and so be free of each other after all; he could go out and get children and I would be able to die because we would go on forever after all. My legs won't hold me and my face has flaked away, I cry and my hands shake and I soil my bed, when I let go for a minute I can feel all my flesh flowing downward, trying to sink into the earth, I would like to go but I have to resist because I need to see my boy. If I had Thad here I could let go, if I made it right with Thad then it would be all right to die because I would rise up again, all of us would rise up again, my bosom son would consent to life and all our hopes would rise up and continue, clothed in the children of Thad's flesh; if only he would come, he will come, oh Thad. Nurse? He is coming, I know it, I think I can see him standing by my bed. Thad? Thad? Please answer, Thad. Oh, Edward, it hasn't any of it been what I expected, it's not what I expected at all.

§§§§ §§§§

To begin with the house seemed not smaller but larger than it had in all his memories; the stairs were dark, the hall above was dark; to his right the parlor and the music room were dark and in the dining room beyond only one light burned. At last the house was empty of her but even so he wavered in the doorway, almost overwhelmed by the remembered consciousness of Mama, lying in wait in her room upstairs; for the last few years of his life in the house her presence had overshadowed everything else so that while he did not necessarily see her she was in every room for him, she would lie down between him and all his lovers, curling about his brain: do you know what you're doing, Thad, could you bring this woman home to me, what do you want from her and are you sure; even separated from her by miles, by years, he was aware of her accumulated pain and bitterness, her weakness and her wants and so long as she lived in the world he could run to the ends of the earth but he would always be in danger of being drawn into her needs, her pretensions and her potential for disappointment and so engulfed, he would disappear from independent life without a trace; now the shadows were deep but she was gone and once he understood that, the house seemed enormous to him; he would close the door quietly and go through the hall on tiptoe, and with great timidity try his voice in all those empty rooms. He took his key out of the lock, noting that it should have been changed years ago, and called: "Nell?"

Lila Melyn answered from the parlor; when he came into the doorway and saw her for the first time he assumed she had been tangled on the sofa with that sailor, who was coughing with his back turned, hastily reassembling himself; later Thad would remember seeing his dead sister's face hidden somewhere in that pale, regretful moon, and beyond, another presence, not yet clear. At the time he thought only: Already, perhaps because he was too old to see that dogged virginity born of innocence and ignorance.

"Uncle Thad?"

She was standing now, covered with embarrassment, and over her shoulder Thad could see the dining room; they had already moved the table and the chairs to one side to make a space for the trestle where his mother's coffin would lie. Because she was the most efficient, Flodie had gone ahead with the arrangements before anybody could stop her, deciding all by herself that every one of them would want to look into Mama's beautiful face one last time before she went into the earth. She had resurrected Mama's grey velvet gown with the chinchilla trim and steamed it; she had taken it down to the funeral home, bickering with the cosmetician and the hairdresser, commanding a masterpiece. They were all to gather around Mama's open casket; she would hold them together once more, as she had held them together in life. Cora had protested because she never liked to think about death, much less see it, she may even have feared that Mama would rise up and reproach her; Edward thought they all ought to remember her as she had been in her best moments, in her favorite photographs, but it was Nell who had burst into tears on the telephone, Long Distance, and from New York Thad had issued his orders. After all, he was the oldest and head of the family, and while his reasons were his own, he would not consent to have his mother laid out in the house unless the coffin was closed. Still, looking into Lila Melyn's sad, adolescent face, he wondered if he wasn't going to have to go on seeing his mother's face for the rest of his life after all. He looked from the girl to the sailor and understood too well not necessarily what they had been doing but what she was trying to do; he wanted to think she was only another adolescent, experimenting, but he began to think rather that through some family flaw, certain of Mama's kin would always be condemned to solitude, damned to disappointment but destined to try all their lives to get close enough to take warmth from at least one other soul.

He said, too sharply: "Where's your aunt?"

"Um."

Lila Melyn was awkward and anxious, tugging at her sweater and trying to smooth her hair and bobbing all at once; Thad thought he recognized a vestigial curtsey; she cut through it all with a sweet, painful smile, saying, "Oh, Uncle Thad, I'd like you to meet Jimmy Turano; Jimmy, this is my Uncle Thad."

The sailor, who was older, rubbed his chin. "I was just going."

Thad nodded without looking at him. "Lila, where are all your aunts?"

"I guess they're still at the funeral home. I was supposed to let you in."

"Call them and tell them I'm on the way over."

The boy had faded; for a second they were alone and then Lila Melyn said, with a certain resignation, "You won't have to, here they come."

And there they were in the hallway, all shaped strangely alike, except for Nell, all of them, even Nell, showing the same high forehead and the same characteristic profile; it was as if, stamped as they were, they had been equally marked to fall short in one way or another, to fail themselves or some irretrievable future which had been promised them; still they came hurrying into the room as if there were nothing but happy memories between them, and his sisters rushed on Thad with loving gurgles. Cora and Flodie put their small, dark mouths on his cheek, leaving the perfect stamp of Mama's mouth in two different shades. Edward shook his hand but with mistrust, as if already gauging his brother's patience; Thad understood that Edward was embarrassed by his own swollen pot, his slanted, retreating teeth and the fact that his hand was cold and slippery while Thad's was firm, he saw that Edward knew how much his suit cost and this was going to embarrass Edward even further, as if Thad's success was in itself an accusation; he shook Thad's hand and let it go quickly, backing off as if in the next second Thad would lash out at him for being less than he should be, for being soft and hiding himself in this dreary southern town. Only Nell hugged Thad without reservation, pressing herself into him with all her bones.

When Nell had let go they all fell back in a little ring and Thad was conscious, for the first time, of all of them massed against him because he had separated himself from them and left home all those years ago while, disparate as they were, they were together here, they were constant; whatever their reasons, they had stayed behind. He said, in some confusion:

"I came as soon as I could."

Edward mumbled, "I know how these things are."

Cora was saying, with some acerbity, "It's a pity you couldn't have been here at the end, Edward says she was asking for you."

Edward repeated, "She was asking for you." He could not bring himself to say that she had clutched all his fingers and called him Thad and cursed him for not forgiving her.

"It's been just dreadful," Cora was saying, "we had to keep running out there every minute, we never knew when she was going to go."

"But she looks just beautiful now," Flodie said with determination. She had his hand, trying to make him listen. "I wish you could see her, we laid her out in that grey velvet robe? You know, the one with the grey fur around the collar."

"She wouldn't eat a thing," Cora said, "Lord knows I ran my legs off, trying to find something that would appeal to her."

"You should have seen her," Flodie went on, "she was so sweet at the end."

Thad knew without asking that Flodie meant: once she had died, because at Flodie's back he saw the tired, patient face of Nell, who had in fact been there at the end and had seen their mother's face go black and the body empty itself of all its fluids, had held her hand and listened to her railing; Nell, meeting his eyes, looked away quickly because she had always loved him and didn't want him to have to deal with the details, because once she had told him there would be no way to convey the rest: that Mama had, at last, fallen silent, perhaps stunned at the moment she let go by the unexpected peace in relinquishment; she may not have wanted to try and tell him because, no matter how many times she rehearsed that final peaceful moment, no matter how carefully she thought about Mama, silent, herself holding her breath and bending close to trace the lines of Mama's face, she could not be absolutely sure whether Mama had been still alive or in transition, or whether she might have been already dead. Years later, as his own death neared, Thad would think that if she had understood at all, Mama had understood only at the last minute that all her life had spun itself out to bring her to the second when she would meet the power foreordained to take her; all her life Mama had planned and schemed and been frustrated or disappointed in the fulfillment of all her schemes when all the time she had needed rather to acknowledge that it would come to this and so, understanding, be willing to continue. At the moment, however, standing in the newly empty house, he was happy to let Nell's eyes escape his because, whatever their mother's death had been like, he knew that right now he needed to spare both himself and Nell from having to recall or examine it.

"Well," Cora said too heartily, "*I* need a drink," and Nell, freed, hurried out to get glasses and ice.

Edward was clearing his throat apologetically. "Vivian ought to be on her way over, she says she's been dying to meet you."

Cora had found the decanters. "Punk said tell you he's sorry, he had this fishing trip . . ."

Flodie was still talking, undeterred. "She looks like she used to look on Christmas, you know, she would come down in the velvet gown?"

". . . he just can't stand funerals."

". . . she just had to get Terence to sleep."

Flodie overrode them both. "And Papa would come up behind her and slip a new locket around her neck."

Cora was begging for a smile: "I don't think he'd show up if it was his own."

"Terence has gotten so he even looks like me."

Flodie pushed on. "We used to have such a wonderful time."

Perhaps made uncomfortable by Thad's gaze, Edward picked it up: "We used to run around like a bunch of wild Indians."

"We used to give Mama fits."

Thad had a flickering vision: Mama with the shades down, lying with pads on her eyes and one hand across her brow.

Even Nell was smiling. "Flodie and Edward were the worst."

Although she was secretly convinced that she looked younger than either Flodie or Nell, Cora let herself become the older sister, chiding: "You were terrible. Spying on poor old Lila and her dates."

Weary, feeling subtly threatened, Thad cut in. "I wonder if I could have something to eat."

Cora looked over the rim of her glass at Thad. "I suppose you think you were safe. Mama knew all those girls of yours by name."

In the background Lila Melyn was drifting; now Flodie tried to bring her into the circle. "Honey, you should have seen your old uncle here, he was a real heartbreaker."

"All those girls." Cora's mouth was getting smaller and smaller. "Time was when you could hardly wait to grow up so you could marry Mama."

"Why so did I." Edward considered. "Terence used to, but I think he's grown out of it."

"No wonder Mama was so jealous of that Sally," Cora said. "I remember you used to take her out in the Electric, you'd be gone for hours."

Nell was dreaming. "I wonder whatever happened to the Electric."

"Papa sold it," Cora said.

"I wish Papa could see us all here together," Flodie said.

Cora scratched her eyelid. "Except for poor Lila, of course."

"It's so *nice* we can be together."

"Oh, we used to have such good times."

"I miss Biggie, don't you?"

". . . miss everything, don't you?"

Their voices were fusing and when Thad nodded, he could not be sure which one of them he was answering; he was totally dislocated now, unless he fixed on something they were going to pull him back into their faulty memories, they would all be captive in the past and he would emerge, if he emerged at all, both weakened and diminished; all those years spent in New York, all his hours accumulated in the forge of loneliness would be as nothing and he would begin crying for Mama as he had when he was a little boy, crying in the expectation that she would come and she could make him better, when he had known from that same childhood that he must answer for himself; he saw them closing in and beyond their circle he saw the face of his niece, pale with that same helplessness, and because he could not tolerate their vulnerability or his own comprehension of her future, he cut them all off, saying, sharply, "This is all very well, but before I go back there have to be a few decisions made."

Arrested, they dropped back, resentful and waiting, and because he could not bear their silence any better than he could their reminiscences, he said, "About the child, for instance," and Flodie said, quickly, "Why, whatever do you mean?" and Cora said, sharply, "Thad, we've done the best we could."

"It isn't easy," Flodie began, but Thad said:

"I don't think it's doing her any good, being on her own down here."

Flodie answered quickly. "She has us."

Lila Melyn was staring blankly but Nell stepped closer to her with a protective gesture; they would face his wrath together.

"Yes," Cora said. "She has us."

"I think she needs more to draw on than you girls and this old house."

Flodie was quick: "That's very easy for you to say, Thad, sitting off there in New York."

"You don't know what it's been like." Cora went on, piously, "We're trying to do what her poor mother would have wanted."

Flodie snapped, "Besides, I've never seen *you* going out of your way for her."

"Well, maybe it's time I did."

Flodie was saying, "After all, we're doing our best for her, the same as Mama did for us."

Looking at his sister, Thad saw floating about her head the mists of nostalgia and self-delusion and in his quickening anger at her, at Cora, at all of them, he said, "You don't know what she was doing when I came here tonight."

Nell tried to raise her voice to room level, saying, "She was waiting to let you in."

"What was she doing while you were all down there at the funeral home fussing with your mother?"

Flodie said, "She's already told you, Lila was supposed to wait and let you in."

"She was in here with a sailor."

Cora put one hand to her breast. "No."

Flodie said, "A sailor!"

Edward took it up, embroidering, "A sailor, with her own grandmother lying down there, not even cold . . ."

Nell gave Thad a look of great pain, pleading, and perhaps understanding that he was blind to her, put her hands over her face.

Thad never looked at her; instead he fixed on Cora and Flodie, enraged by their cheap surprise. "You know damn well there was a sailor here, some light-handed bastard from the base, and tomorrow it will be a soldier and the next day it might even be the garbage man . . ."

Nell cried out: *"Thad."*

". . . or some bum off the waterfront, for all you care . . ."

Edward's voice trickled into the silence. "Poor beautiful Mama, and all the time *this* kind of thing . . ."

". . . and all you can think of is yourselves."

Thad was aware of Edward maundering, of his two sisters fluttering, trying to fend him off with pale, painted fingertips, he may have seen Nell's grief as she put her arm around Lila Melyn, he may even have understood in part what was happening to the child herself; he would tell himself afterward that it was for her sake after all, but he would have to admit to himself that at the time it had not been for her but because of them, for his own sake, that he had persisted, enraged not by their follies but by all their hopes, both angered and increasingly threatened, so that his voice rose until the room was filled with his rage and he was shouting: "It's time you stopped thinking of yourselves, God damn it, I am going to take this child out of here and put her where she'll be safe." He was fleetingly aware of Nell, recoiling as if from a blow, but he had to keep on, if only to save himself. "She's leaving here with me and I'm going to put her in a decent boarding school."

The girl was crying; so was Nell; the other two sisters were protesting but he could see their minds already at work, they were exploring the possibilities, and under the welter of sounds in the room he heard Edward saying, gravely, as if it had been his own idea, "You're right, Thad, I think you're absolutely right."

Spent, Thad let his eyes close for a split second, and as he did so, saw a pattern of red-and-black that made him understand how hard he had pushed his heart, driving his blood pressure so high that all of them had been in danger. He took two breaths and, wavering, opened his eyes and for the first time looked directly into Nell's wounded face. "Oh," he said. "Nell."

The others had dropped back, buzzing, and, left with his youngest sister, struck for the first time by doubt and beginning regret, Thad repeated: "Nell?"

She looked at him, stricken, deprived, but already trying to say, without crying: "Whatever you think will be best for her."

EDWARD

It's all very well for him, sitting up there in those hundred-dollar shoes, it's all very well for him to sit up there in New York where he never has to lift a finger to help himself or anybody else, it's all very well for him to sit up there and judge because he doesn't know what it's like, he ran off up there where it's safe and so he doesn't have an idiot child's conception of what it's like to stay in one place and do what people want. I can just see him calling in his secretary and dictating that note, I can see him signing it and wrapping it around the check, he would be turning that profile of his and thinking something noble: Poor Edward, this will make a better person of him. Poor Edward, this will shut him up. Well I will take his money, I will even thank him because Vivian says I have to, the next time I see him I will probably even smile, but I will never, ever change my mind about him, he ran out on us and for his sins I hope all the devils in hell will climb up on his shoulders and take the skin of his face off shred by shred and then maybe he will know what it feels like to be Edward instead of Thad; if he wants to be noble let him, if he wants to buy me off I will take his money but I will never sell out and I will never forgive him for writing that note:

Hope this little bit will help.

Two thousand dollars, and he writes, Hope this little bit will help. Here, Edward, here's this money, it isn't much, but . . . Does he have any idea what two thousand dollars *is?* Poor Edward, have some money, Edward, and try to forget what you said to me on the long distance telephone, and forgive me for being so goddam noble, I can't help being better than you are because I have never been up against it the way you are. Hundred dollar Italian leather shoes.

Well it wasn't my fault what I said, it was Vivian's, she had this thing fixed in her head about what Mama had, and what Mama was going to leave us in her will, and when I got home with it, Mama's beautiful silver service and Mama's favorite three-legged gilt chair with the brocaded dragons on the seat, all she was going to say was how did I get that mess home on the street car, and then I had to tell her I paid two dollars for a cab. But I was thinking how I could be alone with Mama now, instead of having to go out to that dreadful place and look at her wild hands and all those wrinkles weighing down her face, I could sit in the brocaded chair and keep her just the way I wanted, well and beautiful and safe inside my head; I should have known; when I left to hear them read the will Vivian pushed me out the door, saying, Now we are going to have it, she will reward you for being faithful, going out there every Sunday of the month for all those years. She did reward me, too, she remembered exactly what I wanted, I had always wanted them, for Vivian: she would entertain for me, I would see her reflected in the pier glass, sitting in the three-legged chair and smiling as she poured the tea; when I got to our house Flodie was already reading off the list of things Mama had marked for each of us, and Flodie was crying and Cora was crying and pretty soon I couldn't help it so I started crying and poor Nelly came over and led me into the dining room, saying, This is what Mama wanted you to have, and there was the silver tea service sitting on the gilt three-legged chair, so I knew Mama had remembered, and that meant she loved me after all. I was so happy, I took those things home to Vivian and it should have been enough, but she was in the bedroom, cutting down one of my jackets to make a sports coat for Terence, her red-gold hair was like a halo right up to the second that she looked up from the machine and asked me what Mama had left us and I told her and then watched her start to crackle, saying: Is that all?

I tried, I said: Vivian, she didn't have much. It cost a fortune, keeping her in that hospital . . .

She said, You know what I thought about *that*.

I said, She's my mother and it's none of your business.

Then her hands started going around the way they do, all red nails and long white fingers, she was showing me the bedroom, the whole apartment, the way we have lived for all these years and saying, And I suppose *this* is none of your business?

I looked at Mama's pretty Dresden couple, on our dresser, I thought about the pier table and all the other lovely things we had, I said, Vivian, this is our *home*.

Oh well, I should have known, I should have seen where she was leading me, she said, And that's enough for you.

I do the best I can.

I expected so much *more*.

Vivian, we can't always help the way things go.

She was standing up now, she had the jacket in front of her and she was saying, Oh Edward, can't you see what they're doing to you?

I didn't want to see, her suspicions were so ugly that I didn't want to listen, brothers and sisters love each other and they never cheat; I wanted to tell her but there is no way to stop Vivian once she gets started, you have to let her keep on going until finally she runs down and you are able to get away from her, I thought maybe I could pretend to be straightening the dresser so I wouldn't have to look at her but when Vivian is talking she wants you rooted, you have to stand in one place and listen and if you don't stand in one place and listen, if you try and change the subject or sneak away somewhere quiet to wait until she is finished then she stores it up and sooner or later she catches up with you and she will start all over again from the beginning and you have to go through it all all over again except that it will take longer because she says everything she said last time plus everything she will say this time plus she will never ever forgive you for trying to change the subject or closing your eyes in the middle of her talking or running away, except she will call it: Walking out on her. So I had to stay, she is so beautiful when she is like that, before we were married she used to twine herself around me like wisteria but now it is the only time she is really alive to me, her face is transparent white and she is furious with me because I work in the office at the supermarket now and we have to live in an apartment and go everywhere on the streetcar or the bus, but it's not for herself, it's never for herself; she talks about her and me, what I should do for her, what she should expect from me but behind her face with that one thin layer of skin between I can see what she is really fighting for: Terence; this is all for Terence; she says, You don't know what it's *like* to be a mother; I say, Vivian, I . . .

That day she said, Edward, you know as well as I do they are cheating you.

Vivian, this is all she *had*.

Don't you tell me that. She lifted her hand, I almost thought she was going to hit me but instead she swept it across the dresser, grabbing Mama's little Dresden shepherdess, she said:

They have been stealing from you for years.

Well I didn't want to hear her talking like that, it hurt me and then I started to think it all over: What had happened to it all; we used to have three servants and two cars and a pony cart, and everywhere we went people knew we were Papa's children, they respected us; we were brought up to live decently and here I was in this three-room apartment with Vivian about to cry and Terence off God knows where because Vivian says he's ashamed to bring his friends home to a poky little place like this, but Cora is driving around in a Cadillac and Thad is rich and I began to think maybe she was right, it wasn't just all gone with the years, it had gone *somewhere,* and if all I had was a few old thises and thats of Mama's and too many bills, then what *happened* to it all? Vivian was wild, she was raving, she had that shepherdess in her hand and I couldn't help thinking if I didn't stop her in the next second she was going to let fly and ruin everything, so I said, You're right, Vivian, you're absolutely right, now put that back down where you found it and I will try and get us our share.

It's the least they can do, she said, We deserve a decent share.

So first I called Cora, she is the oldest one of us that is still living in town and so when she wants to she calls herself the head of the family but she didn't want to be the head of the family this time, she said, I don't know what you're talking about, there isn't any money, you know as well as I do that there never was.

I was worked up by that time, I said, Come on, Cora, where did it all go?

Then she lost her temper and said if her word wasn't going to satisfy me then nobody's was but if I was so dead set on it I might as well call up Thad, he was mister Gotrocks after all and by the way, if I found out anything she didn't know would I please telephone her so she and Punk could decide what they were going to do?

I was still upset but I was more or less wrung out by that time so I said, Vivian, honey, let's us go down to the Captain's Dock the way we used to, just you and Terence and me, we'll have a crabmeat salad and then come back and think this through, but she was like a stone, she wouldn't listen, I took her hand and said, Vivian? and she still wouldn't even turn her head, all she did was say, through her teeth, You know perfectly well we can't afford it, and I knew right then that she was going to force the issue, it was going to cost us a fortune, but I was going to have to dial Long Distance and talk to our brother Thad.

Then she put her hand on me as I started to talk to the operator and I was so surprised, so warmed that I did as she said and called Collect.

You can bet Thad was surprised.—Edward? Oh, Edward.

Yes, I said, it's me.

Well how are you Edward.

I could hear him breathing at the other end, just waiting, he was thinking: Edward. What does he want? I suppose he thought I was going to beg or something, I was going to butter him up and then ask for something because I thought that was what he was doing up there on Wall Street, for us to call up there and him to listen and then start handing it out; it would never occur to him that I would call him up on just plain business or to say how was he, we were fine; he would always think of Edward with his hand out because he was so tight with his money, he had sucked it all up somewhere inside him so he still had every penny and then some, he had some of ours up in there with it and that was why he could afford to be so noble, that was why he was so rich when we couldn't even afford to go out to dinner at the Captain's Dock, I thought about it all and how he was swelled with money and I was empty but all swelled up too, like one of those starving Chinese, bloating on all that remembered bitterness, in another minute I was going to bust and so I let it all out into the silence, saying:

I want my money.

What money?

You know, Mama's money.

Edward, there wasn't any money, there hasn't been any money for years.

I was still filled, I had to let it out, I held my breath for a minute trying to keep it in but before I could stop myself it all came out in a whoosh: You've been stealing our money, you've been cheating us for years.

It was all gone, I was limp as a dishrag, hanging over the phone like a wet balloon, but Thad couldn't see me, he was still chewing on that last little bit and I just hung there on the silence until finally I heard his voice coming back, tired and slow, he was saying, Oh my God.

I wanted to say Oh Thad I didn't mean it, but I couldn't, Vivian was watching like a tigress, and I wanted to say I'm sorry, but I couldn't do that either because I had let it all out now and there was nothing left, nothing but the silence and then Thad's voice dropping into it and then another silence and then Thad's voice sieved through all those wires, thin and sad like it was the end of the world: Edward, there isn't any, but don't worry, I'll take care of you.

There wasn't anything left for me to say so I put my mind on my fingers and finally I was able to bunch some muscles together, just enough so I could hang up on him, then all I wanted to do was crawl off in the corner behind Mama's gilded chair and die, but Vivian was right there, saying, Well, what did he say? It took me a long time to get enough breath to push some voice out but there she was hanging on my fingers and finally to get her off I said, He said he'd see, and I guess that was enough for her for the time being because she took me to bed right then and there with Terence due home from school almost any minute, he could have come right in and put his books down on the other twin bed, but Vivian was so happy she didn't even care, I didn't either, I was so tired I just lay there and she did everything, and then when Terence came in about five instead of three, she didn't even fuss at him about where had he been; we went down to the Captain's Dock for an early dinner and Vivian laughed and Terence laughed but all I could think of was Thad's voice and how he has always made me do things that would make him better than I was, and I couldn't even think about how all the money was coming for all I hated him; I hated him and I was going to hate the money but at least we could use it to pay off the bedroom suite and the new icebox and Terence's Victrola that we had to get so he would have something to entertain his friends.

If I had it my way, if I didn't have us all to think of, I would have sent the money back, what right did he have to sit up there in New York with no cares and no responsibilities and write me off with a two-thousand-dollar check? I opened the note and the check fell out and I was ashamed, God I was ashamed, but I knew better than anybody that there was no sending it back, I was going to have to use it to try and get us out of the hole we keep sliding into, no matter how much we owe or how much we get we always seem to need something more. It came on a Saturday morning, Vivian was off somewhere and Terence was sitting there in his yellow bathrobe watching me turn out the envelope, except that when I looked up I could never catch him watching, he would pretend to read. But I knew he was watching and I said, This is two thousand dollars, Terence, and he still wouldn't look at me, he just said, Swell, so I thought he must know what I felt like and what Thad must think about me; I thought I knew what Terence thought of me and I had to explain, I said, You understand, don't you, Terence, I did it for us. Terence is getting very handsome, he looked into the windowpane, using it like a mirror, and he combed his hair and kept on combing it and wouldn't say anything. Finally I said, We're going to see our way clear now, we might even save up some for your college, things are going to go uphill from now on, and he left off combing, saying: Sure Edward. Do you think we could use some of the money to buy a car?

Well we didn't, what we did was, when it came I thought we would use it pay off our debts and get a little next egg but Vivian came home at lunch and she danced around with the check and after lunch she brought out some folders and said, Oh Edward, how wonderful, look, I've been saving these for a surprise. I looked at them and then I told her we couldn't afford it, we couldn't begin to afford it and in the next minute she turned to fire right in front of me, she was talking, shouting, screaming without even drawing a breath, her words were going in and out between my bones like little tongues of flame; Terence had faded and she was alone with me, taking me down to my bones, and I had to stop her, I couldn't stand it, she was going to leave me standing there in my bones with nothing left, none of the past or Mama, or her and me in love, she wasn't even going to like me, she might not even *tolerate* me in another minute and because I couldn't bear it I screamed louder than she did, yelling: All right, against her screaming; I lifted my voice and howled, above her howling, All right, Vivian, anything you say.

I had to go to bed for the rest of the day and Vivian brought me things to drink and Terence even brought the paper in for me, and Vivian said I must have been running around with a fever or I wouldn't have been so dragged out like that, but Sunday I was better and Sunday afternoon we went out and looked at it, this tract? They are building all these little houses, grass and all they don't take up much more room than the place we're living now, but at least they are houses, *houses,* with a little bit of yard outside and a corrugated plastic carport, and once we move all our things and Mama's things into it everything will be better because it's what Vivian and I have really needed right from the beginning, a little place we can call our own; when we invite the family over they won't always be making up excuses, the place is going to be so pretty that they'll all be falling all over themselves to come. Vivian is going to take a job so we can swing it, and Terence has promised to sell papers or something to help pay for the car insurance and the gas and all; after all, if we're going to live that far out then we're going to need a way to get there, if we only use half of Thad's check for the down payment on the house, then we can put the rest of the money into a little car. After all, Vivian has to have some way to get to work and get the groceries home, and Terence can use it for his dates and when we get time I can take Terence around and show him some of the places I used to talk about: where we had the river camp and where Thad and Cora used to ride their horses and where Nurse took us in the pony cart, and on Saturdays when it's nice we can pack a lunch and Terence and Vivian and I will all drive out to the beach.

§§§§ §§§§

As he grew older Punk seemed to curl in around his habits and so-lidify, until he made a circle about himself; even his needs made a

232

circle, and while they involved Cora they also excluded her from anything beyond a certain physical presence and particular things which must be accomplished for his comfort: an omelet at breakfast, the pitcher of martinis before dinner, dinner itself; then five nights out of seven he would finish the day with several long Scotches and go off to bed, leaving Cora to spin out the last hours of the evening with Alden, pretending that neither he nor she needed anything beyond the snugness of their living room and the knowledge that they had pledged to go through life together: the three of them, even though at the moment Punk was drunk and snoring above their heads. When she went to join him at eleven, he would either wake and warm to her or else he wouldn't, he slept or made love with the same self-centered indifference, excluding Cora even as he embraced her, leaving her each night to prop her head up in the darkness, open-eyed and thinking dimly that this was not precisely what she had contracted for all those years ago, but unable to put her finger on just what had gone wrong. On one of those evenings she had not gone up at eleven, sitting in the living room with Alden instead, nibbling at the edges of the silence and deciding, finally, that she had come upon a solution for all of them. She got up to show Alden something she was reading, standing by his chair with the sense that she was about to do something right; then, without being totally clear what she intended, she bent and put her face against the top of his smooth, silvering hair. He lifted his mouth instinctively, as he must have to dozens of women, sliding into an embrace as if from habit, withdrawing almost as soon as he remembered who she was. "Cora."

"Oh Alden," she said, implying: *he's drunk, you must be lonely,* but when she did go on it was to say, "It hasn't worked out, Alden, why can't we make it work out?"

He let her go, handsome and regretful and at the same time anxious to keep her in the ways he had always been able to keep her. "I love you, Cora, but we have to do it our way. You know."

She sighed. "You mean the three of us."

He was pleading. "If we made love I'd have to move out of here."

"Punk wouldn't know, he wouldn't even care."

"If we made love Punk would know."

She pressed him. "What if he didn't?"

"I would know, and I'd have to move out of here. Cora?" His voice lifted, he was asking her to turn and tell him everything was going to be all right.

It was going to be all right and they both already knew it, because Cora had begun to straighten the room as they talked, puffing up the pillows and altering the position of a lamp so it would be just where they liked it, putting the empty glasses and the dirty ashtrays on a tray so that when they all came in here in the morning with their coffee it would be exactly the way they all expected; when they looked up from their papers there would be no vestigial apparitions hanging in the air to shame them: Cora on the couch with her garters showing, Alden forgetting himself.

Cora had emptied the last ashtray without saying anything and Alden felt he had to say: "It's because I *do* love you, Cora."

She was at the door now, turning to say, "Don't worry, Alden. I have to walk the dog."

For the rest, Cora was fairly well content; for better or worse she had her two men, she had her pretty house and her clothes, and she had rafts of friends. She played bridge once a week and devoted one afternoon to the garden club, and recently the girls had started lunching at the Hacienda Beach Club on Wednesdays, having martinis on the Spanish tiles besides the pool and then moving on in to the dining room for crabmeat salads on avocado, or Dover sole chosen to balance off dessert because they had to remember their figures now. When they left the dining room they always held in their stomachs and tittered, conscious of the eyes of the darling new manager; Lawson looked Spanish although he was from New York somewhere, and he had a way of warming ladies with his eyes, complimenting smooth skins and tightened bellies without saying a word. He was only in his twenties but even the men had to agree he was doing wonders, going to any lengths to help them plan their parties, moving heaven and earth to decorate the dining room for Gemma's luau or the hobo party Cora gave for Punk at Christmas of that year. All the best people came and, looking at Alden in his ragged shirt and lidless boater, at Punk, with his burnt-cork chin and light-bulb nose, seeing all their friends in tatters, dancing, Cora felt very rich indeed.

From the beginning she had moved in the circles she would have chosen, all her friends had husbands in business or one of the professions, they all lived in big houses and went away for a month in the summer, and all the girls had cars of their own now because they needed them for shopping and bridge parties, appointments at the hairdresser and afternoons spent by the pool. Relaxing, buttered and spread out in the sunshine alongside the others, Cora felt sleek and privileged, perhaps ever better off than the rest because more than one of the others had said, Lucky Cora, she has two men instead of only one. Still most of them had one commodity it was too late for Cora to come by; they had at least one son or daughter, and some had two. In the beginning they had been only hindrances: reasons why Gemma couldn't go to the fashion luncheon in Atlanta, or why Ella Arnold had to refuse the bridge playoff; she had to take Polly to the orthodontist, all the way to Savannah, they drove miles. At first Cora, listening to their complaints, had thanked her stars and never fully understood the underlying pride when Gemma Farmer said Jimmie was sick and needed her; after all, Gemma had been the first to say: You have *two* men instead of one. But the children were older now, sliding through their teens, and Cora's friends used them as currency: Jimmie was doing beautifully at Porter, when he came home for the holidays they were going to have to match him up with Ellen's girl, after all, she was going to need an escort for the graduation party Ellen was planning, and with next year's deb list in the works, they had to think ahead . . . Excluded, Cora slid in a word or two about gifts from her men but the girls let that slip by without even a murmur and continued playing, moving their children about like pawns in a new, engrossing game, so that finally Cora was forced to develop new resources, saying, "Oh, I hope Lila—" She started to say: *gets invited to some of the right parties when she comes home from school,* but she knew at once that was a mistake and so she swallowed her breath and finished: "—wants all your children on her list." The others were on her immediately, saying What list, and so she continued, creating: "I'm giving a dance for her seventeenth birthday, I thought we might have it right here at the club."

Lila wouldn't be home again until June, her birthday was months away and so Cora was able to talk about her with added enthusiasm, she would not be coming down to the pool the next second to refute or rebuke Cora with her moon face, her ungainly hips, the wet, longing look she almost always wore. None of Cora's friends had seen her since one Christmas years before, when she had passed the nuts at a cocktail party, and Cora herself had begun to forget what Lila looked like, so they were all able to talk about Cora's niece as just another of the girls, no taller, no fatter, no more lonely or anxious than Marguerite's daughter Tillie, or Ellen Arnold's girl; Cora could send a small monthly check and when Lila sent a thank-you in exchange she would be able to put her own tokens into circulation, saying, "Lila says they're having an assembly on sex. At that age. Imagine." Or: "Poor thing is worried to death she won't have a date for the prom, you ought to see the dress I sent her, it's adorable."

As the weather got warmer Cora and her friends spent more time at the club, playing bridge by the pool in their straw hats and flowered bathing suits until nearly one; although they never swam they had to shower, watching the brown skin on their arms shrivel as they soaped off the suntan oil and then emerging, feeling privileged, sybaritic as they changed into their pastel linen sheaths for the procession into the dining room. Lawson would be waiting with the menus, all gallantry and deference but gauging each one with an almost obscene flattery as he seated her; when they were all seated and fluttering he would suggest the most expensive entrée of the day and in their excitement, or gratitude, they would all insist on it and then sign for the meal without a second thought. Cora would have preferred to pass that entire spring and summer sunning, showering, eating in a dreamy suspension, but Gemma turned to her at lunch one day and said, "When is that birthday dance you're giving, Cora? I don't want it to conflict with Jeannine's graduation party, the children get jaded if there are too many parties in one week."

Cora hesitated, saying, "Why, on her birthday, I suppose," and then, because she couldn't remember exactly when Lila's birthday was she said, "Or the nearest Saturday," plunging on. "I thought it might be nice to have it the last Saturday in June."

"Oh, Lawson," Gemma said, hailing the manager before Cora could stop her. "I wondered if you could come and talk to Mrs. Gresham, she's planning a summer supper dance."

Cora saw Lawson start up from his desk at the door to the dining room, and for reasons which at the time would have surprised her she flushed, saying sharply, "Not now, Lawson. I'll come out tomorrow morning."

They made an appointment for nine-thirty; it would give Cora a chance to get the details settled before the girls arrived with the scorepads and the cards; with her business done, she could slide easily into the day's routine. The club at that time of day had a different aspect; it was still cool and so quiet that Cora could hear the wind in the black Australian pines; the sky was bright and unsullied and there was nobody there except a few young mothers browning on beach towels while the life guard splashed with their small children at the shallow end of the pool. The dining room was dim and chilly as a cave and, waiting, Cora was oppressed by the silence, distracted by the note on Lawson's desk calendar. She would have expected: Mrs. Gresham, or: Important party, but the note, scribbled in pencil, said only, Cora, 9:30 A.M.; she could feel herself warming almost against her will so it was only reasonable for her to reach for a chair, a little giddy, as the door to the kitchen opened and Lawson came across all those miles of flowered carpet with a tight, unreadable grin.

"Mrs. Gresham," he said.

"I'm here to plan the supper dance. I'd like it to be the last Saturday in June."

"For Mr. Gresham?" He sat down behind the desk, looking abstractedly at his calendar; Cora thought wildly: My name; he's going to look down and see my first name.

"A sort of a sweet sixteen party."

He was fooling with his pencil, sliding it back and forth behind his ear. "You look too young to have a daughter that old."

Cora said, "I am. It's for my niece."

They were both silent for several seconds, while Lawson pretended to go over the party schedule for the month. He ran his pencil down a list of dates and then looked up unexpectedly, saying, "Mrs. Gresham, I hope you won't take this the wrong way, but would you like to go to bed with me?"

Cora could feel herself turning colors; she was sorting through all the possible varieties of responses: rage, laughter, injured dignity, before she could settle on one of them she heard herself saying, "Yes, Lawson. Yes I would."

So she lay on his bed in his room at the top of the Spanish tower and let him make love to her while she listened to other people's children splashing in the pool, and when she rose to dress it was with a certain satisfaction; she smoothed her dress, thinking of Punk, Alden, what the girls would say, and as she looked back at her new lover, still lounging on the bed, she heard a clear, smug voice inside her sounding like a bell: All right.

After that she had something to look forward to. If they were to continue it would have to be on her own initiative, as Lawson would never telephone her house for fear of catching Punk at home or reaching her during one of her luncheons, and they could not afford to indicate anything, one way or the other, while they were together

237

at the club, so it was up to Cora to call. She would put if off because she did not like to be dependent, he ought to care enough to pursue her no matter what the risks; she would put if off because it made her feel awkward and embarrassed to be making the advances, or because she thought abstractedly that she really shouldn't, but sooner or later she would call him and they would meet at a rooming house Lawson knew where they could go in without seeing the landlady, and he could take his pleasure on a wide, old-fashioned bed in a ramshackle upstairs room while Cora dreamed all the while, watching the light move on the ceiling as the afternoon breeze took the window shades.

When Lila came home in June Cora was so immersed in possession that she barely remembered to tell the girl about the dance.

"I thought it would be a sort of a sweet sixteen party, all my friends' children are going to come."

"I'm going to be seventeen, Aunt Cora."

Cora thought abstractedly: I wish she wouldn't call me Aunt, she's so huge. "Gemma Farmer's boy is going to be your escort, he goes to Porter and he's just adorable."

"Aunt Cora, I don't think I would do very well at a party."

"I thought they wouldn't bring presents even though it *is* your birthday, some people think they can get off with just the present and never have you back." Cora looked at her niece, who was standing with her arms at her sides, silent and miserable. "Oh honey, I *wish* you could take off a little weight."

"Aunt Cora, nobody will dance with me."

"Of course they will. We'll get you one of those strapless formals, you know, you have a pretty bosom and it will take their minds off your hips. I guess you'd better wear flats, honey, so you won't look so tall . . ."

"I don't want a party."

"And maybe we can do something about your hair . . ." Cora was forced to look at the girl closely now, she saw the dull hair, the plain, heroic face, the enlarged pores around the nose; she saw, further, the extent of Lila's hopelessness and understood as well as the girl did that it would never work out, but now, with Lawson in her bed, it ceased to matter as much as it had. "Honey, you know we have to go on with the party, the invitations have gone out . . ." She went on quickly, retrenching, "but I'll tell you what. We can make it a joint party, we'll still have your friends but we'll have all my friends too, it can be a birthday gala for you and Punk." She went on, only faintly aware of the girl's beginning smile, her almost overwhelming relief. "We might even have Nell and Flo and Randolph, and if you want to . . ." She considered, already thinking: It will be better in the long run, I can wear my green dress with the sequinned top, and Lawson and I will pretend not to speak. ". . . if you want to, you and your young friends can run along the minute supper's over, and not have to stay around and be polite." She continued weaving, not even aware when Lila stopped listening; she wasn't even listening herself, she was thinking about Lawson, they had bumped into teach other at the specialty market that same morning, the clerk had said, "Mrs. Gresham, I believe you haven't met Mister Lawson, he's the new manager out at the Hacienda?" and Cora and Lawson had exchanged cold looks of complicity as Cora said, indifferently, "Yes, thank you, we've already met." The dance would go off more or less the way she expected, with Nell taking Lila home in a cab the minute supper was over and all of her friends proving that friends can be counted on, making it the funniest, gayest, most raucous party the club had seen so far. As she and Punk danced the last number together in the darkened dining room, she saw over his shoulder that Lawson was watching, and conceived that both of them were linked by the same thought: If they chose to, Cora would nod and Lawson would just cut in right in front of everybody, he and Cora would dance away to his room upstairs without a backward look.

She had already begun to realize that it was not enough to exchange looks with Lawson in crowded places, or to squint at her friends from beneath her sun hat, thinking with a covert pride: If they only knew. Why, if nobody knew then it didn't much matter that she was having her affair right under their noses, nor did it matter that she had at last gotten even with Punk for all those nights of drunken snoring; there was nobody to appreciate those complicated, pervasive ties which bound her and Alden, keeping him chaste inside her house; there was nobody to share the details and so put Lawson into jeopardy, making him appreciate what they had won; her affair, all those clandestine afternoons at the rooming house would be as nothing if nobody knew and so by late summer she had decided she would have to tell at least one other person in order to make it seem real. It might have been any one of the girls but in the end she chose Gemma, who had been going on at length about her new cottage in

North Carolina, it was in the middle of the mountains, right on the edge of a lake.

"Of course you'll want to bring that sweet niece of yours, I can't guarantee Jimmie will be around much, but she'll have such a good time in the water that it won't matter."

"Oh Gemma I can't," Cora said, with infinite condescension, "it's not that I wouldn't love to, but I couldn't possibly leave town."

"Why on earth not?"

Cora lowered her head, saying from beneath her straw brim, "Because I have a lover now, and I couldn't bear to be away from him."

"Who on earth."

Cora was smiling, reborn in achievement. "Lawson."

They were both smiling now. Gemma said, "Oh my God."

"For the past six months."

"But what about Punk?"

Cora looked at her nails. "This doesn't have anything to do with Punk, and besides, I want what I want."

"All right," Gemma said, delighted, "but I could never do a thing like that."

"I suppose Howard . . ."

Gemma evaded her. "I could never do a thing like that because of Jimmie, it would kill him if he knew."

"Kids," Cora said.

Lawson must have felt some of the same things she had about needing someone to pry at the edges of their secret; he may have grown bored or he may have decided that it was time to put an end to it, because he came to Cora's house in broad daylight that same week, not even pretending to care who saw. He came in the guise of asking her to help him plan the Indian Summer Dance because her own party at the club had been such a success. That excuse would do for the neighbors, who saw him arrive at high noon and would see him leave more than an hour later, but Cora knew she would have to do better for Punk and Alden, and, facing Lawson there in the front hall, she cast around in her mind for the safest place to take him: her room? The discarded studio couch in the attic? She decided finally on the guest room even though she knew as she changed the sheets and put on fresh ones after he had left her that there was no place in her house to have him, it was not set up for adultery. Sure enough, even though she was at pains to cover her tracks, she knew as soon as they settled down in the parlor after dinner that Alden knew. She tried to divert him with tidbits from the evening paper but instead of listening he cleared his throat uncomfortably, trying to think of a way to begin; she wanted to stop him, telling him there wasn't any way, but he said, miserably, "I saw him."

She shrugged. "I suppose he wanted you to. Well, what are you going to do about it?"

"Cora, you can't do this to Punk."

She looked at him coldly; they were both thinking: Punk probably wouldn't care, or he wouldn't care enough.

"All right." He came over and got on his knees on the floor next to her, awkwardly taking her hand and bending his head over it, so she was forced to look at his thinning crown; he put his face against her hand and held it there without moving for several seconds, getting up finally and saying, from his height, "Then you can't do it to me."

There were a number of things she wanted to say, had in fact rehearsed for just such a moment, but she saw that he didn't want to play to her, he had made his plea and he wasn't going to feed her any more lines, so all her speeches dissolved in smoke before she could fix on any one of them; she thought with a beginning wash of guilt that she had not been unfaithful to Punk but to Alden, or Alden's idea of fidelity, and looking into his face she saw that if she wanted to keep him, if she wanted to keep either one of them she was going to have to mend it, and mend it quickly; she could feel Alden receding, and with him the room, the house and all her comforts were receding, and because she had more or less accomplished what she had set out do do, putting the whole incident into currency, she said without regret:

"It's all right, Alden, I'm going to break it off."

§§§§ §§§§

When she was small Lila Melyn played bride just like anybody else, pulling a lace curtain across her cheek to hide a face which would be luminous under the wedding veil, embroidering on the weddings she knew by heart to create her own, yet despite all her fabrications she was puzzled all her life by a repeated dream. She would never know who she was supposed to be marrying in the dream, whether it was

Uncle Harry, Rhett Butler, Gaylord Ravenal, but she was getting ready, she would move through the unreal corridors in tattered white chiffon which swept the granite floors, picking up city grime. She was in a deserted office building down town, brass strips marked off the granite floor in squares but her skirts swept across the brass lines and erased them, so she could see more or less where she was going but she couldn't tell where she had been; it was always dawn and she would be alone in the lobby except for an old Negro with a string mop whom she would recognize as Brewster, although Brewster had probably been murdered in his young manhood years before she was ever born. Brewster would see her standing uncertainly in her shredded wedding gown and after an unbearable pause he would shamble forward and she would bow her head to suffer his congratulatory kiss. Waking, she would think: God is trying to tell me something, but to the end of her life she would never be sure precisely what it meant.

She wasn't sure how she knew about her grandmother's wedding but she knew it in the same way she knew the rest of the family history; even though her frame was larger and her profile deviated from the others' she knew the Lyons, their lives in the house were stamped inside her, marking her to the bones. She knew that Lily and Thaddeus Lyon had knelt side by side on satin pillows in the old church in Charleston at the beginning of the golden age, there were banks on banks of white flowers and a Trumpet Voluntary and all the best families rustled and whispered in the walnut pews. Old Aunt Florence had stayed at the house during the ceremony, not because she disliked Thad Lyon but because, as she said, somebody had to see to the nuts and silver-frosted petits fours, somebody had to set the tapers alight and start the silver fountain bubbling with champagne. Nobody had told her so but Lila Melyn liked to believe that Uncle Harry had been the best man, jumping into the carriage with the couple at the last minute to ride off with them, lickety-split, into their new life. The picture showed only the two of them, Lily small and dark with a calla-lily shape and Thad strong and handsome; nobody had doubted that they would live together in happiness for the rest of their lives.

She used to brood over the pictures of her own mother's wedding, taken by a professional photographer and mounted in a satin-covered book; there were all her aunts and uncles looking better than they ever were in formal clothes, the women wearing headbands with central gems and egret sprays; the oblique light struck glints in the beaten satin dresses, and gleaming at the center was her mother Lila, encased in satin, pale and chaste as a new kid glove. Fifteen hundred people had come to see her marry Simon Millard in the National Cathederal, the reception was in the ballroom of the Wardman Park, and if Cora got too drunk and embarrassed the family it was to be expected, after all, those were the Twenties, everybody was too wild. Mama Lyon had been the first to say it but ever afterward all the Lyons would accept it, believing that none of them were really to blame for the tragedies, the foolish acts and petty disasters they created for the rest of their lives; after all, their breeding was beyond reproach, their rearing was the best Papa could afford, they could not be prey to weakness or foolishness, to evil or susceptibility to evil for they were Lyons; they had been betrayed by the uncertain times, the times alone were to blame.

From childhood Lila Melyn thought not about the details of the ceremony, which were to be assumed, but about life afterward; she would have somebody to lie down next to, some warm, comforting shape beside her in the bed, she could press her whole length against him for as long as she wanted to and so have someone to help her pass the night. If she woke in the dark, crying, she wouldn't have to wait for her mother and then cry harder, understanding that nobody was going to come; there would be somebody right there to ask her what was the matter and tell her it was going to be all right. He would be in rooms when she came into them and if she called his name he would not tell her to go away, the way her aunts did; he would look up and speak. If the details of the marriage were blurred in her mind, lost in the mists of hope, one thing was clear to her: never again would she have to be alone.

As it turned out, she was going to be married at nineteen to a man who would turn out to be something less than any of them had expected, standing before a Justice of the Peace in the shabby parlor of a waterfront hotel. Her groom would wear blue serge and she would have an aqua felt hat with feathers dyed to match, and aqua gloves chosen to bright her plain beige suit; she would stand proudly as her mother had stood even though she was almost twice her mother's size; she would be married with her eyes moist for want of love and her spreading bottom encased in gabardine.

243

Flodie was bitterly disappointed when she heard. She called Cora, saying, "You'll never guess. Thad just called."

Distracted, Cora said, "He's decided to give us all a hundred thousand dollars."

"Lila Melyn is getting married."

"Oh good. I can give her a kitchen shower, and of course she'll want Punk to give her away, we can have the reception at the club."

"Next week," Flodie said, with a vindictive satisfaction. "Somewhere outside of Washington."

"But she can't do that, all her friends are here."

"It seems the boy wants a little tiny wedding," Flodie said wearily. "I don't know."

"Well then Punk and I can give a party at the club when they come back from their honeymoon."

"They're not coming back *here*."

Cora hes°   °d, readjusting. "Well, we'd better get up there to make sure she ⌣ɹys something decent for the wedding. The pictures will have to be in all the papers here."

"She doesn't even want a white dress," Flodie said.

Without needing to discuss it, they had each secretly decided that the poor child *had* to get married; why else would she have her wedding in some out-of-the-way little town?

"Well, I hope it's somebody she met at college."

"Nell took the message, and you know how vague she is. I think he works in a gas station," Flodie said.

"Punk will have a fit."

"But he's going to school at night, or else he's going to start going to school at night." Flodie added, "Ranny says we all have to be very nice to him."

Cora's voice flicked like a knife. "What else would you *expect* Ranny to say?"

"Punk is no bargain either, and don't you forget it," Flodie said, but by that time Cora had already hung up.

Edward said he couldn't possibly afford a trip all the way up there just for a wedding, even if it was his only niece, and besides, what was the matter with her, why couldn't she do it down here, she could get married by a J.P. if she was so hellbent on being married by a J.P. but at least she could have a proper reception the way Mama would have wanted it with everybody's friends and all the

244

family coming to the house to meet her and the boy, after all, she was the last receptacle of the family name.

Cora said, "I think he's Polish."

". . . she could probably even wear our mother's gown."

"My God, Edward," Cora said.

"Well, her veil at least."

"I told you, she wants to be married in a tailored suit."

"Well I'm sorry but Vivian and I can't afford a trip all the way up there right now, not with Terence's lessons and the new car. You take her Mama's Chinese plates, you know the ones, those can be her present from Vivian and Terence and me, she always admired Mama's Chinese plates."

"She's going to need a hell of a lot more than Chinese plates," Cora said.

Naturally Edward called Nell about the plates, just to be sure they were earmarked as his gift and because he knew Nell could be counted on to wrap and mail them. She said,

"Oh Edward, isn't it wonderful?"

"Cora seemed to think he wasn't up to the mark."

"Of course he is," Nell said, "all our family have made good marriages."

"Of course we have," Edward said. "Well you just tell her how sorry I am I can't be there? I wouldn't miss it for the world, but it's inventory time at the market, and I'm going to have to be down there day and night."

"It's going to be a lovely wedding," Nell said.

She said the same thing to Cora the next day; Cora was waiting in the front hall with Flodie while Nell found the family cake knife and the punch ladle for Cora to take with her to Annapolis, or wherever it was. Rummaging in the silver drawer, Nell thought she ought to be flying up with Cora, instead of waiting to go in the car with everybody else; if she had the money she would run ahead so she could be there to help her niece or protect her; alone with the girl, Cora might hold up the fabric of her love for scrutiny and without somebody there to stay her hand she was just as liable to strike out, ruining it like a piece of muslin slashed with a razor blade. When she came back with the silver her two sisters were still where she had left them, standing in such uncompromising attitudes that she said, with some force:

"It's going to be a lovely wedding, I just know it."

"Honey, we don't know a thing about this boy."

Nell handed her the knife, saying firmly, "All weddings are lovely."

Flodie snorted. "And all brides are beautiful."

"It may be just dreadful," Cora said, "But if she insists on going through with it I might as well be there to see that it gets done right."

Flodie said, "I suppose no matter what you do it's going to be a little tacky."

"Flodie!"

Cora drew herself up, looking almost the mother of the bride in her pheasant hat and the tweed suit with the matching coat. "Well, I'm going to do my best."

Flodie had her hand to her mouth. "Lord, Cora."

"What's the matter?"

"For a minute you looked just like Mama," Flodie said.

I called up Uncle Thad first, since he is the one who is paying my way through college, and when I told him I was going to get married he didn't say How wonderful, but he didn't say, Who is he, which is what my aunts would say; Who are his people, as if that had anything to do with it. He said, Well, all right, as long as you think you know what you're doing, and then I said, He, uh, works in a gas station, and after he didn't hit the ceiling I said, Don't you want to meet him, but he only said, It doesn't matter who he is as long as you really want him, I wish I'd known that at your age; he has a voice that is sharp and dry, like static, and I thought I heard him saying, Lord knows I would be the last one to discourage you. I said, His name is Sim Stevens and we're going to be married a week from Saturday in this place we both like a lot, I was hoping you could come down for the wedding. Then there was this long, empty period, just telephone, and finally more static, Uncle Thad clearing his throat and saying, I'm sorry, that's not one of the things I do. I said, I'm going to ask the whole family, and he said, I know. He knew I would understand; he keeps to himself, he doesn't give much but he is always there, like a monument, if he had been my father he would have been there no matter what, he never would have let go of life the way Daddy did. He never makes promises either, the rest of them were always promising and promising, you could string out your

246

whole life on those promises and nine times out of ten whatever it was will never come; Uncle Thad doesn't promise, I'm not even sure he likes me, but it doesn't matter because I can count on him, if he tells me not to expect anything then I don't expect anything; that means that when he says something is going to be all right, then it really is going to be all right, and if he says he can't come to my wedding then he has good reasons, and that's all right.

I'm sorry but I'm glad, Uncle Thad is so small and neat and sort of contained that Sim could never measure up, next to Uncle Thad he is only going to look country and somehow *less,* but without Uncle Thad around to remind me what he could be, he can hold his own against the rest of them; I mean, he could live for a hundred years and never get that look Edward has, when Edward gives you that wet hand you have to pull away quick because he is probably sweating tears and in another minute they're going to rub off on you; Uncle Alden is cold and sad and Uncle Punk carries meanness like a fever but Sim is kind and I think he loves me, so I don't care what they think. At least there will be one Lyon less, Lord knows it's going to be hard enough on Sim, having to meet the rest of them all in a lump; they still scare me some of the time even though they're the only family I have and I've had all these years to get used to them, I mean, they have all gone to a lot of trouble for me and I love them all but it's easier to take them one at a time, you don't have to see that same face over and over with every one of them looking disappointed in you before you even know what it is you haven't done. Well it doesn't matter what they think this time, I don't care what any of them say, I'm going to marry Sim Stevens and he's going to love me, I can quit college and I won't have to worry about what I'm going to do when I graduate, I can stay home and take care of Sim, and when we lie down together nothing else will matter, I know it won't.

I used to think I would find somebody that looked like Daddy and it would happen the way Champy says it's supposed to, all lightning and hot flashes, You're beautiful, I love you, but now I'm not so sure it ever does; it isn't exactly who you meet it's when, and when you have been alone too long and you can't stand *not* being married another minute, somebody comes along that you think needs you and you need him. Sim isn't Daddy, he isn't even half of Daddy and I loved Daddy, I will never get over him, but for everything he was, he didn't have whatever it took to stay around and take care of me; he just left, and no matter what happens, I think Sim will stay around and take care of me. Champy says that isn't what it's for, but I'm not all that sure she knows, she has her father and two brothers and all those dates and I could talk for hours and never make her see because she doesn't know what need is; we have talked about everything, but there is no way for me to tell. We don't go around together all that much but we have roomed together ever since boarding school, and when the lights go out we lie in our bunks and talk about everything we know; first I tell and then she tells and then I tell, but we walk right past Daddy, we skirt around him every time and Champy doesn't know how close we've been; there is no way to tell her I still think I may bump into him around the next corner, and when I find him I can go back to being whoever I was before he killed himself and I started to change, not exactly change but fail; if he had stayed around maybe I would have grown up to be as quick and good-looking as Champy, I would be able to talk without turning red and I could even go into a room without worrying about bumping into things.

I don't really tell her about Sim either, she's seen him but she doesn't have to know that the first thing he wanted was for me to let him; she would say, Ha, I told you, he's only marrying you so he can get into your pants. Well maybe he did want me but I wouldn't, because you don't, and besides, Champy and I have talked and talked about it, what you did, what the man did, but I kept on worrying about whether I had it straight; I might get it wrong and Sim would drop me, or if I got it right he might say, OK, if you're *that* kind, it would give him an excuse to drop me; after we're married, then we'll be married, and it won't matter so much whether I get it exactly right because we'll have lots of time. Now that we're engaged he says he's glad, he says that kind of thing is important if you're going to marry somebody, so instead we go out in his car and we get as close as we can and then talk. Once I asked him if he ever and he said not with anybody you would care about, if they would do it with you before they were married then they would do it with anybody, and nobody wants to marry a girl who is That Kind.

I don't know, I probably would have been any kind of girl he wanted if it would make him marry me; I have lived in other people's houses for so long that I am sick for a place of my own; I have lived with women for so long that I am going to bust if I don't get someplace where I can hear a man's voice buzzing, and if I can't have a man in the room with me every minute then I have to be able to think one is about to come through the door; Champy has plenty of men so she can take her time, but I've been waiting all my life, I have been going around with my arms open, and if it wasn't Sim it was going to have to be somebody soon because I have been wandering for years and I have to find somebody to take my hand and lead me home. I used to sit in that damn dormitory, I would say goodbye to Champy and then hang out the window; after about two minutes she would come out three stories below with her hair shining and some boy stroking the sleeve of that beaver coat; Jacky or Arnold or Bill would bend slightly to open the car door for her and it always looked like forever, like the pictures in all those ads; I would have to watch them from inside my own body, stringy hair and to much behind. After they had driven away and I couldn't even hear the motor I would sit on my bed and think until my mouth watered, if somebody didn't come for me soon, not just somebody, *anybody,* I thought I was going to die. I would sign myself out for the movies and then I'd go down to the car Uncle Thad let me buy with what was left of Grandmother Millard's legacy and I'd put the top down and start to drive, I'd drive until midnight when we had to sign in and if it was a weekend I'd start out in the morning and drive, I drove until finally I ran out of gas around high noon last September and I pulled into some gas station or other and somebody in a coverall came out to help me and it was Sim.

He didn't know who I was, he didn't know I always turned red and bumped into things, he didn't even know how big I was because I was still sitting in the car; I had on my bandanna and my sunglasses and my favorite lipstick, Rosy Future; he smiled, so I guess from the neck up I looked pretty good. He took his sweet time and I didn't have anything else to do so I just sat there in the sun while he checked the oil and water and the battery, and then I sat while he did the windshield; he is big and rawboned and towheaded and he smiled and I smiled because I thought he was kind of cute, and when I drove off he said, Hurry back, hear? the way they always do. I came back the next day, Sunday, and the next Saturday; all we really said to each other was, I wonder if you would check the tires: me, and him: These back ones are pretty slick, how many miles do you have on this thing? He would say, Hurry back, hear? and I would say, OK. I didn't have to say any more right then and neither did he; I could go back to the dorm and think about driving out there the next time, and it didn't matter that he never said anything that mattered and it didn't even matter that Champy had a weekend date at Princeton or an invitation to the Winter Carnival six months ahead, I could sit around and think about Sim and after a while I could go back there and sit in the sun while he did things to the car. It didn't matter about him not finishing high school or working in the gas station because he liked me, when he saw me he would smile; even when I got out of the car and he saw how big I was he looked right at me and he still smiled, he was the only boy who has ever looked at me like that; we didn't know anything about each other, we hadn't even been anywhere together but I already knew that if he ever asked me I was going to marry him.

By the end of October he had run out of things to do to the car and it got too cool for me to sit outside so he invited me to come sit in the office with him, we could have coffee while he waited for the next car to come, and by the middle of November we decided it was silly for me to just come out and sit in the office like that, I could come when he was off duty and we could go to the movies or something, so we did that, and then we parked and he moved over and put his arms around me and he was so warm and strong that I thought I would die if I ever had to let him go; now we have been going together for almost a year, last month one of us said it was dumb for me to have to keep driving back and forth between the gas station and the college when I don't even like the college, I could be perfectly happy in his trailer, and one thing led to another and we decided to get married, and I don't know what my aunts are going to say but it's already settled and if they come up here and try to stop me I'll kill them, and besides, Champy says he's very sweet.

I don't know, she's big and she's warm and she loves me, so I decided why not? Besides, I'm tired of doing for myself.

Meeting her niece in the lobby of the shabby waterfront hotel, Cora ran forward and put her arms around Lila, big as she was, because she thought she ought to; after all, Mama had brought them all up to believe that all families were loving, all weddings were beautiful and a reunion, no matter how diffuse or diffident the parties, was always marked with an embrace and a kiss on the cheek. She may have been confused by Lila's response; the girl hadn't seen her aunt in some months and seldom thought of her, so that she was unpre-

pared for the moment's pause on recognition and then Cora's determined progress across the room, and, unprepared, was unable to
raise her arms in response and just barely remembered to offer her
cheek.

"Punk and Alden send all their love," Cora said, backing away
and looking past Lila. "Where's the lucky boy?"

Off-guard, Lila jerked her head as if to see who was standing
behind her. "Oh," she said in some embarrassment. "You mean Sim.
I'm sorry, he's taking next week off for the honeymoon so he has to
work every night this week."

"But of course he'll be off for the rehearsal dinner."

"Rehearsal dinner?"

"You know, the night before." Cora was busy with her gloves
but now she looked up. "The boy's parents give it." She saw that
something was wrong and she went on quickly, "It doesn't have to be
big."

Lila was working at her own gloves now; she had on a blue
tweed, a three-quarter length coat with a matching skirt, with a softer
blue sweater and a string of pearls; she looked very pretty for Lila,
but it could all crumple in just a few seconds unless they both
worked very hard, and there was lurking at the back of both their
minds the certainty that the wedding itself could collapse just as
quickly; because she had to, Lila said, for the last time speaking to
her aunt in complete honesty:

"Aunt Cora, I don't even know where Sim's parents are."

But Cora was already involved in the complicated work of suspension, saying, "Oh. Well. Well, I'll tell you what, Punk and I are
dying to give a party for you and we'll give the rehearsal dinner."

"But Sim can't come."

"For the rest of the wedding party, then, people expect a little
something when they've traveled all this way. You know, the ushers
and all."

"We thought we wouldn't bother with any ushers," Lila said,
because it would be too hard for her to say: I don't know whether
Sim has any friends.

"Oh, every wedding needs somebody," Cora said. "A best man,
at least. I know," she went on, already thinking how sweet it would
be, "Alden would adore to be best man, and Punk, Punk would love
to give you away."

"If you think he wouldn't mind," Lila said because she had no choice, "but I don't want a rehearsal party if Sim can't come. How about something after the wedding?"

"But your reception. The cake."

Lila blushed. "We were just going to have a drink and leave."

"Oh honey, *no*." Cora was already ransacking her purse for her jeweled reading glasses, a notebook, a small mechanical pencil, and she began making notes with a sense of importance for she saw now that if the wedding was going to come off she would have to bring·it off, she would have to see to the cake and the pianist and the nut cups and the napkins with bridal bells in silver because it was too late to have the couple's names put on, she was going to have to work from now to Saturday to get it right and if she could just remember everything then maybe it would be a lovely wedding after all, the marriage might even turn out and she would be able to point to it years later, saying, *It was all because of me.* "Get me the phone book," she said with relish, "we have a lot to do."

Lila was uncomfortable. "Aunt Cora, you don't need to . . ."

"Don't be silly, that's what family is for." She sat in the dusty lobby proposing, and because none of it mattered particularly Lila let her, thinking if she could just keep her aunt away from Sim until it was all over, everything would be all right. When Cora had it settled she lifted her head slightly, the light glinted off her glasses frames and her profile was so neat and hard that she looked for a second like an intelligent jeweled bug, waving the gold pencil and saying, "Now, where in God's name are we going to pick up a white dress?"

". . . but I don't . . ."

". . . a short white dress if you must, honey, but a white dress."

Lila drew herself up slowly, mottled pink with misery. "Aunt Cora, I'm sorry, I'm being married in a suit, I have it all picked out."

Cora gave her a quick, efficient glance, as if to see how this would affect her plans, and then made a tick on her pad. "Oh well, if you insist. Well, if you're wearing a suit, I'll have to pick up something that will fit in, I think corsages would be more appropriate than nosegays, don't you?" She looked at Lila so there would be no doubt; she had already written her speeches for Gemma and the other girls: *Just two young kids crazy in love, Punk and I stood up for them, it was the sweetest thing.* "I mean, for the matron of honor."

"Oh Aunt Cora, I . . ." Wanted Champy to do it. Lila was

watching her aunt carefully now; she wanted to do the wedding right, she had to do it right because no matter what she felt, no matter what she thought of them, this small jeweled woman and her two sisters and assorted uncles were the only family she had, and she had to be married in the bosom of that family because families always love each other and weddings are always happy, the one was going to follow from the other, so that without being sure why, she had to find some way to tell her aunt anything she wanted was all right; but Cora was already threading her way through the silence, saying, grudgingly: "That is, if you *want* me to."

"Of course I do," Lila said.

". . . but I do wish you'd give in and wear white."

"Please don't ask me any more."

Cora drew back, surprised by the force in the girl's voice, and then she recognized the expression she had seen too many times when Punk, teasing, had pushed the child too far; if she insisted, she might lose everything she had gained. It ought to be enough to say to her friends, "It was small but it was *sweet,* so much nicer than those big old weddings where the poor bride doesn't know a soul." So Cora reached out for Lila's hand but touched her sleeve instead, saying, "It's all right, honey, people always get upset at weddings, it's the strain."

They all met at the hotel first thing Saturday because of course it was a sweet little place but none of them really wanted to *stay* there, Punk and Alden and Randolph were going to entertain Sim in the lobby while her aunts took Lila upstairs to help her dress. There would be punch and sandwiches in the dining room afterward and then Lila and Sim would cut the cake and leave. Afterward Punk and Alden were going to take Cora to Annapolis for a baseball game at the Academy and Cora, watching the midshipmen in their khakis, all rising in the stands, would think: Why in God's name didn't she marry one of them; if she were an officer's wife we wouldn't have to worry about her any more. As it was, Sim was better-looking than she had expected, he reminded her a little of Lawson, but without Lawson's brutal callousness, so that he looked not only vulnerable but malleable, as if, punched in the right places, he might be prodded into an acceptable shape.

It should have been a happy occasion, the aunts giggling girlishly, helping their niece lay out the lacy underwear and seeing to it that she had the turquoise jabot right, but of course they were all tired and nervous and both Cora and Flodie were slightly hung over and perhaps a little put out with Lila for not getting married in her home town, which would have made it a better party and a lot less trouble for all. It might have worked out all right anyway, if Flodie hadn't looked at Cora over the slither of dress boxes, saying, "You weren't half so excited when I married Ranny," and if Cora, still put out about the white dress, had not snapped back: "Well, you weren't my favorite niece." Flodie was quick with, "You mean your *only* niece," but Cora was just as quick, with a charge from childhood: "That's not fair."

Lila was still powdering her shoulders, unaware, but Nell fluttered between her sisters in distress, knowing there was nothing she could say to stop Flodie, who was already on the attack: "You've never given Ranny the time of day." Cora fell into her familiar whine: "You know I wanted to do more for you, honey, it's just that Punk and Randolph never got along, and . . ." "And Ranny can't stand Punk. Come to think of it, neither can I," Flo said with satisfaction. "The way he treats everybody, the baby, for example." They both should have had the sense to stop then but they were too tired and spiteful and Cora said, "Well at least he never ran out on her the way you did, marrying any old second-rater just to get out of the house." Nell cried, "Flodie, Cora, *please,*" but Flodie was swelling as they watched, saying, "I suppose you don't see that *she's* marrying a second-rater just to get away from you." Cora smiled sweetly. "And you." They moved around Lila as if around a statue but now the girl rose, marbled and urgent in her lacy slip, saying, too loud, "I guess I forgot to tell you, Sim is only working in the gas station to earn enough to go back to college on the G.I. Bill." Nell said quickly, "That's wonderful," and Cora, still angry, turned on her niece, saying, "If you ask me, it's too late." "I'm going to work to put him through, he might go for an M.A." Flodie was saying, *sotto voce,* ". . . if you don't get stuck with a baby right off," but Lila Melyn went on in a rising urgency: "Or a Ph.D."

She could see them all sniping around her, in a minute the little knot of women would explode, sending shrapnel in all directions, and she could let them, she could tell them all to go to hell and walk away, she would run down to see Sim standing with her uncles in the dining room the sheep among the wolves, she would dart in and grab him and run away to someplace safe. Or she could let it be what they all needed, or expected, going downstairs with her jabot neatly arranged to please them all, with her least favorite aunt at her left, her matron of honor, and the other two following; she recoiled from them, she wanted to leave, but this was her family, she would never have any other, and if she cut herself off from her past with them then she would have to admit to herself that none of them had ever loved her, except Nell, and her life up to this point had been a waste, and if she did this she might lose her future too; unless she acquiesced to their vision she was going to have to scream and run; she might lose everything, she might even lose Sim, and she had to keep him, she had to have him at all costs. Flodie was at her left, crackling, Nell had put one pleading hand on hers, and she realized now that even if she was sure, she was not equipped to go anywhere; her knees were unsteady and she would have to run out in her slip. So, acquiescing, she sowed the seeds of later trouble, saying, to distract him: "Sim is going to be a college professor." Somebody else said, "That's wonderful," and so they were able to finish dressing her and they went on downstairs together, maintaining the fiction of a happy family wedding which they would be able to look back on with nostalgia in later, more rueful days.

It was a lovely wedding, really, they all stood in the dust-filled sunlight and the J.P. gave a little talk about the purpose of marriage and joined Lila's hand to Sim's with a look that made Flodie snuffle and poor Nell smile through a glaze of tears; even Punk was mild today, handing Lila over with a bemused look, dazed by the morning sunlight and fixed, perhaps, on some past moment none of them could see. The party afterward was as pretty as it could be, with white streamers on the table and the little family so concentrated on the ritual of the moment that none of them comprehended the beauty of the day: the clarity of the air, or the blaze of the water just outside. Lila's roommate came, Alicia Champlain in a dirty raincoat and sneakers; the aunts all loved her because she had such beautiful manners and besides, her father was important in the State Legislature; Sim was patient and very sweet, he worked hard to find something nice to say to every one of those relatives and Lila stood at his side in a dignity that reminded all the family of her mother; she smiled at them all, holding Sim's hand tight and letting them say anything they wanted because she was married now, she had somebody to lie down next to for as long as she could make it last; she had somebody to lie down next to even if only for a while.

IV

Lee

§§§§ §§§§

Entering the last third of his life, Thad spent most of his unoccupied hours listening; he filled his days as best he could and when the office closed and the last friend left his club he would go home, he would sit alone in his living room and after a while everything would stop: his breath would stop and he would be convinced his heart had stopped with it and he would sit, listening in a void, until at last his concentration was broken by some small sound, the refrigerator starting, or a noise filtering up all those stories from the street, and then with a rush in his ears it would begin again. Shaken, he would get up and pace, struck as he had never been before by an almost intolerable sense of emptiness, for he knew now that he was waiting; he was empty and all his life had been spent waiting for something to come and fill him up. He remembered those remote Sundays before the war, when he had tried to shore up against the hours his ritual pleasures and old friends, and he thought he understood more or less what he had been trying to do, but nothing he could find now seemed to serve the purpose. Now on Sundays he would go without expectations to a chic little church near his building, being over-generous at the offertory and giving the responses with some acerbity because he was still waiting, the fulfillment or whatever it was had not come; he began to play golf again for the first time since the war; trembling with embarrassment, he signed up for a twenty-lesson course in ballroom dancing. Although he was surprised by his own soft-headedness, he found himself turning back to his family, or the idea of family, and because he could not bear Edward or any of his sisters, he fixed instead on his niece, sending her a set of silver goblets from Tiffany's as a first anniversary present. She wrote to thank him with such warmth that his mouth watered with unexpected gratitude and she had added, more or less offhand: *Come down and visit us some time, we'd love to see you.* He debated for as long as he could make himself and then gave in and wrote, asking her when it would be convenient for him to come.

He was not sure what either of them would do when he got there but it had occurred to him that her parents were dead too, Edward was her uncle and his sisters were her only aunts, so she was no better fixed for relatives than he was; if they looked at each other and understood that, perhaps it would be enough. If it worked out, he could be concerned from a distance, an infrequent visitor to their marriage but one who had, at least, a marriage he could visit; he could send them presents at Christmas and carry their children's pictures in his wallet. He would have, at last, some species of family, rather, all the family he would care to have; there would be no responsibilities and no demands. He would ask nothing of them, except perhaps that when he died, Lila might come to New York and close his eyes.

Because he didn't want to make too much of it, he arranged to see several people in Washington on business, thinking that the conferences alone would justify the trip. When he had finished he checked out of the Hay-Adams House and rented a car and drove toward the Eastern Shore, consulting maps and asking at filling stations until finally he came to the crossroads she had indicated, and then he doubled back to the nearest store and asked again because he couldn't quite believe it; they were living in a trailer camp. Wary, he left his car outside the gate and went on foot between the rows of trailers, depressed by the tinny radio music and the unrelenting chatter that came at him from all those sordid little boxes on wheels, angered by the clothes drying everywhere and the women in pants with pincurls like snails nailed flat to their heads with bobby pins. He was depressed further by the obvious attempts to fix up the place, garish little window boxes and cheerful signs, reading: Bide-a-Wee, and Arnold's Acres, and, at the end of the last row, Stevens Rest; he faltered, thinking perhaps the best thing would be for him to go on back to the car and drive straight on to the airport; he could wire from New York, pretending he had been forced to cancel the trip. He would send her a pretty present, something practical instead of those damn silly goblets, something she could use in the trailer, to make her more comfortable while she did whatever it was that she did. But that was her name on the last sign, that was probably her face behind the tiny window, she may have seen him, and her trailer was set away from the others, surrounded by a ridiculous picket fence and flowering bushes and other signs of such hope that he knew he was going to have to go on in and go through with it. Just then she opened the door and he was surprised all over again to see how big she was, and more surprised to see that she was not at all embarrassed to have him see her here.

"Uncle Thad," she said, and she could have been welcoming him to the big old house, standing between the columns with outstretched hands, "I'm so glad you could come."

Inside, the place was as sweet and pretty as she could make it, with scraps of curtains at the window and little flowered cushions on a leatherette bench which looked as if it probably opened into a bed.

"And look, we even have a guest room, this opens out into a bed." Her face was huge and hopeful. "If you want to, you can stay here."

"That's very kind," he said, lying, "but I've already checked into a motel."

"Oh well." She blushed.

They talked, neither of them would remember about what, and after a while she said, "We'll eat as soon as Sim comes, he's got to wait for the night man to come on."

"Where is he working?"

She blushed again, and found it necessary to say, "It's just a temporary thing."

They were sitting more or less knee to knee in the tiny living space, she had pulled out a chair from somewhere and enthroned him and she was on the bench; she had managed some crackers and Camembert and an unopened bottle of Scotch for him. Feeling claustrophobic, enclosed in the flowered cushions and the tinny walls, Thad looked at his niece and past her for as far as his eyes were allowed to go; brought up short at the end of the trailer, he let his glance come back to her face. He knew that his mother, all his sisters had been overreachers, but he was so oppressed by the smallness, the *compactness* of the space in which this girl had chosen to content herself that he wished he could take her by the wrists and pull her outside with him, he would make her jump the tiny picket fence and run away; he wished there were some way to say to her, My dear, you have to want *enough*. Because there was not he said instead:

"Do you have everything you need?"

"I beg your pardon?" She understood him perfectly; when she looked at him her eyes were clear.

"I thought, if there was anything you wanted . . ."

"Oh, we're fine."

" . . . if you wanted to take a few classes, go back to the university part-time . . ."

She said, "Sim wants me at home for now."

He went on with an increasing sense of frustration. "If there's anything I can do, anything you need . . ."

"Oh no, Uncle Thad, we have everything we want and besides, Sim would never accept anything from anybody else."

She got up quickly, to cut off the conversation, and while he watched she began to prepare their dinner, opening a canned ham and surrounding it with lettuce and pineapple slices, putting a casserole into an oven he hadn't even noticed. He wanted to take them both out to a restaurant but she had already refused him, and so he watched her make her preparations, sighing as she opened a jar of crabapples and made up corn muffins from a mix. He wanted to say more but he knew she wouldn't let him, and so when she sat down again they talked about Cora and Nell and Flodie and Edward, exchanging scraps of information until they had run out of things to say; when they fell silent at last she refilled his wine glass and then they both sat; it occurred to him now that they were both waiting and he saw also, looking not at her midsection but at the rounded shape she made, head and shoulders and hips, that she was probably pregnant; he saw as well that there was nothing he could do for her, at least not now. She was contented, so preoccupied and self-contained that she would probably forget his visit as soon as he was gone; as for her adopting him, or him adopting them, he could see now that there was no point to it and no hope for it, but after all, he had never really expected it.

They sat in silence until Sim came; as he opened the door Lila started up, flushed with embarrassment: "Oh, Uncle Thad, I must have been daydreaming," and he murmured, "I must have dozed off." Then Sim was inside with them, blond and warm and even bigger than she was; she put her arms around him in absolute unselfconsciousness and then the two of them turned, hips bumping, so she could present him.

"Sim," she said, "this is my Uncle Thad."

The boy turned red and nodded, putting out a hand, and Thad stood to shake hands with him; his hand was big and warm, without any particular vitality or power, and Thad couldn't stop himself from thinking: God, if I were only this uncomplicated.

"Uncle Thad," Lila was saying, as if it were not only necessary but important, "this is my husband, Sim."

Looking at them, he thought he understood what she was trying to do; he didn't know why she thought she could accomplish it here, with this slow-moving boy, but he knew she was trying to make all the world she would ever need inside this trailer, and although she may have known as well as Thad did that it wouldn't last, he wished her luck with it for as long as she was able, or wanted, to hold it together. When he got back to New York he would send them a package of cheeses and fancy foods; patés and caviars were the only thing he could give them right now, if he wanted any assurance of acceptance.

FLODIE

Well I suppose it was my own damn fault that I lost him, there were too many people there, they were so thick you couldn't see the flowers, much less whoever it was you came with, and besides, I was mad at him about something or other so I kept hurrying on ahead and even when he caught up and tried to take my arm I would pull away, I didn't want him to walk with me, and then when it was time to go I looked back to see whether he was still following, I was going to say, Randolph, come *on*. He was there when we ran into Cora, he was there when we bought the bleeding heart, so it must have happened after we had the fight and I started hurrying on ahead; anyway, one of those times I wasn't looking, maybe it was *because* I wasn't looking, the son of a bitch just sort of faded away.

It was stupid of me to want to go to the garden show in the first place, we don't even have a window box, much less some place to put one of those marble urns, but Mama used to set such great store by it, and it's the one place I can still bump into some of the girls we used to run with, I put on my best flowered hat and when I bump into them I can be just as good as they are; we nod and nod, without really saying anything, and then we smile and smile. Besides, it is held in the Poulnot gardens, one of the few places I can still take

Randolph and say: See, Ranny, this is where we used to play. They took the LeFevres' for a shopping plaza, junior *and* senior sold out, they said they needed the extra acreage for the parking lot, at the prices they were getting the LeFevres would have been just as glad to throw in our house too; Mama used to talk about protecting our neighborhood, but I know by now that even the quality will sell out if the price is right. So they took the LeFevres', there is a six-lane highway running through the park where we used to ride our ponies, but even though the Chamber of Commerce bought the Poulnot house for state headquarters, they have kept the greenhouse and the garden just as beautiful as they ever were. From the outside the house looks more or less the same, except for the gold letters, and if you turn your back on the booths and the big-hat ladies with those poison smiles and baskets full of flowers, if you look down the lawn toward the river and squint your eyes, you can almost see it the way it was when we were little; Nell and Edward and I would come over to play with Clara, we would hide in the banyans and sooner or later we would lose Edward, if I shut out the music and the ladies jabbering I could almost hear him crying somewhere off in the trees.

So we were going along at the flower show, there was an exhibit from every single garden club in the state, and the greenhouse was full of orchids and prize plants grown by one Johnny-come-lately or another, there were hardly any names I recognized; I was thinking, if I had married Morris I could have stayed home and grown calendulas or Spanish bayonets. We had just bumped into Cora with that friend of hers, Gemma Farmer, I thought we might all go into the tea shop together for a lemonade, but Cora was in a terrible hurry to get to her dessert bridge, the way she treated me you wouldn't think we were long-lost sisters, you would think we had barely met. So Ranny and I went on down the walk, just like we had better things to do, and I was so upset we had to buy the bleeding heart, and then I carried that along, thinking, Lord, look what this has all come to. There were all kinds of rude people around, rich trash trampling the flowers, and it crossed my mind that they didn't belong here, I did, I might have married somebody else and come here to live; I might have lived here anyway, if Papa hadn't lost all his money when he did; it was the war, the land crash, by the time the Depression came there was nothing left to lose; I was thinking, God, we've got nothing left to lose, when out of a clear sky Ranny said, If it would make you happy, you could quit work and join one of these ladies' clubs. I guess I flew off, I turned on him and said: If I quit work, I couldn't afford to join *anything.* He went white around the mouth and I stepped out fast because otherwise he would try and make it up with me and I would end up crying in front of everybody, right there on the main walk to Clara Poulnot's house. So I stepped out without him, when I looked back he had stopped to look at the century plant, I could have told him he could stand there all day and all night and never see it bloom; I went on in to see the annuals, and when I looked around again there was no sign of him, I don't know where he had gone but he was gone.

Maybe if he had snapped back at me we could have had a fight, we would have had *something,* but Randolph would never be angry with me, he would never be *anything;* if I tried to pick a fight he would say, Honey, you know how I hate a fuss. I tried to get him to put himself forward more at the office, but he would only say, You can't always expect things to get better, honey, you ought to be grateful when they stay the same. Well maybe he was right, but it was so much the same that I couldn't stand it. We would get up and dress and eat and go to work and come home and Randolph would sit down with the paper while I made dinner. I would look out there in the living room and there he would be, sitting like a piece of furniture that you never should have bought, or a pet dog that has gotten too big to live in the house.

Oh, we got along all right, like brother and sister, or good friends, except that we did the one thing; maybe that was the trouble. Each time we did it I would think, If it were only better, or different, but it was always the same, it was probably his fault but there was no way to say anything because it would only hurt his feelings; I don't know, half the time it was like being married to nobody at all. I suppose that's why I married him in the first place, I looked at that face like a blank page and I would think: Once I get him, I can turn him into anything I want, but then we got married, it was like dripping castles in the sand, I would get him ready to ask for a raise or run for office and something would come along like a wave, WHOOSH, and whatever it was I hoped for would be wiped away.

So I got away from Nelly and the baby and our empty house, I got away from being an old maid but I didn't get *to* anywhere, as it turns out, except for the apartment, even Ranny said it was too damn small. I thought when Ranny got promoted I would quit my job and we would move to a pretty house over on the Drive where Cora lives. After he got to be division head we would move into one of the big old houses on the river, Cora would come to visit and when she got inside the door she would look up, at the chandeliers and the rising stairs; she would look around my gracious old home and she would feel smaller, the way I do every time I go into her house. I would give lots of parties, we would be surrounded by all the right people, they would call me Mrs. Askew but they would be thinking, Florence LYON; I would take the place I should have had years ago.

When we moved in the apartment I said, It's awfully small, Ranny, but he said, We'll move as soon as we have kids. We just never quite had them; I remember saying there were other things that were more important, we had to pay for the honeymoon, and we were saving for the club, when Cora proposed us we had to put up a bond, but it didn't matter how many times we had them over, we put up with Punk until we were blue, they would just thank us and that would be the end of that. We got a car but we never really went anywhere, and when Ranny used to say, Children, I would say, Money, or, The war, or, Randolph, there are more important things, but I can't remember exactly what they were. After a while I thought why not go ahead and have a baby, at least it would be something different for a change, but it turned out that whatever it was, the chance, we were so careful for so long that I guess we lost it, nothing happened, and that was Ranny's fault too, he should have fought me from the first. Then I thought maybe the job, here we were married all these years with nothing to show for it, and maybe it would be better if he was better at his job. Lord knows I did all I could, I even got a job somewhere else so I wouldn't show him up; I could work rings around him if I wanted to, but I didn't want to work all the rest of my life, I wanted him to be the one. Maybe I should have stayed around that office to keep an eye on him because he couldn't do it without me, he let all those opportunities slip by, he let everything slip by. I don't know, maybe if it hadn't been for the war, all those veterans came back and they all got promoted over Randolph's head. I said, Ranny, you've got to put up a *fight,* but he would only slouch down behind his paper, it happened every time I thought I had us headed somewhere. Every time I had him lined up for a promotion he would just let go. I don't know, I got married, I got out of the house, what else did I want? Whatever it was, I never got it, Ranny was never enough. Maybe nothing is ever enough.

When I lost him at the flower show my first thought was the river, in my mind I threw up my arms and started screaming, I've lost somebody, *Help,* but in my mind I could see all those flowered heads turning to stare. They would rush toward me and suddenly Ranny would turn up after all, he would have been somewhere: looking at the herbs, or behind a bush. He would say, What's the matter, honey, I was right here all the time, and I would be humiliated, right in front of everyone. So I didn't call for help, I didn't even go and look for him, I would be bound to run into somebody and they would say, What's the matter, Flodie, did you lose something? Or they would say, What's the matter, Nell, and I would have to say, I'm *Flodie,* and my husband's lost; it would be too embarrassing, and so I just went along home without Randolph, and stayed up half the night waiting dinner, because I thought he had just stepped out for a minute, in another minute he was going to come.

He didn't come, he had just faded away. It was like being married to nobody, you go along for years without really noticing a person, and after a while they just fade away. The only trouble was, I began to miss him, I had his *absence,* which was worse than having him around. I waited all night for him to come, I was just sick, and the next morning I thought about calling the office to tell them he was sick and then I thought: What if they say, He's not sick at all, Mrs. Askew, he's right here at his desk. I couldn't stand the shame. I thought about calling Cora and then I thought, she would smile that sleek cat smile and say: So he finally got away. Well she could go to hell. Nell would never say a thing to hurt me, it would just remind her of Cleve and if she cried I would end up crying and I couldn't stand the idea of the two of us moaning around together, just like the old days, so I kept it to myself, and when Cora called up out of the blue to ask Randolph and me to a party at the club, the *club,* I just squinched up my eyes and pounded my fists on my thighs and told her no, we couldn't, Ranny was in bed with the flu. So I didn't call the office, I didn't call anybody, I just ate alone and went to work and came home and ate alone and went to bed and thought eventually I would hear. He would be in the hospital, they had found him behind a bush in Clara's garden, he had been stricken with some disease; either that or he had been run over by a truck. I kept thinking I would wake up and find him in the bed beside me, I had imagined the whole thing; I might hear a knock, I would go to the door and there he would be, covered with shame and explanations, either that or he would be covered with honors, presents for me; he would say, My God, Florence, there's been a terrible mistake.

I didn't call the police, either, not until Ranny's boss called from the office, it took them two weeks to notice he was missing, *two weeks*. I said Mr. Askew was under the weather but he hoped he would be in to work on Monday, I would do my best, and then I knew I had to call the police. I had been putting it off because I knew what would happen, they would say, When was the last time you saw him, and I wouldn't be able to remember, exactly, whether it was looking at the century plant or one of those times when I wouldn't let him catch up with me, maybe I had looked back and seen him hurrying after me, red in the face; maybe it was when he caught up and I tried to pretend I didn't know who he was. They would take down my story and they wouldn't say anything but I could see it in their eyes: Couldn't keep your husband, could you, lady? Five'll get you ten he ran away.

He didn't run away, he would never run away. He just disappeared.

As it turned out they were very nice about it, they never accused me. They brought him back as if that kind of thing happened every day. The policemen came to the door and said, Is this your husband, lady?

I looked at him, it had been two weeks but he looked the same, blank and a little confused, and I said, Yes, that's my husband.

They said, Found him in the railroad station, he wasn't in his right mind.

I guess I was supposed to do something or say something but I didn't, I just looked at Randolph and Randolph looked at me.

I must have looked like I wasn't going to take him in or something because the sergeant put his hand on my arm and said, He's all right now, Mrs. Askew, you'd better take him on inside.

I said, Of course, but I guess I still couldn't move. He finally pushed Randolph on into the living room and then he pulled me out in the hall and whispered, behind his hand:

It happens all the time, lady. People disappear. Be glad you got him back.

I am glad, I am.

He winked. Remember, he wasn't in his right mind.

If you say so, I said, and closed the door. Then I turned to

Ranny, he was just standing in the middle of our living room with his hands hanging out of his sleeves, I said, Oh, Randolph.

He said, I'm sorry, Florence, I wasn't in my right mind.

I said, I know you weren't, or you wouldn't have done it.

He said, I had amnesia.

I said, I know you did.

I guess I was supposed to run over and hug him but I couldn't, I was standing there with the front door closed behind me and all those two weeks jammed up together with the two of us in that room, I kept thinking about the misery, the embarrassment, I remembered how the police sergeant had tipped me the wink and I looked at Randolph and he looked at me. I knew better than to say anything, but I had to, I looked him in the eye and said: You didn't have amnesia.

He didn't even have the grace to hesitate, he said, No I didn't; he said it without even taking time to draw a breath.

I said, Oh, Randolph.

I'm sorry, Florence, I just couldn't stand getting up every morning and having everything the same.

I thought you liked having everything the same.

He didn't say anything, he just blushed.

I said, You mean, having me the same.

He said, I'm sorry.

About running away, or about being married to me?

I could see he didn't want to go on, but he did, he seemed to have to: Both.

I was backing now, trying to find the right thing to say; he was fighting back and it made him look better, much better, I thought: If I only had a plan. I put out my hand, to make him come to me, and when he wouldn't come I said, I'll be better, Randolph, I'll . . . I know, we'll get a dog.

He was very quiet, he looked bigger than he had for a long time; I couldn't believe it when he said, No, I think we are going to get a divorce.

So I'm living home now, I see him every once in a while when I'm on my lunch hour, he looks thin and younger, I think he's going with one of the secretaries; he's bought himself a plaid sports jacket and he even has a snap-brim hat, and it is like gall and wormwood to me to see him like that, why didn't he fall in the river if he was going to do this to me, why didn't he have the decency to get run over by a truck? I kept it to myself as long as I could, and after it went to court and got in the papers I tried to go along as if nothing was really different. I hung onto my job and my apartment and I kept myself to myself, I would get up and eat and sit all alone in that well of bitterness, until finally Nelly came to see me and she said, You're silly to sit up here in your pride, when you could be so comfortable at home, and I wanted to say, What do you know, get out, but I looked at her and she looked at me and we both broke down and cried. Well I was tired of the apartment anyway, everything we had was tacky, tacky, and the ceilings were too low.

LILA MELYN

I love him but he's slow, he hasn't got a mean bone in him but sometimes he's so slow it drives you crazy. I'll tell him something and he doesn't understand it, he just looks at me with those wide, mild eyes, either that or I think he understands and when I ask him about it, it turns out he wasn't even listening. There we were in that tiny trailer with a new baby and no room to turn around; I saw it wasn't going to work as soon as I got home from the hospital, but when I tried to tell him, he never even heard. Her things were all over the place and when she cried the whole trailer seemed to fill up until there wasn't any room for me. Champy came out to see the baby and I could see how nervous it made her, she crossed her legs and chewed her cuticles and finally she said, I can't stand it another minute, bring that baby and let's go out for a drive. I couldn't stand it either, I used to wrap her up and take her places, once we spent the day in the dorm with Champy, I put her in Champy's bottom drawer and the two of us almost forgot about her, we sat there on the beds and talked about everything I had missed for the whole last year. Another time I took her to an art exhibition, I had to carry her around to look at all those paintings because they wouldn't let me take the carriage inside; we used to go shopping a lot, I would drive to the nearest town and we would go around to all the stores. When it got really cold outside it was a lot worse; we had to be inside a lot, and if I didn't get to the Laundromat to dry the diapers I would have to hang them inside, sometimes it seemed like there was nothing in the world but the baby crying and all those steamy diapers, hanging like shrouds. When I got to one of the windows it would be covered with sweat and I would have to wipe it off before I could even see outside. At first I used to try to tell Sim, but it was so much with me that I thought he felt it too and I didn't need to say anything more; I was scared to death he would think I was a nag. Maybe he really didn't notice, he was gone all day and by the time he came back the baby would be asleep and I would have everything put away, but Lord knows I told him enough times.

Then on our anniversary we put the baby in the back of the car and went to a drive-in for dinner and then stayed out for a drive-in movie; when we got back I looked at that trailer, I thought, Dear Lord, I can't go back in there, I just can't, and I stood outside and started to cry.

When he asked me what was the matter I said, If we have to live here one week longer I'm going right out of my mind.

He just put his arm around me and said, Why honey, I thought you loved this place; he was so surprised I wanted to shake him, you'd think I had never mentioned it before. Then he said, Don't cry, honey, we'll see about it, I promise, and then he put both arms around me until I said, I'm OK, and we went inside.

Now the baby is a year old, and I think she probably looks like my father, dark-eyed and quick; she has soft brown hair and a beautiful face and when she looks at me I can see what she's telling me: You're letting it all go by, I am going to grow up to be beautiful, and you're already getting old.

We were still in the trailer and finally I decided to take things into my own hands. I waited until we were in bed, with my head on his arm, and I said, Sim, I'm going to take the baby down to see the family, we'll be back when you find us a decent place to live. He didn't listen, he only buried his face in me and said, Oh, honey. I don't think he believed I would really go. I let a few more weeks go by and when nothing happened I made the reservation, maybe I thought when he saw we were really going he would rush out and find something but he didn't, he just looked at me and said, Honey, what's the matter?

I said, I told you I was going, I've been talking about it for weeks.

He said, I thought that was just talk.

Just *talk*. I was crying, I said, All these weeks, and you haven't even tried . . .

He was looking at me the way he does, he lets his head drop between his shoulders, like a bull, or an ox; he should have put his arms around me or apologized, anything. Instead he said, I didn't think you really meant it.

Well, I flew off, I said, Of course I meant it, what if I didn't come back, it would serve you right if I went off and never came back.

He didn't put his arms around me even then, he just sighed the way he does and said, Oh honey, you know you'll be back.

I didn't want to admit it but it crossed my mind that I might not go back, I would get down there and see how it was in the house, I think I thought the house could hold us all; I would ask Uncle Punk or somebody to find Sim a job and then the three of us could just move in; we would live there alongside Aunt Nell for as long as we needed to, without ever getting in each other's way. Sim would like it when he got there, maybe he could get something better than this mechanic's job; I would almost rather see him up in the front of the lot in a checkered suit, selling cars. When we left he promised to wire as soon as he found something, but the baby and I have been down here for a month now, and the only time I hear from Sim is when I call him up. I would ask him to write but I can't bear to get his letters, they're like letters from a child. I thought once we got settled I could get him enrolled in night classes, if he kept at it he could end up with a college degree, but I'm beginning to wonder whether we'll ever be settled anywhere; when I call him I talk about everything *but* that, waiting for him to bring it up. He never does, so I have to ask him, finally: Have you found a place? Then he sounds tired, or pained, as if I do nothing but nag him about it, and he says, Honey, I'm doing the best I can.

When we came in on the train the town had changed so much I hardly recognized it; there are two new bridges over the river, and the railroad tracks are lined with factories now, where there used to be just the patent medicine plant and the sneaker factory. Somebody has put up a housing project about a half-mile from our house, I came by in the car on the way in and saw little colored children playing outside on the doorsteps. The buildings were all painted white with little bushes out front, everything looked so fresh and hopeful that I couldn't understand why Aunt Flodie was so upset about it, she just set her jaw and drove on by. I felt a lot worse about what has happened to the house next door; it's been a rooming house for as long as I can remember but somebody new has bought it, they've taken off the portico and put in some glass bricks to make it look modern, and there's even a neon sign now, it says, RIVER ROAD HOUSE: GUESTS. They've cut down the big tree in front of our house, Aunt Flodie says the city did it, it was interfering with the wires, but we have two new places to eat in the neighborhood and my first night home, Aunt Nell stayed with the baby while Aunt Flodie and I went out to the new movie house around the corner; there is a luminous mural and the seats roll back so people can get in front of you without bumping your knees. Still my room looked the same as it had before I went away to boarding school, and Aunt Nell has fixed up the room across the hall for the baby, with lavender walls and a little bassinette with a lavender quilt; I didn't have the heart to tell her the sides were so low the baby was going to fall out on her head almost any minute, and now every time I put her away I have to push it against the dresser and put chairs all around to keep her in, and half the time I get so worried that I get up and bring her into the bed with me. It's so strange, being in my old room with my own baby, I slept here alone for so long; I thought what it would be like making love with Sim in this house where nothing has happened to anybody for so many years, I thought I could ask him to come down as soon as he got his vacation, and when he saw how nice it was he would want to stay.

I guess I was so taken with the changes and all the rest that I didn't see what else has been happening. I came down here with the idea that this was my home and these were my people, I would slip back into my place and everything would be more or less the way it ought to be. Sim would come to be part of it too, and our baby could grow up in the same house where her great-grandmother lived, and brought up her grandmother and all her great-aunts and uncles; maybe I actually thought they were all down here waiting for us, imagine, all the Lyons that are left sitting around waiting for the baby and me. I know when the train came in I was so anxious to see them all that I could hardly breathe. I suppose I thought they would all be at the station to meet us, either that or somebody would pick me up and everybody else would be waiting at the house. I would let them all kiss me and then I'd set the baby down on the rug and she would take at least two steps before she sat down; when she does that her skirts look just like a flower, and even Uncle Punk would have to say how beautiful she was. I couldn't expect much from Vivian, she would be jealous when Edward touched the baby's hair and said, Why, she looks just like Mama; then somebody, probably Aunt Nell, would say, Oh, *aren't* you glad they're here. Well of course we haven't seen a hair of Edward and it took weeks for Aunt Cora to get around to us, I should have remembered that was the way it used to be. But there have been changes nobody will talk about; Aunt Flo came to meet me and she wouldn't talk about Randolph, it turns out she is living with Aunt Nell in the house, and Aunt Nell has gotten thinner, she at least was glad to see us, but when she hugs me or the baby her arms twine around us like vines and I wonder if she will ever let us go. When I finally did see Aunt Cora I could see she has lost her figure, it is all pulled in and pushed out in the same old places, but she is thicker by several inches, I don't think she even knows; there is something the matter with Alden, he's gone white and he looks so frail that I wonder if he's going to make it, but none of them will talk about it, Aunt Cora and Uncle Punk keep him up late and drag him around to all the parties and try to pretend he isn't sick; only Uncle Punk is more or less the same.

I don't know why I expected anything of Punk in the first place, I suppose when you don't have anywhere to turn, you'll pin your hopes on anything that will stand still long enough. I was dying to see him as soon as I got settled, I wanted to ask him what he could find for Sim, but I had to wait around for weeks before Aunt Cora got worked up to ask us over; she called once the night I got there and had some nighties sent over from the store, they were too fussy-looking for a baby and the baby is already much too big for them. I suppose she thought she could get away with that, but I called up last week, and I hung on the phone until finally she had to invite me over just to get me off the line. I thought I would take the baby but Aunt Nell offered to keep her at the last minute, she said after all, Punk and Cora have never been able to stand children, and Lord knows that's the truth. They keep that damn dog of theirs on the end of their bed at night, he's so old now that he smells bad, and there's a filthy spot on the living room couch where they let him sit. Nobody seems to notice when he forgets himself and wets the rug, but as soon as I came in Uncle Punk said, Well, Lana Turner, what's that on your coat? I looked down and said, Oh, I guess it's something the baby spilled, and he made a terrible face and turned away, you would have thought I'd brought a dead rat into the house. It was a little better when I followed Aunt Cora out into the kitchen, we talked about housekeeping and recipes, but she didn't want to hear about the baby at all.

After dinner we went out into the living room, and when I sat down in the wing chair she said it was high time I started calling her Cora, Aunt Cora made her sound too old. Then she said it would be lovely to give a shower for the baby at the club, so I thought that was as good a time as any to bring up Sim; I had to ask Uncle Punk about him before he could get too drunk and go on up to bed. I should have known better, he wouldn't even listen, he started calling me Lay-la, Lee-la, Loo-la, the way he did when I was in high school because it always made me mad. Then he said, Where *is* your boyfriend, honey, and when I said, Back home, he said, Ah-ha-*ha,* he looked like that little man on the front of *Esquire,* with the moustache and the leer. I kept at it because I had to, I tried to explain about Sim measuring up to any job he started, if he could just find something better to *start* with, but when Uncle Punk said, So your boyfriend couldn't take care of you, I got furious, I thought maybe I had gotten old enough to stand up and give him hell for once, but before I could open my mouth he had kissed Aunt Cora on the forehead and started up to bed. When he was gone Alden came over and stood by my chair, saying, Maybe I can do something for him, what sort of training has he had. I had to say, None; Aunt Cora got embarrassed and went out in the kitchen to do the dishes, but Alden stayed and said, I may be able to find him something, I still have a few connections, but he looked so frail that I knew I shouldn't depend on him, it was going to be hard enough for him to keep on going, without something extra to have to worry about. I found out by accident that he's only going to the office half a day now, he went out to the bathroom during dinner and Uncle Punk started to complain about it, Aunt Cora had to shush him before Alden came back and heard. I thanked him for offering, and said if there was anything he could do I would certainly call on him, and when Aunt Cora came back with the Cointreau and three snifters, I said I had better be getting back and it certainly was nice to see them all at least once before I went home.

I have to go home; there is nothing for me here. Besides, when I got back from Aunt Cora's, Aunt Nell had the baby up, there it was ten o'clock at night and she had my baby sitting on her lap in the kitchen, big as life, she was feeding her a Hershey bar. I said, Oh, Aunt Nell, you know that isn't good for her, but she just held the baby tighter and said, It won't hurt her just this once. I suppose I was keyed up from playing footsie with Punk all night, I tried to take the baby from her and the baby started to yell, Aunt Nell looked like she was about to cry too, she said, It's only a little chocolate. I could hear my voice getting bigger, I yelled, Well she can't have it; she said, She was so sweet, she begged for it so I had to let her have it just this once, and the baby was going mu-mu-muh and trying to hang on to her. I thought we would all be crying in another minute so I handed the baby back to her, saying, All right, all right, just this once. I thought that would be the end of it but she took that baby away from me with such a hungry look that it scared me, I knew I was going to have to get her out of there. I know Aunt Nell means well, she's always been all love, but I have to have my way with my own baby, she's my baby and for all I know she's all I'll ever have. If I have to go back and live in that trailer to keep her, then I'll go back and live in the trailer. I love Aunt Nell, I might as well admit she's the only one who's ever cared one single damn about me, I know she means well but Lee is my baby, and I have to get her out of here.

§§§§ §§§§

Perhaps the thing that troubled Alden most about his illness was the fact that all his life he had hated mess. Lying in the hospital, he knew perfectly well how disgusting it was for Cora to have to clean up the bathroom after he had haemorrhaged; at the time he had been troubled by that prospect almost as much as he had been by the helpless loss of so much of his blood. He had kept his lips together and tried to contain it, even as they had all tried to contain his illness for so long, ignoring the diet because it was too much trouble for Cora to have to cook two meals every time they sat down at the table and besides, the food he was supposed to have was so bland and boring that the sight of it would have depressed them all. He had the idea that refusing Cora's dinners would be like refusing all the years they had spent together in mutual independence, and so he had preferred to sit down and eat whatever Cora served him; it would have been degrading to have to say, looking at her curry or her exquisite paella, Oh, I can't eat that. When the pains troubled him too much he would come to the table with a can of Metrecal, offering the fiction that he was watching his figure; Punk would poke a finger at his ribs, saying, I wish Cora would take some of your skinny pills; then Cora would bridle and the three of them would laugh. And so they had gone on for as long as they could, pretending there was no illness. Alden would not let them see him wince and he would sneak away to take his medicine, concealing all the details with the idea that if only he could keep it all hidden, the illness itself might cease to exist.

Instead it escaped him, coming out in a rush of blood, and at the time it crossed his mind that it might be better if he let it all out at once; then they would come to the door in the morning and find him dead, it would be a terrible mess for them, but at least that would be the end of it. But Cora heard him choking after the first rush and scratched at the door, whispering, Are you all right? He wanted to tell her to go away, he wanted to call out, I'm just fine; after all, none of them were ever sick, but he was strangling, and when he didn't answer she opened the door and saw the blood and threw her arms around him, crying, "Stop it, *stop* it." Sobbing, she called an ambulance and he was on his way to the hospital within minutes, already too late to die. Through the worst hours he would carry with him the cameo of Cora's face after they got him onto the stretcher; she was blanched and distraught, trapped in helplessness, and in the deeps of that first night of his illness he vowed without knowing how he would achieve it that he would never again let her look at him that way.

For the first week or so after the operation both of them visited him twice a day, Cora with a pile of magazines and silly presents, Punk proffering a flask of martinis which Alden would have to re- fuse; exasperated, Punk would say, "But it's the best medicine in the world," and then Cora would pat Alden on the knee and say, "Now Punk, you leave my boy alone." Then together they would lay elabo- rate plans for what they would do as soon as Alden got well and then after a while they would forget him, nattering to each other about the business of the day. Finally the nurse would come with the bedpan, releasing them; Punk would back out in hurried embarrass- ment, leaving Cora to bend and kiss Alden on the ear, whispering, "This is a terrible place, I can hardly wait until you get out of here." They had already agreed that he should not come straight home; it would be better for him to go to a convalescent home until he was fit, they would know just what to do for him. Once he was moved, Punk came less frequently; he had always said hospitals made him nervous, so naturally Alden would understand. Cora was faithful, coming every day, but only at mid-afternoon, when it would not interfere with her routines. She always brought him a present, coming in full of vitality and smelling of the out-of-doors. She still talked about what they would do as soon as he got out of this place, but lying on the hospital bed with all its cranks and apparatus for his comfort, conscious of the stiff linen and the rubber sheet underneath, Alden found it hard to pay attention to her; he thought he was seeping into the bed, becoming one with it, and he found it impossible to conceive of any sort of future, or to care what happened next. When Cora talked about what they were going to do next summer, he closed his eyes and tried to go along with her, thinking dutifully of summer, but it meant no more to him than childhood dreams of going to the moon.

"You have to get better," she said one day, clutching his hand until he winced.

Blinking, he sat up to look at her. "Of course I'll get better."

They both knew by then what the surgeons had found; he would get better, he might even get well enough to live out another year at home with her and Punk, but he would never be himself again, he would need close attention and constant help; he would need at least some measure of help for whatever was left of his life. "I'll be out of here in no time," Alden said.

To his surprise, Cora burst into tears.

"Cora, Cora, it's not that bad. Nothing is that bad."

She kept on crying. "I don't know how to tell you."

"What, Cora. What is it?"

"Poor Maurice." She was fumbling in her purse. "I brought you his collar."

"What's the matter with him?"

"We hated to do it without asking you, but he was so sick." She was sobbing.

"He was old, Cora. What happened?"

"He was so pathetic." When she spoke again Alden could hardly hear her; she said "We had to have him put away."

"I see," he said, and he did see; he didn't know how they would manage it, or how they were going to break it to him, but he would never go back to their house. (Later, he would sit propped up in a brass bed, looking with failing sight around an unfamiliar room. Downstairs a dumpy middle-aged woman would move around her kitchen, making trays for him; she would care for him and she would care for him well, because she was doing it for pay and, further, because she had a good heart and tried to imagine how he felt. Later, in that strange bedroom, Alden would wonder whether he would have fared better with blood relatives, whether, after all, he should have taken that dangerous step and married, but he would never know because he had never wanted the responsibility. Fair's fair, he would think, in the intermittent lulls in his depression and pain.)

"He's had a good life," Cora said on that day in the convalescent home. "He was so sick, it was the only thing we could do."

"Yes," said Alden, wondering what excuses they had made to themselves, understanding finally that in all his life he had never loved anyone well enough to take him into his home, ailing; he had chosen to remain autonomous, with nothing given and nothing asked, and it was because Cora and Punk had permitted this that he had made his solitary life in their home. He had never accepted anyone in toto, with misfiring bodily functions and apprehensions and pain, not even them, and because he could never give this kind of love he knew he had no right to expect it from her or anybody else.

"Poor Maurice," he said, because she was waiting. "It was the only thing you could do."

§§§§ §§§§

It seemed to Edward that the little stucco house didn't really belong to him; he had reconciled himself to the mortgage payments, he would be making them all his life, but he had assumed that once he was in the house with his things around him, it would be more or less his own. Instead he felt like an intruder. He hated coming home, the rooms were too small and filled with Vivian and Terence; he imagined he heard them talking about him behind closed doors. He would look at Vivian, wanting to cry: What do you *want* from me? Whatever it was, he suspected it was almost accomplished; he might as well be a mote of dust for all he saw reflected in her eyes.

There seemed to be no place for him; if he wanted to read the paper in the living room, Terence would be lying on the couch with his feet up, or Vivian would come in to clean. If he moved to the dining ell she would want him to move so she could set the table. If it was fair he could take a folding chair out to the carport, but more often than not Terence would be there, polishing the car with professional verve, making it obvious that Edward was in the way. Terence worked with his shirt off and everything, his competence, even the lines of his body would be a reproach to Edward because he had filled out, his stomach was tight and his hair crackled; he measured off Edward's life like a yardstick, saying, with never a word: You are getting old.

Most nights Edward had to sleep on the tweed jackknife couch in the living room. The two tiny bedrooms had a common wall, and whenever Edward snored or turned in the spool bed, trying to embrace his wife, Terence would thump on the plasterboard and Vivian would turn with her hair down and the color high on her cheeks and whisper: "He's a growing boy, Edward, he needs his sleep." So on week nights Edward would creep in from work some time after midnight and put himself to bed on the couch, lying down in his pajamas and grappling with a blanket which he could never get to cover him satisfactorily, no matter what he tried.

Weekends were more complicated, because Edward was around the house all day, and he had to be quiet in the mornings so Terence could sleep. At night the boy would have friends in; Vivian had fixed up the other bedroom with posters and a record player, but Terence never seemed to like to use it. Instead he and his friends sat around the living room in tight bleached jeans and figured shirts, fingering ducktail haircuts and not looking at Edward when he spoke. Once he heard a tongue click and looked back to see one of the boys watching him; the boy dipped his head as if to say: Poor sap. Edward would beg Vivian to go out to dinner or a movie because he knew it would be hours before the boys left and he could go to sleep. She would let him take her out but the boys were always there long after they got back and Vivian retreated to her room; Edward would have to go to Terence's room, catnapping on the spread with his shoes on until Terence woke him, saying with contempt: "You can come out now, Edward, they're all gone." The studio couch would be permeated with cigarette smoke and greasy from fragmented potato chips, and Edward, too tired to get his pillow from the closet, would have to lie down with his cheek pressed against the stale upholstery.

He was surprised to find that Vivian hated the parties as much as he did. They were both hiding out in the bedroom, Vivian buffing her nails by the window, Edward sitting off-balance on the edge of the bed.

"Vivian, it's getting to be too much."

She said, "That music is enough to drive you out of your mind."

Edward went on, encouraged. "If you spoke to him, Vivian. He won't listen to me."

Vivian's eyes were blue and distant. "Let him have his fun, it's more than we ever had."

Edward knew he was on dangerous ground but he pressed on. "Sometimes I think all you care about is that boy." His breath left him and he rocked, vertiginous.

Her eyes frightened him. "Edward, he is my own flesh and blood."

He sat in absolute silence, and when she did not go on to compare, or attack, he thanked his stars and got up, saying, quietly, "I guess I'll go on to bed."

"You do that," Vivian said.

So he curled up on Terence's bed until Terence rousted him out and then he went to the couch, thinking this would have to do until the boy finished high school; then he would see to it that there were some changes made because he knew he had to have more room.

Still that wasn't the worst thing. What bothered Edward most was that every time he left the house, even for a few minutes, he would find that Vivian had done away with every trace of him. The pier table was in storage now; the three-legged chair was in the attic and he was not sure what had happened to the Chinese plates or the Dresden set, and while he was out Vivian would have emptied all the ashtrays and pounded his imprint from the pillows, throwing out the evening paper and putting away his crossword puzzle books, and if he wanted to see any trace of himself he would have to take out Papa's watch; Thad had refused it, perhaps seeing that Edward could not take his eyes off it, and so it had come to him.

He had bought the crossword puzzle books in the hopes of finishing something for once; if he could just get one done then he could put it aside, saying: There, but he had never in all his life been able to say: There, not about anything. Even when Vivian didn't throw away the puzzle books he couldn't seem to finish one, they were so hard, and he never finished the by-the-numbers painting Terence had gotten for Christmas and handed over to him with a derisive grin, and he could never finish anything at the hotel, either; he began to think of himself as a clump of loose ends, all dangling like cords from the hotel switchboard, he would just begin to get one of them taken care of when another would let go. Harassed by phone calls and messages, he would watch the mail and the keys pile up, and by the end of his shift he would be running back and forth from switchboard to counter to boxes with his eyes wide and his arms flashing and when the midnight clerk came on, Edward would greet him with a little whimper of relief, reading his eyes as he did so: How could you let things get in such a mess?

Despite all this, Edward had his hopes. Like his mother he had lived all his life on expectations and so he refused to deal with any particular day as he lived through it but thought instead about next year. Next year Terence would be ready for college, and Edward knew that once Terence went off to the University there would be more room for him in the house, there would be more room for everything; there would be no more glances and whispers, no sour words lying unsaid in the corners of the rooms. Vivian would quit work and when he came in she would be glad to see him. Since he would only be home for the holidays, Terence could sleep in the living room: Edward would be back in the spool bed and he would have made Terence's room into a study. He might get down the three-legged chair and the Chinese plates from the attic; he would take the pier table and his other things out of storage and make the room into a proper setting where he could sit up late, drinking port and talking to his wife like any gentleman. He had his hopes for Terence too; he had never been able to get the boy to take the Lyon name or call him anything but Edward, but once he went to college, Terence would in some small way assume a part of the family responsibility, he would be Edward's accomplishment and as such would have accepted the charge. Edward would be able to go to his mother's grave without embarrassment, he would run his fingers over the draped urn and say, I have sent my stepson to college; given a son of my own, I could have done as well. He is going to make us proud.

During this period Edward would talk, whenever Terence let him, about Thad's career at the University, playing up remembered stories of all-night parties and homecomings and the night when Thad, at least he thought it was Thad, had filled up the fountain in the memorial quadrangle with champagne. He gestured widely, calling up fast girls and racy cars with shining spokes, but he could never be sure whether Terence was listening. If he said, sharply: "Terence," the boy would look up, saying "Huh?" "Were you listening?" "Sure, Edward. Sure." Searching his eyes, Edward would see an edge of resentment and would draw back because, whether or not he liked to admit it, he was a little afraid of Terence now, he was not altogether sure he could get Terence to go to college any more than he could get him to speak respectfully to his mother or carry out the garbage when it was his turn. Still, so long as Terence did not refuse he could go on thinking about it, and he clung to that for as long as he could. He decided, in the summer before the boy's senior year in high school, that he needed some kind of wedge, and so he fixed on the boat.

Terence had been after both of them about the boat, you could get a lightweight aluminum model that fit right on top of the car, and if there were two of you, you could take it out past the surf and ride around in the sunshine, confounding swimmers and throwing out glittering spray. Edward couldn't afford it any more than he could afford the house, or the car, but when he mentioned this to Vivian she looked at him with those clear, cool eyes and said, "I've been meaning to tell you, Edward, I've had a promotion, there will be a lot more money from now on." Then she produced the money from a savings account he didn't even know she had, and Edward went down with Terence to pick out the boat. He remembered that when he was in high school he had been a pretty keen swimmer, he and his friends had gone out to the new beach pavilion for high school dances and afterwards they would all go into the water together, fearless in the black water, watching the phosphorescence flow over their hands. In his early childhood there had been nothing there, nothing but scrub palmettos and blue sky and bright waves, and there was somewhere at the back of his mind the idea that if he went to the beach with Terence, and the two of them went in the water together, things would be as they should be once more, with the pure sand washed clean and both of them washed clean.

Terence agreed that he couldn't get the boat in the water by himself and so that Saturday the two of them got in the car together and rode out to the beach. Terence went along happily enough, not exactly talking to him but not refusing to talk either, so Edward was able to drive along in an increasing aura of camaraderie, thinking that after all these years he had found the key to the boy's confidence, perhaps it would be the key to everything. Terence had been hitchhiking to the beach every day since school ended but now the two of them would be able to go out together on Saturdays, father and son laughing and pushing the boat out through the breakers, skinning aboard and firing off the motor; when they got out far enough, they would fish. Edward's skin would begin to tan and he thought his muscles would harden, the exercise would be good for him; he would bide his time and some afternoon, when they were both sitting on the blanket eating hot dogs, he would say: I want you to go for an interview at the University, you are going to have all the advantages I never had. He wasn't quite satisfied with the speech yet, it didn't seem to matter how hard he worked and polished; perhaps it did not ring true. Still they had all summer, if they got on well together they might keep coming out on into the fall, and when Edward presented Terence to the dean for his interview, he would be able to say: This is my son. He would have to say it, for this was all the son he would ever have.

When Mama was well enough for us all to leave her, Papa used to bring everybody out here in the carriage, it used to be a long way in those days, we would have to get up before it got light and we never got home until after dark. We took the big hamper Biggie had packed for us, with everything wrapped in white napkins, and Papa would peel down to his striped bathing suit and run out into the water just like one of the kids, I remember him and Thad throwing water and the two of them wrestling on the beach. The girls always sat in the shade to protect their complexions, but after an hour or two they wouldn't be able to stand it and they would be in the water along with everybody else. I don't know what Brewster did all day but he would come back for us around five, I think he had a friend in a shack up on one of the keys because he would always be grinning and there would be whiskey on his breath. Papa used to take me out in the water and hold me up, he was white from being indoors so much, but his arms were strong. That was before they built the pavilion, there was hardly anybody here, it was like there was nobody else in the world. If it was an unusual day we might run into one or two carriages, but usually there was nothing but the oyster-shell road and palmettos and sandspurs sticking up on either side, when I was in high school they would come out here and race cars right on the beach, now all you can see for miles is motels and hot dog stands and people in their smelly cars. I think we will ruin the land if we work at it hard enough, but maybe when you finish college you can afford to go someplace that isn't spoiled. Oh, look what they've done to the old pavilion, look at that.

He looked to Terence for a response, but Terence was staring ahead as if Edward had not said anything, and maybe he hadn't, even though he thought he had been saying it all out loud, for the boy's benefit. If he had, Terence seemed to be unaffected; when Edward looked over at him a second time he was glowering out the window, perhaps wondering why he had not been allowed to drive. When Terence has been to college, he thought, we'll have more to talk about.

They got the boat into the water easily enough, and Terence seemed to like it, because he said sure, they could go out together again some time, next time Edward had his day off. He did leave Edward alone on the blanket for the better part of the afternoon, but he was only a kid; Edward thought he was up at the refreshment stand talking to some boys he knew, but for one reason or another he did not want to look. Terence came back about five and the two of them got the boat back on top of the car, Edward pink and sore around the neck and wrists even though he had been careful enough to put on his shirt and trousers before lying down. They went home in silence, Edward mulling, Terence thinking God knew what.

Edward thought later that if he had only been content with the one Saturday, if he had remembered that one day on the water and been content to let it go at that, it might have been all right, but he came out to the carport the next Saturday to find Terence already warming up the car. He reached for the door handle and Terence would have backed out leaving him behind except that the motor stalled and while Terence was cursing and trying to get it started, Edward got in.

"What do you want?"

Edward said, with his heart failing, "What do you mean, what do I want? You can't get that boat in the water all by yourself."

"Have it your way," Terence said, and they were off.

Carrying the boat down on the beach, Edward thought the place could not be any more beautiful; the sand was still fresh and there was nobody else on it but a fisherman casting into the surf; there were a few people lazing in the shadows of the pavilion but the water ahead was bright and empty and Edward's heart expanded. "This is what it was like when we used to come."

"You told me," Terence said.

The boy was edgy today; once they put the boat down and spread the blanket he darted and wandered as if he could not get free of Edward fast enough. Edward had thought they would go ahead and put the boat in the water but Terence shifted from one foot to the other and said why didn't they just wait. They folded their clothes on the blanket and stood facing each other in their suits.

"You should have seen the pavilion in the old days," Edward said. "Guy Lombardo played here once, in 1928."

"You told me."

"I like . . ." He stopped, wanting to find words to dress his hopes, but failing that he said, "I like coming out here." He looked at the boy in a growing fondness. "Are you coming in?"

"Not yet." Stripped, Terence was tanned and compact-looking, and his careless ease made Edward conscious of his own pale body, laced with black hairs, shrivelled and sagging in his leaden wool trunks. "You go on out," Terence said. "I'll be along."

Plunging backward in the long shallows, Edward gave himself to the water, already soothed by the remembered burn of the salt, the familiar, receding line of the building on the beach.

"Stay loose," Terence said over his shoulder.

"I . . ." Edward started to say ". . . will," but something in the boy's voice, in his posture as he walked up the beach to the pavilion, arrested him and he came to his feet in the water, listening hard.

But for the first time in more years than he could remember he could not hear any of the time-smoothed words he had used to soothe himself, and as he shook his head to clear it of the water he looked at the beach again, bloating with an eerie, concentrated knowledge that he had never been to this place in his childhood, that he had never seen the beach or the pavilion or, in fact, the boy before. He blinked at the narrow beach, the crumbling building stripped of memories, thinking how ugly they all were.

In front of the pavilion the boy stood in the sand, talking broadly to an older man, and something raw and unfamiliar about the way they stood, leaning into each other without touching, repulsed him and his voice leaped: "TERENCE," and came out in a roar that surprised him because he had been sure the sound would die somewhere between them, perhaps on the last small, incoming wave. The boy heard and approached, wading through the unfamiliar-looking water, his hair ducktailed and his penis cradled, suggestively, in the low-cut candy-striped bathing suit. The beach belonged to him now, and in him Edward saw the emblem, the concretization of his own defeat; the boy was out of his control, had never been in his control, any more than was his fabrication of the future, and he knew as well that it was not so much that the boy was false as that his own conception of the boy was false, and if this was so then his life with Vivian was false and worse, so were his pictures of the past; it had never been good, it could never have been as good as he wanted, he had never been able to swim and in the old days his father and Thad had swung him, screaming, out over the water and then let go, and in high school he had gone to a dance at the pavilion but it was only as an appendage to Punk and Cora, who were too drunk, Punk had given him two beers and he had lurked at the edges like a miserable ghost; he was miserable now and he knew he must have been miserable on most of those remembered golden days, and he almost doubled over with the pain, crying aloud in his rage and chagrin.

Terence was impatient, tanned and insolent. "What do you want."

If he had been another man Edward might have reached out, there, in the water, and drowned the boy, but he knew he would never be able to go back to Vivian and read the truth about himself in her face; as it was he only said, "Cramp. I'm going home."

Terence seemed just as glad. "I'm staying. Ronnie and I . . ."

"I thought you would." Coming out of the water, Edward had to pick his way because the angle of the beach and buildings, even the slope of the sky had changed ever so slightly so that he was leaning just a little off center, unable to point to any particular change but aware of distress at the centers of his equilibrium, as if he were being forced to walk around in somebody else's thick glasses with everything refracted so sharply that nothing would ever again look the same. His ears had filled as if with water and he could barely hear Terence saying:

"Leave me the car?"

"No. You'll have to find your own way back."

LILA MELYN

Of course it was my fault because I got after him and once I got after him I kept after him. Sometimes I could step off and hear myself, I sounded just like one of those terrible housewives in the soap operas, but I couldn't help it because we had been married all this time and nothing was any different, we were no better off than we had been, just older, and I suppose I should have been satisfied but I couldn't help myself, I wanted more, I wanted to *be* more. In the beginning I used to tell myself, Everybody has to start somewhere; then I told myself I had to be patient, it was only a matter of time; I tried to tell myself everybody has to struggle, but there we were in that tiny little place and we weren't even struggling, it was a step up from the trailer but except for that we were no better off than we had been that first year, we were out there in the sticks in a tiny little match-box house just like all the other matchbox houses and Lee had to play outside in the dirt because nobody cared enough to keep up the grass.

Champy used to come out to see me, she would sit on the arm of the couch and cross her legs and I could see what was going through her mind. I never apologized, I never tried to explain, but she always felt she had to say: You've got all the important things, a husband who loves you and a beautiful little girl. Part of it was put on, but I guess she has a right to be tragic about things, that handsome boy from the wonderful family turned out to be randy as a rat, they found him in a downtown hotel with two high school girls and it took all of Champy's father's money to hush up the divorce. I suppose she came to see me because she was lonely, or she didn't have anything else to do, she would sit there in her fur jacket and try to pretend we were still girls together and when she couldn't stand it another minute she would take me out to lunch. I used to look at her and think: I don't mind for myself, but I would like Lee to be like Champy when she gets to college, not like me. Then when Sim would come in that night I would start; I tried not to nag but I had to make him want something better, if I didn't, Lee was going to grow up in that damn development, saying *he don't* and *ain't* just like all the other kids, she would forget her mother had ever been to college and she would never even know her family was just as good as Champy's, before the war they all had maids. I did everything I could to keep from nagging but it was like moving a mountain and after a while I would end up yelling, Why don't you *ever,* or, If you would *only,* and Sim would bow his head like some big child so I didn't even know if he was listening; that just made me madder and madder, by the end I was saying awful things, I don't know why he didn't hate me. But no matter what else you said about Sim, he was very sweet, he would always try to make it up, it seemed important to him to make it up; I don't think he really minded what I said as long as the house was comfortable and the meals were regular and things went on more or less the same. As long as he could come home at night and take Lee on his lap in the big chair and have me bring him things, he didn't care.

So I suppose it was my fault because I did care, Champy was going to business school to keep her mind off things and I got one of the girls in the development to give Lee lunches and take care of her after school and I went too. The two of us would finish up the typing and the shorthand classes and then we would go someplace for lunch, it was almost glamorous after the way Sim and I had been living. In the afternoons Champy would go shopping, I went along like a poor relation, if I tried on something I liked Champy would offer to loan me the money but I would never let her, I had my pride. I would just watch her put on resort clothes or jersey sheaths that slithered down over her hips and my stomach would ache, I was thinking about Lee. When the course was over Champy signed up for art appreciation at the Corcoran, she even joined a Great Books group for a while, but I went out and found a part-time job. As soon as I could afford it I started having my hair done and I bought myself a few things, after all I had to have something decent to wear to work. For a while I was even on a diet, Sim complained because we never had potatoes any more, I honestly don't think he noticed what was happening to me until he came to the table at night and found out there were no potatoes and no more pies; he never said I looked thinner or better or even different. I suppose I have no right to say anything about that because I wasn't noticing either, right up until the last minute I didn't see what was happening to him. All I saw was that my jobs were getting better and better; I still had hopes, I thought maybe if I threw it up to him, but by that time it was not something either of us planned, it was a condition of life: I would complain and he would not do anything.

As it turns out I'm a damn good secretary, I haven't been out of work since I got that first job with the shoe people, I suppose it helped split Sim and me but it's given me something to fall back on and even if it did split us, I'm not so sure that was a mistake. I suppose he felt it, me being in an office when he was getting himself dirty down there at the brake-lining place, and if he'd said anything at the beginning I probably would have quit. But he never did come out with it, all he ever said was that he wished I would just stay home and cook, and I told him when we could afford it I would think about it; he would just sigh and give me that hopeless look. He seemed to go along with anything I did, I suppose I got the idea that he would put up with anything I said to him and finally I came home and told Lee I had a new job, Sim was right there in the room but I actually heard myself saying, I'll be making more than Daddy gets. I didn't even think about what I was saying until I heard him yell:

Son of a bitch.

I jumped a foot because I had forgotten he was even in the room. I said, Honey, what's the matter?

You talk like I was a piece of furniture.

Sim I didn't mean to . . .

He was standing over me, he was so red in the face it scared me, because I had never seen him mad. He said, Just remember this, you goddam snot, I'm not a piece of furniture.

Then he went out and slammed the door.

I suppose I should have known then, I waited up until he finally came in, it was almost four, I hugged him and I apologized and cried, I wasn't really listening for what he would say, maybe I was afraid to hear it, I just assumed he had forgiven me. Now that I think of it I know he didn't, he just let me hug him and kiss him and he never said anything. But I wouldn't see it, I had to wait until it hit me in the face, I came home in the middle of the day, sick, Lee was in school and I thought the house was empty but there they were, in my bed. She was a cheap little girl who used to baby sit for us, she said *he don't* and *ain't* but she was soft and round and she had a pretty face. When he sent her out and we tried to talk about it I tried everything and finally I said, Honey, she'll only pull you down. Then he set his shoulders and glared at me, saying: Maybe I *want* to be pulled down.

So there it was, and I don't have to go and see the two of them to know exactly what he meant, and now that we are divorced and they are married I can't bear to see them together. When it's time to pick Lee up I send a cab for her because I would rather die than go in there and see the two of them, with no pretensions and no hopes, I know they are snuggled around each other, completely happy in that miserable place because they don't want anything, Sim has never wanted anything.

I should never have pushed him and I'm sorry, the whole thing was my fault for tormenting him, it was all my fault. I should be sorry and I know I'm grateful, because he gave me Lee, she's not going to be fat the way I am, she has soft brown hair and I think I can see Daddy in her face. We have quite a nice apartment, it's small but I have a few things of Grandmother Millard's so she can have her friends home and not be ashamed. If I'm lucky I'll be able to get her into a good college, even though I don't have the money to send her to boarding school.

After the divorce Uncle Thad offered me money but I turned him down, I guess I was upset. We had gone up to see him the weekend Sim got married, maybe I thought I would like New York and Lee and I might live there; maybe I only wanted to get out of town. I don't know why Uncle Thad invited us, except that I wrote and asked if we could come and he wrote back and said he had been just about to ask. I don't know what I hoped for, maybe I thought we were going to have a good time, maybe I even thought we could live together and maybe he thought so too, but I couldn't seem to put anything where Uncle Thad wanted it, Lee ran around the apartment and touched all his things and I could see him trying not to say anything about it and that got on my nerves. We would sit there after Lee went to bed, trying to pretend we were comfortable together. I think he wanted it to be true as much as I did, but the silences would stretch until he rattled his paper or covered his mouth to hide that dry cough; in the end he had nothing to say to me and I had nothing to say to him. Then Lee bumped into a photograph and broke the glass and he couldn't help himself, he shouted and I heard myself yell: She didn't *want* to break the goddam thing, and then we both apologized but we were both so nervous I knew it wouldn't work, and the next day I said we had to be going and he said he was sorry, we both looked at each other when we said it and we both meant it, but there was no power on earth that could make it possible for us to be any closer than we were: two people who had ended up in the same place at the same time more or less by mistake. At the airport he asked if there was any way he could help; he meant money, but I was frazzled by then, I was so upset with him for being upset with Lee that I said No, even though I could see that I was hurting him. He wouldn't give up, he said if there was ever anything he could do, and I promised to let him know but we both knew I wouldn't't. Maybe when Lee is ready for college he will beat down his pride and offer me money again; then I will let him pay a part of the expenses and we can both feel a little better about the whole thing, but there was nothing we could do for each other right then. I had thought New York might be a good place for Lee and me, I had thought Uncle Thad might be able to help me and who knows, maybe he thought so too; I had even told myself he was lonely and I had something to offer him, but I suppose I have known all along that when it comes right down to it everybody has to go the whole way more or less alone.

CORA

I begged him not to do it, I knew it would be the end of everything, if he went then of course that meant I could go too, I could go any time from then on, nothing but a whiff of dust, and I have never liked to think about things like that; poor stupid Lila, going the way she did when she still had her figure and the most of her looks, she just laid down and let it happen to her. Of course it was his fault, I have been after him about his weight for years but he was stubborn, stubborn, talking to that man was like talking to a brick wall; he ignored what I said to him for so many years that he wouldn't listen to that either, even though I kept telling him what the doctor said, it could be a matter of life and death. I knew we would have to start taking better care of ourselves, everybody does after a certain age, but when I would bring it up he wouldn't listen, I could talk and talk and he wouldn't hear a word, it was almost as if he didn't care. I think he had the same idea about it I had, we would both pop off in our sleep some night and they could bury us together in the family plot, Thad wouldn't be caught dead down here, so Punk could take his place. I thought if we didn't just slip away in the night then we would probably go out like two lights in a car crash and that would be the end of it, we wouldn't feel anything and neither of us would have to be alone. Then, after Alden, every once in a while I would wake up in the night, thinking: But what if we didn't? What if he, and I had to be alone? What if I. Who would put away his shirts for him, who would put him to bed; who would put up with him then, if I? I should have known better. Punk has always been selfish, selfish, I bet he never gave it a thought.

And then of course he always has wanted to be the center of attention; he had to go all by himself so he could leave somebody behind to cry. Well who in hell does he think is going to cry for me? Self-centered. He couldn't even do it while Alden was still around to

292

help take care of things, he had to wait until it would really make a difference; he waited until things were going along better than they had been for years. I mean, we all went along like everybody does, thinking the next year would be better. Well, maybe it was, even though it was never as good as you thought it was going to be; what was important was, Punk and I had reached the point where we didn't have to think so much about next year. Poor Alden had passed away and we didn't have poor little Maurice to worry about, there were just the two of us in the house with no responsibilities, we could live one day at a time and for the first time since the beginning we were more or less content. I don't know whether it was age or time or some patience we never had before, but we could eat dinner and then fall asleep in front of the television every night without even wanting to go out to the movies or some party, we didn't worry every minute about whether we would rather be out somewhere. Well, maybe it was age after all, but age turns out to have its advantages; I still have my figure, I keep myself up but I don't have to worry so much about the wrinkles because everybody my age has wrinkles, and I know I look a damn sight better than most of them. I can see how my friends' sons look at me, they think I am an old bag but I can see from their eyes that they know I'm a good-looking old bag, and I can take their admiration without having to worry about whether they would like to go to bed with me; I know I look fine and right now that's enough, the men don't matter any more. I suppose Punk felt some of the same thing, I know he used to have his girl-friends, I never saw any of them, I never even had a hint, but I know damn well he wasn't a hundred per cent faithful, nobody is, but he was more or less past caring for that last couple of years; we were able to sit at home with our highballs and be happy because we had everything we needed and we didn't want anything in particular, it was sweet, really, I have never known so much peace. But then that night Punk let it happen and that was the end of everything.

We had broiled chicken and mashed potatoes for dinner, we were cutting down on the rich stuff and the hot stuff because we couldn't seem to take it any more; we had a Jello salad and vanilla ice cream, Punk's favorite, he said it was the best meal he had had in weeks, he had two helpings of potatoes because it had the cheese on top, the way he liked it, I took a chance and sprinkled on a little tarragon. We listened to the six o'clock news while we were eating and we didn't even squabble over the political report the way we used to like to, we just sat there and talked about that scandal with Liz and Richard, they were just getting together, I said it was terrible and Punk said tsk tsk tsk; we were mellow as two old cook pots, bubbling away together: it was sweet, sweet. Then I washed up and Punk took his bourbon highball out into the living room and read the paper; when I finished I went out and picked up *House and Garden,* Huntley and Brinkley were on but we weren't really watching, it was just a nice background and I felt snug and happy the way I did on all those nights, you know, doing the same thing, and then I heard this noise, it was so funny that for a minute I didn't even know where it was coming from. I looked over to see if Punk had heard it and it was him, I screamed at him, Punk, what in God's name is the *matter* with you? But he didn't answer, he couldn't even move, he was all red and he just looked at me. I thought maybe he was only choking on a piece of chicken and then I saw it in his eyes, it was the same look Alden had when I went to visit him right before he passed away. I said God, oh my God, and ran over to help him but it was too late, he had already keeled over and I hung on to him for a minute, I was crying, please don't, Punk, please, please don't, but he wasn't listening because it had already happened to him; I knew I had to get somebody so I put a pillow under his head and then I ran and called the ambulance.

Of course it was a stroke, it was like the weight of the world was shoved right into my stomach, I thought I would never see him again, but they got him better, I went and spent every afternoon with him and as it turned out, I even got him back for a while. I got to have him for the last six months, he could only say a couple of things and his whole right side was paralyzed, but I brought the television up into his room and after I fed him supper I would eat on a TV tray and then we would both sit up together and go to sleep in front of the TV, just the way we always had; in the daytime he would sit in the bed and follow me with his eyes and every time I came close, he would put out his hand, it was really very sweet, it was like having the baby after all. I suppose I had the idea that I had him back forever, we could keep going on like that and it wasn't really going to be so different because we never talked much after dinner even before he had the stroke, we watched the same things and turned the TV off at the same time we always had and in a way things were better, I could see from Punk's eyes how much he depended on me now. I don't know whether I thought about depending on him, but then one night we were watching Jackie Gleason, it was a Saturday and I remembered all those parties we used to go to at the club; I said, Remember that hobo party we gave for your birthday, Punk. Punk? I looked over at him and he was going, his head was back and his eyes were all whites, I tried to stop him because I knew what it was going to do to me but before I could even reach out to touch him he was gone and I never want to think about what I felt right then, it was like having a tooth ripped right out of its socket, he left a big, black hole. He was so cross sometimes I wanted to kill him, compared to a lot of men I suppose he wasn't much, but I don't know, maybe he was all I ever was.

I don't know, you go along for a long time not seeing somebody, without even thinking about them, and then you're thrown back with them and it turns out they are a lot more than you remembered; I mean my sisters, they turned out to be a lot more loyal than my friends. Oh, Gemma and all the rest of them came around as soon as they heard, they even made their husbands go with them to the funeral; they all brought around patés and custard pies their maids had baked, they made a big point of having me over for dinner and saying, Cora, you ought to get out more often, you ought to meet some men, but even that was only for a while; it was Flodie who came over to the house when I called her, and first she said to me, Now you know what it's like to lose somebody; she had a funny cat-like look when she said it, but she coped when I couldn't, notifying Punk's brother in Omaha and telephoning the doctor and the funeral home, she called the newspapers and she came back the next day in her black bouclé, smoothing her hair and opening the door to all my friends, she would make sure I had my hair combed and my face dusted before she let them come upstairs. Gemma came in the bedroom and threw her arms around me and cried as if she had lost somebody of her own, but it was Nell who took Punk's best suit down to the funeral home and stood by while they laid him out. Flodie was sweeter than I have ever seen her, she even said to me, after the funeral: You could always come back and live with us. I thought about it and then I looked at her in her black bouclé, with dandruff showing, shoes a little bit too cheap; I looked over at Nell, who is letting herself get grey even though she's at least ten years younger than me, I thought about the house and everything I did to get away from it and I said *No,* louder than I ever meant to, and then I started crying until I thought I would never stop. Flo was sweet as could be, she patted me and forgave me right away, saying it was only nerves, and she still calls me up every single Sunday night to talk; she hasn't mentioned me moving back in there since that time at the funeral, maybe she thinks it would be a bad idea, maybe she only thinks one offer should be enough.

Well for a while I thought I could handle it alone. I was miserable, I was empty, I thought it was only missing Punk but after a while I had to admit to myself that it was plain old loneliness, I was rattling around in that house and after a while I couldn't even be sure I was really there because nobody called and nobody came, one day could run right into the next before I even heard the sound of my own voice. At first the girls were nice as could be, they would take me out to lunch and tuck me in at dinner parties, the dinner parties were the first to go because nobody likes an extra woman at the table, they are afraid you will grab off their husband or some damn thing. After a while even the lunch invitations tapered off, maybe they didn't like to look at me and think they could be going the same way any minute, at the last tick of some poor husband's heart. I think they just got tired of having to think about me; when you go out of your way to be nice to somebody you expect them to show something for it, they are supposed to get better, or different, so you don't have to keep on thinking about them; everybody likes to be kind but nobody wants to have to keep on doing something about somebody for the whole rest of their life. At first I thought I could move on out and be somebody without Punk, I could give cocktail parties to get off my obligations and parties for friends' children, I might even meet a man; I should have known better, there weren't any men, and the ones there were looked like they were scared to death: another widow on the market, waiting to grab them off. After a while there weren't any invitations either, Gemma and the rest of them had more or less done their duty, they would look me up every once in a while at a Garden Club meeting but it was as if they couldn't quite make out who I was, I was fading fast and pretty soon I would just disappear.

So I get up in the morning and rattle around the house until night comes, and then I fall asleep in front of the television and I get up the next morning without anybody there to care whether I get up or not, and then I rattle around the house some more. Maybe if Punk and I had gone ahead and had a child that lived. Maybe if I had gone to college, the way Papa wanted me to, instead of getting married right away; maybe if I had something I could do, some kind of job. Or we could have tried to take Alden back after the operation, it was going to be so hard and we couldn't afford a private nurse but maybe he would have gotten better after all, he might be around to talk to me now. But the house is empty; except for Flodie nobody ever calls, and when I go to the door to talk to a salesman or ask the mailman if he's sure that's all he has for me, just those brochures, he looks at me as if I am hardly there at all and I think I am going to disappear soon if I don't get out of here; if I stay here I know I'll get older and older and smaller and smaller, I'll stay inside my bathrobe and eat dinners out of cans and one day the mailman or somebody will come in and find me dead and that will be the end of it. So I am going back to live in the old house, with the girls. They don't know it yet, but I'm sure it's a good idea, after all I am the oldest sister, and they need somebody to take charge; they've been living there in a perfect mess, God knows what-all in their wardrobes, and the television right out where anybody could see it, you'd think they'd forgotten who they are. It's going to be good for all of us, I can feel it, they are going to be grateful and I, I don't know; Nell is a namby-pamby and I've never been able to stand Flo, but if I stay here I'll just disappear.

§§§§ §§§§

Trapped in the old house, Nell found it harder and harder to keep up with everything; at a time when she would have liked to relax a little, she had Flodie, who would insist that they dine in the dining room just like they did in the old days, and then would complain about a spot of grease left on the waxy surface of the table, or biscuit crumbs which would attract roaches unless Nell went around with the dustpan and the handbrush after dinner and tried to get them up. Biggie had left them for good and all some time after Mama went to the hospital, and the day worker they had lasted through the '40s, and some time in the '50s got herself a job in the tire factory, which sent fumes over the entire city (Nell would wake in the night, clutching at her throat and thinking: My God, what's that, and then she would recognize the smell). Nell had one cleaning woman after another after that, but nobody would stay long because they all said the house was just too much for one person, and besides, she couldn't afford to pay them enough to make it worth their while. After Flodie came back she would come down in her robe on a Saturday morning and make a pass with a dustcloth, but actually she was flogging Nell from room to room: faster, faster. When Nell would turn and suggest mildly that Flo could vacuum for a change, or help her put on fresh sheets, Flo would draw herself up indignantly, saying: Why Nell, I'm ashamed of you, you know perfectly well I'm the breadwinner in the family, and this is my day off. Now she had Cora too, Cora, who had come in tears but remained to ensconce herself in Mama's bedroom, paying to have it repainted in a color which was not Mama's color but *looked* like Mama's color, and resurrecting the chaise, which she had reupholstered in grey velvet instead of Mama's pink; Nell, looking at the room, would think life was not so different after all.

Cora began by being something of a help, making croquettes and fussy Jello salads for their dinners, but as the weeks went by and she was assured of her future with her sisters, she became less and less particular about cleaning up after herself, and in the end retrenched to the point where she had little to do with any of the meals except for the days when she would dash down just before supper to make up some last-minute masterpiece which would cut everybody's appetite and dirty all the pots. Nell was usually in the kitchen until well after nine, cleaning up, and then she would come into the chintzy living room to find Flodie in the most comfortable chair with her feet over one arm and Cora stretched out on the davenport which Nell had called her own for so many years.

Cleaning the dining room chandelier or the bronzed Grace which crowned the newel post, straightening out Flo's wardrobe or picking up one of Cora's negligees, Nell realized that things had gotten out of hand, the house had gotten out of hand and she would never again be in control. She had bathrooms to clean, dishes to do, beds to change, and even with all that taken care of there was dust piling up in the back bedrooms where she never had time to clean; she couldn't take care of it all, and if she didn't take care of it soon it was going to start rolling out into the hallway and down the stairs, it would choke them all, cascading through the parlors and filling the dining room; she had not the means or strength to stop it and she knew they were going to have to get out soon, if they didn't then the dust was going to roll on, out into the street, and all the world would know of her defeat. There were three of them now, Flodie was a businesswoman and would be able to take care of the arrangements,

Cora could help take care of the extra costs; neither of them seemed any happier in the house than she did and so, in those quiet months before Edward's divorce, Nell began laying plans for her escape.

Once she mentioned it, both her sisters agreed the neighborhood was going downhill; the man in the filling station called Cora by her first name and the other night some hoodlum had followed Flodie all the way home from the bus. When she was alone Nell had never been afraid, but now she and her sisters fed, each on the others' imaginations, so that they had a new sense of being weak women together; they were beginning to be uneasy about their safety, making a ritual check of all the locks before they went to bed and waking in turn to sit upright in the dark, listening with their eyes wide and their mouths open for alien sounds in the night. It was easy enough for Nell to tempt them with the newspaper announcement; the new Co-op would be as sound as a fortress, with a doorman and an operator at the desk who would not let anybody in to see an occupant unless the occupant approved the visitor. The girls murmured together over the brochure, admiring the shimmering white facing and the picture windows high above the filthy river, the rows of royal palms which would be transplanted, full-grown, to dress the building's entrance. There would be a pharmacy and a specialty shop right on the ground floor, so if you didn't want to, you wouldn't even have to go out. The apartment Nell wanted had a big foyer and a long living-dining room and three bedrooms, one for each; it was going to be expensive, but if they could get enough for the house they would be able to swing it, and Cora and Flo between them would be able to make up the monthly maintenance charge.

The girls were happy enough to talk about it, they even began to speculate about the social opportunities: distinguished bachelors, maybe even a handsome widower, but Nell ran into trouble whenever she tried to get ready for the move. They would not let her have a dealer in to appraise the furniture, and she had to agree that they would take all of Mama's really fine pieces with them; it might be a little crowded but they would look just beautiful in the apartment. Cora cried when she talked about calling the Goodwill to take the old clothes out of the attic, and Flodie fought like a tiger to keep Nell from going through Papa's papers. In the end Nell had to retreat to her brochures, praying for strength to handle it all when the apartments were ready, doing her best to keep pace with the grime on the windows and the dust which would not stop rolling out between the

baseboards and the floor. Once they saw the place, it would be easier.

They put on bright linens and straw hats and white gloves and
went to the apartments the first day they opened; the building was on
the river, there was a little plaza where the residents could stroll
without having to worry about panhandlers or muggers or the kind of
men who come up and speak to women on the street. Flo and Cora
murmured over the empty rooms and Nell, seeing the light glancing
off the white, unsullied ceiling, thought she was very, very close;
Cora whirled in front of the plate-glass window, saying, "I can
hardly wait."

Going home, Flodie and Cora chattered while Nell sat in the
back seat, chewing over all her attempted escapes. Papa had always
wanted her to go to college, but before she could break free Mama
was failing, and Mama took all of her time. Cleve showed her the
way, but then he abandoned her and so she had to stay in the house
and wait for him, and for years after that she was so shattered by the
fact that he had never come that she didn't have the heart to try
again. Then Lila came home, dying, and then there was Lila Melyn;
the two of them had made a pleasant life together, she and the fat
child, and Nell forgot for a time that there was any life outside the
house. But now her sisters were talking about a Dispos-all and a
dishwasher and Fibreglass drapes for the picture window; they were
talking with easy cold-heartedness about selling the big house and everything in it, hurrying ahead with such relish that Nell herself felt
new misgivings. She lifted her head as they turned into the drive,
looking up at the house where she had spent her life and then choking off her voice because she almost cried out: Stop, I've changed my
mind.

As it turned out, there was no need; there had never really been
any need. They wrote Thad for permission and called the realtor;
they drafted an ad for the Sunday paper, but as it turned out they
never had a chance to call it in. They were waked in the night by the
sound of the doorbell and then pounding because they could not get
there fast enough to satisfy the people waiting on the porch. Sitting
upright in bed, in a beginning sweat, Nell remembered all the midnight alarms she had ever read about and she wanted to stay where
she was and pray that her sisters hadn't even heard, but the two of
them were already murmuring in the hallway outside her room, they
would expect her to come out to give them moral support, and so she

put on her robe and followed them downstairs. It turned out to be Vivian; she had Terence with her and between them they held Edward, who was white and incoherent, vibrating with a fear which touched Nell and took her so that she shrank from him, even as Cora said, "For God's sake, Vivian, what's the matter?" and Vivian thrust Edward into the hallway to join his sisters, saying, "Here, you take him. I've had enough."

EDWARD

It's all my fault. Mama always said I had to think about my responsibilities, Thad used to tell me and *tell* me about all those things I should have been doing instead of whatever it was I was trying to do at the time but it was all so hard, and now I am in this big old house without a decent job to fill my time and outside the neighborhood is going to rack and ruin, my poor sisters are getting old and wrinkled because we don't have the money for all those creams, or whatever it was that Mama used to keep herself so young and beautiful, we can't even afford to have the stained glass window fixed, or paint the house, because I don't have any money; I never had any money and it was all my fault. If I had only gone to the University, but the Land Crash, we never really had the money anyway; maybe if I had let Thad say whatever it was, if he had kept me in New York, but he was so God damn superior, father knowit-all, he told me terrible things about our family: After all, Edward, I am more or less your godfather. For God's sake, Thad, why can't you leave me alone? And besides, the Depression, and besides, Vivian, I wasted all those years with Vivian and by that time we were in the war . . .

They never knew how hard I worked. If they knew Vivian never would have, Terence wouldn't look at me the way he did; I worked day and night for those two, turning myself inside out to scrape the last little bits of money off my guts, I would look at their two faces and think if only I could get finished, if only I could buy them the right things, I might be able to let down for a while and get some rest. I would be able to come in at night and sit down in my soft chair and have Vivian smile at me. I wanted to give her everything and it looked like I would never even be able to give her *enough*. All those years. All those years and now Terence hates me and when I try to call the house Vivian won't even come to the phone. Maybe if I had been more forceful, but she was beautiful, she was the only woman who ever, and I wanted, and now I don't even know whether she ever loved me or if she was pretending right from that first night. If we had had the baby, Vivian would have, and Mama could pin it all on the baby instead of me, he would be the one who had to carry on the responsibility, the last receptacle of the family name, why did it always have to be me? What was I supposed to do, Mama, have the baby by myself? At the end she wouldn't even let me, but by that time it was too late anyway, I had dried up, I am nothing but a bunch of dead branches hanging from a dead tree.

Here I am with nothing to show for all those years; all I have to show is this white mark above my eyebrow, I don't know if Terence hit me, Terence would never hit me, so I guess I just fell. I went over there the other day, she wouldn't let me in and I was afraid anyway, it used to be like going into an open mouth; Vivian would wake me in the night and scream, or else it was me screaming and she woke me up to make me stop, I think I've been sick, and at the end either she and Terence made me sit up for my dinners, like a dog, or else she was down on her knees begging me to eat, and either she and Terence put me out in the yard, it was cold and I howled around the house, or else it was in my head; all I know is I am back here and it is bitter, bitter, there is very little left.

Lord knows I want to be some help with the cooking and the dishes, I would like to help Nell but she is so sweet and patient, they all look so tired; they like the dishes dried just *so,* and whenever I try to cook something or help a little bit I just get in the way. I thought I might find another job but I can't seem to get anything and besides I hate to go out looking, people stare down their noses at you, and it's so hard. I was going to help them around the house instead, I could do some painting, I could fix the kitchen floor, but after the first room Cora said thank you very much but she was afraid there was no more money to buy paint and besides, they like the kitchen floor the way it is; when I go out in the yard to see what I can do about the garden all I find are beer cans and broken glass, they have let the grass all die and people keep throwing things from the rooming houses on either side of us, you would think this was a public dump. I used to think I could rake it all out but when I went out the other night it was piled up worse than ever and there were these two kids doing it in the bushes right behind our house. If I were a lawyer I could take care of it, I would be able to protect us, the neighborhood is going to rack and ruin and we need protection; I would like to be able to build a proper wall but I can't seem to get a job, not anywhere, and terrible things are happening on our property, Mama would have to see them from her bedroom window if she were still alive. Or if I had gone on to be a doctor we would have plenty of money now; I could have operated and saved Mama; I could have brought her back here to live and made her proud, but now she's dead and I can't even get a job, the neighborhood is going to rack and ruin, with cheap trash living on all sides, and I can't even take out the garbage for fear something terrible will happen to me; Nell has to take it, and it's just Providence that nothing has happened to her so far.

If I could afford it I would fix up the old house so we could be proud of it, plenty of people live in fine old houses in bad neighborhoods, but they have plenty of money and they build strong walls; I can't afford to build a wall, I can't even afford to take my sisters out to dinner for a change, there's no money left. It's all gone, Thad has it now, he is sitting up there in New York on top of all that money and he doesn't even send us a Christmas card. He's so rich he doesn't even think about the rest of us, he doesn't care whether we live or die. Well some day when I feel a little better I am going to go up there and face him, and then my sisters and I will get our due, he can't keep on living up there untouched by all of this, he doesn't have the right. I am going to get a haircut and put on my best suit and face up to my brother and tell him the truth. I'm going to say, You are still our brother, Thad, and I'm tired of taking all the blame. If I'm responsible for all this rack and ruin then you are responsible for me, so you are responsible for all this after all. I'll just tell him, and he'll have to see. But Mama, is Mama ever going to see? She'll say, Oh. Thad, I never expected anything from Thad. It was you, Edward, it was always you, and look how you have failed. You just let it go. I'll admit it, I'm afraid of her, I'm afraid of Thad too and I'm afraid of everything that's happening to me, I can't get a job and I can't keep the house the way it ought to be and I can't even keep my body any more, my hands shake all the time and I have to keep on running to the bathroom, my muscles have all shrunk to nothing and there is white skin hanging down from all my bones; when I look down at my body I hate it, I hate myself and I want to die but I can't do that either, if I die then I will have to face Mama, she will seek me out and find me no matter where I try to hide; when I meet her in whatever world there is to come she will say, It's all your fault, Edward, everything has gone to hell in a handbasket and it's all your fault.

FLODIE

Well he's not worth the paper he's printed on, you never know when he's going to cry at the dinner table and I have to open the jars in this household because his wrists are so weak, but maybe Edward is going to be some use to us after all. In times like these you need a man around the house, even if it is only Edward; I hear there are people buying dope from some diddybop right in front of the store where we buy our cakes and sugar, and there are some women doing things for money over in the Breault house, at least I think they are, and the music coming out of the place next door is enough to drive you right straight out of your mind. Mr. Breault would have a fit, he used to wear a tuxedo to all the parties we went to over there, and she was small and round and sweet as Mama, she was usually just coming out of mourning for somebody or other, she almost always had on dove grey, but if it was a big party she would wear white, and now there are terrible things going on right where we used to dance. Well maybe the Breaults wouldn't care, they moved away a long time ago, and as soon as they left the house started to go downhill, and that's part of the problem with this neighborhood, the people who cared have all moved out, first it was the Breaults and then the Le-Fevres and then the rest of them, and as soon as they moved out things began to happen to their houses, everything started to go downhill; we are the only ones left in the neighborhood, and this is the only house that hasn't been broken up into rented rooms or degraded in some other way; Papa built this house, he built this house for Mama and all her children, and maybe it is our business to stay here and keep it the way it was.

Somebody has to maintain a few standards. The house ought to be painted soon, but except for that and needing a little yard work, it looks as good as it ever did, and more or less the same things are going on inside, even after all these years. Cora and Edward and I still sit down to dinner at the old mahogany table, and Nell brings out the dishes she has fixed for us, we do without some of the side dishes and at least one of the starches, but we have hot bread on the table every night. After dinner we go into the family sitting room and watch the television, the music programs mostly, because you cannot trust anything they tell you on the news, and sometimes Cora makes divinity the way Mama did when she was well enough. Then we sit around until bedtime, just a nice family, but when I have to say good night and go to bed alone everything changes. I lie there and I can feel the whole house spreading out around me, every loose board and every weak lock and every faulty window screen, and when there's a noise it's like a hot flash going over me. When I was little the worst thing that could happen in the night would be Uncle Harry drunk and falling over something in the dark, but now it could be a rapist scratching at the basement window, or a murderer just waiting to come in and lay us waste, everything has changed and nothing is too terrible to happen. We are trying our best but when I go to bed I can hear all the sounds in the neighborhood, dirty laughter and cheap music, somebody is throwing bottles next door and I can lie flat on my sheet and feel everything draining right out of my toes and fingertips, pretty soon there will be nothing left of any of us, we'll just be old shells waiting for some punk to break in and finish us off, maybe somebody will throw a lighted match into a corner and the whole place will go, it will be as if none of it ever happened, and we were never even here.

Well it's a little better now; they all know there is a man in the house, they must have seen Edward going out with the garbage and potting around the yard, it's enough to drive you crazy; they don't know it's only Edward, so they're going to have to think twice before they try and break in here, and if they do it anyway I'm going to yell a lot, I'll go and get Edward and if he is too weak or too stupid to fight for us I can push him downstairs in front of me, like a shield, and when we find whoever it is I'll give Edward a shove so he bowls right into them, they'll think he is fighting and if they don't get scared and run right away I can call the police while they're still tangled up with Edward, before they figure out that he isn't fighting at all.

I never used to think about things like this. When we were all little, this house was the safest place in the world; we had Papa and Thad, Cora told me about Papa's silver derringer and there was always Brewster, sleeping over the carriage house; there were men to spare and we slept with all our doors unlocked because this whole town was just as safe as a garden, it was like a park filled with our friends and people who were paid to take care of us and all our friends: maids, nurses, sweet colored men who would make jokes with you while they were grooming the horses or shining the family's cars. We knew everybody in town and they all knew us, if they didn't know us they knew who we belonged to, they would be able to tell by the way our eyes were set, or by the family nose, every time we went out when we were little somebody would say, I know you, you're Thad Lyon's children. I remember one night Nell and I sneaked out and went barefooted all the way down to the little gazebo by the river to listen to the band concert, we came home down the warm streets with bare feet and nothing but little blouses on over our nighties, we cut through people's gardens without thinking twice about it, going through the warm grass without even feeling it, and when we came up through the back garden the house rose up in the dark just like a big white ship, there were lights in almost all the windows and when the breeze took the trees you could pretend it was the house that was moving, we would get on board in a minute and sneak up to our beds so we would be there when Papa came in to kiss us, we would be safe in the ship and nothing could ever hurt us then.

Now the gazebo is gone and Papa is gone and our house is full of noises, I can go to work in the morning and go to ten stores on my lunch hour and walk halfway home before I get on the bus and even when I get off at our corner I won't see a single face I know, or anybody that knows me, for that matter; a colored man can come and sit down right next to me on the bus and if I smile at him to show there's no harm done he will give me a look like a knife in the gullet, when I've never done one single living thing to him; I have to worry about whether we've locked all the doors and checked all the windows and I can't even go down to the mailbox by myself at night without wondering if I am going to get hit in the head; my sisters and I were not brought up to live in times like these, it's just too terrible, and I can't even say whose fault it is. We were brought up to be ladies, Mama taught us to embroider and how to curtsey, she taught us to undress underneath our nighties so not even our sisters could see us, and to depend on men to open doors for us and servants to do our cleaning for us and here we are, the four of us in this old house without even anybody to do the yard for us, much less scrub the kitchen floor, and I don't even know whose fault it was: ours, for believing what she told us? Hers, for not knowing what to expect? At least I had the sense to go out and learn typing and short-hand; when Mama was a girl no lady worked. Well, no lady ever had to worry about whether she was going to get raped going to the mail-box, either; it's all changed, I take my turn scouring the toilet bowls and scrubbing the kitchen floor, I haven't done a curtsey in more than forty years but I can't really blame Mama, she thought she was doing her best for us; still we were brushed and combed and patted, we had dancing lessons, we were all trained up for a life that was never going to happen the way she thought it should, how could it, nothing could ever be as good as Mama promised, so maybe we were cheated, we were cheated from the start.

What did she know anyway, she never had to cope with beer cans in the garden, or roadhouse noises from next door. Last night I was lying here in my bedroom and suddenly I sat bolt upright, there was the most godawful sound, some hick on dope and yelling like the damned, and then I realized it was somebody's victrola from next door, I thought it was going to drive me right straight out of my mind. I kept waiting for it to go away and when I couldn't stand it another minute I got out the phone book and called them up. Well first they said they didn't know anything about it, and when I made a fuss they put this young kid on the phone; I said, I live next door and I'm trying to sleep and would you mind terribly, and then he said something so awful I would never repeat it and I said, All right, if that's the way you feel about it, I'm going to call the police; well he just laughed, and there was not one single thing I could do. Then when I called the police they were very nice but they said they couldn't do anything, and when I said why not they said Lady, if we answered all the calls we get about noisy neighbors we wouldn't have any time for the *real* problems, and when I said I had never heard of such a thing they said they were terribly sorry but that was just the way it was. So I had to go back to bed and lie there and listen; for a minute I thought I might just wake up Edward and send him over but I knew he wouldn't go, he can't do anything, so I had to lie here on my own bed in my own house that I was born in and listen to that music that was so loud it was like it was right inside my own room; we're all getting older and everything is going to pieces, we can't seem to stop it and now I can't even say whose fault it is.

All right, maybe Mama did expect too much for us, but how could she know? How could anybody know it was going to turn out like this? It's not her fault, it's not my fault, it's not even Edward's fault, for letting go. It's the times, the terrible, terrible times; all the young people are doing things we never even dreamed of, they have no shame and half of them are on dope, they can't even get anybody to fight for this country any more, and decent people aren't safe out on the streets. Papa built this big house for us and Mama moved in and wanted so much for all of us and now here we all are, living here, no better and no different than we ever were, maybe a little bit worse, and the whole world is going right on outside as if we never even lived. Well if they can do without us, we can do without them; I've never given up on anything and I say the hell with them. I've put up with halfway measures and compromises for too long now, and now I'm going to have things the way I want. I'm coming up for early retirement in September, I'm supposed to get a bonus, and we'll do all right on my money, along with Cora's insurance and the money Thad sends Nell, and as soon as I am at home all day, things are going to start to change. We used to talk about selling this old place and moving into an apartment, I guess Nell thinks it would be easier, without so much to clean, but I have lived in an apartment, and that's like giving up, we would have to get rid of everything and we would end up in one of those little boxes with nothing left to make us any different from anybody else; we wouldn't be any better than anybody else if we didn't have the house; it may be run down but at least the house has style, the house is all we ever were.

So I'm going to take my money and the money I have in savings, that I got from Randolph, and I'm going to do a few things around here, starting with air conditioning, it will take about six units, three on each floor, but when we have them all in we will be able to keep the windows shut even in the hottest weather, and I won't have to listen to that caterwauling going on next door. We can have some carpenter work done, extra bolts for all the doors, and there are some aluminum grills you can get now that look like the ones in New Orleans, I am going to order those and then get Edward up off his lazy bottom and follow him around while he drills the holes and puts them in. I don't like bumping into the types you meet in the markets around here, so either I will take the car out to River Acres to do my shopping or else I'll order things by phone, and when we want an outing we will all drive someplace where we can sit on the grass without somebody coming up and being rude. I know where Mama's dressing gowns were put away, there's one in particular that I remember, and I don't think it would hurt us to sit around like ladies and gentlemen and have tea in the afternoons, and another thing, the minute Edward gets better we are going to have heavy cream and butter puff pastries from the bakery for our tea; we'll be able to afford it because he doesn't know it, but the minute he gets better, Edward is going to go out and get a decent job.

EDWARD

It's too hard.

NELL

I wasn't as upset by Edward as the girls were, after all, I had Mama all that time, I would have been happy to let him go, but at the beginning they kept saying he wasn't sick, all he needed was a little rest, and then they couldn't understand why he didn't get any better when he was safe in the house for all those weeks with us to look after him and nothing to worry about but himself. After a while they just lost patience with him, they decided it was all in his mind, he wanted to be sick, and so they began to bully him, sending him off places for weekends and out to look for jobs, but each time he came back, it was too far or too hard, and they began to be frightened, if they couldn't handle whatever it was that was the matter with him, then it might get out of hand and spread to them; if they couldn't fix him, they would end up just like Edward, wandering around and moving furniture, trying to get it exactly the way it was when we were all little and living here. So first they kept trying to talk him out of it, they would make up errands for him, or come home with puzzle books and leather burning equipment to get him interested in something outside himself, and when that didn't work they tried to get him to go to one doctor after another, they would tell him it was for a checkup or to see about those funny brown spots on the backs of his hands but he knew, and they knew; then after he went to the doctor they would watch him like hawks, to be sure he took his pills, and to spite them he would forget his pills; then when nothing seemed to work they would come up to me, separately, and say: We've got to get rid of him, but as soon as I tried to make them sit down and figure out how to do it, Cora would say: We can't, it would be too embarrassing, or Flodie would say: We couldn't do that to Mama, she would just die. I suppose I should have insisted but there was no more money left for a private hospital, and no member of our family has ever had to go to a state institution; when we were little we would tease each other about Chattahoochee, we always shrieked and said the name too loud because we were all frightened by the same image: black Bedlam, with ourselves chained to the walls.

He was very sweet most of the time, but even at the beginning he could be annoying, he would come into the kitchen when I was cooking and look over my shoulder at the vegetables, saying, Biggie always used to cube everything; then he would forget everything that had happened to him in the last ten years and say, At our house, Vivian always turns the roast up high for a few minutes, to seal in the juices, and he'd give me a beautiful smile; then he would tsk-tsk over the peeling linoleum and say, If Thad were a man he would come down here and take care of things, he has the money but he doesn't know what his responsibilities are; then I would look into his eyes and see that he had fallen short of Thad, or Thad had fallen short of him, I was never sure which one it was, but he would cock his head as if he were expecting something, he had been expecting something all along and if he could just figure out what it was, he could make it come. After a while he would wander off into the dining room and fool around with the candlesticks, trying to remember how it was.

Flodie kept thinking she could shape him up if she could just be stern enough, she would try to make Edward do things for her, like putting bookshelves in her bedroom, or changing all the locks. She would give him directions and then get absolutely furious when he stared at her without even trying to understand; she would jam the hammer into his hand and say, over and over, Nail, Edward, you take the *hammer* and hit the *nail,* talking through her teeth until finally I had to go in and rescue him, saying, I don't think he's up to it today. So there was that, the more impatient she got the worse he was at anything she set for him; there was that and then there was the way he stared at Cora, as if he was trying to make out something hidden in her face. He kept surprising her in rooms, toward the end he would take her for Mama and ask her to forgive him, heaven only knows what for. I came in once and found them, he had his face pressed against her skirt and she was swatting at him and saying, I'm not Mama, I have worked all my *life* not to be Mama, now for God's sake will you let go of me and go away? I suppose he made her feel trapped, when I know all she wants is to get married again and get away from here; it was partly that, and partly that she has never been able to stand Edward, he's so weak, but after a while it got so that she would jump every time he came up behind her, Flodie and I would have to laugh, she would swat him and then say Get away, get away, but it never put him off, not even for a minute, he just kept after her. Our sister Cora wants things the way she wants them, and even though she wouldn't talk about how we were going to do it, she was the first one to come out and say Edward was going to have to go.

I suppose she wanted it from the beginning, maybe we all did, he reminded us of too much pain, but we couldn't seem to do anything, maybe we were waiting for somebody else to come along. As it turned out we had to take the first steps ourselves. He was missing for two days, we found him in the bottom of the coat closet under the stairs, where he used to hide when we were kids. He didn't recognize us, all he said was, *Thad,* and I suppose that has always been part of it. When we were little Edward would run to Mama and blame Thad for everything, and if it was all still Thad's fault, then Thad was going to have to come down here and take care of him; I don't know what he wanted, all I know is that when Thad did come, Edward looked up at him and smiled as if it was all he had wanted all along. As it turned out I was the one who had to call him, because I'm the only one who has never talked against him, my sisters weren't about to get on that phone and say out of all their bitterness: We never said it, Thad, and if we did, we didn't mean anything by it; we need you Thad, you're going to have to come down here and help. So I made them go and sit in the kitchen while I made the call.

§§§§ §§§§

When Thad came Edward was still in the closet, although they had made him more comfortable, and once again, as at the christening, Thad stepped forward with regret and in increasing pain, assuming a responsibility of which he had been overpoweringly conscious all his life and which, despite his best efforts, he had never been able to discharge. He was aware of his sisters fluttering at his elbows, saying, "Oh Thad, you've got to . . ." and, "Thad, thank heaven," but he

311

brushed past them, going to the closet where Nell stood, looking down at their brother on the coats; he understood now that he had failed him, but he understood as well that the potential for this failure had always been so great that much as he had wanted to, responsible as he had felt, he could never have helped Edward, any more than Edward could have been helped by him. Still he said, "Edward?" and Edward, who had not spoken for three days, looked up and said, "Oh Thad, thank God it's you."

NELL

When Thad finally came it was smooth, it was all so fast that Edward was in the hospital, looking around in confusion and turning his hands, he had already had his shot and they were taking his particulars for the record before he even realized what we had done. We had all kissed him and promised he would be better soon, all of us except Thad, and we were on our way out before he even began to scream.

When we got back to the house Cora tried to make a party, going for the glasses and decanters we keep in the dining room, but our brother Thad was not going to be distracted, I think he saw a way to cut his ties, to end all of it for all of us, because he was saying, This is as good a time as any. Flodie was on him in a second, I've never seen her look so sharp: Time for what? He said, You know, this place is nothing but a liability, it's been a white elephant for years. Cora put down the decanters, saying, *Thad,* but he kept on anyway: It's only dragging you down. But before he could finish Flodie attacked: What right do you have, you ran out on us forty-five years ago. He only brushed her aside, pretending not to hear. I'll be glad to help with the details. Then Cora, who would like nothing better than to get out of here, my sister Cora began to cry, she pulled on his arm and her voice went up high: Thad, it would be just like killing Mama, and Flodie hit him, crying, What do you know, you selfish son of a bitch, and so he turned to me. Maybe he thought we could help each other, but Cora was crying, Flodie wanted to tear into him, and I thought: Why should we? Why should I, after all? As long as my sisters want to live here I might as well stay around to help, and keep things going; sometimes I think about not having to clean these rooms, but what would I do instead, go out and look for

Cleve? Thad was waiting, I knew what he wanted me to say, but I just shook my head. I've lived here for too long and besides, where else would I go?

§§§§ §§§§

Before he went into the Army, Thad's mother had tried to stop him, rearing up in bed and crying: *You can't go.*

You can't stop me.

You can't go, you're too much like Harry.

What do you mean?

She had held out her arms to him with real love, saying: *You are too beautiful, you'll be stricken down in your youth.*

Then, precisely because he was young, he had looked at her in accumulated bitterness, saying: *That might not be so bad. At least I would get out of here for once and all.*

Now, looking at his sisters, he thought he recognized Mama in Cora's eyes; unless he was mistaken Flodie had dragged out one of their mother's dressing gowns, and even Nell had settled, moving around the drawing room as if she had never dreamed of living any place else. They had made him promise to let them keep the house and now they were trying to draw him in too, sitting in his mother's curve-backed chairs and brooding over her decanters, offering to let him stay as long as he wanted, and, seeing the three of them, he remembered his mother's statement, or curse, when he had come back after all, because someone had to help get Papa into the ground. He had come back matured, or hardened: he had come back determined never to spend another night under her roof, and although she may not have recognized him she had seen this one thing because she had lamented: *You are changed, I can see it. You should have gone while you were still beautiful, you should have died in the war.*

Heedless, Cora was saying, "You can even have your own room, you owe it to yourself to see some of your old friends."

"I don't have any . . ."

Flodie cut him off. "Belle LeFevre is widowed now, and living back in town."

"You ought to get married, Thad." Cora looked him straight in the eye. "It's never too late to get married, you know."

Flodie said, "I know, we could give a party."

313

"My God."

Cora had taken off Punk's rings and now she was looking down at her bare white hand. "People have found some very rewarding companionships in their golden years."

"A party, just like Mama used to have."

"Oh my God."

So here he was in her house again despite all his best efforts, and here were his sisters, busily engaged in putting on the imagined past as if the true past had never been, as if there had been nothing to be learned from it. He remembered looking at his sister Lila's child, and then at Lee, thinking that there must be some advance in each generation; he had always wanted to think that life must not only progress but improve, but looking into the changeless faces of his sisters, he knew he had to kiss them hastily and get out of that house because if he stayed he would have to admit to himself that this might not be so.

It was after dark and they were worried about him, particularly when he refused to take a cab, but he was so impatient to be free of them that he walked out by himself, angered by their warnings that the neighborhood was not safe. What did they know; hadn't he lived here for some twenty years? In the dark, most of the changes were obscured, a few of the details had changed but none of the major shapes had changed, so that he was able to walk in an increasing sense of familiarity right up to the minute that the two kids jumped him, coming from the friendly shadows of the trees. They were both junkies, one black, one white; the black one had his forearm across Thad's throat, the white one was in front of him holding a razor, and he faced the razor with such relief that he knew now what he had been waiting for all his life; he had been waiting for death and the joy which he had assumed for some years must be in the next world because he had been born wanting, he had lived all his life wanting, and he had never found it in this one, no matter where he looked; postulating on his own want he closed his eyes, privileged, touched for the first time with a sense of God, and, shaken by the potential, the possibilities, he waited for the boy in front of him to sever him from his body. Instead the boy with the razor flipped up his necktie, slashing it off with contempt as if to show him how easy it would have been; then the boy holding him fished in all his pockets and came up with Thad's wallet, and then they threw him down and stomped him and after that they ran away, leaving him to stagger to his hands and knees, shaking his head like a dog and stifling his voice to keep from crying out because he had been so close, only to be bilked at the last minute.

Lifting his head he saw, or imagined he saw, Uncle Harry, forever young, forever handsome in the white suit, forever going away; he would have just rounded that same corner, and Thad understood that if he had to live then he must continue to live, he would do his best to make a decent job of it because it seemed quite possible that it was, after all, the function of the living to redeem the dead; he remembered his mother the last time he had seen her, saying, *You should have gone while you were still beautiful,* and now he answered: *That might not have been so bad.*

He could imagine the girls if he went back to the house, they would fuss over him, they would beg him to stay until he felt better, Flodie would not be able to keep from saying: I told you so. He got to his feet as soon as he was able and took a cab to the police station; he would not stay long enough to press charges, instead he would call from the station to reconfirm his reservation and leave town without saying anything more to the rest of them.

NELL

What would Mama say if she could see her children now?

LEE

So here we are in this lousy rooming house, I don't know exactly why we aren't staying at the big house, since Mother says it's so goddam wonderful and everybody always falls on her with open arms and starts to slobber the minute she comes to the door, but ever since we got here she's been like some damn fool debutante getting ready for a date, she says we have to get unpacked and clean ourselves up and then we'll go on over and surprise them, but I can hear her now, telephoning Nell or one of them, she's crying right out there in the hall. I don't know, maybe she only wants me to get cleaned up before she has to show me to her fabulous relatives, maybe she really is ashamed of the way I look, or maybe she's not so sure of them? That one I did meet, Thad, was not what you would call thrilled to see us, but he wasn't so wonderful either, he was short and his eyes were too close together and he was cross as hell with both of us, so maybe we are waiting here until they can get themselves fixed up a little? They can all change into pretty dresses and fix their eyes so they don't look so close together and they can make me a lemon pie or some goddam thing and I will be so thrilled to see them that I will fall in love with them and this great house I've heard so much about, I will stretch my arms out until they go around my old mother and I will say Oh Mommy, I love it, I love it, I want to move in here with all your relatives and be just like them, we will all live down here forever and ever and I'll never go back to any of those places you had to come and get me out of, I'll never see any of those people ever again. Forty-something years old and she hasn't figured out that changing the air doesn't change the people, they have to be what they have to be.

Hell, why does she get so upset about it? I always come out the other side. The first time it was this summer cottage, some kids and I broke in and lived there for about a week and it was sweet as hell, everybody did exactly what they wanted and there was nobody around to tell them not to, nobody gave a damn, but the mother can't stand it when she doesn't know where I am every living minute, she is scared to death that the minute I get out of her sight I'm going to get hurt or something, or else I might get out from under and do something she is going to have to be ashamed of, so that time she put on her space shoes and her field glasses and she slogged around and asked and looked and looked and asked until she found me and dragged me out of that terrible place. Then I had to go to the boarding school and sneak grass when I could get it, which was seldom, and spend most of my afternoons with Sir Walter Scott, the place was filled with kids that their parents blew it and they were paying a pile of dough to get the school to do it for them instead but it was already too late, it was too late for all of them so we used to get out anyway, we were going to get out and do what we wanted no matter what they paid. There were a lot of places after that, new towns, new kinds of schools, but I would always crack out and she would have to come and get me, she would come and get me no matter where I hid; you have to kind of admire her for that, it's like a bulldog that always gets its man. What she doesn't get is that as long as she takes out after me I am going to have to keep going, I have to keep going until she gives up and I'm free, then when she finally gives up and I know I can cut out without being followed, I might even want to come back, I will have done the one thing and I can have it my way from then on.

This last time you would have thought I had stuck her full of daggers, she got me home and ranted for an hour; she does that thing where you throw yourself down on the bed and kick your feet and cry I've failed, and the kid is supposed to feel terrible but hell, maybe she *has* failed, or if she hasn't failed then maybe something or somebody else has failed along the way, all those people that come in and try and hurt you when you're all sitting around grooving on each other and saying isn't it great that you're all together somewhere that you can never ever be hurt. What they can't stand is that you won't do what they expect you to, you won't want what they think you ought to want, they are giving you hell because none of their things are turning out the way they thought they would. Well whose fault is that? Who gives a shit? I'm not fat like she is, my hair is almost down to my ass and from here things look pretty good. I even got myself into a couple of colleges in spite of everything, and I might make it if I feel like it, or I might not, I don't *have* to do anything because it doesn't matter if you do anything or not.

The thing was, she was rolling around on the bed crying so hard about how she'd failed, it had failed, that I had to do something to make her feel better and so I got her to shut up so I could tell her I would come down here with her for this goddam funeral. It's my Great-uncle Edward or somebody, I don't know who the hell he is, except that Mother says he was very nice to her when she was a little girl. The minute I said I would she sat up, she felt all better, she started telling me how I was going to love these aunts that had been so wonderful to her when she was little and then she went into this little poem or song about knowing what and where I came from, and valuing my roots, how you had to know your past because it is what we are all built on, or some goddam thing, and then she had the nerve to tell me that I was going to love these aunts; why the hell does she think I'n going to love them when I've never clapped eyes on them? She is a OK lady when she's at the office, she has brains, but there she was sitting on the bed with this whole family to tell me about as if that was going to make us love each other on sight when we haven't exactly kept in touch, and she went all squashy at the center, like some piece of fruit that is going bad; I listened until I couldn't stand it and then I got out in a hurry because I thought I was going to throw up. But we had the house at meals and the aunts while we were doing dishes and those slaves or whatever it was they used to have; we had Uncle Thad, the World War One hero, and Aunt Nell the family martyr and Uncle Punk's Last Illness, she goes on and on about them as if she thinks there is some lesson to be learned from her goddam family, when she knows as well as I do that there are no lessons to be learned, only families; all the way down she had to tell me about Great-grandfather Lyon, and how he was one of the founders of this city, and how the house was a wedding present to my great-grandmother, but he built it too close to the business district, and that's why the neighborhood has gone down, she told me about what a great lady my great-grandmother was, she wore a size four-and-a-half shoe and her bare foot never touched the ground, and she goes on and on about Great-great Uncle Harry, who swam out to some ship or other in the Civil War; I don't see what any of that has to do with me.